The Human Age

The Human Age

Wyndham Lewis

The Human Age

Book One

Childermass

Calder Publications
London
Riverrun Press
New York

First published in 1928 and reprinted in 1956 by
Methuen in hardcover.
Jupiter edition published by Calder and Boyars Ltd 1962.
Reprinted in this edition in 2000 by John Calder Publisher,
London and Riverrun Press, New York.

British Library Cataloguing in Publication Data is available.
Library of Congress Cataloging in Publication Data is
available

Printed and bound in Canada by Webcom Ltd, Toronto.

Childermass

Scene

OUTSIDE HEAVEN

THE CITY LIES IN A PLAIN, ornamented with mountains. These appear as a fringe of crystals to the heavenly north. One minute bronze cone has a black plume of smoke. Beyond the oasis-plain is the desert. The sand-devils perform up to its northern and southern borders. The alluvial bench has recently gained, in the celestial region, upon the wall of the dunes. The 'pulse of Asia' never ceases beating. But the outer Aeolian element has been worsted locally by the element of the oasis.

The approach to the so-called Yang Gate is over a ridge of nummulitic limestone. From its red crest the city and its walls are seen as though in an isometric plan. Two miles across, a tract of mist and dust separates this ridge from the river. It is here that in a shimmering obscurity the emigrant mass is collected within sight of the walls of the magnetic city. To the accompaniment of innumerable lowing horns along the banks of the river, a chorus of mournful messages, the day breaks. At the dully sparkling margin, their feet in the hot waves, stand the watermen, signalling from shore to shore. An exhausted movement disturbs the night-camp stretching on either side of the highway—which when it reaches the abrupt sides of the ridge turns at right angles northward. Mules and oxen are being driven out on to the road: like the tiny scratches of a needle upon this drum, having the horizon as its perimeter, cries are carried to the neighbourhood of the river.

The western horizon behind the ridge, where the camp ends inland, but southward from the highroad, is a mist that seems to thunder. A heavy murmur resembling the rolling of ritualistic drums shakes the atmosphere. It is the outposts or investing belt of Beelzebub, threatening Heaven from that direction, but at a distance of a hundred leagues, composed of his resonant subjects. Occasionally upon a long-winded blast the frittered corpse of a mosquito may be borne. As it strikes the heavenly soil a small sanguine flame bursts up, and is consumed or rescued. A dark ganglion of the bodies of anopheles, mayflies, locusts, ephemerids, will sometimes be hurled down upon the road; a whiff of plague and splenic fever, the diabolic flame, and the nodal obscenity is gone.

With the gait of Cartophilus some homing solitary shadow is continually arriving in the restless dust of the turnpike, challenged at the tollgate thrown across it at the first milestone from the water-front. Like black drops falling into a cistern these slow but incessant forms feed the camp to overflowing. Where the highway terminates at the riverside is a ferry-station. Facing this on the metropolitan shore is, to the right, the citadel, rising plumb from the water, a crown of silver rock, as florets towers arranged around its summit.

At the ferry-station there is a frail figure planted on the discoloured stones facing the stream. Hatless, feet thrust into old leather slippers, the brown vamp prolonged up the instep by a japanned tongue of black, it might be a morning in the breezy popular summer, a visitor halted on the quay of the holiday-port, to watch the early-morning catch. Sandy-grey hair in dejected spandrils strays in rusty wisps: a thin rank moustache is pressed by the wind, bearing first from one direction then another, back against the small self-possessed mouth. Shoulders high and studious, the right arm hugs, as a paradoxical ally, a humble limb of nature, an oaken sapling Wicklow-bred. The suit of nondescript dark grey for ordinary day-wear, well-cut and a little shabby, is coquettishly tight and small, on the trunk and limbs of a child. Reaching up with a girlish hand to the stick cuddled under the miniature oxter, with the other hand the glasses are shaded against the light, as the eyes follow the flight of a wild duck along the city walls northward, the knee slightly flexed to allow the body to move gracefully from the slender hips.

Speculations as to the habitat and sport-status of the celestial water-fowl.—Food (fish-fry, frogs?). Speculations as to fish-life in these waters, lifeless they seem: more speculations involving chemistry of waters.—A crowded punt is making inshore, at a spot fifty yards above the ferry. A band of swarthy peons disembark, carrying picks and spades. They enter a box-shaped skip, their backs forming a top-heavy wall above its sides. It begins moving inland upon its toy track.

A longshoreman fidgets at the movements of the small observer, finally thrusting first one long-booted leg and then another into his bark, a giant clog whose peaked toe wavers as he enters its shell, he walks off wagging his buttocks as he churns the rudder-paddle upon the rusty tide, an offended aquatic creature. A stone's-throw out he stops, faces the shore, studying sombrely in perspective the man-sparrow, who multiplies precise movements, an organism which in place of speech has evolved a peripatetic system of response to a dead environment. It has wandered beside this Styx, a lost automaton rather than a lost soul. It has taken the measure of its universe: man is the measure: it rears itself up, steadily confronts and moves along these shadows.

A new voice hails him of an old friend, spanking noisily the opaque air, at his back. The maternal warmth of early life gushes unexpectedly from a mouth opened somewhere near him in the atmosphere.

'Pullman? I thought so! Well I'm damned!'

The guttural cheery reports stop. A pink young mask flushed in welcome, the blue eyes engagingly dilated, comes smiling round, working from the rear uncertainly, not certain of Pullman, yet claiming him as a pink fragment of its past. Pullman reddens. The *wellimedammd* falls like a refreshing rain: his tongue, suddenly galvanic, raps out its response:

'I hope not!' The nondescript brevity of clattering morse hammers out on his palate message and counter-message, in harsh English. Eye in eye they dart and scent each other's minds, like nozzling dogs.

'Where did you spring from?'

'I thought I'd take a turn. I couldn't sleep.'

'What are you doing here?'

'I'm damned if I know!'

They laugh. Damned if he knows if he's damned, and damned if he cares! So this is Heaven?

Here we are and that's that!

And let the devil take the hindmost!

And be damned to him for God's Ape!

God's in his Heaven—all's well with us!—Lullabys.

Pullman from the old days, dear old Pulley, Satters is sentimental: he contorts himself, smiling, into a hundred shapes of restless shyness, wriggling back into familiarity.

'From behind I recognized you at once.'

He lurches and cranes his neck, calling the behind to witness.

'The moment you spoke I knew you,' says Pullman. 'Before I saw you I said "Satters!" It's like knowing who's speaking on the telephone—not one of my accomplishments—or I should say wasn't. Thank Heaven for small mercies they've no telephones here!' His mouth continues to work abstractedly, back amongst the telephones. 'I never know who I'm talking to till they say who they are.'

'Nor do I.' (*Nordouai*, like deep Greek vocables.)

Satterthwaite is in knee-cords, football stogies, tasselled golf stockings, a Fair Isle jumper, a frogged mess jacket, a Mons Star pinned upon the left breast, and a Rugby cap, the tinsel rusted, of out-size, canted forward.

'Where the devil did you get that outlandish kit from?'

'I know——!' He looks down without seeing. 'I'm damned if I know!'

Satters takes the laugh imposed by Humour with orthodox boyish eagerness. The ridiculous but charming self sacrificed by all gentlemen with hasty grace to the god of fun corkscrews in a painful bashfulness. Grin gripped in grin, they avoid each other's gaze, swaying.

'Is it too preposterous?' Loftily ill-at-ease, Satters makes a detached inventory.

'No more preposterous than everything else here.'

'No we're all in the same boat—that's comforting, at least.' Satters seeks comfort in a veiled examination of his friend, prosecuted in discreet instalments, between blows delivered upon the dusty surface of his garments. As his hand falls upon his chest the medal dances, while a loud hollow sound is thumped up.

'One would say one was hollow!' he says. He delivers a blow in the neighbourhood of the Star. 'Sounds somehow empty doesn't it?' Again he strikes, and listens.

Pullman smiles with condescension.

Satters passes his hand over either bulging jacket-breast.

'The beastly things *fit*! That's the really shattering part! If only they hadn't I might have.'

'A tree is known by its fruit they say!' Pullman flashes a moment the Chinese grimace, the accepted civilized grotesque of malice, and they laugh together, they are unkind.

'I've got used to them. I raised Hell to start with! I refused to keep them on; I told them I thought it was most unfair.'

'As indeed it is!'

'Most! I told the old Bailiff off. He must have thought —— He didn't seem to mind though as a matter of fact. It seemed rather to amuse him.'

At the word *Bailiff* Pullman withdraws into a hypnotic

9

fixity of expression, as if something precise for him alone had been mentioned under an unexpected enigma.

'Well, there it is!' These details are dismissed. Satters sighs a *that's-that* sigh. 'I've got used to this along with the rest: haven't you?'

Pullman is now included more directly. For a moment his friend's eyes rest upon his person with meaning. Pullman stands fast, shoulders high and squared, small calves in inflexible arcs, eyes still hypnotic.

'Quite.'

'I suppose in the end we shall get more suitable. I'm afraid——'

Hiding behind the joke-self Satters peeps out laughing. He's *afraid*; he stops, gracefully timid; the object of his fear is immaterial. Taking off his cap he begins striking it against his leg, dust puffing from it in magical abundance, a cornucopia of reddish powder.

'Yes. At all events we can hope. You can't be at the same time in the oven and in the mill.'

'What?'

'You can't be in two places at once.'

'Rather not.'

Under his eyelashes Satters doubtfully surveys his friend, a respectful strangeness superseding the first familiarity. The ice is broken fresh bearings have to be taken. New worlds for old—all is in the melting-pot.

'Temporarily at least I have decided to forget. And forgive.'

Pullman laughs a quick bark of icy hysteria; they both laugh for a moment. Pullman stamps his right foot softly. He works his toes up and down in the slipper. His head twists sharply towards the river as though in pain; turning back in act to speak he comes to a halt in his former attitude, and is silent.

Satters grown redder, with the bashfulness of a tongue-tied junior, *autres temps autres mœurs*, holds his cap with

10

both hands awkwardly in front of him, schoolboy fashion, swinging his body with an arch girlish oscillation. More forward with truth, Pullman continues to gaze at the clothes. Satters looks up obliquely, blushing—it is Pullman's turn; he asks:

'Isn't that the stick you always used to have, Pulley? Why, you're going a bit on top?' He points to the crown of his own head, florid with fat yellow curls. 'I thought you were—let's see, what was it? eighteen months about wasn't it?—senior to me. Or was it as much as that? I've got a pretty good thatch still.'

'You have indeed. Yes, they've done you well in that matter.' He carries his hand gingerly to his occiput, fingering himself. 'I don't know why they've given me a bald head. I suppose—— It's got much worse since I've been here. I shall be a patriarch if I don't soon get passed in.'

'How long have you been here?'

'Weeks. A month nearly—not quite.' Both pairs of eyes withdrawn into the respective shells, faces towards the ground, with one movement they now wheel and begin walking in step away from the quay slowly, Satters with a long-legged slouch, Pullman with a slowing-down of his light-limbed machine, hugging, high-shouldered, his stick. Their feet sink into the exuviae and migrating sand, dust and gypsum, of the riverside, kicking, first one and then the other, a stone or fragment of jetsam of the camp or flood, Pullman outwards towards the shore, Satters inland campwards. Their minds continue to work in silent rhythm, according to the system of habit set in motion by their meeting.

'This is rather beastly, isn't it?' Satters uses the rapid half-voice of confidence, of the social equal and confederate. Pullman, with the same half-voice, without touching his friend with his eyes, jerks his chin up quickly towards the city.

'Beastly!'

The little word snaps out of its trap as fresh as paint. He snatches his mouth away as he discharges it, crossly fixing the lateral horizon. Beastly—the judgment of the gentleman. Satters' face is 'grave as a judge'. He dawdles along moodily, throwing out large mailed thonged and studded feet, for which there is no plump buoyant ball— all dressed up and nothing to kick. Pullman bends down and plucks a small panicled flower, of the Egyptian privet. He puts it to his nose, exquisite with pinched-in nostrils, half-closing his eyes to sniff. Offering it to Satters between his thumb and index finger he says:

'This is camphire; have you see it before here? That's its book-name. It has some other. *Bible* camphire, you know. It has rather a jolly smell. They use it in the camp, ground in hot water, to dye their beards and moustaches.'

'No, really? How sweet! Is it effective?' They laugh a little: Satters, half-closing his eyes, and stumbling in consequence, dabs at his nostril with the flower. With a voluptuous arrogance he affects to absorb himself in extracting perfume from the camphire.

Pullman comes to a stop, his feet firmly set side by side in the worn slippers, pushing down, shovelling into the hot sandy nap, the small legs braced and arched, knotted in little business-like muscles, shoulders high, hands pressed into jacket-pockets, and gazes across the river. Satters makes a collapsed zigzag at his side, in silence.

Stretching into the distance away from the citadel, to the celestial north, are a double belt of battlements. As they recede they withdraw from the shore of the river. They are strengthened with numerous buttresses, a process at their tops finned like the biretta of a Roman priest. Their surface shines damply as though with some sebaceous moisture.

The sheer profile of the city is intricate and uneven. Above the walls appears, naissant, armorial, and unreal, a high-hatched outcropping of huddled balconies, black

rufous brown vermilion and white; the upper stages of wicker towers; helmet-like hoods of tinted stucco; tamarisks; the smaragdine and olive of tropical vegetations; tinselled banners; gigantic grey sea-green and speckled cones, rising like truncated eggs from a system of profuse nests; and a florid zoologic symbolism—reptilian heads of painted wood, filled-out tinfoil or alloy, that strike round beneath the gusts of wind, and pigs made of inflated skins, in flight, bumped and tossed by serpents, among the pennants and embossed banners. The severe crests of bulky ziggurats rise here and there above this charivari of roof-life, perceived beyond and between the protecting walls. It is without human life, like a city after a tragic exodus.

Rising at the side of a wide cone is the dark needle of a gothic spire, surmounted by an emblematic cock, a gold point that glitters in the sky. There is a faint pulsation of a bell. Pullman sketches a cross upon his breast, bowing his head and then raising it.

'That is the sanctus bell. It comes from that spire. It's the English Church.' He points at the spire.

'Are you a Catholic?' asks Satters, his eyes feeding in wonder upon the ritualist of which he has just had a glimpse.

'Yes, a Roman Catholic,' Pullman answers.

'How does it feel to be Roman?'—'Just the same—Christian.'

As they are standing close together, Pullman becomes conscious of a pungent smell. It is the sticky vegetable odour of small babies in a close room, a distillation of the secretions and excrements of the earliest human life. It is Satters' smell, the new smell that Satters has. Taking him by the arm he feels the warmth of elastic animal matter in big thick-meated resistent layers beneath his fingers but his friend's face is fastened stupidly upon the gilded cock, a wide-eyed suckling. The wet cherry-mouth has burst open and displays its juicy fibres. Feeling the hand

15

that has crawled in and settled upon his biceps Satters
points to the cock, asking with drunken fixity:

'It comes from the spire? Not the spire!'

'Yes, from the spire, it is the English church.'

'English.'

'So I've always understood. It was built in the fifteenth
century. Come along.'

'Was that place——' Satters' face is fixing itself, the
jaw dropped. Pulley sharpens his voice to cut into the
gathering membrane of this stupor.

'Yes, that place has *always* been there. But the church
was built in the fifteenth century. It's a fifteenth-century
church—that's what I mean.'

Distant and strong-minded, not-sniffing, not-offended,
a tart smart tight little governess.—His stick clipped
under the hunched shoulder, striking into his rapid self-
possessed finicky-sturdy one-time, Pullman propels the
reluctant muscle-taking-root away from the spot of its
threatened settlement beneath the spell of the cock.

'Isn't it b-b-bright?' Satters is forced away backwards,
sagging and open-mouthed. The golden ornament for
him is now dominating the sky.

He sees an imposing bird hovering above the city.

'The Catholic emblem. I don't think it's very bright
is it? Your young eyes can see further than mine.' Pullman blinks sedately.

'Come along; it's best to keep moving here.'

A veteran rat trotting in an aerial gutter, he catches a
glimpse of glittering chasms but averts his eyes, his
present business the periplus of the roof. He is guiding,
dutiful senior, the young rat to their eyrie their coign of
vantage. Once they get there he will rest, and have a
dream perhaps, of gigantic apparitions inhabiting the
dangerous hollows inside the world. Meanwhile action is
everything; to keep moving is the idea, this is his law of
existence—to rattle along these beaten tracks. Has he not

16

the golden secret, who knows as he does the right road to the proper place in record time, barring accidents? But the glamour of this outcast plan, rigid and forbidden, whose lines are marked out through the solid walls of matter, contrary to the purposes of nature, is lost on the newcomer. He only has eyes for the abyss. Intoxicated with the spaces plunging all round them, in passionate distances expressed as bright dizzy drops, let in at spy-holes or thrown up as reflections, he walks upon air, truant in mind from the too-concrete circuit.

It is ancestral, as all order is. Born to march and counter-march, two-dimensional and hieratic almost, he has had a revelation starting at the gold point occupied by the cock. He has reached chaos, the natural goal.

Greedy mouth and lush eyeball tell their tale swimmy and silly where to act is impertinent; he is right off the map in a Seventh Heaven or Dimension. Circumspect Pullman gets the back of the backslider towards the magnetic city with gentle ju-jitsu. He easily masters his heavy-weight friend; a few deft pressures here and there do it.

'How's your tummy? a bit wonky?' he presses without looking where the answer would have come from; he knows it's not much good.

This is the sound that comforts him—Satters is as deaf as a post: so he twitters, supposing that Pullman sees: 'Oh, isn't it prett-ty!': Pullman fixes his eye on the track at right angles they are now following, with a look of great reserve. The track is interesting if nothing else, he did not know it was there.

'Which way?' he tramples harshly against Pullman laughing helplessly in feeble apologetic fun.

'No that's not it. Straight ahead. Steady! To your left.'

Satters is wrenched at by the other, certain of his ground. Pullman's is the gait now of a man who has lost interest, he slows down but still carries out the elementary duty of keeping the other's head leeward as regards the magnetic attack. Satters flings his feet out, supposing each yard twice as spacious as it is. So for him his foot always comes down too soon or falls short.

When the bird was exploded—that the effect at least of its sudden disappearance—a mellow effulgence became evident to Satters. The gold dust generated from the destruction of the clockwork cock thickens the air with reddish particles. It gilds the clouds on whose cambered paths they stog and plod, leg and leg. They are in mud now. Their backs are turned, but the apocalyptic coloration has outrun them.

'I think it's too lovely. I think this is *too* lovely! Oh, Pulley, I do think this is too divine! *and* lovely!'

Satters' lips flower in desperate unctuous ravishment. Pullman says:

'Look, let's slow down a little. You feel a bit shaky don't you?'

They stop, and Satters sways, laughing.

'Stamp! Stamp your feet!'

Satters raises his feet with difficulty, making lubberly passes above the level of the ground, which see-saws, and stamps them down quickly and blindly.

'Don't try and go too fast.'

After a few steps he rears up before Pullman's shadow as it bars his path then trips and sits down abruptly. Pullman kneels beside the stricken Satters who sits staring and pointing while he blabs on blindly saluting all the lovely sights. He recognizes Pullman and crows at him as he notices any unusual movement on that object's part but he resists attempts to raise his person from the sitting position. Pullman, prescribing quiet, sits down beside him, drumming on the ground with the point of his stick held penwise along the underside of the index. Satters grabs at it and falls upon his side. There with an exhausted grunt he falls asleep.

After an interval of several minutes Pullman turns the point of the stick in the direction of the sleeper and pokes him lazily about the ribs.

'Come along, you've had your forty winks. That's done it hasn't it?' he calls. 'It's all O.K.?'

Satters struggles into a sitting position staring about him with frowning effort.

'Yes it's me!' Pullman smiles and nods. 'You met me just now!'

Satters boggles a little at the ingratiating presence, but there is recognition in the staring infant-eye.

'There's nothing like a short sharp nap at the right moment!' Pullman exclaims and dropping over upon his hands swings himself rigidly up and up to a tiptoe erectness; then, stalking and stretching tense-legged, in a succession of classical art-poses suggestive of shadow-archery, he approaches Satters. He relaxes like the collapse of a little house of cards, extends a friendly lackadaisical hand, and sings out:

'Up again, come jump to it! Be a man for a spell and after that you can once more be a feller! A good hard walk will do you good. You'll be surprised.'

Seeing the outstretched hand is disregarded, he takes the cheerless sodden trunk by its top, and like a drayman testing the weight of a barrel begins canting it a little this way and that.

'Houeep! the old firm! gently does it, over she goes!' he chanties to pass off the fresh character of his unceremonious overhead help, conjuring up a capstan, appropriately for this human sheet-anchor he has now tacked on to him. The good ship *Pulley* wants again to be under way.

Satters makes no objection but he is heavy and has not much power himself. His breathing is rapid and his wind short, too, but they get him up, and he leans confidingly, with an absent grin, against his staunch attendant, who

19

comes briskly over on to his blind side with many soft and trivial encouragements—to *walk*, to put his best foot foremost, to shake a leg while the going is good, with a 'Let's foot it', and 'Try Shanks's mare', and 'Suffer me to lead Apes in Hell for I'll never make a match of it now' and so forth.

Satters starts off badly, striking his feet down all over the place, but after a trial or two he finds his sea-legs and develops a gait of his own which is manfully rachitic, if at first absurdly arrogant.

'Steady!' the watchful Pullman cries. 'First the left and then the right!'

Down goes the left, with a shell-shock waggle, and hits the earth toe-first.

'Always lead off with the left!'

And so he does and they make some progress. At long last Satters' clodhoppers tumble with regularity, the earth is crisp and firm. The water clears out of his eyes which become stolid china-blue. His lips return to a meat-tasting smacking and kissing pulp rather than the rose of Sharon of infant-ecstasy.

There is still, for Satters, a slight radiation in the sky, the afterglow of catastrophe. But it approximates to the heavy red fog of the normal scene.

'That must be the light I see! It shines in my face.' He shades his eyes affectedly. 'It's a bore not having a proper night here. Don't you find that?'

He has learnt wonderfully quickly but he tends to walk too fast. Pullman corrects him.

'Easy! easy! You mustn't run before you can walk! That's better!'

He is obedient; a correct vitality is distributed throughout the machine; he gets back quickly the dead accuracy required for walking flexibly from the hips and as though born a biped.

'It's a dud climate. Can you sleep? I wish I could.'

Satters' voice is chopped thick and lisping, that of a husky tart. 'I dread the nightsth!'

'Take care.'

Satters trips; a sound is shaken out of him.

He now walks as well as he ever will, without assistance. They are turned back by Pullman and regain the riverside path.

Ahead of them, unnoticed until now, a heavy fly-boat is disembarking a working-party of the peons despatched at daybreak from the celestial port for field-work and employment in the camp.

Grey-faced, a cracked parchment with beards of a like material, ragged wisps and lamellations of the skin, bandage-like turbans of the same shade, or long-peaked caps, their eyes are blank, like discoloured stones. A number of figures are collected with picks and shovels, baulks, a wheelbarrow in the shape of a steep trough, a gleaming sickle, two long-handled sledges and one heavy beetle-hammer. Their spindle limbs are in worn braided dungaree suitings. One holds by the bridle an ass, which trumpets with sedate hysteria. Electrified at each brazen blare, its attendant stiffens. He is shaken out of an attitude to which on each occasion he returns, throwing him into a gaunt runaway perspective, that of a master-acrobat tilted statuesquely at an angle of forty-five degrees from the upright awaiting the onset of the swarming troupe destined for his head and shoulders. SHAM 101 is painted in letters of garnet-red upon the hull of the fly-boat. An ape crouches, chained, its hand on the tiller.

Satters hangs back his body a frightened and shrinking herd of muscles, forced on from without by masterful Miss Pullman towards these condensations of the red dusty fog—to the frightened war-time soul of the startled Satters, angels of Mons, devils of Mons, enemies, ghosts of battle.

21

'They're all right; don't be alarmed.'

Pullman advances with wary precision with asides and injunctions as he feels his charge start or falter.

'It's a crowd of peons on their way to the camp. They're used to us.'

'I suppose they are.'

'It's time they were if they're not.'

Pullman rattles as they come nearer—slowing them down to an easy pace.

'They're a particularly feeble lot—they seem scarcely material. We could almost walk through them! Don't look.'

'I can't help.'

'I know but when you come across them you ought to make a point of looking away or pretending you don't see them. They'll let you alone then.'

Satters' dilated eyes continue to fix the gang they are approaching, taken forward intrepidly full of veteran hints and easy warnings of pitfalls by Pullman.

'I have known them to become quite offensive, the monkey's usually the difficulty,' he gossips. 'Hunamans or hanumans they call them: funny name, isn't it, like houyhnhnms! It's hindu I believe, it's an Ape-god. They are the mascots of the river-crossing. In the eyes of all these people they're sacred, you have to be careful not to attract their attention they're extremely nervous little beasts probably because they're so spoilt. You can sometimes see numbers of them running about where the ferry draws up, across the water. Have you ever noticed them?'

The peons stand rigid an archaic waxworks.

'They're extraordinarily awkward I've often watched them working. Their hands are all thumbs for exterior objects.'

'Who? Have you?' asks Satters, without taking his eyes off the grouped exhibits to obey the lecturer.

'They have no idea of how to handle saws.'

'Don't they? They have them. There are three more.'

Calm and masterful in the presence of inferior natures Pullman gives expression to his liberal beliefs.

'They're too hard on them.'

He frowns on the oppressor, there is a ganger in the boat.

'I saw one beaten unmercifully once, he didn't bleed he just turned black poor devil.'

To the left of the group there were three Satters had not noticed, articulated with the stiffest joints they were stalking slowly in but advancing very little, he could not understand whether the mist was too heavy which they seemed carrying with them like a red atmosphere.

'Take care, there's nothing to be afraid of but they do get cross if you stare too much.'

Satters' eyes are attracted to these halted human shells as though to a suddenly perceived vacuum but with them it is not the abstract abyss. The bold spanking rhythm of Satters' forward roll degenerates into sluggish pretence, stimulated by his trainer. His vertigo increases as they draw near to the peons. Pullman idles coolly forward, blandly receptive in his Zoo of men, but he says, 'Don't look!' frequently, mistrusting the mysterious inflammability of all more instinctive organisms.

Satters in the dirty mirror of the fog sees a hundred images, in the aggregate, sometimes as few as twenty, it depends if his gaze is steadfast. Here and there their surfaces collapse altogether as his eyes fall upon them, the whole appearance vanishes, the man is gone. But as the pressure withdraws of the full-blown human glance the shadow reassembles, in the same stark posture, every way as before, at the same spot—obliquely he is able to observe it coming back jerkily into position. One figure is fainter than any of the rest, he is a thin and shabby mustard yellow, in colouring a flat daguerreotype or one of the personnel of a pre-war film, split tarnished and transparent from travel and barter. He comes and goes; sometimes he is there, then he flickers out. He is a tall man of no occupation, in the foreground. He falls like a yellow smear upon one much firmer than himself behind, or invades him like a rusty putrefaction, but never blots out the stronger person. Some are mere upright shadows; they accompany the rest as the supers of the clan. Satters watches them sidelong to see if they will come out. They have no tools—as followers, or a residue of thin dependants. The principals are entrusted with the heavy instruments; there is the hammer and there is the sickle; they can hardly lift them as they stand tense and separate where they are stationed.

The perspiration coming into the hollow of Satters' palm moistens his friend's fingers, convulsively clutched. The effort to understand is thrown upon the large blue circular eyes entirely: but the blue disk is a simple register; it has been filled with a family of pain-photisms, a hundred odd, it is a nest of vipers absolutely—oh, they are unreal! what are these objects that have got in? signal the muscles of the helpless eye: it distends in alarm; it is nothing but a shocked astonished apparatus, asking itself if it has begun to work improperly. It was too unkind to have brought him here in laryngeal sub-speech he sets up a silent howl, it is too unkind! He is terribly sorry he came he need not have it is Pulley's fault. It was most terribly unkind of Pulley who should have known what to expect, they are miles away.

The images take on for him abruptly a menacing distinctness; the monotonous breathing of the group turns into a heave that with a person would be a sigh; all this collection are inflated with a breath of unexpected sadness; a darker shade rushes into the pigments, as it were, of them, like a wind springing up in their immaterial passionless trances, whistling upon their lips, at some order, denying them more repose—since they have a life after their fashion, however faded; and a thrill of dismay responds in Satters, the spell lifts, he presses against Pullman, forcing him off the track in panic. At this point it is slightly raised above the surrounding level and they both stumble down. Stubbornly holding his ground, Pullman, asserting himself, butts and rolls the stampeding colossus back upon the footpath.

'We must hold our ground,' easily he remarks as he does so, without looking at Satters. 'Don't show you're afraid of them whatever you do. Where are your fighting glands? They're quite inoffensive.'

Jacking him high and dry with a final hustling bounce, he jumps up beside him.

Satters directs a milky, indignant, half-conscious glare at his placid guide. His hand settles round Pullman's in a moist vice-like mass.

'Don't look—Oh, what's that? Look at *that* jolly little bird sitting on *that* bough! I wonder what *he* is. *He* looks like a blackbird. Or is *he* a magpie?'

Miss Pullman kisses her fingers in the direction of the bird.

'There's for luck in case you are; let's take no chances!'

No chances are taken, Satters is confused by the blandishments. Pullman continues to kiss his hand.

There is a sudden hissing like that of cats or geese. With a noisy intake of the breath Satters halts, pulverizing the cindery track as he pulls up with the reversed iron-horseshoes of his heels.

A slow animation flexes and disturbs the tableau, a clockwork spring released or a trumpet blown in other spaces. The figures move clumsily as though to rehearse their occupations, each in its kind, but first to stretch their joints, and practise ankle neck and wrist. Several, slowly lurching from one foot to the other and back, persevere.

'Satters!'

The call falls flat, Satters now is planted where he can watch in spite of himself; the elements of the group—he with the sickle, he with the ass, and the darker silhouette dancing inside the shafts of the barrow, which creaks and rolls slowly—are sharply fixed upon his senses, wound up to concert pitch. He stands shivering, his hands at his side, in front of this group-mechanism, or takes refuge in victorian abandon upon the arm of the gentleman: the yellow wraith the most immaterial—so thin as to be scarcely actual, but sluggishly active at last—is near enough for him to be able by stretching out a hand to finger it.

Pullman is rising to the occasion; he has disengaged his arm and throws it round his companion's heaving shoulders.

'Satters! You must come at once!'

Two of the figures leaning upon spades, their legs straddled wide, stretch their necks with the movement of roosters. After several recoils, chins extended, from the stumpy spouts of their mouths, jutting in a taut muscular process, a mournful deep-fetched drawl issues:

'Zuuur! I say! . . . Zuuur!'

The one holding the sickle swings it, a shining pendulum, back and forth, with clockwork regularity, exaggerating its weight, his face screwed into a vacant grin.

'They're like parrots; they learn "Yes sir" and "No sir" and like to show off their English. Look alive. They really may get unpleasant if we stop here.'

The ass pumps an ear-splitting complaint into its downy snout, scouring the loud sound up and down in an insane seesaw. The halter with which he is held seems to have some mechanical connection with the performance. Blinking gently and stupidly, he then hangs his neck and head over the ground, detached from his strange cry.

The man swinging the sickle begins intoning, with the

same straining forth of the neck to hasten an emesis, or to pump from the inside what he would utter—'Oyez! Oyez! Oyez!'

A figure standing out from the others, barring the way of the two interlopers, upon the uncertain track, comes to life. His neck sticks out there is a black flash and a stream of sputum stained with betel-nut strikes Satters upon the cheek. As quickly, almost at once, as he spits, come the two admonitory words, huffy and quick:

'Be off!'

Satters screams and starts back: Pullman bustles with him sideways, straining away from the danger zone and succeeds in getting him slowly out of reach, which is difficult because of his trembling and the weak response of his legs.

Frowning at the aggressor imperiously, his eye fixed technically hypnotic upon the root of his nose, Pullman shouts:

'Get back! Get back! You hear! Beat it! You hear! Yes!'

They clear the figure blocking their way and making a small circuit regain the track.

'You must learn to deal with these fear-neuroses you're a bad case. Look sharp here comes another.'

Leaving the shafts of the wheelbarrow where he has stood, an agile figure, leaping from spot to spot, overtakes them in an uneven series of cavorts, drops upon his haunches in their path, and head wagging peers up into Satters' face. Halted once more, Satters stares down: the other continues to roll his head and squint up innocently.

'Take no notice!' Pullman drags at Satters shouting at the peon, 'Get back! Go back. What do you think you're doing here, this is not your place! Shadow! go back to your barrow!'

The quizzing frog-figure shoots out a reptilian neck as they begin to move away, launching his dart of black spittle as the other has done. It enters Satters' nostril and breaks round his lips, a viscous fluid scented and bitter. Pullman, moving to cover his friend, receives on his sleeve some of the discharge. Satters with a loud infant-bellow puts his hand to his face. Lolling and wagging his turbaned poll as he goes, in self-applause, this member of the gang returns in a dozen parabolic bounds to his position in the group, between the shafts of the barrow, returning to his immobility. A cackle of exultant geese rises from his companions.

As Satters and Pullman retire a hollow drone follows them from the first of the party to speak.

'Zuuur! I say! Zuuur!'

Cool and masculine, with an eye for the hostile units and one 'visibly distressed' for the cataleptic Tom Tug delivered into his custody, Miss Pullman urges Satters along. He draws out of his left breast-pocket a small handkerchief, attentively wiping his charge's face. A small index pushed daintily into it scours gently the corners of the mouth.

'Spit!' Pullman slows down and spits slightly himself in genteel encouragement. 'Spit out that filth!'

Shivering like a frightened horse, bathed in perspiration, Satters abandons himself to his attentive guide, walking along without looking where he is going, while his breath comes in uneven gasps. Told to spit he complies, dribbling as he does so, blowing as he spits.

'Again!'

He continues to dribble and spit, Pullman wipes his mouth with the handkerchief.

'That's right.'

The peons become a part of the sodden unsteady phantasm of the past upon the spot. In the course of a minute they have convulsively faded. Satters forgets too, what is hidden by his mountainous trembling shoulders and presently even the trembling is gone. Pullman is all movement, dainty quick and aloof. He never looks at the object of his solicitude but busies himself in the abstract. Satters is treated as an absentee—with high and unwavering devotion. Fresh as a daisy, he reasserts their ordinary solid life-spell in common acts and great homeliness, of housewife-order.

A small grip, with a metallic glitter of trickling water like iron-filings flowing in the bottom of its parched channel, holds up or confuses Satters as to its true width. He stands deciding if it is really to be leaped or not: at once the weaker vessel is assisted over it by way of a convenient stone, without noticing how he passed it, so discreet was the kind help. A rusty finger from the broken stave of a cask claws and catches in Satters' stocking. Pullman, model Abigail, kneels down and removes it. Satters acquiesces, measuring the busy figure with bovine eyes, he does not see what it is doing.

His heart warms to reality. He embraces the dependence, only divined in moist flashes of emotion. Pulley is always speaking, when he is not far away and wrapped up in thought, no doubt. He is soothed and sleepy. How hot it is! He is tired. He leans confidingly on this gentle patron. And at length his voice starts lisping softly once more with a silken coo:

'You must think me a dreadful baby Pulley! I am so terribly sorry! I simply can't get used to those people you don't seem to mind, I think you're *marvellous*. I always did Pulley I always looked up to you most terribly, I do so adore being with you I can't tell you how much!'

Pullman keeps his collected business-like air, only smiling distantly in faint acknowledgment. This is his and Satters' normal posthumous relationship; it is the normal way.

Pullman looks back, to discover that the party of peons with whom they have had the encounter is no longer there. So they went probably—he is not sure which way; they may not have been there—that unfortunately always has to be reckoned with.—If they keep on they will come to the hill.

'You'll soon get used to them. But I recommend you, when you come across them, to pretend you don't see anything at all they don't expect you to see them! Many of them don't know they exist. If you don't take any notice they continue to think they're not there and of course then it's all right. But you mustn't take any notice. Spit again! that's right. How long did you say you'd been here, Satters?'

'Oh, ten days, I told you, that's why I'm so ashamed at being such a baby, that's one reason.'

They cross a soggy stretch of ground unexpectedly and cannot talk, picking their way. Pullman several times is parted from one of his slippers, having to stop to reinsert his foot and prise it up with humped toes.

'They hardly seem human do they? I think there's something uncanny about them!' Satters exclaims emptily. He half glances back with sudden apprehension. They could not be in front: though he has lost his sense of their position. There is the river gleaming underneath, however, but the mist has rolled over on to it. It seems canted a little towards them, a table of light beneath a block of fog. There is no city.

Pullman laughs with short superiority.

'Yes, they are unearthly,' he said. 'What they say about them is that they are the masses of personalities whom God, having created them, is unable to destroy, but who are not distinct enough to remain more than what you see. Indistinct ideas don't you know,' he adds loftily.

Satters crushes his hand under his friend's arm and whispers:

'How strange it all is, Pulley! How *fearfully weird* all this is!'

Dramatized, the dreary voice produces a sound like the

wind soughing, for the private ear of Pullman, the expression of whose profile undergoes no change.

'Even you Pulley must feel a little less a little more unimportant and oh! just of absolutely no consequence at all, like a fly at times aren't you? don't you *ever* want to just slink away? You must have blue moments.'

Pullman's profile as they trudge forward refuses the most insignificant response.

'I'm absolutely prostrated I can't describe how utterly— ever since I arrived I've been like that; as a matter of fact —*all the time*—I can't help it—at least until I met you.'

He shudders against Pullman: the hushed, scared mask of the overblown neuter stumbling beside the little hero stares out of its human refuge but is not encouraged: though, squeezing Satters' hand with one arm and the stick beneath the other, Pullman continues, with the dogmatism of his great class of business-like pelmanic seers, stunted in action for that purpose. Satters listens, his mouth gaping luxuriously in veneration, far far off— in fact from the bench of the infants' class, with a little hinnie to be tanned and a curly poll to be patted.

'It's all a matter of distinctness the Bailiff says: and I think he's right.'

'How clever you are Pulley; you seem to understand everything!' tumbles out in a gush of adulation, eyes swimming and hot hand clutching. 'Do you know I can give you no idea how terribly bucked I am at having met you like this! I think I'm most terribly lucky!' A flattering pressure on Pullman's arm, an immense baby-face of wonder and respect turned with all its engines of unmeaning melting expressiveness in his direction.

After a few throbbing moments:

'Do you think we should be called distinct Pulley? You are, I know. I do think you're perfectly wonderful!'

Pullman smiles, slightly turns his head, running an indulgent critical eye sidelong over his friend.

31

'I can't say I've ever seen anything quite like you!
You'll pass muster I think.'

Satters laughs to himself, giving self a comfortable
hug: reality is divine!—when it's self: it now possesses a
semi-official seal or the next thing to it.

The fog has somewhat lifted, as several working parties
of peons are disembarking immediately ahead of them
they strike inland. They pick their way to a track that
runs parallel to the shore at a distance of two hundred
yards or less, but sometimes it seems very much more. It
is backed by a small line of copper-red bluffs. They look
up at them.

'What are those hills?'

'Hills? Where? There are no hills. They're nothing!'
Pullman crossly exclaims.

'I didn't know.'

'Nothing at all, not hills.'

The distance to the city varies; Satters repeatedly looks
over, lunging his head to catch it at its changes and at
last says:

'Doesn't that look smaller sometimes?'

'What?' Pullman looks round indignantly.

'Sometimes it looks smaller to me than others.'

'Certainly not! Whatever makes you think!'

The whole city like a film-scene slides away perceptibly
several inches to the rear, as their eyes are fixed upon it.

'There!' exclaims Satters pointing.

'Oh that! I know, it looks like it. But it isn't so. It's
only the atmosphere.'

Satters leans heavily upon the sage Pullman's arm.

'If it weren't for the nights I believe I could manage.
They absolutely defeat me,' he expands in sibilant con-
fidences. 'What? No, the *nightsth*! the nights are per-
fectly shattering don't you find that. If I could get to sleep
I shouldn't mind so much.' He stumbles, rolling against
Pullman as he speaks, closing in. 'Are you sure I don't

bore you I'm certain I must. It's perfect hell sometimes. Do you mind don't let's go so fast. Thanks. Tell me if I bore you too dreadfully—do you live in a hut or a dug-out? I think the camp's beastly unhealthy.—There are six others in my dug-out six without me, I never see them except when I turn in, then we never say anything none of them have much to say ever. They don't seem to take to me. What? there's one I could strangle at times he makes a maddening *grud-grud-grud* noise he sleeps like a porpoise and keeps me awake or that's one of the things. There are two of them I believe nothing could up-set they remind me of you. I envy them terribly one's a doctor. What—he's a dago. A *doctor* that's right he goes by the name of Carlo, he speaks English, of course: badly, he says *hich-hreit* for "right". The other's rather a bounder yes English. They're older men of course I sup-pose that has something to do. There's one of them one of the others quite young, he's even worse than I am poor lamb, I rather like him but he's always too ill to answer or take any notice; he never speaks. I say do you mind don't let's hare along like this; I'm most awfully sorry to be such a nuisance.'

They stand still while he pants, his tongue hanging between jutting feline cheeks, stopping twice to smile apo-logetically to Pullman, putting his tongue back, then hanging it out again.

'That's better!'

Pullman walks slowly forward; Satters on his arm, now winded, recommences:

'Meeting you's put me fit for the rest of the day! It's most awfully kind of you not to go so fast!—You must think me a perfectly diabolical baby Pulley! It is so jolly to have someone to talk to—don't you agree? It's so differ-ent when one's not by oneself in *every way*—don't you think so? If you can find somebody who. I spent an abso-lutely shattering day yesterday. But that's nothing to the

33

nights. It's no use. The nights here—when the night comes I simply lie down and howl my eyes out, when I can't do that any more I sit bolt upright. For hours I'm too nervous to lie. Sometimes I pray. I know it sounds idiotic. I pray with my eyes open! It's beastly it's not like praying, I don't know what it's like, I do it. What's that? So long as you're with me I shall be all right. I sort of feel you were sent me Pulley it's absurd I know. What? do you mind? Oh do let's not part Pulley! Will you promise?'

Pullman's face does not register. Satters flushes and casts his eyes down, while his gait becomes a strenuous canter.

'I shouldn't have said that! Please forget what I have just said Pullman!'

Pullman's ears do not function; he has disconnected them for the present. Satters peers a moment sideways then he sighs and continues:

'Since we met I've behaved in an idiotic way I agree, I've been a perfectly ghastly baby I don't know how you tolerate me. I've had no one to talk to for so long you see that must be it I suppose you're perfectly splendid about me, I'm not—I'm sure you must despise me to a perfectly frantic extent, I should! Say if you do. You can always hoof me out if I become too impossible, I shouldn't mind I should hate it, but. You do despise me—*anybody!* —You don't say much!' Critically and coquettishly obliquely ogling stern Miss Pullman. 'I believe you're sorry you met me or aren't you I wish I knew!' he lisps in luscious contralto, the kitchen-maid's passionate arch complaint. 'You must be! What did you say? I believe you're cursing yourself for a fool for stopping when you saw me aren't you? I know you are! I *do* understand how awful it must be to have to listen but it's no use whatever. I simply can't go on any longer I must tell somebody or I should go mad! If it weren't—what did you say? I'm a coward I suppose. Would you say I was no really and truly? No I mean a moral coward I think I am. Oh I don't know I'm an absolute wash-out. I have no illusions about myself thank God for that. I think what they say's bunk about you know what one's done—I did my bit as they chose to call it, I can't stick this though it's a hundred times worse. But the nights those dreadful nights that's what simply pulverizes me, I can't face them it's no good.'

Pullman has apparently heard nothing. Satters wonders if he is a little deaf and raises his voice.

'May I ask you something or are you absolutely sick to death of listening to me? Pullman!'

Pullman proceeds imperturbable, reconnoitring ahead to left and right. He says at last, recalling himself:

'Have you tried lying with your arms out? you make a cross.'

'Have I tried! There's nothing I haven't. There's nothing you can tell me about *sleep*—or it's opposite!'

'I've known that to answer.'

Pullman slows down, peering ahead, wary, responsible. A dusky figure, distinct for a moment, passes them, face averted, moujik-effect.

'It doesn't with me.'

As the disembarking peons have rapidly proceeded inland they once more make for the riverside.

'Pulley, if you lost your temper with me I don't know what I should do I'm so terribly sensitive, if you really became cross and horrid. I believe I should go mad, never never be cross with me promise me that, but we should part. I can't bear the thought of our parting—not just yet at least, we shan't shall we? Oh do answer you do terrify me Pulley when you're so silent!'

A slight frown gathers upon Pullman's face. Satters' eyes become fixed upon the city. He trips repeatedly.

'I do wish you'd stop looking over there,' Miss Pullman scolds. 'It's best not to look; haven't you found that out yet?—most people never do—haven't you noticed?' Faint injured surprise gives his questions a personal direction, but his face stares in unrecognizing passivity ahead. 'It's unlucky.'

'That's right.—Really, I haven't seen——— What's unlucky? I know. It is. It's most frightfully unlucky!'

'Most. Then why do you keep staring at it!'

'I'm not. *You* looked.—It was *you* who looked. I do think you're unfair! I shouldn't have looked if——' His mouth works in silence; mastering his large lips he violently spits: *'Can't I speak?'* His body corkscrews towards the maddening culprit, a thick spiral.

'You are the best judge of that! I shouldn't take so much upon myself——'

'I'm not well can't you see? Don't you understand are you absolutely blind as well as dumb? You march on without speaking as though you were some stupid machine!' Satters stops aggressively. 'You can leave me here thank you very much. Yes. I'd much rather be alone I would really! Please go on, I'd much rather. I'm not your robot. I can get along quite nicely by myself! No your services are not. Really, it's not at all necessary!'

Pullman without looking stops. Satters starts forward, with enraged speed; Pullman follows suit, closely in his rear, as though at the word of command.

'You're not looking where you're going,' Pullman hisses in his ear.

'Oh do leave me alone!' Satters stamps. 'Can't you see I'm feeling rotten! I'm not a *child*.' The last he explodes hotly in two raucous pants, the child long, as *chaaarld*.

'No.'

Faint and withering, having the last word, Pullman's 'No' issues like fine cigarette smoke, impalpable and automatic.—They proceed in an electric silence. Pullman's right arm has the aegis draped on it, but he holds it phenomenally still, skewered with his stick; at most

36

summer thunder, at rare intervals, issues from it, to recall Satters to a sense of his mortal state.

Three boys approach them irregularly, coming out of the High Street, their legs convulsed, the copious pepper-and-salt flannel trousers struck, from inside, hither and thither violently. Satters sees that one is Marcus. Their school-books are wedged horizontally between their waists and the inside of the elbow-joint. The ribbons of their boaters have diagonal stripes of black and yellow.

'Are you going in?' Marcus calls. His hat blows off.

The High Street is a tunnel, or the street that is called Straight; there are booths; it is an eastern bazaar. Satters is going in, but stops. The boys stop.

'Don't look at them! They are peons,' Pullman mutters huffily. He cannot see Pullman.

Marcus pounces upon his straw-yard, as it spins stolidly off on its rim, revolving upon its plaited umbo.

'Peons. Who?' Satters looks hard at the boys. Their faces are grey and elementary, their eyes mere disks of verdigris; he recognizes that they are peons.

'They are scarcely human,' he remarks.

'No, they are the multitudes of personalities which God, having created, is unable to destroy,' the voice of the immaterial guide declaims, but Satters fixes his eyes for the moment upon the sunlight which is opaque as milk upon the tropic pavement, in which the restless feet of the impostors are hidden, as they charleston sideways.

From behind the other two Marcus approaches him charlestoning stealthily and slowly.

'It's a pity your people are broke! Poor old bean!'

Satters is about to retort; his hat blows off. It stands at a slight angle from the vertical, stuck upon its disproportionate flange. As he lowers his trunk towards it his left leg sweeps upward behind, in deliberately clockwork arc. He snatches it *tang!* out of the pavement, his hand pecking down upon it as slick as a bird's bill. As the stiff trunk goes up again the leg comes down and the foot reaches the ground beside the other. With a hollow report he cracks the hat back where it fits upon his schoolboy pate, imbedding the talons of its serrated edge in the taut scalp.

'Lend us half a crown!' Marcus mocks. 'I say Satters, lend us half a crown like a good fellow!'

'We're in a hurry,' Satters hears Pullman say, blotted in his rear. 'Please don't detain us with your idiotic requests.'

'I like that! I'm stony. No that's right, stony broke. Don't you believe me?'

'Not with a name like Marcus Morriss!' Satters feels Pullman's sneer upon the back of his neck. He sneers quickly at Marcus, following suit, swelling a little. There is a pause. Pullman sneers again, near his ear. Satters repeats his. There is a pause.

'Don't you think so? But what business is it of yours anyway Mr. Nosey I should like to know? You weren't asked.'

'Mr. Parker!' Pullman sneers. 'How nicely you express yourself! Such a little gentleman!'

'Yes Nosey Parker yourself!' Satters sneers.

Satters could smack Marcus with his great red servile face, provoking him whenever they meet. But the reason is obvious.

Marcus keeps his eyes fixed over Satters' shoulders at the principal. Pullman, out of sight, sneers slowly, with set purpose and a wealth of meaning.

Satters turns his head; out of the tail of his eye he can catch sight of a large face manœuvring. It is Pullman's head, very large. It appears to slip off Satters' shoulder, whistling as it drops, he only sees its sinking silhouette.

Marcus stands stiffly in front of him charlestoning in hieratic St. Vitus' dance: then he moves forward, on the tips of his toes, brushes against Satters, leering over his wide high straight shoulders as he wobbles past.

'House-tart!' he purrs.

'You unspeakable bully! You——' Satters pants.

'Satters!' Pullman's voice reaches him in sharp reproach. Pullman is a long way off, a small shapely figure; he has a basket, he is shaking his head violently. 'Look sharp! What are you waiting for?'

The two other 'boys' charleston in time with each other.

'Craddocks is out of bounds!' Marcus cries warningly and alarmingly on his flank, marking time in spiral jig.

'Since when?'

'He looks awfully ratty. Say you're a friend of mine.'

'Right ho!' Satters starts after Pullman. 'Thanks most awfully, Marcus. But we're not going there!'

'Aren't you? Good egg! Well, tra la la!'

'Well, cheerioh!'

He is out of breath as he reaches Pullman.

Pullman is undersized for a large school; he is a very small boy; he has a slight moustache as at present: signs of irritation are not wanting in his impatience, attending his lumbering chum.

'Didn't you spot them? Didn't you see they were peons?' he pipes imperiously and crossly.

'No!' Satters, sheepish, bays. He remains breathless as he comes to rest, beating his breast.

'What of it?' he asks gruffly.

'What of it?' the little Pullman squeaks indignantly. 'Why you're not supposed to talk to peons; yes, you're not. But I don't care.'

The little stickler for the correct-at-all-costs is down on the peons, that's what it is; he doesn't know about Satters' meetings at night, behind the coal-scuttle; but he's right in his way. For being right he is *au fait* with some things Satters is afraid—though to hell with them all he will do as he likes!

'Marcus wasn't a peon.' (It was Marcus, after all, with whom.)

39

'Wasn't he?'

Satters feels a sneering breath upon the sweat of his neck; Pullman goes 'h'ch! h'ch! h'ch!' the air blocked in little cheap snorts of offensively sluggish contempt.

Satters, impressed, steals a glance over his shoulder in some consternation. The opening is a blank semicircle of light.

'Marcus? No! Was that a peon?'

'Please yourself!'

There are intersections of the tunnel that are cliffs of sunlight. Their sharp sides section the covered market, dropping plumb into its black aisle. These solid luminous slices have the consistency of smoked glass: apparitions gradually take shape in their substance, hesitate or arrive with fixity, become delicately plastic, increase their size, burst out of the wall like an inky exploding chrysalid, scuttling past the two schoolboys: near-sighted or dazzled, in a busy rush they often collide. Or figures at their side plunge into the glassy surface of the light. As they do so they are metamorphosed from black disquieting figures of mysterious Orientals (hangers-on or lotus-eating Arabian merchants) into transparent angelical presences, which fade slowly in the material of the milky wall. The two get in close beneath the eave of a shop to avoid accidents. Satters surreptitiously reaches out his hand to the cutting edge of the light. It is hard it's more like marble. It is *not* sunlight or it is frozen beams. He hastily withdraws his hand, looking to see if Pullman has noticed.

'Perhaps he *was* now you come to think of it. Don't be cross Pulley; I can't tell them. Was that really a peon though? How horrible.'

Pullman seems unwilling to reply outright. He peers into his basket, his eyes concealed under the wide harrovian hat-brim of the new honey-white straw.

'It depends on what you call a peon,' he mutters.

'But Marcus didn't look like one.'

'No, perhaps not!'

Grim little Pullman gravely turns over his eggs.

'No really you must be wrong. It was Marcus right enough.'

'To all appearance!'

'But I know Marcus as well as I know you! If that wasn't Marcus——'

Pullman is sneering under his hat.

'That may be. Better, perhaps! But what is "Marcus"?'

'Marcus? Old Marcus is in Mansell's——'

'But *what* is Marcus?'

'How do you mean what? Marcus.—Oh you *are* tiresome today!'

Pullman continues to fidget with his basket, and does not look up.

'But were the others peons, then, I mean the same sort of——'

'It's as you like.'

Satters leans up for support against a Turkish rug that is displayed at full stretch. Pullman is slowly going into his shell, and apt to be rough or just silent when he is, that's the way he talked before; so Satters proposes mildly, with every respectful inducement:

'What is a peon then, really?'

The response commences at once.

'It is the multitude of personalities which God has created, ever since the beginning of time, and is unable now to destroy,' Pullman mumbles under protest, saying his lesson, over his basket, in which he stirs about with his finger.

'How about Marcus then?'

'Well *how* about him?'

'Well, did I just imagine Marcus—you know what I mean, or don't you?—I'm afraid!'

41

'Did *you* create Marcus, do you mean?' Pullman's voice improves and grows distinct, but his head is sunk. He talks to his eggs as he turns them over.

'Oh all right don't beastly well talk if you don't wan't to! No, I don't mean that, that I—what did you say?'

'Why not? In your dreams you create all sorts of people. Why not in the other thing?'

'Why not in the what?'

'Why, in the other dream.'

Pullman looks up. Satters gazes into a sallow vacant mask, on which lines of sour malice are disappearing, till it is blank and elementary, in fact the face of a clay doll.

'Why, you are a peon!' Satters cries pointedly, clapping his hands.

Pullman recovers at his cry, and his face, with muscular initiative, shrinks as though in the grip of a colossal sneeze. The screwed-up cuticle is a pinched blister of a head-piece: it unclenches, and the normal Pullman-mask emerges, but still sallow, battered and stiff-lipped.

'And you're an ass! No.' Pullman mouths, as though about to sneeze, peaking his nostrils. 'What made you say that? Was I asleep?'

With his free hand he removes his glasses, and kneads the dough of his eyelids with his knuckles vigorously.

'Were you?'

'Drat the left!' He hops. 'Leg.' He stretches his legs. 'One has to keep moving here and no mistake! Asleep? No. Somnolent, you know. I must have dozed. It's the infernal heat. When we're asleep there's not much left of us, that's a fact. We may be less than the dust for all I know—*Socrates awake and Socrates asleep* what is it?'

'I suppose so.'

Satters coughs. He examines Pullman's plausible face askance. He leans back offhandedly, bellying the tautly drawn rug inward with the hemispheres of his lowering shoulders, in flabby trance. He closes his eyes.

'Then I could create you as well, couldn't I?' he drawls, and yawns.

'I expect so.'

Pullman squints at him with vixenish reserve and yawns.

'Are peons—— What was I going to say? Are the peons——'

'Men?'

'No not men; I mean are they always peons?'

Pullman is in a huff; he moves the previous question. The dialogue prevents him from leaving.

'They are not *always* peons.'

'*Always* is a big order. Once a peon, always a peon: is that what you mean? Not necessarily.'

'Yes I expect sometimes—— They are human like us, aren't they, in a way, Pulley?'

'Not like us.'

'Not like us? What is the difference? Are we very different? I believe we only think we're so different.'

Pullman is bending over his basket.

'I have to go to Craddocks.'

'It's out of bounds.—What is this place Pulley? I forgot to ask you.'

'This? It's the city of the dead I imagine. Can't be too sure——'

Pullman ducks. As he speaks the lambent grain of the wall falls into violent movement, then it collapses, a white triturated dust puffs into the bazaar. Satters plunges into the dissolving surface after the small darting figure with the basket. He closes his eyes, there is a soft rush in his ears, there is an empty instant of time, and he is hurled from the sinking fabric.

For a few seconds he is confused. He is still aware, as an image, of the scene from which he has been expelled. But the river is there in front of him: the city is reflected in it, as it is near. Pullman tramples beside him, bareheaded, in his slippers. The strangeness of the abrupt readjustment is overcome almost immediately. Then at once the present drives out everything except itself, so that inside a minute it for him is the real.

Pullman takes no notice of him. They continue their methodic advance, but Pullman is now leading. Satters begins to lag behind, eyes on the ground.

A strange voice rises upon the atmosphere, in apostrophe:

'Tempter, I am new to you! You see me for the first time. What is your opinion? I should think you were about fed up! *No news?*'

The voice bawls a little the final remark. Satters looks up and gazes about him his face lengthened with fear. Pullman stalks forward.

There is a silence, full of the immense negative of the unseen Tempter. Satters wheezes.

'Depart!—Be off!' A pause, then quickly: 'Exceed! Evade! *Erump!*'

The words are pronounced meticulously, in the even voice of the dominie. It's old Pulley! Satters' face relaxes. He eyes with mischievous satisfaction the unconscious figure. The words are Pullman's but the voice and the manner those of a stranger.

Pullman scratches his chin. He stares round quickly at Satters and catches his eye scuttling back into his head. Satters coughs. Next moment Pullman crossly jerks the mute figure at his side, while its smell in his nostrils affects him with a gripping queasiness. Frowning, he eructates slightly twice, then again, expelling the sensation—planting his slippered feet, as he advances, with additional firmness. He whistles a few bars of a chimes. As a person guilty of a spasm of wind in a select company, but who covers the breach with a stolid eye, so Pullman disregards his lapse from the rational.

Looking over at the city with a frowning intentness he begins in a stern monotone:

'That shore is not for us yet!' He looks back at Satters, stressing the weightiness of these conclusions. 'Some say even it is a mirage.' He eructates again, a little genteel crack. 'It's in another dimension.'

The studious, dapper, high-shouldered machine struts forward, swelling with disciplines.

'What's that?'

'It's not there really.'

Satters swings his head round violently towards the metropolis across the water.

'Where?'

He imagines the bazaar, there are a double set of images.

'The waves are years, the water is "Time-stuff", as they call it; that is the idea. I don't credit—I mean the idea is not mine, that's the sort of thing they say, I only tell you——'

'Tempter!' Suddenly Satters laughs in hoarse retrospective mockery. 'Tempter!' He points, with violent clownish grin, at his companion.

Pullman turns on him squarely, his little mouth working for a moment hysterically in suspense of the will, a silent stutter, his amused eyes contemplating Satters. The stutter breaks, in a compact volume, and is poured out in one breath:

'Yes *Old Scratch!*' (Quite right! Old Scratch!)

He turns away his head, once more they are back in their respective orderly rôles. His compulsory absence from the scene where they are walking is quite recognized by Pullman—such absences are regrettable, but, realized, they take on a different complexion. Some minutes pass in the grinding plod of Satters' stogies and the opaque soft patter of his slippered companion.

'Had I been managing this show,' says Pullman, practical and chatty, 'I shouldn't have placed the city there, within sight of the camp. You can't help looking at it, every one finds that, it is an obvious difficulty. Yet most people when they look at it feel as you do.—This river bank is always empty, except for the peons.'

The time-stuff crashes softly in the stillness, the murmur to the west is like a filmy wall of sound only. The city is always hushed. The sound of a pick or oar-splash arrives at the end of its sound-wave journey as though at the end of a corridor. Satters espies a dark human stork, wading, net extended.

'I should like to paddle, like that fellow! Do *you* see *him*? No, there! I suppose you've never paddled—I mean here? Is that possible? I mean possible. When is it—what? Not now of course I meant. I should adore.'

'No.'

Pullman is the iron girder supporting these delicate unstable effects, refusing collapse. *He* is there! That is sufficient. He puts his foot down. *Not.* Not that.

Satters reels, tears flooding his eyes. His mouth works in infant rage, fighting to keep its shape. Words burst out of it towards the familiar autocrat.

'I know but I think you're too unkind. I hate you! You are *too*—— You are a selfish—— Why did you bring me out here—in this heat? There was no prospect! I loathe walking, it hurts my feet and makes me hot—you must have had some reason! You stalk along there and never speak to me you are unbearable! I absolutely detest you!'

'Paddle if you like.'

'I shan't paddle now. You want to see me get my legs dirty! You nasty-cross-beast!'

They stagger forward, two intoxicated silhouettes, at ten yards cut out red in the mist. The mist is thickened round their knees with a cloudy gossamer that has begun to arrive from inland, moving north by east. Only trunks and thighs of human figures are henceforth visible. There are torsos moving with bemused slowness on all sides, their helmet-capped testudinate heads jut this way and that. In thin clockwork cadence the exhausted splash of the waves is a sound that is a cold ribbon just existing in the massive heat. The delicate surf falls with the abrupt crash of glass, section by section.

Pullman refuses speech; they get along splendidly with regard to space, but the time is another matter. The bluffs have gone, a red rocky haugh sweeps right and left, from the river-brim to the dexter nearside horizon. They spank ahead, but in and out, in great journeys between steadfast landmarks.

'That's a good tree,' Pullman assures Satters, and they make for it.

'It looks to me just an ordinary—ordinary.'

'I know, but it has endurance. It would take something to make that cave in or—move away you know. Whereas.'

As they reach the tree it vanishes, like a reflection upon the air: they pass above its position.

'I made sure,' mutters Pullman.

He looks keenly at a flag-pole with a yard askew and a pennant.

'That looks all right,' he breathes as they make for it along a zigzag path. 'This is a bad bit. The last time I was here I lost my stick.'

'No really?'

'It's a fact. It's the most troublesome stretch of all.'

'I shall be glad when we're through it won't you?'

'There's worse to come.'

They are blown against a fence, surrounding an empty circular parclose, irregularly planted with high posts. The gust flattens and then releases them; as its elastic pressure abruptly relaxes they rush back-foremost into a void for a few steps, recovering from this reverse winded and giddy.

'It's a sort of vortex you know'—the breathless Pullman stirs his finger round in the air. 'Its centre is over there, where you see that cloud of dust.'

47

'Do let's get along don't you think? Why does this path twist so much? I suppose we must follow.' Satters indicates the habit of the track they have engaged on to baulk unaccountably a promising expanse, without anything to show why its course has been altered, in favour of a rough approach. By its vagaries they are pitchforked into bad patches of rocky litter.

'Yes, it's better. All these tracks have been made by the peons. They know the place inside out.'

The scene is steadily redistributed, vamped from position to position intermittently at its boundaries. It revolves upon itself in a slow material maelstrom. Satters sickly clings to his strapping little champion: sounds rise on all hands like the sharp screech of ripping calico, the piercing alto of the slate-pencil, or the bassooning of imposing masses, frictioning each other as they slowly turn in concerted circles.

Never before have there been so many objects of uncertain credentials or origin: as it grows more intricate Pullman whisks them forwards, peering into the sky for lost stars twirling about as he has to face two ways at once on the *qui vive* for the new setting, fearing above all reflections, on the look-out for optical traps, lynx-eyed for threatening ambushes of anomalous times behind the orderly furniture of Space or hidden in objects to confute the solid at the last moment, every inch a pilot.

They get no nearer the flag-pole. Pullman alters their course. A tree is perceived not far ahead. They reach it in determined tramp. It slips back into the air spinning down to an impalpable thread, as a whipped top loses body then snuffs out in a flashing spasm.

'Where did that go?' exclaims Pullman, looking keenly round.

'Over there,' cries Satters nervously, pointing to a tree.

Pullman gives it a capable glance in its new position.

A boulder entrenches itself in the path they are ascend-

48

ing; as they near it it skids away in precipitate perspective to nothing.

Stopping composedly, Pullman removes and wipes his glasses, his eyes while he is doing so never ceasing to shoot out vigilantly to every quarter of the compass.

'This is a thoroughly bad bit.'

Satters is dazed; he now answers his leader's behests mechanically his mouth dropped open.

Soon things grow easier, they come again upon the railheads of miniature tracks. The features of the higher ground, with the regular wall of low bluffs, return. They seem to escape very quickly. Satters looks up and the new setting has come up to them; surely this is where they were?

'Where's the river?' he inquires at once, in his normal voice.

'That's napoo.'

'Oh! Why? Shan't we?'

'It will be all right; we shall find it never fear the old river's never far off. But you don't see it here.'

'Isn't it there? I see.'

'I'm afraid not! I wish it were.'

The strain slackens, Satters' eyes sunset swimmingly on either side of his nose; but they roll ajar with each lurch ahead, the eyelids working upon a balance, doll-like to open and shut.

'Damn this bitch of a track!' cries Pullman through his teeth.

'There's nothing like it!' mutters Satters thickly. 'Don't let's go back that would be too much! Do let's go on, I feel good for another ten miles or even more.'

'There aren't ten more.'

'How do you mean?'

'We should find ourselves circling back.'

'How about those mountains over there?'

Pullman casts his eye in the direction of the distant volcanoes.

'We couldn't reach them.'

'How long would it take?'

'They're not in our part of Time at all. We couldn't reach them if we walked on here for ever. We should just be turning round.'

'But we see them. I don't understand how.'

'We can see the stars can't we?' Pullman exclaims testily. He adds in a calmer voice: 'If we had the necessary instruments we could see their mountains. Well, if our eyes here are so adjusted to Time——'

Satters revives: as he is paying no attention Pullman stops.

They are back upon the normal riverside, to blaze their itinerary while it is there.

Pullman disengages the gossamer that is collecting upon his legs. Satters' torpor passes, cosy security the order of the day. It is balmy though so hot. The water's lovely. Pulley is there! How he loves! This careful pal, destined to be met by him, specially despatched, perhaps by God Himself—who knows?

Satters day-dreams and stares and steins while he clings to his new-found instrument for all he's worth.

Pulley has been most terribly helpful and kind there's no use excusing himself Pulley has been most terribly helpful and kind—most terribly helpful and he's been kind. He's been most terribly kind and helpful, there are two things, he's been most kind he's been terribly helpful, he's kind he can't help being—he's terribly. He's been most fearfully tiresome when he likes and he's been tiresome too but who doesn't when they're not? He has been most terribly. But who does ever? Oh I don't know! There can be no mistake about it all's not on one side when it's not all smooth sailing it shouldn't be—there are one-sided housetops—brickholds and there are mutual arrangements not one-sided I mean they are mutual. That is his or he should say theirs. He's sure it was so.

He's been terribly kind and helpful. Every fellow's not then in the camp he's sure this is the first. One doesn't know when, to be well off. As well off.

'I'm jolly glad we met!'

Statement for statement, once and for all, it's as good as you'll find! I mean it (I am glad!) to sound silly.

'Oh Pullman look how wet I've got my jacket and my!'

Big rich-voiced pleasure yodels vainly. Duty stares away into its Nirvana: Pullman takes no notice, in fact.

But Satters intercedes, soft-cheeked, why Pulley *should*? why should Pulley? why on earth should Pulley! and he loves to be bossed to be Pulley-bossed, he adores, and to be jolly helpless is young and heavenly, to be like that when so many fellows. Really he's jolly lucky there are so many. Fellows and fellows and fellows—*and* fellows. There are great stacks of fellows of course.

'I'm wet but you don't notice! Just turn your back while I wring out.'

Pulley p'raps does but he shows no sign. He is always thinking about ways and means.

'I'm not sure if we haven't come too far north!' Little Pullman's brows are knit.

'Have we?'

'I'm not at all sure. I can't make out where we went wrong.'

The girl-who-took-the-wrong-turning laughs softly to herself. Pullman turns round at this, but with gentle banter Satters takes cover behind his broad fat back, and giggling wrings out the last drops from its tail at his feet, and shoves the horrid damp thing back in its place inside and buttons up.

'I believe we should have turned to the left.'

'Should we?'

How perfectly sweet he is Satters laughs and takes his arm, he rubs his lazy eyes with the backs of his sleepy awkward paws and yawns; stretched open at the beefy gills, his little ox-tongue quivering in the gap, he pats at his mouth, palm out, with absent-minded knocks, to stop himself. He ends on a feline bellow of content.

'Should we (yah-yah-yaaaah!) to the left, do you think? It's too late now.'

Pullman frowns harder as he feels the big hand lie in ponderous surrender, hot and heavy against his ribs. He starts slowly advancing, as he calculates.

Satters sweetens his lips and eyes, to nestle up, dawdling in tow:

'It was jolly meeting you Pulley!' he presses. But they are to start completely afresh as though they had just met for the first time and nothing disappointing had ever happened; the honeymoon note wells up, in moist contralto. There is no fatigue. He gathers himself neck and crop for the new push.

'Pulley do believe me when I say I don't know what I should have done if we hadn't, I do really mean that, it was too marvellous our meeting like that! I do think also it is so romantic after such a long time it was ages.' He is pensive, he suppurates the old days. 'Did you forget me Pulley I mean absolutely—I never forgot you. But it is terribly strange our meeting in that way all the same don't you agree, I had no idea you were in the camp. I can't tell you how glad I am. Are *yoooo*?'

Shyly he squeezes Pullman's arm. At the contact of the immense and burning hand, patches of caressed body spring into goose-flesh, locally shuddering. A sensation of brisk change establishes itself in his arteries, but Pullman's face is discreetly blank.

'I'm glad we met.' Negligent and quick, eyes turned away, Pullman catches in his hand a floating gossamer. Lifting it, he blows it upward.

'Chimaera! What masses of this stuff there is! *God has passed*, they say—in the night.' He returns to the personal, abrupt and to the point. 'I dreamed about you last night.' He half-stabs the perspective of the figure beside him with a regard that is the glancing edge of a concession. 'When you turned up just now—that accounts for it—I thought we had an appointment to meet! You know how one thinks. It must have been the dream.' He picks off another drifting gossamer. 'Oddly enough you were just as you are at present. I remember the cap.'

'How marvellous, Pulley! Fancy your dreaming that we met! Was I short or tall?—I always dream of myself as short—and weeny!' He pouts.

'A sort of tot.'

'Yes a disgusting little fellow.'

'You were in every respect as you are at present as a matter of fact,' Pullman without looking blankly remarks. 'It was a confused dream. What was it? It was a nightmare, I suppose. We had an adventure—I've been trying to. *What* was it?'

'Oh do try and remember! I should most awfully like to hear it! Do try and remember what it was, Pulley! I believe in dreams most awfully don't you? Some I think are horrid. I had a perfectly *beastly* one last night.'

The beastliness of the dream becomes exoteric in his disgusted lips. He dawdles. A big moody schoolboy, his eyes probing the ground, full of adolescent sadness, Satters allows himself to be led along. Big dreamy-eyes and business-like little Miss Pullman, the new governess, out for a pococuranting stone-kicking promenade, rapt in childhood's dreams away from the horrid crowds.

'Shall we try and get passed through together?' Pullman asks with the minimum of eagerness.

'Oh, Pulley! Do let's!' Satters lisps, throwing a baby ravishment into his gaze. 'That would be too divine! Can we?' The flattering light of ravishment quickly, mechanically, dies; his head is hung again in appropriate disillusion.

'I don't see why not, if you'd like to. That's for you to say.'

'Is it? do you really mean it you don't do you? Oh Pulley you know I would! Don't you?'—(a squeeze)—'Do let's!' Satters stickily lisps. 'You're a perfect darling Pulley!' in a florid whisper, on a hot and baby-scented breath.

Pullman's hair is growing quickly on the top of his head, pigment welling up from the follicles. A large ribbed curl develops gradually upon his right temple. A transformation is in progress in his face: the lines become fainter, colour returning, conforming to the time-universe at his side that has attached itself. He brightens, he takes the air more freshly into his lungs.

Satters revives to pour out, in a rich whining sibillation, leaning heavily upon Pullman's arm:

'Oh I do wish we could Pulley that would be too lovely! Are you sure it would be all right, do let's try!' He looks up into the face of responsibility, bowed forward and slouching for that purpose, with swimming bright-eyes, his large beef-eating hands shyly clinging to the fragile fingers of the arm he holds.

Pullman tosses his head, and releasing his hand without thinking roughly from Satters' clutch, sweeps the now flourishing lock off his forehead, from which the eczema is departing. He is unconscious. Stern and erect, he dreams the hero-dream, plans a busy afternoon for self and charge. But the discarded hand is snatched back angrily by its owner.

Pregnant women's bodies saturated with milk; and Pullman more delicately flushed, with a more sparkling sedateness, provided with a softer, more silken, covering of hair, every minute: Satters examines, under his lids, with resentful eyes, the second of these *eternities*, in ferment at his side. Savagely he strikes out at the hot gossamer, the stuff-of-God surviving the daybreak, which in some places floats in blue clouds in the draught near the surface of the earth. Pullman swims familiarly in the floating down, as though the fluff of his own small wayward moustache, and the silk of the new hair, gave him the right to breast its impalpable drifting body with that composure.

Uncertainly once more the china-blue set in massive earthenware, with its pink glaze from frosty football fields, is clouded. Satters buries his hands in his trouser-pockets: he sets his eyes in sullen staring torpor to show he doesn't care: and silently withdraws into his private nursery. There all speaks Satters, and he beats out the matter in relentless day-dreaming dialogue with Pullman's image, for it is time he did.

Pulley has been most terribly helpful and kind, terribly kind and most awfully helpful. He has been kind and in a sense helpful, though not so helpful. At the start he was helpful and kind now he pushes his hand off his arm as though he had some infectious disease, he forgets he is not alone, but why not, if he feels horrid? He has allowed Pulley to be helpful because he knew how kind without which he would not be worth bothering and it is not fair to take advantage of his wish to be kind as Pulley has. To come helping him like that was rotten if he did not intend to wherever they were be awfully decent as he thought he was. Not that he minds but from the start it was understood. If Pulley did not want to come along it was up to him; it isn't as though he were without experience, he should say instead of being horrid and never answering when he spoke and thinking of himself all the time instead of understanding just a little. He is a selfish.

In burning appropriate soliloquy the first neuter show-baby hen-pecks his dolly Pulley to himself and comes out of his nursery, with a cave-man scowl for the rejuvenating mask at his side. The less stable ghost to which he has been attached, it seems, does not look at him now at all.

It is most upsetting because he is tactful to be treated so unkindly; Pulley knows he would not have come all this way simply to be upset. It is most unkind and terribly upsetting. Satters sulkily drops into The Well; it's the only way; he has nothing to say to Pulley who has become a perfectly crashing bore and it's better to go into one's well, well one's shell there's nothing else to do.

The protohistoric jowl which carries the fat flower-lips whose favourite food is prunes and prisms juts out in bull-dog trance; Satters dawdles displeased; he will not take any interest, he does not care which way he goes, but Nannie urges him a little with a deft hand, and says:

'Are you tired?'

Satters violently shakes his sulky head: the lips addressed to the acquisition of the paphian *Mimp* quiver.

'Are you sure? You look a little dark under the eyes and absent-minded, and you're so silent. I can see I shall have to look after you; I'm not certain you should be out in this heat at all.'

But Satters has stood enough of it; there is another Satters. Out of the nursery Satters-number-two shoulders his way to show this Nannie! A guttural roll ascended into his voice, he grumbles suddenly forth:

'It's a bit late in the day to think about that! God it's hot!' He stops forcibly, mopping his face. 'Where are we going? I'd give something for an ice drink! My kingdom for an ice-julep, or grenadine frappée, what?'

The war-time officer of the Mons Star and mess-kit, in blues, sick and to be petted, makes his appearance. The stage shakes. Ma'mselle of Armenteers, the faded cartoonesque byword, is there almost palpably in the cheerio of his accents, the feminine expelled, or just a mascot—and she is really Pulley, embalmed in the zero-hour of those in whose life she was one of the last apparitions.

56

Nurse Pullman is silent, she notices nothing, except that her eyebrows rise. What coarse expressions the child picks up; I'm sure I don't know where he gets them, Nurse's distant distrait shadow-smile conveys. Pullman half hero's-nurse, half nursery-governess, advances frowning.

'Let's get out of this beastly stuff can't we?' Satters exclaims, picking from round his mouth fibres of gossamer. 'It's getting down my throat.'

'It'll do you no harm.'

'I daresay. But—— Pfui! What is the beastly stuff? Is it spiders'——?'

Pullman gives his eye the cock of the uplifted martyr, detached into the cloudy ceiling of the masterpiece, as he says:

'It is the dissolving body of God's chimaera. That is the correct description, if we are to believe——'

Satters blows, then spits angrily.

They soon get into a space where there is much less of the drifting funicles of gossamer.

The volume of perspiration discharged by Satters is presently doubled: a violent itching of the neck and back supervenes. This is detected by Pullman; it is with difficulty that he masters his concern. Blowing his nose repeatedly, he expels in stout blasts a slight snuffling prurience. The starting water disappears in the décolleté cleft of Satters' shirt: but he sweeps the bubbling sweat upward from his cheeks with a khaki handkerchief, which he wrings with lowering sensuality, lips in the Græco-Roman gymnastic adolescent pout. Pullman's feet slacken their relentless tattoo; he hesitates, taking a few perfunctory touch-and-run looks, for the form, at the drooping decomposed calf, and carries his eyes up into the hot sky: but he comes to a quiet halt, and remarks loudly, not to look that way:

'How hot you are!'

'Yes, I appear to be.'

'But you do on the whole feel much better for your walk?'

Satters stands and drips like a snow man in a thaw, from the nose and chin. He puts his handkerchief in the way of the water.

'I wonder where it all comes from? There's pints of it.'

Sagacious, quiet-voiced, plodding Miss Pullman remarks in rapid undertone, uncertain if such a truth could convey anything to The Child:

'We're nine-tenths water.'

Satters sullenly impounds the sensational truth: as evidence of its telling quality, his eyes, darkened immediately with a balance of alarm, contemplate sections of his person, suddenly that of a man-of-water. *Nine-tenths!*—so nine-tenths would soon no longer be there! He fingers the clots of his moist shirt over his midriff daintily.

The terrors of existence after all grow no lighter in this old schoolfellow's company with water on the brain. *Wisely* up till now has he baulked such friendship and kept to himself! He sighs simply and softly.

His guide with a careless little sweep of the hand places the cracked and dirty ground at his disposal.

'Let's have a rest. You're not up to it, that's evident. I suggest we take it horizontally till you are cooler.'

His heart full, with one black look, the junior partner tumbles down with a grunt. Pullman reduces himself abstractedly to a shrunk and huddled shell, just out of touching distance, a matter of a fathom and a stand-offish fraction, sniffs and is silent. They are on the edge of a space blackened by a recent fire, a charred midden for their immediate prospect. Pullman squats alert and cool, his stick shoulders and arms a compact circle, within which the head knees and trunk at different levels are collected. Satters at his side is an animal chaos, heaving and melting, restlessly adjusting itself to the tumpy uncompromising earth, thrusting up into him the sharp edges of its minerals.

'Have you got your *Bailiff's Paper*,' breathes Pullman in frosty unconcern, looking away. 'You know, the questionnaire you were served out with——?'

Satters gazes up at him. Always asking for something!

'Do you mind if I look at it?'

'What?'

'The paper with the questions. Weren't you given one?'

Satters worms his hand sulkily into a pocket, the opening compressed over the thick butt of his footballing hip, contorts himself grunting, scratches under the army cords, hauls out painfully at the end of his hand, secured by the inward pressure of his finger-tips, a crumpled parchment.

'Is this what you mean?'

'That's it.'

He tosses it over to Pullman.

'What's it all about? I haven't filled it in.' He coughs and waves at a shadowy filament bearing down upon his face. War-time Satters has come to stay, as the complement of the Pullman now emerging: impatient and masterful he shows himself, but Pullman is not to know. 'It's too deep for me. Phew! This heat gets me down! You look as cool as—— How do you do it?' He blows. 'What are we supposed to do with that?'

Pullman examines it.

'Shall I fill it in for you?'

The other looks up quickly, scowling.

'Fill it in? No, why fill it in? There's no tearing hurry is there? Here, give it to me. I'll——'

Pullman hands it back to him with unruffled pointed dignity. Satters bends over it, beads of perspiration hanging in disequilibrium upon his forehead, then plunging down splashing the crumpled paper. Pullman lays his stick beside him with deliberation, then charging his hand with an ounce of stony sand, riddles it slowly through his ten fingers, with a lazy rolling movement of the sieve from side to side, as it trickles away.

Satters reads: ' "*Have you been inclined to say—There is no Judgment and there is no Judge? What is your opinion at present on this point? Is or is not?*" Oh!'

'Well?' Pullman is cold.

'Well, what does that mean for the love of Mike?'

'What it says—you must write "Is".'

'Oh you must write Is? That's all is it.' He reads, frowning:

' "*State whether in life you were Polytheist, Pantheist, Atheist, Agnostic, Theist, or Deist.*" What on earth? I say. Help!'

'What do you say?'

'Was I Polytheist—Pantheist—what's the difference?'

'Between which? Theism and Deism?' Pullman looks over patiently at the big furrowed and perspiring brow, the chaotic locks, of Satters the dunce, the Owl of the Remove, the chump, the bufflehead who is always bottom. 'Both are heretical metaphysical doctrines. Theism believes in an immanent spiritual power, Deism separates its God from Nature.'

Satters looks up.

'Pullman, have a little pity on my youth! How am I expected to know, at my time of life? What shall I stick down then? Theist?'

'No. Write—"*None of these.*" '

'Is that the proper answer? If you make me put the wrong thing I shall say you told me.'

'You can. That's the proper way to answer it.'

'It's a sort of catch then, is it? What's the idea?'

'It's quite simple. It is supposed that in life you were addicted to crossword puzzles and during the period of enforced idleness, as the Bailiff puts it, in the camp here, it will help to keep you amused. It's not intended to be taken seriously.'

Satters looks at Pullman camped sphinx-like in front of him, with suspicion. This spaewife he has met is not the old Pulley. Not the Pulley he first supposed he was with. He has been deceived. It is Pulley, good old Pulley, and it isn't. At the start it was. He squints crossly.

'Oh is that all?'

Pullman is a year or two under thirty. This is apparent now from his face, and especially the freshly-waving cinder-brown hair. He is as composed as before, but his fixity is now disturbed by a constant tossing of the head, to throw up the silken tentacles of a lock of hair from his right temple. His right hand flashes up repeatedly to drive it back. It is the mechanical tossing and fidgeting of athletes and acrobats with similar nerve-racking spectacular locks, and Satters as he watches is referred back to that delicious youth in emerald tights upon a circus-trapeze flinging his divine body into a lake of blue air, milky with tobacco-smoke. Satters shuts his eyes tight, as a schoolboy would clench his hand upon a winged insect about to escape, and breathlessly follows the divine body, of bright green indiarubber. The minute green figure, its legs merged in mermaid fashion for flight, is projected again and again through the air for him, no larger than a fly. Then it stands shuffling its feet upon the performer's aerial platform, dashing back the lock of hair with an impatient spasm of the head. But Satters begins to dislike this figure; in the end it reminds him of its prototype; it tosses its head once too often. He opens his eyes and coughs viciously in the direction of Pullman.

He turns to a brooding lament; of course of one who has been terribly helpful and kind, but kind as he certainly has been not so terribly helpful. Pulley has been most terribly helpful and kind, but what a hateful beast Pulley has turned out after all to be why not confess it?— Oh! will that bloody man *never* stop? (He glares round in black protest at the tossing that proceeds unchecked. The scowl is transformed into a bilious covert backstairs grin.) Why, actually he's starting to put his hand up and fumble with his *moustache*, like a whisker-proud youngster with the first bass-crack in his elfin choirboy twitter; its sprouty contours visibly straggle less; it is neat and quite immature. Like two downy buds, one on either lip, it sprouts, plain to see, more restrained every minute, and the lock is a positive ad. for a hair-tonic—he'll be quite a big boy soon and expect to be carried about told the time and be taken down to the beach of that filthy Styx to sail paper-boats and make mudpies or listen spellbound and all Eton-collared respect to the bollockybilling and yarning of the crusted old salts, if such types haunt this treacherous health-resort. A disgusted heave of the torso shows what *he* thinks, as he lurches over expressively and slams down in churlish abandon. This new-fangled backward-growing matinee-idol's not had so terribly much to say for himself since they've met when one comes to think of it in cold blood and that's rather odd; there's something needs clearing up. What are they supposed to be doing anyway out in this heat? It isn't as though it were pleasant or violently exciting traipsing about in this ghastly place; it's a revolting occupation— that is a point that this sheikh may eventually condescend to clear up, I hope so in case not.—But he's had enough not to stand it and that's flat; it's a bore. I'm fed to the teeth wails the war-time soul. The way Pulley's monkeying about with himself is his own affair but his offhand beastly way of treating him is extremely unkind and most unfair, what's more. In the way of mateyness and all that, what has Pulley?—he should like to answer that. He has never shown, he's been jolly decent to Pulley—it's always the same. The way he ignores him or pretends to—oh he is beastly that's what he means. He's been terribly kind and in some ways most helpful he really has been most terribly helpful and kind to Pulley, who is a selfish he is hateful. Were he any one else. It is his good-nature.

Stealthily Satters lifts his hand, first scratching his neck, then it passes up higher. A deep mass of hair is met with, impending above the left ear. It is deliciously soft! He strokes it. Reassured, a light sigh escapes from him. He casts his eyes down and gently fans his lashes. Again he lifts his eyes in the direction of Pullman. His eyes fall more gently on the Styx-side sheikh, he observes their meeting in retrospect, his ears repeat the cheerful reports of their voices—they were all right, as things were they hit it off, they were friends at once as they had been; he remembered good old Pulley at school rather not! What's happening is a bore but he lowers his eyes again in a luscious decline, with handsome ginger lashes all a-flutter, and peace enters into the soul all-perplexed.

'Is there anything you find puzzling in the paper?'

The voice is the old-time Pulley's voice; it is helpful and kind.

'The paper!' Satters looks down at the paper. He is glad to have it to look at. He crinkles schoolboy brows above it applying the dunce's massage to his prickly chump, fag-fashion.

He reads in an aggrieved voice, stopping at 'subversive' and swallowing in dumbshow drily:

' "*Whether you bring with you any subversive designs upon the celestial state. If so, of what nature are those designs?*'"—I call that a silly question—I should like to change *this bloody heat!*'

'Put that down, then,' rattles Miss Pullman, as quick as thought.

Satters laughs. He throws the paper aside, and rolls over upon his back, his hands forming a suety nest for his head, the jutting bongrace of his out-size cap blotting out the upper half of his face with its crescent shadow.

'You haven't caught the spirit of that document.'

'No I haven't that's a fact!'

Pullman drops upon an elbow, making a slender raking profile, more suitable for confidences or easy conversation.

'The Bailiff encourages jokes,' mildly expansive, he proceeds, warming to this congenial instruction. 'If you want to get into his good books you will find that that's the way. He's really not so black as he's painted. Haven't you ever gone down there and listened to him? I mean for a whole morning, say? When I feel a bit under the weather I go there. He cheers me up remarkably. I was very surprised at first to find—you hardly expect to find a sense of humour in such a person. He really can be extremely entertaining at times. He says himself that people come there as if he were a music-hall.' Pullman indicates the paper with his stick. 'That particular question he expects you to take as a joke. He put it in on account of that faction—you know that sort of bolshie crowd that lives in an enclosure away from the rest——'

'I know the—that classical crowd,' rolls roughly the war-time Satters, frowning upon bolshies, conshies, highbrows, and all strange cattle.

'Classical! Well yes, they call themselves that. They dress themselves up to look like peripatetics, you know Aristotle's school, who used to walk about; they weren't allowed to sit down—that's why they were called peripatetics—there's nothing else very classical about them. That's the lot I mean anyway, they poison the air of this place. I can't understand why the Bailiff puts up with it. I shouldn't.'

'It's damn funny; I shouldn't either.' Satters yawns convulsively.

He stretches out his hand and picks up the paper. He reads:

Chest measurement.
Waist ditto.
Neck ditto.
Biceps ditto.

With the fumbling circumspection of the bedridden, the shoulders huddled, his right hand travels over his body. It squeezes the twin-pudding of the biceps. With the help of the other hand it constricts the waist-line while, extensors at full stretch, he flattens himself along the ground. Making a callipers of his index and thumb, he fixes them upon his neck, the thumb standing steadily upon the sterno-mastoid surface, while the point of the index seeks, underneath, the antipode required for the diameter. He removes this claw carefully, then holds it up before his face, a battered semicircle, disposing it in profile, the horny flukes stuck aslant in the red flesh, each podgy dactyl crowding out its neighbour. It remains there, the object of moody inspection. Gracefully relaxing, the index cranes out, a duck's neck emulating the lines of the swan, the remaining fingers drooping behind it. He stares at it, with little movement on either side, the face and hand suspended in front of each other, the arm a crazy bridge for them.

With pathetic aspiration, the index yearns forward again, then tries a graceful droop. The hand is turned over on its back, its mounts bulging with fatality, the scored and padded underside stiff with fat, above swollen annulate wrists.

'Look at that fist! No, I ask you!'

Pullman flashes an eye over the pendant pincer, as it is revolving back till it hangs with its fat legs dangling again.

'Yes the hands put on weight here. The feet too.'

He points this remark by advancing his own miniature

65

ones, extending them side by side, a neat demure brace, tiptoeing alternately very slightly, in dainty rhythm.

'What does?'

The pulsing of a heavy musical instrument reaches them from the rear, a monotonous flat throb.

'What's your waist?' asks Satters.

'My——? Oh, I'm rather slightly built of course. I should say—— I don't know. That's of no consequence, he's only teasing you.'

'Who?' Satters is examining the paper. 'I say. How can you measure the size of an eye. *Eyes. Size. Colour.* I haven't so much as seen my beastly eyes since I've been here.'

'That means *large* or *small.*'

'What are mine?' gruffly.

'Oh *large.* Very big. Lovely big ones! And *blue.*'

Without turning his head, Satters listens greedily.

'Grey?'

'No *blue.* True-blue!'

Satters' discouragement passes: sounds of suppressed good-humour are heard from him. He rolls and stretches full of lush self-feeling.

'I say look here. I'm not sure this was meant for my young eyes. Is it my mind that's not nice, or isn't that? Well!'

Pullman has an indulgent smile. He leans over, and Satters' finger picks out for him the questionable words.

'What's that mean? Is that——'

'Yes.' Pullman snaps in to cut a long (and toothsome) story short, beaming faintly with lazy indulgence; the babe has found something to keep it quiet!

A silence sets in; Pullman conveys his attention to a remote spot in the riverine middle-distance. There a naval engagement appears to be in progress. A half-dozen large fly-boats are grappled in mid-stream, and the violent swarming of their crews, which is just visible, pouring from one hull, swart and almost flush with the tide, to the other, suggests some description of insect-conflict.

So Pullman mounts guard, alertly abstracted, satisfied that his buxom charge is busy with his game of marbles provided by the joking Bailiff for such occasions. All correct! a perfunctory dart of the eye establishes that: the obscene facetiousness of the form provided for this nursery constantly operates. Pullman returns to the naval battle: he observes dark specks tumbling from the extremity of the largest of the vessels. Evidently the defeated faction being driven overboard: the peons often fight: he sighs: it is no doubt one of their only recreations! Other boats are now approaching the scene of the disturbance, coming out from the celestial shore. His dutiful eye slews for an instant back to his charge. Nothing unusual: but as it is about to flit off again to the distant encounter it is checked. A look of conventional anxiety clouds it as it hovers before returning. *What is this?* the eyebrow curls in a fine voluble question-mark. Impressive danger-signals have made their appearance, but they are trite, he does not trouble to check them. Still they are in for more trouble it is plain.

A stealthy convulsion, which had escaped his notice the first time, is in progress. The symptoms prevail on his attention a little, the inexorable professional eye lights up at contact with a problem.

Satters still sprawls upon his back ripped open down the front to the waist, a hairy rift. The crumpled entrance-form is held stiffly before his nose as though every part of his face were shortsightedly participating in the Bailiff's expansive whim, the paper rattling where it touches some portion nearer than another. Teeth bared, belly shaking, he shivers and jumps in chilly silence, with catching of the breath and fierce hissing sighs. The tears roll down his cheek, ploughing their way through the moist nap of sweat that has collected.

Pullman, the polite faintly-ironical professional question-mark, sits on sentry-go. The face is concealed from him by the parchment form, which knocks incessantly against it with an inanimate rat-tat. This has the appearance of a crushed mask, but without eyeholes, lips, hair, or any furnishings, about to be fitted on, blank but plastic. Pullman peers idly at the dancing parchment; its palsied rat-tat proceeds. The headless figure beneath vibrates in secret enjoyment, so it seems, of a tip-top joke, which it is essential should be kept to itself. It hides its face: it dies of laughing!

Sometimes this monotonous seizure seems hastening to a climax. But it sinks again into its jog-trot of chattering syncopation. Pullman has an uneasy movement, a change of leg, a suppressed sigh. Dismal and vigilant, he gazes sideways at Satters. He has lost interest. The usual typhonic symptoms continue. The front of the thickset trunk is flung up and down in abrupt jumps, eructating with the fierce clockwork spasms of a dog with chorea. Pullman looks away. The disciplinary barges have reached the spot: they bump. There is a fresh excited swarming. A new battle begins. Many black specks catapult out to left and right, vanishing as they meet the glassy river. It is the exodus of the victors probably, before the onset of the city-police.

A new noise has occurred, causing Pullman to return to the patient. Nothing has changed; but a weak voice, the sleek falsetto whimpering of a small child in a day-dream, talking to itself, comes from under the paper. Pullman catches the words, and weighs them mirthlessly, while he watches, ears coldly pricked for more.

'Stones is good! What a *gime*! What a *gime*!'

Still! A displeased expression definitely sets in upon the face of the featherweight sphinx in attendance. It endeavours, to the extent of a displacement sideways and earthwards of the head through a few degrees, no more,

68

to catch a glimpse, under the unsteady edge of the questionnaire, of the hidden face beneath, just for form's sake.

'*Oh stones is good!*' The words of his exclamations conform to the mood that waits upon the Mons Star. The mood is the djinn of the Star.

It is the war-time Satters that is beneath the parchment. The joke is too big for his capacity. Charged with the imbecility of Tommy-laughter rammed home by the facetious queries he continues to go off pop. His body has become a kicking ordnance calibrated for the 'any-old-where' of happy-go-lucky Satters of Armenteers. Now he grovels before Nurse Pullman (so hard-boiled yet kindly), the victim of the devils of Humour, of war pestilence and famine. All outside is blank Nowhere, Pulley is abolished. His lips beneath the paper whimper with the anguish of this false too great joke, his mouth and nostrils full of the Death-gas again, shell-shocked into automaton.

'What a *gime!*' he whimpers wearily from beneath the paper. 'I siy, what a bloody gime!' There is a hard hiccup. 'N'is'n nun! 'Struth!'

A string of hiccups follow, punctual with the intestinal contractions. The skaking parchment comes away from the face, warped in the undirected hand, and part of the moist mask, with its chattering lips, appears beneath.

Pullman bends towards Satters quickly, his eye full of regulation solicitude, the appointed nurse of this hero. He seizes the near hand, which lies inert, buffeted upon the chest.

'Satters! Satters! I say! What's the matter? Do you hear? I say!' He shakes him once or twice gently.

Satters becomes quiet; he is listening.

'Satters! Let's get along; we must go back! It's getting late.' Satters is seen to still himself to receive the messages from the familiar plane. Then slowly he removes the parchment. Their faces confront each other, Pullman's

69

sliding away and coming back an evasive disk; then it is removed completely, discreet and faintly huffy. Satters watches for some minutes without moving, except for the jumping of his diaphragm. There is an interval of silent disquiet.

Satters ostensibly collects himself. Pullman starts slightly as he perceives him rising from the ground. Painfully he has screwed himself in the direction of his friend; he shuffles himself up upon an elbow. With a heave he props his convulsed torso upon a stiff arm, in that position he quivers and flexes in the manner of an acrobat in the midst of his stunt.

'Thanks old boy.' His voice is deliberate: between his remarks there is a struggling massive interval resembling the rushing hiatus between the strokes of a robust and determined clock.

'Thanks; it's most awfully good of you.'

Pullman raises his eyebrows.

'My God! Is that——? No!' A voice of sickly suburban anguish booms the *No*.

A rushing incontinent interval.

'Are you going?'

Quick surprise at threatened departure.

Another interval of rustling momentum.

'Keep it still.'

Pullman looks offended. He turns his head a fraction more away, giving a further portion of the cold shoulder, jacked up with the stick; his eyes transport him to the ill-defined events on the upper flats of the river. These he perseveringly examines, picking out this movement and that upon the ships, with the eye of the practised draught-player.

'H'nch!' A low semi-rational sound comes from Satters, the shadow of a human *Well!*

It is a voice from the intestines, too internal or private to be human. It is a stocktaking sound.

Pullman revolves his head slowly back. The eyes reach their destination last. This is interesting!—Bland inquiry is distributed idly over his face.

'Did you speak?' he asks. 'I thought I heard you say something.'

Satters' eyes level their alarmed blue signals of distress, in direct beams, upon various points of the person of Pullman. They pick out spots, settle in empty fixity, wrench themselves off and fall heavily down upon the next.

'Thanks, I can see quite well.—I can't see properly. Up more, no up!'

Pullman pierces him with steadfast glances of understanding.

'That's right!'

A mystery is in process of consummation, in all its thrilling platitude, Satters speaks in sober quick undertone, the intense commonplace of the voice of the first sexual encounters of two persons. He tosses his head slightly, seeking to drive back the collapsed locks of heavy wet gold. His repulsion distorts, in imitative play, each of his sensual features, till his face has the bitter cast to fit offensive smells and tastes. To discipline his mask, for fear it should disintegrate in some local spasm of its own, he gnaws the underlip.

Expert and patient Pullman detaches his eye to keep in touch with him, then shoots it out again into the distance. If something out of the ordinary is on foot he clearly indicates that he regards it as his business to suppress it. The uncommon play proceeds, between an alert dummy on the one side and a glaring person risen from the ground suddenly to conspect it, sending up ghastly question marks, with the horror that is the due only of an ominous phantom. But all the time the matter-of-fact doll squats there squarely to belie anything of the sort. So, while terror gathers on the one side, the matter-of-fact the normal entrenches itself upon the other.

71

Satters lurches anchored in face of the non-committal Pullman minute after minute. He is rocked with the muscular contractions; on each occasion they rattle the contents of a pocket, the faint cymballing of coppers escapes. Time passes silently, in one-sided scrutiny, the clashing of the metallic material in the pocket, the husky murmur from the river. Cicadas come near them and perform; there are all the usual sounds of a wilderness under its maximum heat, at that time of the day.

Pullman tosses his head, and then with a delicate right hand waves away the negligent locks. When the words start, they grow on a dumb root, as though coming at the end of an embittered submerged discourse. Satters' voice blends with the moderate hum around them and commences on a tone of mutual understanding.

'Put that down!'

The voice-shy panting breath comes out at Pullman flatly, with a muted bang.

'Do you hear?'

Could it hear if it would? Can wood, a little head-wool, a neat waxen ear innocent of cerumen but also drumless, an eye of jade, can linen and shoe-leather respond? The bourgeois lay-figure says *No* with its dapper jutting sleek undisturbed profile.

'Put it—*down*!'

(*Dar-oo-own* is convulsively argumentative.)

'Put that *down*!' Bitter coaxing repeated.

'Put-that-bloody-thing-down-or-I'll-smash-it-you're-asking-for-it-Pullman-and-you'll-get-it!'

The hoarse clatter of staccato command stops slick, yapped by Satters second-loot, back in the battery; but stoical haughty outsider, sternly civilian, with one of the hero-poses of science, the immune figure of Pullman does not respond by the displacement of a single muscle, except to lock nervously its little jaws. It is no robot to jump to smart attention! Its nerves are beneath its own orders!

72

It levitates a fraction of an inch, however, its eye placid and icy.

'Sneaking little cad! Yes you! Contemptible cad!'

The sprig of the lordly new-well-bred has cadded at the crouching Pullman who raises his little nose as though *just* above water-level and gentlemans himself generally as much as the sitting posture admits.

'Scurvy underhand cad!'

Pullman heaves his small dexter shoulder as though to shift a bushel-weight of cads to the left.

'You unspeakable—blaggar!'

Pullman gasps then looks sideways in bewilderment. An error surely!—the tongue has slipped.

'Bll'liar-liar!' Satters shouts loudly after a moment's delay to collect himself, quite clearly.

Pullman looks down demurely, puckering vertically the panels of his delicate dewlap.

'Who licks the Bailiff's boots? Lickspittle!'

Pullman tosses his head up swiftly like an anchored ball and leaves it thrown up, chin jutting.

'Spy!'

Pullman takes on the expression of a spy.

'You think I can't see you. I know you—it's no use your turning your head away. *Your—head——*'

Pullman starts as though shot, Satters stops. *What?* The head—! not the little hairy head that carries the eyes?—it is swivelled swiftly but the memory of the face is a tell-tale phantom projected by Satters. Concealment is vain, Satters *sees* you, he has you in his mind's eye, the game's up!

'Charlatan!'—a count of three. 'Outsider!'

At *charlatan* Pullman squares his jaw and goes through the dumb show of chewing a don't-care straw. He spits.

'You may spit you low hound but I have you taped!'

A dull pause scatters leaden asterisks and zeros, a pattering shrapnel. Pullman preens himself apart, dusts his

73

sleeve. Satters wobbles dreamily, then brings his eye down with a sickly grin upon Pullman, who levitates slightly.

'Why did you bring me out here alone?'

Ah! that is the question now we're coming to it! Alone to be brought out, into the remote heat, with nothing but peons, under the menace of the magnetic city, without an object! That is something like. Pullman smiles a little.

'You know why!'

The head is attacked by Satters' eyes, though the real eyes are not exposed to this fire. *It* knows why it brought, it does, the little skulking hairy ball. Pullman shakes his head at the audience, in the opposite direction.

'Yes you do!'

You know why you brought, Pullman shakes his shoulders.

'So do I!'

I know why you brought. The knowledge of your bringing is privy to me.

'I know!'

It is unspoken, but your object was clear!

'First go off you took me in Mr. Pullman—that once was!'

You are unmasked!

How dreadfully vulgar human beings can be made by all passions, especially this one, Pullman blankly stares and blinks. They let themselves go, and presto they become the coarse animal girding on the ground at our side, hereinafter known as the prosecutor or the accuser, the eternal moralist.

'Oblige me by not behaving like a blag-blaggar-ger-guard! Yes you y-y-you, th-though you pretend to be far-away! Y-y-you damned old Cis-ciss-cissy! Yes you Mister —Pullman!'

Pullman coughs: a scandalized rigor descends upon the averted face.

74

'Y-y-y-y-y-y-you howwid blag-blag-blag-blag-blag-blag-blag-blag-blag-blag—!'

A stein-stammer that can never reach the *guard* of blackguard hammers without stopping *blag*.

Pullman puts his fingers in his ears, shutting out the blagging which passes over into high-pitched continuous stammering, and the fingers are removed with a quiet precision. Satters begins screaming hoarsely, violently hurling his head towards Pullman to drive home *blag bug* or *bag* with panting whistling discharges.

More of Pullman's back shows, still less of his front, where the stick and arms vinculated before in a nervous circle contain the squatting student-god.

With a sweeping gesture to banish something into the utter outer never-never Satters whirls his arms in one smashing all-inclusive clean-sweep and crashes down backwards: a prolonged mournful baying breaks out. Elbows and kneecaps on high, he lies a capsized quadruped, his face stamped out by his heavily-planted paws. Through his tightly-held fingers wind and water come hotly puffing, with sobs.

At last! Pullman relaxes, stretches, dumb-bells once or twice with his dapper fists, with distressed expression passes into circumspect action. He sits a moment, stiffens, gets up on one finicky knee; bending towards his prostrate pal he places his hand upon the slippery forehead above Satters' hands. Slowly he drags the nervous fingers upward, pressing back the damp hair-clots. He sinks into a sitting posture nearer in: then he disposes himself so that he can draw the sobbing head upon his lap. His delicate professional hands compress the temples of his charge, as though to constrict and set bounds to this disorder.

The vomiting of heavy sobs at last decreases in intensity. Pushing back the hair from the face, massaging gently either temple, the amateur male-nurse squats in a Buddha-lethargy, all this chaos subsiding upon his lap. The last sigh grumbles out, the mass is still. Pullman reigns sightless over the Land of Nod, his small fingers stuck into the damp coarse curls, like an absent-minded creator whose craftsman's fingers have sunk into the wet clay he has been kneading into a man.

Five-minutes passes of invisible time, though Pullman follows the shuffling of the vessels upstream, now coming apart with the clumsiness of beetles. A crude disturbance from the direction of the shore rouses the sleeper. Puppy eyes, thick-lidded and weak, open and blink, then close again; smacking his lips to disperse their fishy glue, grunting he bestirs himself in ungainly protest, nestling his head inflexibly into its human pillow. The noise continues: there is a quick beat of feet, a heavy chain collapses in a cascade of iron to the bottom of a fly-boat at the water-edge; barking cries convey question and response.

Stretching, his arms unfolding diagonally in convulsive slow-movement, he opens his eyes once more, the disk of his upturned face still flush with the inert lap in which it is sunk, his great wig-block stuck fast in the miniature vice of Miss Pullman's knees. The yellow sky overhead swims and lowers for him: he follows for a moment with nausea the rush of an impending cloud. Then, focusing upon the disturbing sounds in the neighbourhood, he turns his head with stiff neck and strained eyes, connecting over his shoulder with the intruders.

Pullman is pale; it is the turn of his long queasiness to have its climax. The spongy sweet butter-and-bread perfume of the slumbering Satters ferments and billows inside him. He is holding a little handkerchief to his nose; above its protection his eyes wander with distress hither and thither, contemplating flight.

Satters yawns. He struggles, kicks himself away from Pullman, rolls into a sitting position.

'I feel rotten!' he belches out. A large yawn breaks his

face. 'What's all this? Is it those bloody peons again? Have you a glass of water? Can we get some?'

Pullman is on his feet, standing back. Walking a few yards away, his handkerchief to his mouth, he retches violently. After the emesis he stands for some minutes quite still, his legs forked capably out, his head depressed. Then he slowly raises his face, wipes his lips daintily with the handkerchief and returns.

'How do you feel now?' he asks Satters. 'Fit?'

'Not bad. I've got a bit of a head.'

'That will not last long.'

Satters looks at him uncertainly.

'Let's get along,' Pullman proposes, approaching Satters and stretching out his hand. Satters is helped to his feet. He stands digging his fists into his eyes.

The peons are being borne inland in their primitive motor-truck. Satterthwaite and Pullman resume their walk.

For some minutes they hurry forward, Pullman setting the pace.

'Don't let's go so fast,' pants Satters. 'I'm a bit shaky. What happened?'

'When?'

Satters yawns. Pullman tightens his waist-belt, and spanks the seat of his trousers with his hand.

'Did something happen?'

'Nothing much. You were a little queer,' says Pullman, preoccupied.

'Is that all? Was I?'

He passes his hand over his face to dry it. Then he fans himself, blowing to add to the draught.

'God my poor head! What was it happened exactly? All I can remember——'

'It was nothing. Put it out of your mind. Your brain's got the fit-habit, it's a bore—you should try and break it of—but it's all over.

'Don't walk so fast—do you mind? Oh, you had——'

'Look out! It's slippery.'

'Damn! Yes, I do hate this slime'—he heaves up his massive feet with fastidious high-stepping protest, shakng off the red mucilage. 'It's worse than the sand.—Ugh!—I know it's narrow-minded but I do think this is a revolting mess!'

'It's only here. It's a drain.'

'Is that it?—they ought to drain it off—what are the peons for?'

'It's far worse to the south—it becomes a sort of fen there—it's peculiar, because it is generally so arid here.'

'But what happened? You had——'

'Never mind.'

'Yes but I'm doing my best I want to try—please don't be impatient I'm certain in a moment it will all come back to me I'm most terribly slow especially to-day.'

Pullman walks quicker to outstrip in exercise the mood of inquiry of the patient.

'It's maddening I *wish*—I catted didn't I at first when you were—no—you were sitting. Was I smoking you said you looked—I know!'

Satters comes to a standstill, the light of intelligence burst up in his face. The zest of discovery softens the inrush of hostile fact from memory.

'I remember perfectly you were holding up a mirror somehow for me to look—— Wasn't that it; of course!'

'Don't be absurd.'

'It was a looking-glass you——'

'Hardly! Haven't you ever seen that before?'

'What?—You *had*.'

'You were dreaming evidently. A glass! Why a glass? Where did I get it from?'

'How do I know? You had a glass.—I ought to have. I forget.'

'Well, you thought you saw a glass there is that it? Is that the first?'

'You had you know quite well.'

'Think! Try and bring to mind, now. Don't upset yourself. You often have seen that. Of course! *A large glass.* It is life-size.'

'What?'

'Why, what you thought you——'

'*Life*-size?' A wave of passion not evacuated rushes in. 'Oh you never stop scolding and bullying me I do think it's unkind I can't help it if I don't remember! Life-size *what*—I won't stand it I really shan't if you get so beastly cross! I'll give up trying to be——! I can't explain you know I can't explain in the way that, it isn't as though I had your experience after all is it you forget I'm not. I never said because you were behind you confuse me on purpose it's most unkind. All I said was a glass didn't I, you had—good God I saw didn't I, I can see!'

'As a matter of fact you were mistaken. But you shouldn't let that depress you. Mistakes of that sort. You mustn't allow that to prey on your mind. Every one here in the camp has that; we all have spells of it. It's nothing.'

'What?'

'Haven't you heard people grumbling about it to the Bailiff?'

'Bailiff? No.'

'They often do. I can assure you.' Pullman laughs, appreciation brightening his face. 'It's quite a common symptom it appears in hysterical diseases. Can you wonder at people being hysterical I expect we all are more or less. Portius I think it was yes that was the name, the Bailiff discussed it and cited his authority. He's always very careful to do that by the way which I think is very much in his favour. But you *must* have heard people talking about it! You can't have been here—how long is it?'

'Oh only ten days—I've told you barely that. I haven't

79

honour bright! I keep to myself I've told you Pulley. I don't.'

'Well'—Pullman examines him out of the corner of his eye, sceptical but going on—'people are warned of attacks you know by the appearance of their own image, as though in a mirror. Do you follow? That's where the mirror comes in. I have no mirror. But with us it's rather different, so they say here—whatever *we* may be: I'm telling you what they say that's all; I know nothing more than—— They talk all day long as you know. The Bailiff discussed it a week or two since. He said it had a different significance here—there's no occasion to be alarmed I mean you needn't fancy your reason's going.—You haven't got any!'

Pullman stops talking to enjoy a laugh. He continues, chastening himself:

'That was the Bailiff's way of putting it. But it's all right. You feel quite well now don't you? You see! It's nothing, really. You thought I was holding up a mirror for you to look in that was what happened, it's quite usual; it's disagreeable that's all. Why, I don't know. Afterwards you had an attack. It's quickly over—thank God!'

'Thank God!' mutters Satters.

Pullman surveys with bantering speculation the drooping collop at his side to whom he now gives a jerk. Satters starts, with resentful riposte of the shoulder.

'Thanks! You needn't——! Thanks most awfully for explaining—I heard what you said. Is it wrong of me not to know it all seems most remarkably easy to you but we all have to find out don't we?—perhaps I shall get better I have plenty of time that's one thing I may even be as wise as you some day I shouldn't be surprised.'

At the thought of the wisdom, and the time, they both stop a little puzzled and on their mettle. Pullman alters their course a few points.

'I don't believe you're listening it doesn't matter. I do think I'm wrong I mean because I keep to myself here and never—if I could manage to.'

'Things are slow—but sure.' Pullman laughs airily. 'I shouldn't try.—I've moved on twice. I'm with two Alsatians now. I never talk to them.'

'No?'

'Nop!' Pullman struts stolidly cogitating. 'I think it's better not.' (Taking one consideration with another, it's better not!)

Satters makes big round Red-Riding-Hood eyes to admit the image of the Alsatians, great guardian wolves of stone, with tongues pendent and pricked ears. He breaks off his fixed gaze, snap, to exclaim:

'I've had that before I *have* had that before that's right! What can have possessed me I *am* a moron that's what's the matter. Yes when the beastly thing comes on you lose your senses that's right isn't it? I *knew* when you said "life-size" just now yet it wasn't distinct. I dread that more than all the rest put together which is saying a good deal but I always *forget* it at least I have up to the present thank heaven I do!'

'I have it sometimes,' Pullman remarks after a moment, with condescension. 'I take that opportunity of making my toilet, which is usually much in need of attention.'

Satters is trembling. He laughs loudly with a gulp at the end. He enjoys exultantly the insult to oh! that hateful thing—to treat it like a common glass; he feels he is behaving in that way himself; he exults and laughs throatily.

'I wish I c'd take things the way you do! You have perfectly marvellous self-control you must have Pulley! I only wish——'

'Not so much! Think of the stupid maxim *Nothing is but thinking makes it so.*'

'You're different I tell you; look you must know you—you don't give a tinker's curse do you? I'd give my head to be able—to feel the way——it's no use I've tried my damnedest I *can't* get acclimatized I suppose that's it. But perhaps I shall get better I really feel I might.'

'Where there's a will there's a way! There's another appropriate maxim for you—one maxim covers the *intellect*, the other the *will.* They're a most handy pair. The Bailiff is fond of recommending them.'

Satters has a reaction into lymphatic despair.

'It's all very well for you to talk! You're *not the same.* You know you're not it's no use your saying—— Pulley. Sometimes I'm afraid of you!' Archly: 'I *am.* Quite afraid.'

'But those are maxims for the weak-minded. It's no compliment. You say I'm "different", and so on. I'm the same as you I'm an old hand you know I'm in my second month. It was a little upsetting at first, I admit, when I saw myself for the first time, seated a few yards away, surprised, like myself, at finding me there. I've got used to it that's all. What does it matter?'

'You *are* different of course you are that's all rot.'

'I promise you——'

'I've tried terribly hard to——'

'What?'

'To what yes I express myself so badly you make me worse especially with you I'm hopeless you're so critical, that makes me worse.'

The problem of expression distorts his mouth.

'My mind was made up,' he says, 'I was all in and I should have refused not to be like that any longer but to be always alone with what I can't understand, it's too difficult that is awful. To absolutely pass out absolutely, I have meant to but what is it prevents us, I'm sure it does what is it?'

'What?'

'Oh I don't know!'

Pullman coughs to exercise his throat. Satters notices the cough, then returns to the problem of expression and of confession.

'It's not because I'm a coward because it has nothing to do with it. I am I'm a little funk-coward that has to be faced but it's not that. What? Yes I'm afraid of course I am I wish I could make you understand how abjectly terrified I am then you would be able you'd see.'

'What about? I don't understand, as a matter of fact.'

Satters sulks for a minute. His words are weak. He flings himself upon them.

'Of course you would say that, you don't want to. *What does it all mean* can you tell me? No you can't. Am I mad I wonder if I am, why do I see things that are not there? It must mean something or is it nothing or it's silly to notice as you say?'

'I don't think so, it's nothing to worry about. It is the atmosphere that produces them generally they're hallucinations. They are only mirages, you know, the sort of thing that people see in the desert or at sea—phantom-ships in full sail the oasis that is not there. That's how the Bailiff explains it he ought to know. He says he sees as many as twenty Bailiffs on some occasions. He complains a great deal about the atmosphere and all the Bailiffs he sees!'

Satters jerks his head as though to rid it of the persecutions of an insect. His eyes have grown duller with sallow whites.

'It isn't hysteria then?'

'Sometimes; it depends what it is. What are you talking about now?'

'I'm just a fool of course. I've no grey matter they left it out, all the same I know there's something wrong. There's something on the cross in this show it's a pretty dud Heaven if it's *Heaven*. If!'

83

'What did you expect?'

'Expect—when? I can't say I thought about it.'

'There you are!'

'Yes, but *this*! I'm not such a complete moron as not to be able to—what? That doesn't help matters: I know——'

'Not greatly.'

'Yes but it's something to see——'

'Certainly.'

'I'm not quite a moron.'

'No. Is that how you pronounce it?'

'You needn't try and be so funny—at my expense.'

'I'm sorry, I was flippant and beastly. Go on. I'm listening attentively.'

Bludgeoning the dull ground with his stogies, Satters rolls forward frowning, brows knit, to trample and kick at least some few winged words out, hiding beneath, or embedded in his own thick head.

'You suspect?' Pullman asks civilly, inclining his head as a sign of polite attention.

'Suspect? Yes I *suspect* if you like. I suspect that's about the size of it.'

'*All is not sweet. All is not sound?*'

'All is *not* or do you think it is or what? It isn't in my humble opinion.'

'What is it, then? I'd like to know what it is, so that I may—in what directions do your suspicions lie what is it you suspect?'

'I'm not clever—there's no occasion to rub that in I know that only too well, I wish I were; I'd—well I wouldn't be here long not a minute . . .'

'No? You'd emigrate?—Well what is it that's rotten in the state of Denmark?'

'I haven't the least idea don't ask me to tell you *that*. But I know it's rotten all through from beginning to end. Putrid!'

84

'To know that, as you say, is something. But you must have some idea——'

'I know what I feel—that's all I can tell you. If you want to know, for the first go off I don't know what to make of that Bailiff fellow.'

'Ah!'

'That's for a start. He obsesses me his eyes haunt me I always see them! He hates me I'm certain.'

Pullman laughs with short superiority at once.

'You're not the first to say that. He's the best-hated man anywhere I should say—in this world or out of it. I don't agree with you that's all—I like the beggar!'

'I know I can see you do, there must be some good in him I have no *reason*: he just terrifies me.'

'Lots of people say that. I don't experience anything like that at all I can say no more.'

'Who is he has he ever lived?'

'How can anybody say: some say he is Jacobus del Rio some a Prince of Exile, I have heard him called Trimalchio Loki Herod Karaguez Satan, even some madman said Jesus, there is no knowing what he is. I believe he's just what you see, himself, he is the Bailiff simply, I don't understand the insistence on something factitive behind him or why he is not accepted as he is.'

'Do you think it's possible he may be—no I can't say it I can positively see his eyes, at this minute he's mocking me.'

'He probably isn't whatever it was you were going to say.'

'You have so much more experience than I have and you're so much cleverer and so knowledgeable you simply must be right I can't be right, you see it differently.'

'No.'

'With me it's a sensation under the skin to be near him fills me I've never put it in so many words it's loathing, I fear him but much more still I have that toad-reaction, for me he's a toad oh everything that's disgusting.'

Satters shudders, his voice weakens, the stogies strike down with less assurance.

'That as a matter of fact is the usual thing, it's the way it takes most people to start with at all events.—His is a very difficult position; I don't see how it could be otherwise, quite.'

'I feel myself here somehow——'

'Are you sure——'

'In a *trap*!'

Pullman laughs good-naturedly.

'A trap! Who or what do you suppose is the Trapper?'

Satters thrusts his large hand with difficulty in between Pullman's arm and body, and his giant fingers feel for the X-ray substance of his friend's limb beneath the cloth.

'Don't laugh at me Pulley, I know I'm a baby don't mock me if I talk terrible nonsense—what I'm going to say is.'

His hand tightens its muscles, to secure to itself its frail support.

'Pulley!' Satters whispers nasally. 'Pulley!'

The nasal whisper penetrates his own spine. He shivers at the vibration of his own stage-whisper.

'Yes? *Pulley?*' Pullman mocks, with the air of expecting this frightened word.

'You won't laugh at me if I ask you a perfectly senseless question Pulley are you sure? Is that really you I am talking to am I really—with—*you?*'

A delicate laugh escapes from Pullman.

'You suspect *me* too? Do I seem real? How do I strike you? After all it's only a matter of opinion.'

Satters does not look up: he keeps his eyes travelling upon the ground before them, mounting and descending its uneven surface, counting his steps—three, four, five, six—to himself when he is silent, in the back of his mouth. Sometimes a half-formed numeral jerks out on a catch of the breath or comes down his nose:

'Fai, Tsee, Sayv.'

'Supposing we pinch each other that might enlighten us?' suggests Pullman.

'I don't mean that. I'm not sure I know what——! It's all so dreadfully confusing.'

'That's an advance on what——'

'I've never spoken to any one else here about all this. What's the use, anyway?'

'If it eases your mind.'

'It does it's a tremendous relief; keeping it to myself was horrible all the time.'

'Now it's out you feel better?'

Satters collects himself in silence.

'Nothing I think matters I know that makes me wretched.' He squirms archaically to give the *wretch* play, and further illustrates with a painful grimace. 'I feel it must be my stupidity you make me feel it must yet I can't escape from—— I wonder if you understand what I'm trying to say or not?'

'I do, I think.'

Satters' drowning dull blue eyes fasten upon Pullman's hazel forcibly with the intoxication of despair.

'What is this place we are in?'

It is the awful accent in which Virtue would at length declare itself when at long last it had become conscious of having strayed into a den of Vice.

Pullman sketches several arcs upon the universe with his dapper prospector's eye from left to right and back. With his middle finger he ostentatiously seeks for a fragment that he suspects of having worked its way under his lid. He then replies with the a little surly reluctance of a man compelled at the pistol-point.

'First of all, we're not supposed to talk about that. I don't mind of course. Everybody does. But we are advised to avoid—we're all especially warned on our arrival not to discuss those things except at the place appointed for that purpose that's what it's there for. You're aware of the rule I suppose Satters? Or haven't you heard? You didn't read the si quis to that effect? You don't seem to have inquired much, so you may not———'

Satters nods.

'I have. I've—yes, I've heard. Go ahead.'

'Well it makes no difference I know, one can't help thinking. But what's the use? Do you want to hear theories? You'd hear enough of them and to spare if you went to the Bailiff's court at any time of the day—far too many.'

'I asked you———'

'That's easy, then, if that's all it is; it's just for the sake of talking—not to have it on your mind but to let it escape? I know nothing. I can tell you at once my idea, what shall I say?—by what mechanism we exist—as we are here, now, you and I.'

Satters drops down abruptly into a sitting position. Pullman stops, looking down at him with a mystified patience.

'Tired?'

'Yes, do you mind, let's have a rest.'

Pullman sits down, in the same attitude as at their last halt.

Satters throws himself at full length, propping his head upon his hand in tense prostration. He has again burst out into a violent sweat. With the other hand, which is trembling, he fidgets with a twig, which he uses to trace figures on a bald buff patch of earth.

'I always get giddy like that when I think———'

'Ah, really, is that it that's why you sit down? You take a pew when you put on your thinking-cap so to speak?'

'Put it that way if you like.'

'Yes, I suppose you never in your life have thought of anything of that sort.' Pullman muses at Satters. 'Now that things are apt to force you to, it comes as a shock.'

'I suppose so.'

'So you sit down when the thoughts come to the surface.'

'I usually sit down when.'

'It's much more comfortable.'

Satters heaves a tremulous sigh.

'I wish I *could* think, that's the trouble—I wish I knew what to.'

Pullman looks at him steadily, with the brooding inquiry of the analyst. His mind made up, professional decision arrived at, he remarks:

'There you go again! In my schoolmastering days——'

'Were you a beak?'

'I was a schoolmaster before the war. Afterwards I chucked it.' Pullman interrupts himself to say quickly, 'Do you remember anything about stinks? Well, you know what a Leyden jar is it's the classical apparatus for storing electricity, you've seen it over and over again in the laboratory. There was once upon a time a celebrated physicist, a man of science, called Professor Tyndall. He was manipulating a large battery of Leyden jars, while lecturing. Through some carelessness in handling them he received a very severe electric shock. It was so severe that it knocked him out. For a few moments Professor Tyndall was insensible. You follow? Well, when Professor Tyndall came to, he found himself in the presence of his audience. There was he, there was the audience, there were the Leyden jars. In a flash he realized perfectly what had happened: he knew he had received the battery discharge. The intellectual consciousness, as he called it, of his position returned more promptly than the optical consciousness. What is meant by that is as follows. He recovered himself, so to speak, very nearly at once. He was conscious on the spot of what had occurred. Professor Tyndall had great presence of mind. He was able to address the audience and reassure it immediately. But *while he was reassuring* the audience, his body appeared to him cut up into fragments. For instance, his arms were separated from his trunk, and seemed suspended in the air. He was able to reason and also to speak as though nothing were the matter. But his optic nerve was quite irrational. It reported everything in a fantastic manner. Had he believed what it reported, he would not have been able to address his audience as he did, or in fact address them at all. Do you follow so far? Had it been the optic nerve speaking it would have said, "As you see, I am all in pieces!" As it was, he said, "You see! I am uninjured and quite as usual." Have you followed?'

During this lecture Satters has yawned without intermission. His yawns have increased in intensity, like the crescendo of howls coming from a dog who is compelled to listen to a musical performance or to sounds above a certain pitch. At length Satters has remained with his mouth at full stretch, with difficulty getting it closed as he sees that Pullman is finishing.

'Yes.—That's most awfully interesting.' He yawns again, his eye fixed apologetically upon Pullman, tapping his open mouth repeatedly with his hand. Pullman surveys him with professional equanimity. He continues:

'That used to be one of my stock stories apropos of Leyden jars. The Leyden jars never came upon the scene without my telling it.'

'Really?' Satters drawls, his mouth stretching, while he glances resentfully through his yawn at Pullman, tapping his mouth more carelessly. 'I've got the most diabolical indigestion. I'm sorry to be.'

'Yes. When I got here the story came to my mind. Shall I tell you my reasoning? I said: Tyndall when he was addressing the audience was really disembodied. He had no body at that moment, only bits. He spoke from memory of the normal situation. Do you see the train of thought or not? On the physical side we are, at present, memories of ourselves. Do you get that? We are in fragments, as it were, or anything you like. We are not normal, are we? No. Conscious—we are conscious, though. So there you have a sufficient parallel. We behave as we do *from memory*, that's the idea. We go one better than Tyndall: we put the thing together in its sensational completeness. We behave as though we were now what we used to.be, in life.—I put this to the Bailiff one day. He told me I had grasped an important truth. He was really very nice about my little theory. Two days later I heard him repeating the story of the Leyden jars and in fact advancing my speculation as first-hand truth. I was exceedingly flattered. He did not mention me, I may add. That I thought was very significant and it made me think I'd probably hit the right idea.'

Pullman laughs and lolls lazily.

'Didn't he? Why didn't you stop him? I should, I know. I do think that's *typical*, the unspeakable old humbug don't you Pulley? You know you do really you see through him though you pretend not to. You must, of course, if I do.'

'Why shouldn't he use my illustration? You've got your knife into the Bailiff. You think everything he does is part of some deep-laid——'

'Not at all, it isn't that I'm not so silly as that.—I think it was jolly rotten of him to use what you had said and not say where he'd got it from.'

'Well.' Pullman scratches his chin watching his indignant partisan out of the corner of his eye. 'Now the murder's out is what he said.'

Satters is furious and confused.

'What murder did he mean that time?'

'The murder's out—that some fools would object to it but that I had hit upon the truth I suppose.'

The strong-minded peer of the most upsetting of unsavoury truths conveys a sense of the majesty of evil in his posture and expression: the occupation of such a man would be gone that is archi-evident were truth to turn into a smiling goddess.

'Are they fools? I don't believe a word he says!'

'No?'

But Pullman ignores the slight put upon his own divination and proceeds:

'But I do find his eschatology very difficult to get hold of?'

'I don't know what that is what is it?'

'The doctrine of the last things?'

'The last things?'

'Yes.'

All the last things—the Last Judgment, the last days, le dernier cri, the Last Post, the last rose of summer, Charles the Last Man and with him the Son of the Last Man, Charles too—begin to assemble idly in the ex-schoolmaster's brain in encyclopædic response capitulated under *last*. He blots out the incongruous trooping and says:

'A thousand disincarnate years in fact what is called palingenesis—not to be confused with the stoic *eternal return*—it is a doctrine of Plato, that is what I believe he teaches but I can't be sure.'

Can't you oh can't you! Satters' wide-open eyes shout at Pullman in baffled flashing. The fine puzzled intensity of a face used in constant wrestling with crossword-puzzles is turned away by Pullman from his prostrated audience of one that lies heaving in distress, the roar of yawns breaking from its lips like minute-guns from a foundering vessel: he then says:

'In that view we are palingenetic phantoms.'

Palingenetic phantom No. 2 howls with exhaustion, crashing upon his elastic muzzle with a well-bred hand and crying jocosely:

'Manners!'

'The fire-zone of the dantesque purgatory stretching between the terrestrial and celestial circles is pagan of course and I doubt if the Bailiff would admit it as an allowable opinion that we were behaviourist machines addressed to a static millennium of suffering for purposes of purification, our life staged in some such wilderness as that fixed by pagan thought outside the blessed spheres and the earthly as well, and yet I don't see how else he would account for our position, and he certainly has mentioned a millennium and hinted at a return to earth.'

A return to earth! out of the fire-zones, the restless kissing circles whose uproar you cannot help catching when you are too still, out of the machines of this mad millennium, out of the presence of this imperturbable ghost caressing these abstractions—oh! to be outside again for a refreshing holiday on the earth, there is a chance: almost slyly Satters hazards, in connection with this possibility:

'Does he say that we return to earth?'

'That was when he was referring to us as *lemures* it is true but once I heard him say that he would not be sorry to see the old hole again and there was some reason to suppose that he was then referring to the earth.'

Satters smites his stiff expanding lips and utters a mournful *Yah yah yah!*

'He's dead against the famous stoic *apathy* he won't hear of it. Epicurus' ataraxia he hates even more. The idea of the anaesthesia of death he says revolts him.'

What a man! The something-or-other of death—always death—who on earth is it that is revolted exactly by what? What is he saying now? Apathy, apathy, apathy—and anæsthetics.

'Yes!' Satters almost roars.

Pullman a little flattered plays up to what he takes to be the other's militant mood, he clenches his fist and with a hortative manner, frowning slightly at Satters, pursues:

'*Suffering*—suffering is the secret! He wants us all to *feel* as much as we conveniently can or at any rate on no account entirely to lose our capacity for acute and disagreeable sensation—also agreeable but that is secondary as all the most agreeable sensations are based upon pain in any case as he remarks.'

Satters squints in his direction, sullen and breathless.

'*Still as you go trip on your toe*—it's almost his favourite remark: what he says is "*Vulgar perhaps!* but what I like is a modern six-cylinder up-and-coming hard and hustling big-business man—brisk, efficient, with a great line of talk!"—I'm only repeating his words, but you see the idea—*Professor of Energy* what Stendhal called himself that's what he is: he is really like Napoleon.'

Satters writhes upon the ground now upon his belly howling loudly:

'Napoleon! Yah-yah-yah-yah!'

'Yes. But suffering don't forget is the main thing—people who can't be made to feel or suffer he has no use for—*or what's a Heaven for?* as he once said. He has a very mystical side to him.'

Satters violently flings himself upon his flank so that his back is to Pullman. In musical and delighted tones Pullman's voice reaches his ears.

'You know how gay he almost always is it's amazing—it is dionysiac he says, an *abstemious drunkenness*—he insists that then in fact he is drunk.'

'What with?'

This cataleptic oaf is not worth powder and shot but the subject is too fascinating so.

'What with?' repeats Pullman, 'why with God. It is enthusiasm!'

Rolling in pain as if in answer to these exhortations, Satters bellows:

'A lot there is to be enthusiastic about!'

'Perhaps not for us,' the severe voice rejoins, but it relents and pursues:

'He puzzles me too sometimes I confess. Often he will say things that would be appropriate in the mouth of a cynic. For example I have heard him quote the Roman epitaph *Non fui, fui, non sum, non curo* as though it answered the case and explained his lightheartedness. That seems to contradict the account of his divine inebriation. What can that mean?'

'What what what!' Satters rocks himself and shouts emptily.

Pullman muses with affectionate abstraction.

'He is a strange mixture!' at last he exclaims coming out of his brown study all the serener for his brief plunge into doubt, 'but I am sure you are not right about him. He is an essence he is a quiddity.'

Pullman springs lightly up, moustache wires gallantly fluttering, a hollow fetlock of trouser-leg, a short stiff border of jacket, scant wind-curtain, held gallantly out behind, giving the effect of a statuesque figure in flight.

'Well, shall we be moving? Once more. How do you feel now?' He reverses; the fetlock of trouser-leg swings to the front, the wind, with the deft hand of a tailor, moulds his back, while, skipper of all he surveys, he focuses the city.

'The Bailiff will be rolling up with his court before long what do you say to going and watching the proceedings? It's a fine sight to see him arrive, after we've seen him land we can go and listen for a bit. There's nothing else to do. You may reconsider your opinion. He's not a bad sort you'll find that out I think.'

Satters gets up like a fat arch beauty coyly rising to her feet to be taken out to dance with a slangy masculine *This is us!* He is smiling, a secret smile of conceit. 'Will you walk, will you talk, lady will you walk and talk!' *Yes!*

95

under the breath, why not? Perhaps, of course, we'll see, don't hurry me, I'll be with you in a minute! He drops the dimple of a heavy smile into each cheek—Pullman refuses to look: he says while he is waiting for the lady to get ready:

'Perhaps you'll lose your nervousness. I'm not much of a support, but it's better than being by oneself, there's that about it.'

'I should rather think so!' exclaims Satters. 'Better! It's the best thing that could happen to me for you to take me round.'

'I'm glad you think that. So let's——'

'I'm sick of myself one gets so beastly morbid don't you agree? I simply adore being with you you know I do don't you?'

Pullman sniffs, a weary superior sniff.

'How are you? More yourself?'

'Myself! Rather don't I look it?' Becoming more matey every minute. 'You bring out the best in me! I become well rather childish to be frank when you're not with me and so beastly *morbid*.'

Satters bursts with his great flesh-gauntleted fist into the ladylike aperture between Pullman's coat-sleeve and ribs. It bursts in like a bomb. The ponderous thing, with its crawling energy and heat, conveys to the slight body, in whose side it has lodged itself, the sense of parturition. Heroically weighted with it the pregnant Pullman stoically advances, with responsible measured tread. The thick-tongued voice buzzes, in clinging syllables, its refrain of gratitude:

'I'm terribly grateful to you Pulley for taking so much trouble with me.—You've been most terribly helpful and kind. I'm not worth bothering about as you have, I wonder why you do you must have some reason but I am most terribly grateful.'

A smother of red dust descends on them from the sky.

96

For a few moments they stand crouching against it, its particles pricking their skins. They emerge with spitting puffs. Pullman spanks the seat of his trousers with his free hand, then lightly slaps away the dust and flotsam on his jacket, dancing a little as he advances to clear his trouser-legs of particles. Satters' eyes go musing beefily forward; they distil into the surrounding world, in a thick over-flow, the sweetness of Satters in contact with Pullman. His lips thicken, their swollen contentment weights them like a ripe fruit: the nether lip hangs, longing to drop down in a sick rush to earth, thudding like a thumping pregnant plum. His eyes are as heavy as his lips. He gives Pullman the benefit of his inner contentment.

'I am so terribly glad you like me—I like you very much!'

The delicious confession because of the exciting crudity of words thrills him, it has the sanctity of a pact that a kiss alone could properly seal and he pauses in confusion; then big burning Gretchen he yodels on putting into clumsy brazen words all the sentimental secrecies coveted by the Fausts with jammy and milky appetites in the dark ages of simplicity.

'Everything is different since we have met it all seems to have a meaning, before it hadn't or it was too awful I'm another person, I'm simply terribly happy only I wonder if you are. I'm certain if you wished you could do anything you liked with anybody couldn't you you could with me, you have a most marvellous influence on people you must have—I'm simply clay in your hands and with most people it's the other way about it always has been. You're marvellous!'

The male is marvellous the male is marvellous—let us now praise famous males. I am your cur—you are my man!

Pullman reinforces at all threatened points the protec-tive armour of Anteros.

97

'Even when you're unkind to me I don't mind you are perfectly horrid sometimes!' (Sundry invitations of the heavy female eye in profile. Quarrel motif.) 'You know what we've just been talking about it's too marvellous talking about that to you is quite different to what it would be with any one else, it doesn't seem to matter at all; I get absolutely blue and wretched if I *think* about it for as much as a minute. I could commit shoeinside— that's what Dickie one of the fellows I've been billeted with calls it.—Now you're not listening! I know I've been fearfully weakminded I am a chatterbox but does it matter so much?—What? When you begin talking about oh all those things you know—I lose interest in it on the spot, do you know what I mean?—it all just becomes of no importance. It's most awfully odd I can't account for it. Just now I felt rotten nothing seemed to matter but as soon as you began to explain I felt all right on the spot, it wasn't what you said as a matter of fact I couldn't follow. It's your marvellous way of explaining things you put them beautifully. You make everything so clear even if one doesn't understand. I think you must have a great deal of magnetism!'

The magnetism receives a squeeze.

Satters perceives a butterfly. Snatching his hand out of its tight-fitting nest, wrenching his cap from his head, he flings himself in its pursuit, his great knees sticking together as he runs, buttocks labouring, feet flying out in knock-kneed helter-skelter. He archly contorts himself, establishing a vermiform rhythm between neck and waist. The great corsets and collars of muscle prevent the seductive intention from becoming a complete success.

'Leave that alone!' shouts Pullman after him, perceiving the object of his chase. 'Satters! Come back! Come here! At once! Leave it alone!'

The butterfly escapes.

Satters returns bright-eyed and panting, tossing his

meaty regular Flaxman curls, putting in evidence his croup, smiling the joyful-child smile of the Songs of Innocence—perspiring and 'voluptuous' while he idly trails his cap among the dusty fern fronds. As he gets near his eyes blaze the exultant 'There! did-you-see-me?' smile of radiant infancy, romping lazily back to the apron-string after a vivid escapade.

'Missed him!' he pants.

'A good job, too!' exclaims Miss Pullman, dissatisfied. 'You mustn't go after insects here, especially flies. Didn't you know? You're hopeless! It's stuck up everywhere, the notice about.'

Satters stands, hanging his head, flushed and bashful, basking in the lovely scolding, tongue-tied and happy.

'Why, is it wrong——?' he lisps.

'It's not wrong,' Miss Pullman replies severely. 'It's dangerous. Flies are out of bounds.'

'Fancy that!' exclaims little Cissy Satters ravished pulling cheekily at her apron, roguishly downcast and cunningly civil. 'It's the first I've heard of it. That's the first butterfly I've seen. Is a butterfly a fly?'

Pullman scans the horizon on the look-out for other winged dangers, nursery dragons.

'Yes. Naturally it's a fly.'

Properly trimmed as he has been, with all the observances of an admonished junior, the pleased Satters creeps forward and takes his place by the side of Miss Pullman, kicking out his feet at stones and things with rebellious absent-mindedness, his eyes dutifully lowered, craftily side-glancing. Pullman starts off again by himself this time, spanking the seat of his trousers, from which he suspects some further particles to be not yet expelled. The fine dust has been settling in the coverts of his occiput and temples, and even upon the sparser crown of his head. He dusts here and there with neat taps of his little hand, and proceeds to an equable friction of the hair. Where the

99

scalp is affected with a slight prurience, he very judici-
ously relieves it of the worst of the objectionable sensation with a finger-nail lightly rubbed up and down but
with due regard to a possible dermatitis to be expected
of too forcible a use. When that is done, his attention has
been drawn to his hands. He picks up a splinter of wood,
and improvising a nail-cleaner proceeds to the stealthy
toilet of his finger-nails.

Satters is at his heel, still chidden and tongue-tied.
Why does not Pulley rough-manhandle him some more?
his puffing pout begins to inquire, he has not been scolded
half enough! Pulley is being horrid and cross that's why
he doesn't speak! He's angry with him for having——
How could he know that the beastly flies——?

'Pulley!' Satters the dutiful puppy afraid of being hit
mutters just loud enough to be heard, but so low that he
can pretend that it was an expression of the wind's vague
dreamy unquiet if it turns out that he has been too fresh.

'Pulley!' Again, but no louder, eyes upon the ground,
still a half-step behind to the flank, trudging good-child.

'Yes?' Pullman has heard. He *is* angry.

'Are you cross?'

'What makes you think that?'

'I didn't know—— I thought you might.'

'What?'

'Nothing.'

'I don't see the river,' says Pullman, as they pass from
one compartment to another. How many valleys have
they traversed? Satters comes out of his brooding: they
are among the low blunted bluffs that stud and festoon,
in dejected reds, the back-lands of the littoral. It is a valley of rocks and sand. These are the suburbs of the wilderness, enclosed plots of desert, over each of which a
peculiar solitary sun stands all day, glittering madly upon
its apologetic fragments of vegetation, setting suddenly
without fuss, but after some hours' absence returning,

and without remark glittering again patiently and intensely upon every vestige of life for a new day. Only the wind has a certain versatility.

'I don't see it,' Satters replies, but his eye falls with displeasure upon the contents of the small valley. They go up the middle, he slouches anxiously along, avoiding certain long objects.

'It's getting hotter,' says Pullman.

There is no reply: seeing an explanation is required at once, Pullman frictions his jaw, looks severely at the pleasure-ground of the wind, and remarks:

'How many of those things would you say there were at the foot of that scarp over there? I should say there were about a great hundred: yes, about a great hundred quite that that's what I should think—they look as though they'd crowded in at its foot to get out of the way of the sun.'

Satters is not satisfied with the great hundred, for him there are no numbers. Pullman kicks with light familiarity a large lozenge-shaped rock.

'Concretionary sandstone!' he exclaims slaugily, with jaunty gestures. Satters sheers off, he will not take part. 'They all lie with their long axis one way.' He indicates the direction. 'Do you notice? There are none at right angles.' He looks round at the untidy field of fossils, as they seem. 'It looks as though some one had been here with a pot of red paint. That's oxide of iron. In the Highlands the shepherds use the hematic pigment ground down from the iron ore to mark their sheep.'

He looks down at his feet:

'There may be chalybeate springs here, even, the place is very red.'

He looks directly at Satters, smiling.

'Nature is fond of red!'

Satters is mollified.

'All wild nature is red and green.'

101

Satters responds a little with a wan peep of a smile.

'Are those the bones of animals? They must be pretty big, if they are,' he then asks at last.

'No, they're rocks, the wind blows from that quarter as a rule, it sandpapers them. Look how smooth they are!'

Satters strokes the polished back of one of them. He withdraws his hand quickly, the back is very hot.

The geologist bends down with dainty nonchalance and introduces his hand into one of the three sharp fissures that cut into equal sections the fifteen-foot stone-plantain they are passing.

'You see? They're all cracked. That must mean they are used to extremes of temperature in these parts.'

Satters' attention escapes in passionate yawns, but he affects to shudder as he imagines the vigorous temperatures required to segmentate all this concrete or whatever it was he said with the oxhide was it, red and green. Rather pretty!

'It seems ever so much farther going back,' Satters remarks. He measures the valley with a fishy eye which then meets and does homage to the light-bird's eye of Ka Pullman, flashing back to its nest.

'It always is!'

'Is it?'

'Yes; but it takes no longer.'

Satters looks up quickly as though sharply flicked. He slowly returns his eyes to the ground in front.

'That is, if you don't lose your way.—We *must* get to the river!' Pullman vociferates unexpectedly, starting off at right angles, breaking into a run for a few yards.

Satters right-turns and his hoofs submissively hammer behind the swift slipper-climbing of his guide, as the two scale the lateral terraces of the place, as they *must* get to the river.

'It should be here!' exclaims Pullman with the

youngest eagerness. 'It is here, I am sure!' He is passionate, the river is the real thing, all the rest is a shadow: Satters looks forward to the river, to be in the swim, and stares fervently upward to the little skyline a boy-scout's stone's-throw off.

'It must be here!' pants Pullman. 'It can't be there!'

'Does it curve much?' inquires Satters excitedly.

'There are two rivers!'

'Not really?'

'Yes.'

'We didn't pass this.'

Pullman scrambles sidesteps, rushes and springs. He shouts back:

'You must *will* the river you know; it makes it shorter.'

'Does it?' Satters breathlessly rejoins. 'How do I do, when you say?'

'Just wish frantically for the river with all your might and main! Set your teeth and say to yourself "Every moment and in every respect I get nearer and nearer to the river!" '

'But we *are* near to it!'

'I'm not so sure of that!' Pullman hurls back darkly.

'We *can't be far*!' Satters gasps in the rear in pitiful injured protest.

'We may have got a long way off.'

'We can't have.'

'Why not? When did you last see it?'

'Just now.'

'When was that?'

'When we were sitting down.'

'But that was ages ago!'

Satters is breaking down, the pace is killing, he cannot hypnotize this absent water-course, he is faint: when *was* that that they were sitting? surely not so short, that is, long? His mouth shrinks into his face; his submerged lips start to quiver, he huskily whimpers upwards:

'Don't be ratty!'

'I'm sorry.—I believe it's here after all. Isn't that the city?' As they near the crest Pullman surpasses alpinists and acrobats. He leaps one after another the thick-lying rocks, then swarms up a slippery sandstone body of great bulk. His venturesome figure is outlined against the sky, whipped with the hot wind, his hand grandly shades his eyes, but he is too stock-still as though stopped and there is something in his pose to show that he has met with a setback and been stopped. Satters, burning with curiosity, lumbers dully up, scrambles bulkily panting to the side of the arrested statuette.

'What the devil's this?' Pullman's voice is as sober as before it was all on fire. Satters does not like to say what he sees—he could say what's nowhere to be seen what isn't; he steals a glance at the frowning Pullman, who continues blankly on the look-out.

The squire, Satters, grins as he sees no river, and, rubbing up against his little master, whispers:

'Pulley! Where is the river?'

'Where indeed?' Pullman removes his hand from its place before his eyes and puts it in his pocket. 'This is a bore. What is that there? Can you make it out? I thought I knew this road.'

There is no next valley, either. There is a wide view stretching as far as the eye can reach across flattish country. It is bounded by rain-clouds, they block the horizon. Then there is snow.

'It's like a picture,' Satters suggests, haltingly, afraid the word may not be right.

'Exactly!'

Oh! *snap!* the snubbing little beast! He couldn't have said worse! Pulley *is* in a passion, Satters is sorry he spoke, he'll take good care next time!

Nothing seems to be moving on its surface, their four eyes report, ranging and ratting round in all its corners.

It is a little faded like a very much enlarged rustic colour-print.

Pullman looks knowingly up at Satters and with a slight smile insists—but in a strange coaxing voice for master to squire——

'This is nothing. This will not detain us long—though it's a bore.—It is a large-scale hallucination.' He throws himself into an attitude of detachment. 'I've seen them before.'

'Have you—like this one?'

'It's nothing at all really. It's a time-hallucination—we don't get them often but I've seen several. I daresay it has not much depth, perhaps none, perhaps a few yards—time-yards, I mean! You see how the wind stops in front of us?' He thrusts his hand out. 'That's about as far as it goes. That tree there, you see,' pointing to an oak on the farther side of the crest upon which they stand, and but a few yards off. 'It's not disturbed at all, is it? Its leaves are perfectly still. But it's blowing hard enough here. It stops dead. You see?'

Satters assents.

'You see that ploughman?' Pullman points. 'He has not moved.'

'Perhaps it's a peon.'

'A peon? No, that's not a peon. They never dress like that. On that stile there to our right—can you see that bird, a sort of English rook?'

He whistles off the summit of the rock, alights concertina-ing in flattened perspective, squatting in professional crouch, swiftly assumes the erect position, in an agile detention, stoops and picks up a fragment of sandstone: then, planting his feet wide apart, and swinging dexterously and manfully back, he launches the small brickbat in the direction of the bird.

'You see? No sign of life!' he exclaims, as the brickbat strikes the stile. 'Come along, let's enter it.'

'Hadn't we better—why not walk round it Pulley? I don't like the look of it.'

Pullman stands hunched contemptuous and indignant, beneath, his stick featuring stuck high under his tame arm.

'Why? Of course not. That would take hours. We'll go through it.'

'It may take hours, if we go.'

'Hours? Not at all, at most a few minutes.'

'It looks to me most uninviting and most beastly. I may as well be frank. I don't like these things!'

'Why not? Come along. It's a complete bluff.'

He waves his free hand cavalierly.

'It's hollow! It's only Time!'

'So you say. But how about us? I'll stay here.'

'Well, I'm going in. You do as you like.'

Pullman, striding lightly, passes into the picture.

Satters watches him for a few minutes, then suddenly scrambling down, slipping on the slick surface and dropping in a shameful heap, he gathers himself together and follows. After taking a few steps forward he encounters what by contrast is an icy surface of air. He stops, catches his breath. For a moment the hot wind beats behind him, then he steps into the temperature of the 'picture' or the 'hallucination'. It is moist and chilly but windless.

'It's preternaturally still in here!' Pullman remarks as he catches him up, without looking round. 'It's like being in a vacuum.'

Satters inhales the new air, a critical eye cocked beside his dilated nostril. Having analysed it, he reports:

'It's a little musty isn't it? It's like a damp vault.'

The other sniffs and fixes his eye while he tastes.

Satters looks back. There is an iron railing where they had stood, and apparently a circular verandah. A group of posturing figures, with the silhouettes of ancient fashion-plates, pivot and point to all quarters of the compass, occupied with the view. Their arms stand outstretched, as stiff as cannons, or travel slowly across what they are surveying. One aims a telescope. A butterfly female revolves a grey parasol. Two point in his direction. These figures are swaggering a great deal, for peons, it is his opinion. He is about to draw Pullman's attention, but he sneezes. His face decomposed he looks round at them and inquires casually:

'It's England, isn't it?'

'England?'

Pullman makes his way sturdily across a meadow, treading the green and dewy nap with a step to the manner born, born to the English grass.

'It's supposed to be, no doubt.' He savagely spurns a characteristic buttercup. They make for the ploughman. As they are clambering through a breach in a British hedge of prickly shrubs Pullman meets with an accident. Violently forcing from his path a stiff bramble, as it flies back into position it rakes his wrist. He stops, his leg thrust into the vegetation, and dabs with his handkerchief at the beads of blood upon the scarified flesh.

'I don't like being scratched—at least not by this sort of stuff. You never know what it's made of. It may be anything.'

'Rather!' agrees Satters, as he sits down in the ditch to wait. 'Absolutely anything. It looks like deadly nightshade.'

He gazes with extreme depression up at the rigid lifeless hedge, and Pullman's busy figure, with one small nimble leg stuck into its mild mantrap.

'It's all desiccated, you see. It's not alive.'

Pullman bends back with his finger a black twig.

Satters stamps mournfully on the grass at his feet.

'Nothing here is living,' he mutters for his own benefit, drowsily, noticing that his footprint remains where he has compressed the grass-blades, as it would in a living field.

Pullman vaults over the ditch suddenly, commencing to stamp about on the other side of the grassy balk to rid himself of the material of the false vegetation.

They now ascend the field, following a recently tilled furlong that stretches straight to the man, horse, and plough, where these are transfixed in the act of ploughing.

'Good morning!' Pullman sings out in hearty style as they approach.

His voice echoes in a hollow manner. He goes up to the motionless man and stands at his side, inspecting him carefully from head to foot.

'One would swear he was alive! Also the horse.'

He goes over to the horse. Removing his stick from under his arm he prods it in the flank.

'The flesh gives, you see, just as though the thing were a living horse!'

'I think it moved,' Satters says, turning away.

Pullman looks man to man, a foot from his face, at the ploughman. He has russet side-whiskers and clean-shaven lip; his features are in the frowning sleep of an occupation that requires no consciousness above the animal. His hands grasp the stilts; he has just, with a dreamy rolling movement, reeled to the left hand, in his plodding advance, guiding the ploughshare. The massive horse, shut in by its blinkers, has been arrested in its toiling dream, one hoof in the air. The blue eyes of the man stare away abstractedly into the nothingness always before him in his working-day.

Pullman turns towards Satters.

'*When the sleeper wakes*, you'd say! It's quite uncanny. It's the most lifelike waxwork I've ever seen.'

Satters is dreamy. A painful lethargy taking possession of him like a rough drug engrosses his attention. It attacks his limbs first, he moves restlessly to counter it.

'Don't let's stand here any longer,' he complains.

'No, it's best to keep moving,' Pullman's formula mechanically asserts, and, shaking his shoulders for form's sake, he makes a start. 'We don't want to be stuck like that lot,' he concedes to his friend's startled face.

They move away down the field. Its lower area is untilled, and terminated on one side by a turnpike.

'If we follow that we shan't go far wrong,' Pullman says, and vaults the low gate.

After some minutes' sharp walking they come up with a wagonload of hay accompanied by an undersized wagoner and drawn by a small horse. These are in the same condition as the ploughman: the wagoner saunters forward lazily, his hands thrust under his smock-frock into his breeches-pockets, a straw in his mouth. Nothing moves in this system any more than in that of the plough. They pass close to the inert wagoner.

'Time stands still in this land.'

'I said it was England,' Satters answers, with a lame and sheepish laugh, Pullman smiling. Satters' lethargy increases, he feels his legs wading in dreamy trance. He pulls up energetically and passes his hand over his forehead with masculine friction.

'I say, Pulley, I feel most awfully drowsy! What do you think about all this? I believe if we stop here we shall become like the rest of these people.—Shall we turn back? I don't see how I can go on.'

'What's the use of that? Let's get through it quickly. It can't be very deep.'

'I'm not at all sure I shall be able to stick it.'

'Don't allow yourself to say that—of course you will. It's pure imagination—tell yourself that at once. It's through seeing all these people entranced all round you, the stillness of everything and so forth, it's pure autosuggestion. I don't feel like that so it can't be the place can it? It's you.'

'Oh all right but I know I shan't be able. I'm half asleep already. I think it was absurd ever to come here.'

Pullman affects the harassed air of a man beset by some innocent question, the technique of reply presenting difficulties out of proportion to the truth involved.

'It's like the opposite of insomnia, what you're troubled with. Look, why do you suppose so many people find it difficult to sleep?'

'I can't imagine. I shall be asleep in a moment all right myself.'

'No you won't, I shan't let you. People get it into their heads that they won't sleep, and as a consequence they don't. It's a fear-complex, nothing more: if they could only say to themselves that it doesn't matter if they sleep or not, so long as they're resting, then at once they'd fall asleep. That's the analysis of that.'

Satters bays a long yawn of distress, glancing hurriedly at Pullman, as his lips are closing, with hatred.

'You're just the same, only the other way round. You believe now that you must fatally go to sleep; and sure enough in due course you will hypnotize yourself into sleep. I, on the other hand, shall make it my business to see that you don't!'

Pullman laughs genially to himself.

Satters' heavy footfalls on the macadam echo like steps in a deserted drill-hall.

'It does sound empty in here doesn't it?' says Satters. 'It's like being in an enormous empty building—at night!'

'Of course it does. It *is* empty.' Pullman corrects him at once.

'Your voice sounds awfully far away,' Satters persists.

'That, I'm afraid, is absurd. There's no reason why it should. You've invented that.'

He glances with the mildest severity at the naughty

lying alter-ego detected within Satters to whom he is signalling peremptorily that the game is up.

'Do I sound as though I were speaking in a jug?' asks the obstinate patient.

'No you don't—your voice sounds the same as usual.'

That's another one for the untruthful child within who at last takes the hint. They continue for a little, Pullman setting the pace, bustling along full of tiny bull-dog grit. Occasionally he will stop pointedly and allow Satters to catch him up and pass him before restarting. After a keen glance in every direction, he remarks:

'This is Old England we're in.'

His voice booms upon the Old English air in vacuo: Satters responds with a sickly dumb salute of his closing eye.

'The emphasis is on the *Old*!' Pullman exclaims, gazing in all directions.

A large sheep-dog is trotting, held by the rigor mortis that conditions everything, in the middle of the road.

'Eighteenth Century, I should say. What do you think?' He points to the style of a scarecrow, which owes its wardrobe to some wig-wearing creature. Satters looks away from the scarecrow with what of his eye is left uncovered by the lid.

Pullman whistles to the dog; Satters avoids it, with downcast eyes.

'They had lots of these beasts then.' He pats its back as he passes. Satters believes he hears a growl, but it is Pullman being facetious. Satters looks away in disgust.

They pass a thatched cottage. A diminutive woman is in the act of drawing water from a well. Her quilted petticoat and arch rustic bonnet increase the squat appearance. A stationary man, in gaiters, of the same stature as the woman, is half in and half out of a low door, dark-visaged Old-Weather-Man.

'They're on the small side aren't they?' Pullman nods

111

towards the cottagers with proprietary detachment. The Victorian district-visiting in his blood carries his eye blandly over the top of the honeysuckle of the hedge and makes it insolently free of the picturesque occupants of the cottage, entering straight in at their doors and windows with feudal directness.

'It shows how much bigger we've become.' A conscious massiveness thickens his gait: he rolls a little on his frail pins. 'It's always popularly remarked how all the old armour was made to be worn by quite small people. Here is the proof.—Perhaps it's the Seventeenth Century.'

In turn Pullman's voice slows down, runs along automatically, or starts up with a sudden reinforcement of attention, the idle accompaniment to his busy eye, which ferrets near-sightedly into the details of the homestead.

'That is possible.'

Satters, become a scowling sleep-walker, is led by Pullman, who has taken his arm for the occasion, through this occult village-life, turned into deferential statuary for the time-tourists.

'It's quite likely. Late Seventeenth Century. Several things seem to indicate it!'

Satters *yooahs*, showing his teeth like a greedy dog.

'Really?' He strikes himself a back-handed blow upon the mouth. 'That must have been a fearfully long time ago! My ears are buzzing, Pulley; let's take things easy; do you mind. I feel most uncomfortable.'

'That ploughman's face was very Dix-Septième Siècle.'

Satters' face gathers and furrows, for him to discharge a disquieting impression.

'His face terrified me! I didn't tell you at the time—I felt he knew quite well you were looking at him! Are they dead or what? I feel we ought not to be here—I can't help it.'

'Ought not? Well, we *are*; so.'

'I know. But I feel an intruder. What business have we! Well, I know, none, but we didn't ask—it wasn't as though we wanted to come. Still I feel I'm trespassing.'

Pullman allows a minute for the examination of this point of view then says:

'It's the stillness, I expect. I should rather enjoy it if I could feel I was trespassing. It must be in your case a fear-neurosis, probably on account of the hush and chilly air.'

'Haven't you the sensation that some one is watching us?'

Pullman laughs at that, relieved, encouraging his voice to clatter in self-confident staccato in the stillness, for its tonic properties.

'Who do you suppose would take so much interest in us? We're two little nobodies. Besides, our behaviour has been most correct. We can give an account of ourselves, can't we, if challenged? We are an innocent couple. We're doing nothing here we shouldn't.'

'That may be, but I can't say I feel comfortable all the same.'

'You never do!' Pullman laughs with soft-eyed obsequious banter. 'When you say you feel you're trespassing it's some infantile fixation, I suppose. It's the *out-of-bounds* feeling don't you know—it refers to a time when you were caught stealing apples, I expect. You feel the farmer's in ambush somewhere behind the hedge!'

Holding Satters at arm's-length, his arm payed out to its fullest extent, he daintily warps him forward towards the hedge, where he seizes a honeysuckle by the stem. The plant repels him, whereupon, after a little forcible screwing of it this way and that, he approaches his nostril. After a brief communion with its striped yellow wax he withdraws his nose, very slowly frowning, as though in that close proximity something had passed not at all to his taste.

113

'Scentless!' He utters the privative term deliberately, as if to indicate that perfume had been withheld from his organ by the flower.

Still detaining Satters, airily mortised by a row of flimsy finger-nails, fleshed in the seam of the sleeve, he tiptoes provocatively, with heels coming out of his slippers, and peers over the quickset hedge into the kitchen garden. He fixes his eye upon the washing.

'It's Monday here!' he says. 'That is, if she's a good housewife.'

'Sure to be I should think!' Satters yawns with vicious abandon.

'Yes I should think so,' Pullman agrees, still on tiptoe. With a last look at a billowing white rank of roughly-scalloped underclothes in profile he turns away, remarking—as his severe eye withdraws from one particular inflated pantaloon—with speculative distaste:

'Seventeenth Century!'

He returns, a little conspiratorial, stepping exquisite and feline in his slippers over an old-English cowpatch, to his patiently halted convoy, whom he then releases as a sign to move on.

Two more cottages are passed; at the second a ruddy muscular hatless lout pursues a rushing maiden into an orchard. She has his hat in her hand. They both appear to be falling. Pullman averts his face from this violent scene and examines a cow, its head thrust up into the sharp network of the offside hedge, the shuttle of its underlip, having reached the left-hand extremity of its oscillation, grotesquely protruding, like an organ that had slipped.

Pullman's movements increase in pert force, he lifts his nose to sniff the atmosphere in general, buoyantly advancing upon the balls of his feet.

'The air of Old England suits me—I should say the Old English air!' he exclaims, constricting his nostrils, his moustaches fluttering beneath sensitively like a ragged swarm of olfactory antennæ.

'So it appears,' sneers his sleepy drudge. 'I can't say as much for myself.'

But Pullman throws him a glance of almost vulgar good-nature.

'No? I evidently was built for Time-travel.'

He treads the soil of Time with a light-hearted pioneering step. He has a slightly Dix-Septième Siècle look, he thinks.

'I'm in my element, that's what it amounts to. It's most unexpected.'

His small lips chatter quickly as he prances forward:

'You are slow in the uptake on the Time-track—Time-track.'

Satters rolls heavy-lidded eyes occasionally round upon the conversationalist; a wakeful misgiving disturbs them at the second Time-track.

'Time is giving up its secrets; we're behind the scenes!' Pullman next remarks impressively. 'Would it not be lovely to meet the nomad-angels in their quiddity upon these Time-roads as we might with luck?'

'Don't you feel tired?' Satters pants.

'No I can't honestly say I do. You still are I suppose?' The tail of a flicker of the eye barely reaches Satters. 'We'd better not call a halt here though; I might have to carry you out on my back!'

Pullman consciously develops his glee.

'I know now what it is, one thing about myself I've got wise to that's puzzled me quite a lot from time to time and I'm glad to be privy to. I like other dimensions! That, I'm afraid, has to be taken as proven it's strange, isn't it? I feel as much at home as possible in all this it's childish, I feel ridiculously at home! I could howl for joy—*why*, I haven't the least idea!'

He accelerates, moving with a light and dancing step.

'This two-hundred-year-old air is like an ancient vintage. I feel positively screwed. It is the identical nephalios methe—the drunkenness that is abstemious I've caught it—I know now! It doesn't have that effect at all on you?'

Satters coughs in his slumber-walking, and noticing the hard echo of Pullman's voice ricocheting round on the Time-objects, says:

'What?'

'It gives me that yankee feeling of being on top of the world.'

'Oh! Is that all? So it seems.'

'Yes. The elements must have been very oddly mixed when I came about, in the dark backward, when I come to think. Do wake up! They're all at sixes and sevens here over the birth-question, the Bailiff's solution is unsatisfactory to my mind. I shouldn't be surprised if one day I met my mother, I hope I shall; but I should if I met my father.'

He presses fiercely forward, his neat white teeth with their graceful absence of set or spread ambushed beneath the bristles of the squalid cavalier moustache, as the father-son motif crops up, with savage appeals from its stage-tomtoms.

'I consider *the father* a side-show a mere bagatelle— they are like the reason, overrated and not essential at all, that is the fathers—the male at all if it comes to that.'

He laughs, clearing up the atmosphere. Exit Fathers like a cohort of witches, turning tail at sight of the bristling righteous phalanx of incestuous masculine matrons, with hittite profiles, hanging out like hatchets just clear of the chest, Eton-cropped, short stout necks firmly anchored in asthmatic lungs, with single eyeglasses, and ten diamond corking-pins representing the decaceraphorous beast of the deliverance. They guard the child-herds.

116

Revolutionary cockades bouquet'd with spatulate fig-leaves, symbolic of absolute divorce anti-family son-love and purple passion, dissimulate their abdominal nudity. Pullman barks fiercely: he is the gelded herd-dog. He barks at the heels of the Fathers, bearded despotic but now despatched.

'You don't find it slightly intoxicating?'

Enter unobserved at the other extremity of the stage a small select chorus of stealthy matronly papas. They applaud as one man, community-singing the national anthem of the New Babel jazzed. They take up their position in the nursery modestly as regards The Average, with caressing eyes like head-lights of Santa Claus doing his rounds. Sweetly handwashing they stand aside, retiring Big Businessmen. Featuring as their spokesman, a super-shopwalker offers meat-pale sunkist fleshings of celanese silk stuffed with chocolates, crossword-puzzles, tombola-tickets for crystal-sets, and free-passes for war-films, to the million-headed herd of tiny tots of all ages but one size.

'I think it's perfectly splendid discipline. I'm never quite certain, myself, if it's a pukka White Man's policy. There's the other fellow to be considered even if he's a mere pawn or peon.'

Pullman consents to look towards Satters in his eagerness, a reply being due. They are at cross-purposes over this. Made aware of the hiatus, the dummy remarks, dispirited: 'What would happen if they all came to life suddenly?'

Pullman is all bright tense and controversial.

'You would grant them a measure of Home Rule!' he answers 'unhesitatingly'.

'What?'

'Dominion Status eventually.'

In a long expectant pause Satters is driven at last to drawl out:

117

'They might be rather objectionable—*When the Sleeper Wakes*—possibly some would run amok!'

Pullman advances unmoved at the prospect.

'That always has to be reckoned with.'

He grows more zealous and communicative; he throws Satters one after the other, with rapid patronage, observations made topical by his excitement.

'This running to and fro is most exciting, don't you agree? This to and fro.'

Satters trails his eye skintling and hangdog, to evade his master's novel expansiveness.

'Moods, I suppose,' he mutters. 'It's all the same.'

'Not quite. When was there a distinct privilege—without provocation? They were throughout gages merely, nothing you could bite on, a symbol here and a symbol there. I could never stomach them.'

Satters squints angrily at this.

'And how about the next one?'

'It's all the same—they're all the same!' Pullman exclaims in weary singsong.

They both rest on their oars for an interval, Satters stumbling along short-winded, his breath sawing a little in his throat. Pullman is the first to renew the discussion.

'Our relations to time and space are in the nature of things enlarged; that was to be expected. The removal of the space-barrier makes a tremendous difference, other things being equal.'

As the words are not taken up, he adds, with an effort overcoming the habit of silence which threatens to re-assert itself upon this:

'As a matter of fact I was on the slow side to start with. The possibilities of this additional plasticity only dawned on me after—when I got the Bailiff-habit. That was quite early.'

'You were not like this at first?' Satters inquires with expressionless accents wrung from a mind half-numb.

'Quite at the beginning I might have been anywhere. Do you hear the hammering?'

Satters hears an ominous hollow thumping, he hears it and thrills with every nameless misgiving under the sun, since there is no explanation at all.

'It's a sculptor, I think,' says Pullman evasively, waving his hand towards the sky. 'Sounds like it.—When war was declared I was in Trieste—in Spandau, I should say, at the Berlitz, teaching. That really got away with it and pulled me back half the time I thought I was there. It's most remarkable how two times can be made to fit into one space and that only a functional one; no one can call *this* physical except by courtesy or for convenience. And it seems as natural as possible, ut trigonus in tetragono it beats the bugs! But I was new to it; I used to find myself going to mass at the Bailiff's court—no, really—with the utmost regularity. Everything passed off as at the mass in Spandau except that afterwards I resumed contact with things on the spot. I discovered my mistake by argument usually. However, one morning the Bailiff detected the slip I had made, most cleverly, in my opinion. I was kneeling down. Some one pushed me over, and my glasses broke. The Bailiff took them from me made a pass over them with his hand—like that— and returned them to me whole: séance tenant. It was my first miracle! You can imagine my feelings!'

The hammering proceeds, from underneath it sounds. The blows become as expressive as the midnight blowings of a shunting goods-locomotive, the reports subsiding to whispered taps then thudding up into increasingly loud blows suddenly, with thrilling echoes attached to form a long determined sound.

'Where was that?' asks Satters.

'When? In Spandau,' Pullman answers frowning. 'For two or three days it was there off and on. Once I was in Oxford. I soon shook that off, though even now I forget

119

sometimes—and it's always Spandau of all places!—or is it Trieste? one always suggests the other; I never see them clearly, so I think they must be together in my mind—you know how things grow together in your mind, for no reason; in dreams they always occur together, when you're in one you're in the other. I was not there long—thank God! It's a ghastly hole.'

There is a thunder of blows and a slight vibration under foot.

'It sounds rather near!'

'I know! It does. But that's nothing to go by, *near* and *far* are very relative. I once thought I would like to get back just for a night.—It would be a rotten feeling, don't you think, revisiting the glimpses? It's pure curiosity.'

Satters protests with impatient shrugs like a man in his sleep discouraging a mosquito.

'Nothing would surprise me once they'd started,' he shouts.

'Nor me!' gleefully Pullman agrees like a shot. 'I've served my apprenticeship. I don't think I should be— I *have* been through it, I am wandered too, I am come out all right, come through—very well up to the present.'

'It can't take long can it now?'

'Oh no, of course not now!'

Satters draws his stocking up tighter. Pullman out of the corner of his eyes awaits the new start and falls into step with a nimble skipping shuffle.

'It's unlike anything I felt in the old days—under terrestrial conditions,' he says. 'The sense of freedom one sometimes gets is perfectly staggering, outside. They're wise to draw the line they do—if everybody made a habit of wandering about they'd have to spend half their time looking for lost sheep. Except for the camp—that is, a radius of a mile—all this is not properly organized, that's the fact of the matter one feels the difference almost at

120

once, it's quite wild here. The Time-flats they used to be called to start with. This was a chain of mountains years ago: they were only bubbles. Time is far more dense, of course.'

A woman, standing behind a hedge, a Katinka Queen of the May, in lurid cylinders of muslin, with a merry Mayday squint, watches them pass.

'You must get a method, that is essential,' Pullman remarks. 'A little goes a long way. The trouble is you haven't properly got clear of your old life. It's a common case. I should say you belonged first and foremost to the human dimension, however.'

He examines Satters critically, in the bulk, from head to toe, in a generalized instantaneous stare.

'That accounts for everything.'

It is silent again but considerably warmer. A torrid breeze reaches them from the quarter towards which they have been heading, through the porous denseness of the steep hedge. Satters begins to tear at his throat now, throwing open his male peep-show of bush and buff, as the first currents of the familiar heat play upon his face.

'Do you often experience a longing for life-on-earth? it is the regulation question. I expect you do, that's the snag in your case. You have to get over it. I think you must be what the Bailiff once described as *a natural bug.* —He means spook of course.'

'I'm dead beat. Are we never going to get through this?'

Pullman looks round with surprise.

'Before long I hope. It takes it out of you, certainly, Time. I've got a strong head, it's most necessary. I delight in these Time-spaces, they are passages really. You don't often come across them like this. Reversibility is the proof that the stage of perfection has been reached in machine-construction—it's the same with us, in my opinion. Here we are going backwards aren't we? But in the case of men their perfection involves not only ability to reverse, but to be inverted too—that's theoretic: I don't mean actually to stand on their heads, of course.'

'If you go on like this I shall scream.'

'What? You tempt me to go down on my hands and demonstrate! No, I won't, it's not necessary: only, you *are* a disbelieving Jew!'

Swinging forward now with the presumption of a pocket-Hercules Pullman grins back at Satters, but he pulls himself up and resumes, didactic and chatty:

'We're two hundred years back that's what we are now —but it's under the mark—it's quite a decent amount. It's nothing to speak of really when you come to consider. Have you the sensation of the durational depth? They're not always so well lighted as this—it's an especially clear one. The Time-air *has* a rarity of its own—it's really as though we were on the Matterhorn; that's why it felt so chilly you know when we first struck it, not because it was England—that's what you thought I suppose?'

'Oh do shut up!'

'What. Yes or the Eggishorn or Wetterhorn, that's right—higher, I should say. It is exactly like mountaineering that's the nearest thing to it. This Time-trek is most exacting. Stimulating *for those who like it*—it doesn't suit some people, for them it's quite the opposite—it's too cold for one thing. That's obvious. The centre of the camp's the best place for the real stay-at-home the nearer the better. The magnetism out here again requires stamina of a particular sort; at bottom it's electricity all the way through magnetic and electric, this is all nothing but that—some gold-digger started it to popularize the outskirts. There used to be many more people in the camp than at present. It's left high and dry. So it's a Debatable Land it might be called you know like the bad-lands between the Esk and Sark, chockfull of cut-throats before things were mended and the place policed—do you recall? There are none here. Don't be alarmed. But there *is* a series of culs de sac. There's a big fellow higher up.'

He looks over his shoulder. 'Yes we've got a good way back—two hundred years or more is like five miles up. It actually smells different!'

The road has been narrowing somewhat, and the hedges on either side are appreciably lower.

They reach a stile and Pullman stops.

'This must be the way,' he says.

It is so low that they both straddle over it, Pullman leading like a first-class hurdler his head thrown back and hair flying, the rebellious lock giving one sweeping jump up and down again on his forehead.

'I can't understand why everything is so small,' he says, with a discontented grimace at the puny world. Then, stopped dead, he stands and stares.

'Why we're in a panorama!' he exclaims.

Satters gazes up in drowsy anger.

'A what?'

'It's a panorama! Look at that hedge. Do you see its perspective? It's built in a diminishing perspective! I believe the whole place is meant to be looked at from behind there, where we have just come from.'

The little figure stands uncertain and crestfallen.

'Why then are all these things so lifelike?' he asks, in a tone of injury. The complexion of the Time-scene is altered by the discovery of the device upon which it depends.

'We shall be out of it in a few minutes. Let's hurry up.' He is brisk and cold, full of his normal keenness.

Rallied by the good news, Satters puts his best foot forward. They are soon at the far end of the lovers' walk and come out upon a diminutive highroad. But their heads are now almost level with the tops of the oaks.

Turning back, a by-comparison cyclopean landscape rises behind them.

'This is childish!' Pullman ventilates his disappointment by snapping off the branch of an oak. He examines it.

'It is odd—look at this, it's green. These funny little trees are actually living!'

'I thought they were all the time.'

The turn that things have taken has absolutely roused into active satisfaction salted with malice the drooping squire and he brushes gently in pussycat languish the brick-red outdoor make-up of his ham-pink cheek against the foliage of a friendly little oak while he simpers over with sly content at the discomfited martinet fuming amongst the flower-pots and toy-hedges. A gay nursery atmosphere at once prevails for Satters, he is in no hurry at all now. To prove this he lies down in the road, which is rather than a road a hard dusty track planted in the fashion of a japanese dwarf-garden, with artificially stunted trees and shrubs. He thrusts his arm through the hedge into a meadow and plucks a daisy no larger than a mignonette and dandles it contemplatively, lying back cheekily for a count of nine under Pullman's nose and only opening one eye when addressed.

'You seem to have rather taken to the regions of Time all of a sudden! Supposing we get along. Time is short.'

Satters rolls over laughing. A great outbreak of hollow hammering, accompanied by an oscillation of the earth of the panorama, brings him staggering to his feet. Pullman, legs apart, his weather-eye pedantically open, hands stuck deep and fast in jacket-pockets, sways easily upon his quarter-deck of the good ship Time, and surveys his abject lieutenant zigzagging and next falling into an oak-bush. The hammering becomes more fitful and the tremors then follow it away into the larger areas beyond. Without more ado Pullman turns on his heel and makes for the cross-road which is the nearest landmark. Satters following, now a cowed figure.

Pullman bends forward a little and reads the lettering upon the signpost.

'This is St. John Street Road. I know where I am now, I think.'

Grasping at random the stout limb of a small oak along with some of its leafage, he raises himself above the road-level by swarming a few feet up, his knees roughriding carelessly its trunk, and peers out over the view this has procured for him.

'It seems rather a maze than a way,' says he, 'but I see some buildings, and the half-mile that it pretends to be should not take us above five minutes. Let's make for them across this field.'

The measure is no sooner proposed than its first movement is executed by a smart leap from the oak into the field beyond while, clearing the hedge, Satters follows him.

Removing it from the underside of his sleeve, Pullman holds up a small leaf between his thumb and forefinger, and his eyes undergo an agreeable change.

'You see this?' he says, and Satters nods that he does.

'Where do you suppose that came from?' he inquires, pädagogisch.

'Isn't it a leaf from the tree you hopped up into just now?'

'No it is not,' he replies, without noticing the language selected to refer to his movements. 'It comes from that first hedge I got through, when I did this.' He holds up his bandaged finger. The leaf is insinuated beneath Satters' indifferent nose.

'You would say it came from this hedge here, wouldn't you? It is a miniature leaf—am I right? Yet it comes from the life-size part of the panorama. Do you see the significance of that?'

125

'I can't say I do.'

'You don't? Surely it is very small! It must have got smaller, don't you see, as we came along! It shrinks as the things round it do so.'

He gives Satters a penetrating glance of companionable inquiry, but without result.

'*We* have remained the same size!' he presses knowingly.

'Have we?' Satters yah-yah-yahoos and then giggles. 'Sorry! Are we?'

Pullman administers a glance of the mildest scorn.

'Yes. We are evidently not affected by the same laws as this leaf.'

'Evidently not—though I believe it came from that hedge behind there.'

They step over a hedge into another road and so into a further field in which there are a dozen cows the size of terriers lying about in different positions.

'Ah there they are,' says Pullman, pointing to a little congeries of roofs amid the Time-shrubbery.

Stepping circumspectly amongst the stationary cows they cross a sunken road and enter a turnip-field.

'This is Islington,' announces Pullman as he strides forward over the turnips, his eyes, behind his glasses, fixed upon their destination.

'Shall we see the Angel?—isn't that at Islington?'

'Yes there is an Angel at Islington, I think we've passed the Angel.'

The buildings occupy a cross-roads. They are between five and six feet high. By standing on tip-toe Satters can look over the tallest of these, but Pullman cannot. Passing the hedge in a short jump they find themselves in a roadway in the dust and litter of the surroundings of a large post-house. Standing side by side, they gaze down in silence at the various particulars of the vivacious wax-work. Satters advances his foot incautiously to stir a dog lying in the dust in mid-road, but Pullman prevents him.

Small and nimble figures are going and coming on all hands: ostlers bring horses out of a stable: there are two large wagons full of hay, on the shafts of which miniature carters sit, muffled in banks of clothes, legs dangling, one with the gesture of lazily cracking his whip. A Rowlandson ostler has just spat, and the back of his hand is lifted to his mouth in a sawing movement. There are draymen disposing of casks about the flaps of cellar-doors. In the upper storey of the inn a maid is cleaning a window, her bold posteriors exhibited beyond the sill. The red figure of a lion swings upon a sign, and over the door of the main entrance *The Old Red Lion Tavern* is painted.

'A busy scene!' remarks Pullman.

'It would be if they did anything: as it is it reminds you of Pompeii.'

'The Old Red Lion—do you see?'

'What, the name of the place? yes.'

'That's where Thomas Paine wrote his *Rights of Man*.'

'Who was he?'

'He was a quaker, a great pacifist. His *Rights of Man* was a reply to Burke.'

'I know, the fellow who wrote the speeches?'

'It was at the time of the French Revolution—I daresay I was a century out in my guess.'

'Do you think we've really got into that time?—only why is it all so small? I can't see how they can all stop in the positions they do.'

Pullman allows a few moments to elapse, while he looks fixedly down into the inn-yard.

'It's no doubt magnetism,' he then says. 'This is an etheric phenomenon.'

Slow heavy metallic blows continue to resound in the distance.

Pullman parts with his two hands the thick trees that screen the garden of the inn and looks in. Satters peers over his shoulder. Three figures are gathered about a table immediately beneath them. In the centre of the table an object the size of a large hen's egg, of bright ultramarine, reposes. It is the egg stolen from the Great Mogul the Virgin egg: Satters' inquisitive mouth and eyes fasten upon the egg, there is an effluence that puts on his guard the psychic clown, to touch it spells discovery it suggests, yet his blue eyes that are as large as it are kindled to kindergarten intensity.

One of the three figures standing with its back to them wears powdered hair, with a pigtail and side-curls. Unnoticed by Pullman, whose attention is directed to the blue object, Satters passes his hand between the trees and grasps this figure by the queue with a mischievous wrench. It starts violently as though it had been struck and turns furiously about. Then it discovers the giant hand that has closed on it and which continues to constrict portions of its hair and of the flesh of its neck.

'You shouldn't have done that!' Pullman exclaims, and forces his way at once between the trees.

The little figure, which is about a foot and a half high, stands quite still staring at the portentous red wrist, collecting itself. Pullman seizes Satters' arm and drags the hand away.

'How would you like to be scragged by a giant six times your size?' he asks reproachfully.

The figure looks up at the sound and sees Pullman—he is now inside the garden and planted energetically upon the bowling-green his stick fastened beneath his arm. The mannikin adjusts its collar and carries its hand to the back of its head, where it tidies the little tail of disordered ceremonious hair. Then, in a small distinct voice of some depth, the figure delivers itself, with a slight American accent, as follows, addressing Pullman:

'You, sir, are at least a human being, which is more than can be said for that disgusting lout you are with.'

'Did you ever hear such cheek!' Satters exclaims, his

128

head thrust through the trees. 'Did you hear what he called me?'

Turning violently towards the wicked giant, the other two figures before the table remaining motionless as before, the third shouts again, in a ringing voice of small compass but deep and powerful:

'We may be in Lilliput but you are not a gentleman as was Gulliver, it is evident, from whatever world you may have dropped, you may have been blown off some man but you are not one nor ever will be! You are a lout, as I have already said, and I say it again, sir, in spite of your dimensions.'

Thrust through the trees, large flushed and ominous, Satters' face remains stationary. The eyes, heavily marvelling still at the living toys that it turns out speak and even perorate if you pinch them, observe with fascination and a part of fear the small passionate figure whose clockwork he has set off at full steam now pointing a fragile trembling finger up at him. The large watching face in the frame of the trees becomes charged with spite and a sporting glitter. At the last word of abusive defiance he shoots his hands into the garden and catches the little figure by its middle. Lifting it up through the air he whisks it through the trees and disappears with it into the roadway.

'Sat-ters!' Pullman, starting into indignant action, calls out as he dashes after him. 'Will you leave him alone, do you hear? Put him *down*! Don't be a brute!'

In the roadway Satters grasps in both his hands the funny human plaything, gazing wildly down at it, but with the fierceness and strength of a large athletic rat it struggles, bucking and doubling itself in half upon his thigh. A sharp howl goes up from Satters as the teeth of this refractory monad are fleshed in his hand, and he drops it stamping with pain, both hands tightly squeezed between his legs. Pullman is beside him now.

'What did I say? Why couldn't you leave him alone? Now he's bitten you!'

The insurgent elf has rolled nimbly away and now recovering its feet it starts to run up the road away from the scene of its contretemps.

'I'll get you!' shouts Satters, and his massive body electrified with rage he whirls round and hurls himself in pursuit.

'Satters! Satters!' barks Pullman at his heels.

But in a few strides Satters is up with the fugitive and with a flying kick dashes it forward upon its face, then before Pullman can reach him the football stogies are trampling it in an ecstasy of cruelty beneath them into an inert flattened mass.

'You swine!' Pullman pants as he stops before him and turns away as he sees the mangled creature stamped out of human recognition. As he turns the light is extinguished in a black flash and they are flung upon their faces as the road rises to meet them.

They get up it seems almost immediately, breathless, but the Time-scene has vanished. Pullman observes his companion with distaste and dusts himself. His glasses are still upon his nose, his slippers upon his feet, his stick beside him on the ground. A large helpless woman in distress, Satters rolls his eyes upon him passionately and wildly, while he holds his left hand in his right. Nothing is forthcoming, for Pullman makes no remark but keeps his face steadily turned away; he puts it therefore in his mouth and sucks it. The river is in front of them: led by Pullman they walk towards it, and soon regain the riverside path. As they ascend it in silence, Pullman turns to Satters and points ahead of them.

'You see that shack? We can put ourselves straight there.—We'd better be tidy the Bailiff makes a great point of——'

Satters is sulky now he walks with his head down. His

130

silver football cap replaces his face. The molten twine of its tassel waggles its besom of quicksilver, dangling from the process at the centre of the crown. Pullman glances several times at this emblem. After the last look he asks:

'You left school, when—I forget? I see you got your cap.'

Satters looks up.

'My cap? I suppose so. You had your cap didn't you, Pulley?'

'Yes I got my cap.'

'Now I come to think of it I didn't get my cap,' Satters says argumentatively.

'Didn't you?'

'No, I got my bags.'

'Your bags? Oh, your bags.'

'Yes. My bags. I was supposed to get my cap——'

'It never came off? Rotten luck!'

'It was that swine Crawford. Do you remember him?'

'I can't say I do. He was after my time, I expect.'

'A perfect little beast if ever there was one.'

'Indeed.'

Satters fingers the tassel; he meets Pullman's eye.

'I really don't know what I'm doing with this.'

'You are an athletic impostor!' Pullman laughs.

'It looks like it! I suppose it's another of those rotten jokes they put across here.'

'You got served out with my cap by mistake!'

'I don't want the beastly thing though! It only makes my head hot!' Satters snatches the cap from his head and throws it away.

Pullman stops.

'Now look here. You know you mustn't do that! Pick it up like a good little boy.'

'Why?'

'Because. Go on. We shall be late as it is.'

'But I don't want the beastly thing. Why should I keep it? I never had my cap.'

'Never mind. You've got it now.'

Satters picks up his cap muttering.

'*I* don't believe they know what they're handing out half the time.—Not that it matters.'

'Oh, it matters. Everything has its significance.'

'That's all gutrot you know it is; excuse my violent expression. It's just common gutrot.'

'The Army had an unfortunate effect on you in some ways.'

During this altercation Pullman has been examining other details of Satters' outfit. His eyes return reflectively to the neighbourhood of the left breast of the mess-jacket. As they approach the hut Pullman remarks:

'I got out just after the Mons show. I notice you have the 1914 ribbon; I wonder if we were in the same part of the Line. How odd that would have been! we might have met.'

'Do you mean this?' Satters touches the medal upon the breast of his mess-jacket.

'Yes isn't that a——?' Pullman peers at it short-sightedly.

'Yes that's right.' Satters bites his nails. 'As a matter of fact I didn't go to France till the end of '16. Why they've decorated me with this is more than I can say.'

'You're a military impostor, too!' Pullman laughs.

'I'm an impostor from head to foot!' Satters exclaims, a spirited animosity transfiguring him suddenly. 'All this outfit is a lie every bit of it and a particularly stupid lie at that and as far as I'm concerned it can go back where it came from—*I* haven't any use for it! I tell you what I'm going to do and pretty quick too: that is, peel the bloody stuff off on the spot and get on without it! *I* don't want the beastly things!'

He suits actions to words. The mess-jacket is pulled off in one gesture and flung away, followed by the cap. Lowering his head, the Fair Isle jumper is inverted and

dragged off headlong. There is no shirt, and Satters is now stripped to the waist.

'Satters, you mustn't take those things off!'

'*Mustn't* I?' Satters has unclasped his belt. 'Who said so? I know what you mean! All this tiresome *magic*! I'm sick of it. What are they anyway these precious misfit suitings, is this an Old Clo' show we've got into sometimes I think it is! Anyway here goes.'

'You'll soon see! You know the reason as well as I do. Put them on again like a sensible chap.'

Satters is squatting on the ground, his shoulders between his knees, unlacing the stogies.

'Satters! I'm off if you persevere in this you are maddening. All right have your own way. Good-bye. I'm going to beat it!'

Pullman starts walking rapidly away: Satters looks up aghast at the unprincipled desertion.

'I say! Where are you off to? Aren't you going—— Good enough beat it and be damned to you!'

He returns to the unlacing of his boots which imbued with the privileged sense almost of a skin show themselves stiff and refractory.

Pullman is abreast of the shed for which they have been making when he hears a cry. Looking back he sees the now naked Satters in hot pursuit, waving his arms.

'Hi! Steady on! Not so fast! Wait a minute!'

Pullman plants himself, miniature, erect, jaw set in its impeccable small-scale resolution, and awaits the hurrying naked giant. A formidable elongated bladder of meat, Satters cloppers up his arms flapping fin-like as he runs, useless paddles of dough beating the air up into invisible suds. The red trunk is dark with hair marking its symmetric duality. Pullman's cold steady face receives him.

'Well, are you satisfied?' Pullman looks at him steadfast and bored.

'What do you mean? What's wrong?'

135

'Oh, nothing.'

'It's better this way, much.'

'It's as you think.'

'Why did you push off? Are you cross——?'

The words about to be uttered expire; with a novel discomfort Satters returns the gaze of his friend. Pullman's eyes strike into his with a supercilious tranquillity. 'Cross': those who are cross, those with whom people are cross, exist in another dispensation, the eyes say. Pulley's eyes are unnecessarily bright for a man of his habits; he is cross, damned rotten cross—as usual.

'What are you staring at? You've seen me before!'

The insolent little inquisitor stands his ground, his eyes lighting up the scene, it is felt by Satters, to an extent beyond any requirement he is conscious of. Satters returns to arch movements, as he moves about before the immovable Pullman, upon the balls of his feet. Pulley is the crossest beast he knows just because he took his things off and for some reason he didn't want him to he gets enraged it's typical. Charm will have the last word though —he knows his Pulley; he bends down to pick a camphire bud, as he does so smiling up, hips to the fore. The cross beast follows his action with eyes that are plainly ironic; he rises quickly, stung to radical indignation this time.

'I say look here Pullman, what's the matter please?'

Silence, withering fixity and silence: a nice situation, in or out of the swimming-baths! Pulley has lost his sense of values or it's that beastly conceit of his—he'd forgotten that. He looks up bluffly at the thought: Pullman is in the act of tossing his head! Satters laughs with a big grunting sneer.

'Tempter!' he mocks, his eyes sparkling with resentment. 'Tempter! Where's old Scratch?'

'Taking shape in front of me, I should say!'

Pulley must be trying to mesmerise him! The cold lunar beams of Pulley slowly set fire to an inflammable material somewhere in his interior, back of the eyes. A deep flush establishes itself upon his face; the baby-world of Satters within is in conflagration. What is the secret dump that the ocular bombardment sent over by Pullman has reached? The baby-world of Satters is in flame behind him!

Satters lifts his hand, guided by a new sensation. He places it upon his head, to brush those tiresome tumbling locks away. His hand closes upon those heavy curls—why should it want to seize them?—and as he removes it, it holds fast a bulky half-wig of hair, but brittle and without weight. As he gazes at it it falls in powder from his tightening fingers and subsides in a grey ash upon the ground at his feet. His hand makes the journey again to his head. He sweeps it in an arc from ear to ear, this time a clean sweep. A calcined mass drops down, lighting upon his bare shoulders, and thence, in a few bumps, falls to the earth.

That was the meaning of that hot feeling! Pulley is still planted there before him. The story of Professor Tyndall comes to his mind in an electric flash: it is a magnetic occurrence; he perceives Professor Tyndall standing before his audience, body in pieces—wonderful presence of mind! one eye upon the floating arm, the other upon the upturned faces. Satters hears the well-known Satters-voice, disjoined from him as were the limbs of the Professor, from just near to him, addressing Pulley:

'Hallo! What's happened now? It seems they've cut of the light at the main! Are you cross?'

He hears Pullman reply, with the same imperfect reality:

'You've dropped something! Why not pick it up?'

The well-known Satters-laugh responds to this sally, and he feels himself shaken at its passage.

Satters places his arms akimbo and becomes aware, in

the nadir of his eye, of a paunch that juts out from him towards Pullman and of two prominent sagging paps. A reversal as it were of the physical contretemps of the well-known savant. These objects are part of him, apparently, and yet he disowns them, and proceeds. His sight is not so good as it was, but he wrinkles up his eyes, with a disobliging sneer on his face as he looks Pullman up and down.

'I suppose you think this is a great joke, don't you, Pullman?'

As he speaks he recognizes that his mouth is weighted in an unaccustomed manner. He turns to that to inform himself. Oh! He frowns. There is no question but what it is the pendent cheeks, that are there now, dragging the lips down at either extremity, so that the words lag as they pass out. He works his lips backwards and forwards sharply to render the overloaded organ of speech more elastic. He notices the dental bed is shallower. He swallows with difficulty. He stands aghast, staring stupidly back at Pullman. Pullman's expression does not change. Then he blusters:

'Hrrump! I shouldn't be surprised if this strikes you as remarkably funny Pullman—I can see it does you've been staring hard enough! I hope you've seen what you wanted to, all-correct.'

There is a pause in which Pullman tosses his head several times, like an exaggerated dump invitation to *Comealong*.

'You notice what's happened to my jolly old hair?'

He spurns with his toe the débris of his adolescent locks. He is jaunty, working his bare legs up and down with swimming motion like a gymnast providing his shoe-soles with resin.

'Those're hot! Beastly things especially in this climate. Don't you think—or perhaps you don't, I'm glad to see their backs no that's right uncommonly glad, a German crop is the best for the tropics.' His manner grows intense suddenly, and slightly confidential. 'All those things are *lies*. I said so. They're lies; I never had them you know so why——? That Mons Star I ask you! What a poseur I must have seemed!'

He passes his hand facetiously before his nudity.

'Humpty Dumpty! They don't spare your blushes! Am I——? Oh you're laughing Pullman I do think you're a *cad*! You're not nice! What?'

He laughs with low fierce relish, as though eating thirstily a grape-fruit, his eyes darting with bright icy dashes of understanding to left and right of Pullman.

'Why don't you take yours off? It's six one and half-a-dozen the other, but I'd rather be without. Afraid? *Then they knew they were naked?*'

He guffaws.

'The Old Adam!'

'Yes. The Carrion-Crow, that sort of Adam! Your appearance does not encourage me to make that move!'

Pullman's voice sounds hard and loud, it is that of a martinet it raps with the impatient mark of authority. Satters flinches abashed at the novel ringing of the over-mannish accents. With pity and distaste dryly mixed Pullman examines the galloping decay of the exposed carcass parading before him, he notes its points with the eye of an expert investigating a horse.

'Oh really?' drawls Satters at last, his spirit reasserting itself. 'Is that it my *appearance*——You're a very particular man Pullman one would say! Since when? I daresay if you peeled we should see!'

'I daresay.'

'Hnnnm! We can't all be the Venus of Milo.'

An accordion booms in a funereal ague, shaken and sobbing as it is jolted by the footsteps of the instrumentalist, *Say, poor sinner, lov'st thou Me?* They both look round. It is a peon passing them on the other side of the shed, playing as he walks, crouched over his musical bellows, whose cranky wheezes he listens to very intently.

'*Say* poor *sin*-ner *lov'st* thou *Me?*' Satters booms dismally after him.

'This is too awful!' Pullman exclaims, looking with disgust at the bald hulk in front of him, resounding with Moody and Sankey. The bloated collapsible sections of Satters' trunk pump up and down, reminiscent of a vast decrepit concertina. 'I'll leave you to your own devices I think, there's no point in stopping here. You're impossible!'

In antipathy to what is before him, Pullman has returned from the stage of the youngish don to that of undergraduate-Pulley. It is with the high-spirited flush of first youth that he turns his angry back upon the derelict Satters. He has only taken a step or two when one of the large-sized hands of the naked one descends upon his shoulder; he is spun round to face the other way, the sagging mask of Satters thrust forward with a bitter scowl. It is Bill-Sikes-Satters.

'Here old son not so fast you shan't get away with it this time two can play at that I'm very sorry. Who's "impossible" eh?' the bargee mimics Pullman's exclamation. 'Not quite so much of it! Not so much side no one wants you to stop, I'd sooner you took yourself off straight I would I'm not having any—*impossible*! Sidey little devil! Just keep a civil tongue in your head unless you want me to knock it off see, it wouldn't take much to make me do it, I'll make you laugh the other side of your face. I won't stand too much old buck now then—you just go and be grand somewhere else you old faggot!'

Young Pulley is trembling with anger and as pale as possible, at old the opprobrious adjective his dander rises up to the boil, for half a minute he is quite unable to speak, he is speechless with insulted feelings. Braced in a compact little bristling passion, he remains glaring up at the swaggering jowl rehearsing in mastiff antics in thrust and counter-thrust with locked jaws the barbarities it contemplates if the whipper-snapper does not climb down and sing small a little and say he'll make amends or look sorry or something.

'I see—I see that you're an old ruffian!' at last he vociferates with great withering force. 'How dare you lay your great ugly hand on me!'

His whole being spurts up in haughty speechless choler at the thought of the enormity of this interference. Satters' voice has become so coarse that it has turned out to be a sort of navvy the young gentleman is up against, he is blinded with hot impetuous indignation. Satters is a thing of the past. The time- and class-scales in which they hang in reciprocal action are oscillating violently, as they rush up and down through neighbouring dimensions they sight each other only very imperfectly.

Satters blinks down upon him, hanging great Cromagnon hands beside either naked flank. His eyes travel with stolid stealth over the paradoxical Pullman galvanized into young life and seething with strange haughty vim, who is now close beneath and in front of him. As he remarks the neat terraces of new hair he blinks several times, in dazzled resentful owlishness.

'On you?' he blusters. 'Hoh! I like that! On *you*, did you say? Hoh!'

'Yes, on me, you old brute, you old sot, you disgusting old b-b-bully! How dare you p-p-pull me like that?'

'I pull you?' A shadowy grin comes up into Satters' old-time dour and dismal phiz. 'I'll *pull* you blast you if *pulling's* what you want you upstart swank-pot!'

Deftly the cunning animal-hand of the enraged man of instinct shoots up, his big fingers bury themselves in the hair within such easy reach, the orotund tentacled spring contracts, snapped fast about the silken strands and with a wrench he tugs the struggling head towards him, then plucks it to and fro and up and down with great malicious violence.

'I'll *pull* you!' he booms, straddling bombastically.

Pullman, as violently released, staggers back, a fumbling hand securing his glasses the other grasping his stick. He jumps back, tears starting in his eyes, he tosses the hair off his face, all his person bristles with neat pugnacity. David toe to toe with Goliath, he squares up, moves lithely and rapidly, measuring the insulting bulk of the egregious Satters with methodic deadly eye, with fury cold and grim. At arm's-length he holds his little shillalah grasped at its slender end; he raises it high above his head, his big victim clumsily ducking: he leaps in, the impetuous youngster, and brings the thick end crack down upon the giant's temple who is suddenly groggy before the stars have burst up in an electric bouquet inside his noddy. The ox is felled: Satters as Keystone giant receives the crack exactly in the right spot, he sags forward in obedient overthrow, true to type—as though after a hundred rehearsals, true to a second—and crashes to earth as expected, rolling up a glazed eyeball galore, the correct classical Keystone corpse of Jack-the-Giantkiller comedy. Pullman gazes down through his glasses at the prostrate enemy while the camera could click out a hundred revolutions, ready with his little tingling truncheon. Satters does not stir the whale is worsted by the sprat in deadly knockabout and lies a sheer hulk a Poor Tom Bowling. Light-footed the deceptive pocket-champion steps away. He replaces his waddy in its usual place, clamps it against his rib, shoulders high and squared, and rapidly decamps missing the hut, and making for the uneven stretch of dune beyond.

Fifty yards are covered in berserker canter, he is all aflame. The fierce little victor steams away and leaves the battered monster prone where he lies as he richly has deserved and may all such bullies come to a similar end amen! But with what rapidity his passion deserts him! giving him scarce time to relish the swiftly moving event for it has quickly come and quickly it has almost gone.

His calm pulse announces his restoration to the normal personal mean of circumspect donnish Pullman, with the fading of his aggressive youthful fire the more stable youngish don, studious and alert, with somewhat scanty hair that blows in wisps of uncertain colour, returns, in seventy yards it has absolutely all evaporated, he is cooler than a hotbed of cucumbers.

Now a new sensation possesses him. No normal detail of his equipment has been shed: his glasses are upon his nose, his stick is safely beneath his arm, yet in the personal economy a vivid loss is registered, a state of want declares itself with the indistinct sensation that besets a traveller of having left something in the compartment of the train he has just quitted or refreshment room where he has bought a sandwich, Pullman is beside himself with the ill-defined sense of loss. What is this missing object really? he gropes through all his senses very fussed; continually his mind returns to the large staring uncouth bulk of his friend even Satters: that is not what is missing surely? Indeed it must be though, since it is always back to that fearsome object that his mind is led. But it is not as the Keystone giant he sees him. It is a big-bottomed jolly-cheeked knock-kneed baby, in pursuit of a lovely butterfly. He sees a big school-boy beating a dusty school-cap upon his knee. He hears a rich young voice exclaiming, 'Pulley! Well I'm damned!' But he can bear no more! bravely he advances a few more steps but ever slower, then he stops. He spanks the seat of his trousers, to expel the rough particles that may still be fastened under some thread, or some twig, or to beat out a dust-stain. He adjusts his glasses. Then he turns about and with rapid steps makes his way back to the fallen Satters.

The obese mass still plunged in unconsciousness is

scarcely present to his senses. He passes it and soon reaches the spot where the cap, the Fair Isle jumper, the Mons Star, the stogies, the army cords, the frogged mess-jacket, are strewn. He collects them. Then he returns in the direction of the aged animal carcass in combination with which they result in his present chum who has disappeared and can never be his naked self in this enchantment it is painfully evident. He kneels down beside the body, it is lying upon its face: he turns it over roughly upon its back and pinches the fungus-flesh of the unsightly ears. Satters revives.

'Here, put these things on like a good chap,' says Pullman.

Satters eyes him in sullen shattered state, pompously helpless, but makes no remark at all. He remains stretched out on his back he shows no intention of moving. The face is haggard and obese, in its hairless condition it is reminiscent of an aged mountebank. To Pullman it is scarcely recognizable: he does not look at it, but letting his eyes rest blankly upon the spot beside the sprawling body he continues to press, soberly and without expression:

'Come along. Get this kit on again, like a sensible fellow, we shall be late. Look sharp I'll help you.'

Satters is profoundly silent. He closes his eyes. Still as though it were the celebrated Cavendish at whom you might not look if you wished for a response, Pullman proceeds with eyes studiously averted:

'Don't you think it's time you dressed? It's necessary. I was brutal just now I'm ashamed of myself: I didn't mean that, I apologize, I lost my temper. But we need not part.'

Satters settles sour-lipped and beetle-browed into a fresh coma. Pullman shakes him: then putting down the clothes which he has been holding, he gets up, and placing his hands beneath Satters' shoulders he drags him towards the hut. When he reaches it he kicks open the door with his heel and enters backwards, trailing the sodden bulk behind him which cloppers in sulky bumps and becomes a depressing ugly heap upon the spot with the malice met with in inert things but not expected of the human. He then returns to fetch the clothes.

The hut is low, lighted by a small window, extremely hot, its floor littered with earth and leaves. Pullman enters, closes the door carefully behind him, then, going over to Satters, props his head upon a pillow composed of his jumper and mess-jacket.

'How do you feel? You look rotten.—You had a bad fall.'

'Yes I know.' Satters says no more but he contemplates Pullman with a peaceful philosophic eye of undying dislike.

'Do you think you can manage or shall I help you?'

'Manage what?'

'To get these things on.'

In the dim light Satters can be noticed smiling to himself. He coughs. Pullman leans back against the wall of the hut.

'What's it to do with you?' Satters inquires blankly, from the floor.

'It's in your interest. You must see that. Don't you feel——?'

'Why can't you mind your own business?'

Pullman shrugs his shoulders.

'It's always been my habit to interfere.'

'So it seems.'

Satters does not move.

'Am I to understand——?' Pullman commences, his temper rising. This obstinate old fool is insufferable! He's a good mind to leave him as he deserves——!

'You want me to put those things on?' Satters asks in a husky drawl.

'Yes, that's the idea.'

'Why is that necessary?'

'Simply because—— It's best to have them on, that's all, they prefer it here. It's a bore but there it is!'

'I know. And why is it I have to do that? Because we're held down to this magic we are enslaved . . .'

'I've heard that before. You've been—I can see you've been keeping your ears open more than you pretend. You shouldn't listen to what people say. If you must—— But why magic? Use your intelligence. Did you say *magic—magic*, all the time, in life? You never thought of it then yet you should have said *magic* then just as much shouldn't you or don't you see that? You think it far-fetched. Wasn't life just as much *magic*?'

'No.'

Pullman snorts delicately.

'You think not? But this must be accepted, it's a question of take it or leave it. I told you: we are creatures of imagination we are not real in the sense of men.'

'That wallop you gave me just now seemed real enough.'

'I know, I'm sorry about that I've said so.—Nevertheless, we are not quite real.'

'How do you know?'

'The proof of the pudding's in the eating surely. Look at you! If you're your real self *now*——!'

'A little less of *me*! I'm about fed up with you old son. Leave me out of it—see?'

Pullman moves to the other side of the hut, where he can obtain through the window a command of the shoreline between them and the camp.

'There is the proposition however Satters: those are the terms on which we exist, it seems. It's no use kicking what's the point anyway? Once I left this stick at my kip when I went out. I might as well have left my head! I soon went back for it I promise you! That's the way it is. We are organic with the things around us. This piece of

146

cloth'—he takes up a pinch of his coat sleeve—'is as much me as this flesh. It's a superstition to think the me ends here.' He taps the skin of his hand. 'Even you are a part —as you remarked I was despatched to you! I am a messenger.'

'It's very obliging of you I'm sure!'

'Not at all I can't help it!—When I first came here I was afraid to clean my nails I didn't know what was me and what wasn't. I do it all right now but I had to find out.'

'Rot. You talk rot, you're not right, you don't mind me telling you I hope! I've never heard a man talk such goddam Bedlam rot as you do. It's you who listen to what people tell you not me my poor old son you're potty. *Clean your nails!* Why shouldn't we leave off our coat if it's too hot to wear it? It's easy to leave off one's coat, it's not a difficult feat and what the odds to any one?'

'Yes, it's easy to leave off. But you leave yourself too.'

'Gutrot!' the gut-bag in an attitude of insult barks.

Pullman launches himself violently from the wall towards the door, his eyebrows raised in exasperated arcs.

'Oh you're perfectly *impossible*! Do you understand? You've become the most insufferable old imbecile I've ever met—I wash my hands of you! No I'm damned if I'll put up with you any longer, I'm through.'

Exit Pullman slamming the door behind him.

Outside the hut Pullman halts, after a few quick strides for form's sake. Then he takes up a position ten yards before the door: pulling up his trousers at the knee, he sits down, in his usual attitude, facing it. He arranges himself, then slowly turns his head towards the river.

Twenty minutes elapse without any appreciable movement on his part.—His lips begin moving: at first the words are confused and too low for speech. Then in solemn chanting tones he utters:

147

'Holy things to Holy men! *Holy* are the gifts presented, since they have been visited by the Holy Ghost: *holy* are you also, having been vouchsafed the Holy Ghost; the holy things themselves correspond to the holy persons.'

He pauses, bows his head, crosses himself, emphasizing the triangle of the Trinity with deliberate fingers, and his lips move with the passage of a private effusion. He raises his head, crossing himself again, and his eyes are fixed upon the unpopulated architectures of the magnetic city. He murmurs in measured syllables:

'For truly One alone is Holy, by nature Holy; we too are holy, but not by nature, only by participation, and discipline, and prayer.'

He scrambles lightly upon his knees, lowering himself down first on to one, then the other. He crosses himself and hangs his head, a hurried patter comes up from his moving lips.

A juicy strident laugh bursts out from the hut-door, insulting the stillness. His lips in motion yet, he looks up. Satters fully dressed is propped within, his lush bulk pitched against the jamb, occupying the breach in beefy sinuosity, his curled head bent somewhat to clear the lintel, his eyes cast archly up. The smile of Leonardo's St. John, appropriated to the features of a germanic ploughboy, sustains an expression of heavy mischief. This he coyly diffuses. His crossed legs account for a swirling of ponderous lines, on one side pile-driven for the support of his superior bulk, on the other lazily in reserve, in florid diagonals.

Rising from his knees, Pullman approaches.

'Ah that's right! That's more like it. Shall we go now?'

Satters does not move: he continues to smile, monotonously roguish, in silence.

'It's dreadfully hot for so early in the day. I shouldn't be surprised if we had a thunderstorm.'

148

Satters gives a short sneering snort: *Huch!*

'We shall just do it nicely if we start now.'

Satters repeats the noise.

'How do you feel? Better?'

Satters again reproduces his guttural comment, louder and more winged with contempt.

'Really you seem to have caught a slight cold! It's damp in there, perhaps. Is it in the throat you feel it?'

Satters: 'Grhuuch!'

'Most troublesome it sounds. Still, never say die!'

Da Vinci's deep smile metamorphosed into a violent grin, Satters grunts, his eyes fastened upon Pullman's, who averts his face, first to one side then the other.

'It's tiresome your not being able to speak. You'll be struck like that if you're not careful.'

'Merde!' Satters spits forth from brazen lungs, percussioning with the muscles of his lips.

'Oh!' Pullman glances discreetly down and lightly spanks his knees.

'Yes!'

'A very rudimentary remark! It's a good thing to begin with something simple. It shows you're yourself again, which is the main thing.'

Satters scratches his head, distending his face and elevating his eyebrows in a simian intensity, relishing the scratch.

'Are you cross?' Pullman asks lightly.

Satters stops scratching, uncrosses his legs and comes out of the door.

'Yes. Most!' he says. 'Look here, I want an explanation. What are all these games you've been playing with me? Who put me in there?'

'I did.'

'I thought as much! What for?'

'Oh, fun and fancy. I felt like it.'

'Yes, but what about me?'

'It was with your consent—but I take the full responsibility.'

'Liar!'

'Oh!'

Pullman prances his eyes about as horses with anchored hind legs develop movement in showy rearing, at the spur, Satters being the centre for the eyes' gambols.

'I'll forgive you, shall I?' Satters purrs burningly and richly. He throws his arm round Pullman's neck and goes half-way with the full gamut of reconciliation, bustlingly seductive. The mighty boa hangs and dangles across the diminutive shoulder, in a sausage crescent, while the arch effusive face approaches its laughing carnal kisser to the chaste Pullman, eyeing it guardedly. The lunisolar combination is almost eclipsed with a kiss.

'If yer loves us why don't ye' muck us abart?'

'Behave yourself!' Pullman disengages his neck. 'How about getting along?'

'How about it? Yes, *how* about it! That's what I want to know. Why should we bother? We have the whole day before us. Why don't we go back in there and lie down and have a rest, it's so beautifully cool and I'm sick of the heat.—I don't want to see the old Bailiff, either. Must we go and listen to all that jaw? Why?'

He catches Pullman's hand.

'Come along I'm going do-do I mean bye-bye. I simply want to forget—everything.'

Pullman stands his ground: Satters drops the hand. A vindictive glitter darkens his face, he flings himself into a pouting position, his shoulders against the hut, his hip stuck out, and commences biting his nails, measuring Pullman malevolently with a fishy eye.

'You have about as much pep in you as an old tortoise! Why don't you go and *pray*? I'm sorry I interrupted you!'

'You didn't.'

'No?'

'I was waiting for you.'

'Oh is that all? Well don't wait another time it's hardly worth while!'

'Are you cross?'

Satters levels a sultry glance at the prosaic Ariel fidgeting a yard away impatiently, and divides his attention between his thick-bitten pigmy nails and Pullman's tie.

'Come along, don't be such a *baby*!' Pullman coaxes monotonously.

Baby-Satters bites his fingers and wriggles his body, the Rugby forward's calves swell in response, the stone of scrum-weight of the fleshy behind arches, the sports-pantalettes that fancy can readily furnish in the midst of the ill-assorted museum in place of the breeches take on an infantile helpless—baby-gape, the cap sits awkwardly upon the rough head like a tinsel topee from a Christmas cracker.

Pullman approaches him and takes him by the arm.

'You are really a perfect child, you know, quite charming but a shade ridiculous. Do come now; I'm sure you'll enjoy it once you get there most awfully you see if you don't! Come don't be obstinate.'

'I don't *waant* to!' Satters wails, and stamps.

'Yes, I know, but it will be most awfully jolly. You'll simply die with laughing.'

'I don't *waant* to die!'

'You shan't, you shan't! But you'll absolutely choke yourself with cheeky fun it will be so frightfully amusing!'

'I don't *waant* to choke myself with cheeky fun!'

'Quite! You shan't, then! but you'll be most terribly tickled! Your sides will simply ache!'

'I won't be tickled at all so there! I don't *waant* my sides to ache!'

'They won't ache then we'll see to that! but you'll absolutely have a fit when you see the Bailiff telling off Hyperides!'

151

Satters stamps with a great mock pettishness and screams in Pullman's face:

'But I don't *waant* to see the Bailiff and have a fit!'

Pullman bends forward and whispers in his ear.

'I think you're perfectly horrid!' exclaims Satters. 'I didn't mean that!'

Bracing his little legs in bandy equipoise, and hauling with all his might Pullman gets under way, marching step by step, Satters in tow hanging back with thick twitterings of protest. They are soon clear of the hut. Once in the open Satters gives in; he follows sluggishly, pouting hangdog with much hip-movement.

Thunder and lightning explode from a dense red cloud overhead. It has grown dark. There is a guttural roll followed by dizzy crashes. A violet-white blaze vividly whitewashes everything about them, turning it into a momentary electric world, that starts out and then vanishes. The atmosphere is suddenly chilled; large gobs of frigid rain dash into their faces, smashing or glancing off.

'That's meant for us!' says Pullman, turning up his coat collar and hastening along.

Satters clings to his arm, alarmed and speechless. There is a great defiant roll of shattering intensity, and an immense instantaneous pomp of the most spotless snowy light. Their hands mechanically fly as shields to their eyes, they stand heads down, Satters shuddering against Pullman.

The storm stops.

Pullman looks round, dilates his eyes, works his forehead up and down, rapidly grinds his index finger in the mortar of his ear, delicately lifts the twin lapels of his jacket, and, the two halves limply suspended, rattles them sharply a half-dozen times, removes his glasses and wipes them.

'Very sudden, wasn't it?'

Pullman stretches his legs or takes a turn, up and down,

as though they had spent some time in a confined space. The air is cold.

'They're always like that, short and sweet. How lovely it feels!'

Satters stares at the ground; he is completely dazed.

'Well, that has cleared the atmosphere anyway. The Bailiff refers to it as the water-cart; it's astonishing how sweet and fresh it feels afterwards. It does make a fearful row, though, doesn't it!'

Pullman spanks the embroidered waist of Satters' jacket, saying:

'You're rather wet. You must be careful not to catch another cold.'

Satters delivers dazed blows at different parts of his get-up. Pullman takes him energetically by the arm.

'En route! Come along—we've just time.'

Satters obeys. He is rather deaf. He digs his fat forefinger into his beefy brick-red lug, and rattles his head, which is empty and sings.

'That last clap was the loudest I've ever heard!' He puts his predication forward without visible interest and sneezes vigorously.

'It was rather loud,' Pullman agrees.

'It completely stunned me for the moment.'

'You remember the storms in France?'

'What?'

'They used to wipe out the bombardment. Once I was passing an eight-inch How in action during a storm. It sounded like a pop-gun.'

'I'm as deaf as a post!'

'I'm not surprised.—The Bailiff will be up quite soon now.'

'What?'

'The Bailiff will not be long now!'

Satters brandishes a finger at the departing storm-cloud.

'It's going back.'

'What do you mean?'

'Why, the way it came.'

'How do you mean?'

'That's where it came from—didn't you notice?'

'I can't say I did.'

'Yes, it came from over there.'

He indicates the city.

'*Did* it? I don't see how it could. I think it came from that direction.'

He indicates the tempestuous edges of the opposite horizon, where an opaque apricot haze is aligned a foot above the skyline.

Satters casts a suspicious non-committal glance where Pullman has pointed, and looks quickly away again.

'No, I saw it coming up.—They say the Bailiff sends a storm every morning to clear the atmosphere so that he can be comfortable.'

Pullman, with a wrinkling of his eyes in lazy banter, says:

'What an absurd yarn! But I know that's what they say—some idiots. Many people in this camp as I daresay you've remarked are totally deficient in a sense of humour. The result is that a simple pleasantry is not taken as it's intended at all but they hunt in it for some hidden meaning.—Always something hidden! If they only understood him, the Bailiff's as simple as a child—and as open! He refers to these storms as his *water-cart*. What happens? Out of that comes this absurd story———!'

'What's the point, though, in stunting like that all the time?'

'Really!—None, of course, except to relieve the tension a little.'

'There's a time for everything——— It doesn't seem to me——'

'All I can say is it would be a jolly sight worse for all of

154

us if we had somebody there without a sense of humour. Imagine it!'

'I can't—I suppose you're right.'

'Are you fond of sweets?' Satters asks presently, the storm and its origin having faded away. He drags the sweets up involuntarily out of the depths of a day-dream; lovely little pink and orange ones, his eyes confess. He blushes, ashamed at the thought of the distinct but automatic self pining with such a trifling appetite.

'Not very. I like marrons glacé—-and oh, milk chocolate, sometimes. If you're fond of sweets, though, I know where you can get some very decent toffee.'

'Do you?' Satters clasps his hands in ravishment. 'How *love*-ly! Where?'

A sudden movement of Pullman's jerks him off his balance, he staggers against his guide. They have been approaching a slight elevation in the ground, where some earth has been thrown up, and as they have drawn abreast of it a figure has come into view, lying at full length in its shadow, studying a book, which he is holding almost against his nose.

Pullman says nothing; a look of slight disdain and annoyance has come into his face. He pilots the stumbling Satters rapidly away at a tangent: the latter follows with his head screwed round, inquisitively examining the figure on the ground.

'Don't look at him. He'll follow us if you do.'

'Who is he?'

Pullman appears bored.

'That's Monty Mocatta.'

'Is it?'

'Ach-chew!' Pullman breathes, as though articulating a faint sneeze. 'A joooo! He's mugging something up—probably to curry favour with the Bailiff later in the day.'

'He doesn't look like a Jew,' Satters says, his head still dislocated.

Monty's face, which is leonine, with very high cheek-bones and protruding ears, gazes after them, the book still held in front of his face. He smiles at Satters. Satters can see him smiling.

'I think he looks a nice chap!' Satters says.

Pullman accelerates.

'You wouldn't think so if you had enjoyed as much of his company as I have. There's no shaking him off once he's——he lies in wait for me out here in the morning. I'm lucky if I get rid of him by nightfall.'

Satters gives a last look, stumbles and coquettishly skips. The subject is dropped. They continue to strike inland a little, then turn sharply back towards the river.

They now approach the landing-stage.

Pullman looks at his wrist-watch.

'Just a little over an hour since we started. That's not at all bad going.'

'It must have taken longer than that!'

'No, I don't think so. Why should it?'

'How do you mean?'

'It is difficult to explain, but that's about what I should have said.'

A trumpet-note, an obscene grating vibration, stopping as though a furious hand had been slapped down abruptly upon its mouth, strikes them. An insult from nowhere, a cough of disgusted scorn from some stray functional divinity ambushed in the ether: Satters starts; they both look up at the city, stopping.

'Whatever's that?'

'That is the Bailiff,' Pullman tells him. 'You've never seen them arrive, have you? Let's wait till they have landed.'

Two characters who have occupied the opening scene, they conventionally stand aside to observe the entrance of the massed cast in stately procession, Pullman's manner suggests; withdrawing discreetly a little into the

156

mist, and peering at the massive business of the show as it unfolds itself at the centre of the stage of the Miracle heralded by the sudden detonation of a solitary furious trumpet. Are they observed by their stately silent fellow-actors? Nothing indicates that this is the case. If so, their personal affairs are effaced, as, in attitudes of stylized attention, marking the coming of the new event with whispered asides, they stand for the time being aloof puppets.

All traffic has immediately been suspended upon the highroad: the porters who now throng the approaches to the landing-stage cease work, and attend in silence the coming of the great administrative officer. Some lounge on the bollards or packing-cases; others stand in hushed groups facing the water with a polite forward cant of the head.

The ascent to the Yang Gate is a triple gangway. In the centre is a ramp thirty feet in width; barges are unloading at the wharf at its foot. On either side of the ramp are stairways. Upon the wider of these a procession issuing from the postern beside the main gateway lets itself slowly down with the wavering stealth of a serpent, its head falling gradually towards the white fillet of the landing-stage. It disappears into the waiting ferry. The two banks of oars form a fan on either side, resting upon the water. Then the fan is seen flashing in cadence, somnolently opening and shutting in the silence of the distance: next the massive hull is noticed, through the imperceptible eclipse of one of the rippling fans, to be moving. Its transit is as static a progress as that of the minute hand of a clock. It expands rather than advances. It arrives in silence, without clamour or bustle on the part of the equipage; its nose enters an upholstered socket introduced into the perpendicular front of the landing-stage. The official cortège leaves it. Last comes the litter of the Bailiff, barefooted Nubian carriers sustaining it inflexibly a few inches above the surface of the ground. The procession several hundreds strong makes its way to a circular enclosure, a hundred yards to the right of the highroad.

This place externally is in the form of a peribolos: the wall, not exceeding six feet in height, drops vertically without: within there is a large auditorium on the model of the antique theatre. It is horizontally nook-shafted with regular courses of white limestone, forming a hemicycle of wide shallow seats. On these the petitioners, sitting or half-lying, gather while awaiting their turn, or come there for the spectacle, or accompanying friends due for examination. A sanded path divides the foremost seats which in this case are a double row of rough benches from the heavy railing which encloses the orchestra. A sort of twelve-penny-stool gentlemen are accommodated upon chairs which appear here and there and are often thrust out upon the sanded path. The orchestra is a semicircular paved court. Dividing the tiers of seats into two quadrants is a narrow boarded passage: this central parados takes the place of the lateral parodoi of the antique theatre: it now admits, in single file, or two abreast, the procession. It is closed by a wicket. There are flanking wickets admitting petitioners, from this passage, into the sanded gangway and seats.

Along the diameter of this half-circle rises on a sixty yards frontage the irregular façade of the hustings appropriated to the Bailiff and his staff their booths and sheds. In the centre is the bema occupied by the magistrate. It is in the form of a lofty tapering Punch-and-Judy theatre. This is entered from behind: a dozen steps within ascend to a small railed chamber. From this elevated lob or open loft the Bailiff addresses the petitioners and presides over the business of the day, its floor about five feet above the level of the court. The lower portion of the hull of this structure is divided into two panels beneath its curtained

158

window. On the right-hand panel is painted the symbolical hieroglyph of the cone, the cylinder, and the sphere as described in connection with the tomb of Archimedes. This still-life is surmounted in swash letters by the words *Es bibe lude veni*. The left-hand panel is occupied by a figure of a six-pointed star formed by two equilateral triangles imposed one upon the other. Four of its points are the extremities as it were of symmetrical pairs of lateral wings and the other two are a superior and inferior vertex. The upper vertex has been provided burlesquely with two mithraic horns after the pattern of the statue of Moses. At the common centre of the two triangles a conventional eye has been painted. This is the symbol of the Maha-Yuga, but it has in addition to the horns the representation of a goat-hoof beneath.

The lintel of the magisterial chamber is a border of thick brocade, worked in a pattern of acanthus, the sharp obtrusive extremity of the foliage become a serpent's head. Between these are alternately doric palmets and figures from idalionic amulets of fecundity. Surmounting this is a Phœnician mask of Astarte, equine, with retreating forehead, the protruding lips isolated into a separate, heavily-functional, feature.

The bonnet of the entire structure is, in miniature, the stone bonnet of the tomb of Absalom, only in painted canvas on a wicker frame, tipped with a tuft of black cock's feathers; with, at its base, courses, one above the other, of the locus of a Roman pearl alternating with a pirouette.

Bordering the staring mask of Astarte is a mock entablature, painted a hyacinth yellow. On either hand of the exposed side of the magisterial chamber is, in the same colour, the representation of an ionic pilaster, its inner volutes coinciding with brass bosses of the curtains gathered in a stiff festoon covering the upper half of either jamb. Within the magisterial chamber itself, painted on the inner wall and seen behind the Bailiff as he stands or sits in the front of his narrow lodge, is a life-size figure of the Thracian Bacchus, with leopard-skin and thyrsus.

With restless ceremony the Justice and his suite settle into their places, the positions of the principal functionaries and appellants fixed by rigid custom. Jumping awkwardly from the litter, which is brought to a standstill in the centre of the court, the Bailiff approaches with a quick muscular step the box in which he is to pass the rest of the day. Tapping on the flags of the court with a heavy stick, his neck works in and out as though from a socket, with the darting reptilian rhythm of a chicken. His profile is balanced, as he advances, behind and before by a hump and paunch. He wears a long and sombre caftan. His wide sandalled feet splay outwards as he walks at the angle and in the manner of a frog. No neck is visible, the chin appearing to issue from and return into the swelling gallinaceous chest. Bending with a bird-like dart of the head and a rushing scuffle of flat sprawling feet, he disappears into the back of his box.

To the right of this box is a large booth protected by rank-smelling tatties that flap in the wind advancing in gusts over the bog to the south. The scroll of the law is nailed to a cippus planted between it and the box of the Bailiff. A negro wields a winnowing fan. (This is emblematic as well of the justiciary, dividing chaff from grain; and reminds perhaps the devout of a similar instrument used to beat back the flies from the sacred elements.)

A registrar's hair rises at each oscillation of the fan. He will hoist up his eyebrows also in sympathy, moistening his lips. His papers also rise and fall, sometimes being blown out of his hand. The officials never cease to mop their brows. The Bailiff alone appears cool. But the petitioners for the most part are not inconvenienced by the heat.

160

Notwithstanding the pretentious symbolic devices of the appointments of this court, it is in the nature only of an African bentang or rough moot, deliberately provincial and primitive. Directed to the adjusting of the niceties of salvation, this administrative unit yet displays the untidiness and fatigue of a secular community. An hysteria is noticed to sweep over it whenever its routine is disturbed.

After some minutes the Bailiff reappears in the open chamber above, hanging, a dark-robed polichinelle, over the ledge, which is of a strong and substantial description and serves him as a narrow desk. He now screws his bonneted head from left to right to observe the proceedings of his staff, clucking and snuffling fussily as he does so, tapping nervously with his fingers. Then, placing his stick in the corner, he sits down upon the joint-stool provided for him, resting his sleeved arms on the hand-rail and gazing, his hooked and bloated features exuding an impenetrable melancholy, towards the camp. The lymph of a bottomless obtuseness appears to invade his beaked heavy and shining mask, anæsthetizing it even to the eyes. In his hands he slowly revolves the pivetta used by the atellan actors to mimic the voices of the mimes of classical tragedy. He places it between his lips, letting it lie there, idly sucking it, a baby with its dummy, his eyes expanded to their fullest blankest and blackest. Then agitating his lips, at first with a little low chirping, gathering force and purpose, he suddenly bursts into a deafening gloch-gloch-gloch-gloch! Gloch-gloch! Gloch-gloch! terminating with a withering roulade in the bass.

'Mannaei! Mannaei!'—he claps his hands excitedly, his voice rising to a scream: as he does so a crowd of glass and enamel amulets and medallions, in the shape of the pendants of a lustre, jangle upon his body. His large dark hands are accoutred with rings.

161

The Samaritan, with his justiciary cutlass in the bronze sheath at his hip, springs up from where he has been squatting, his eyes discoloured with sleep, his hair, fixed with a massive comb, producing the effect, for his sallow face, of a carved totemic shaft. He places himself impassibly on the left hand of his master, beneath the window, without looking up. The protonotary scans the list of names for immediate examination.

'Jackie!' the Bailiff calls again. With the slow shimmering volutes of black velvet muscle of the coloured pugilist, Jackie rolls forward. Folding his arms, that sleep henceforth, blood-gorged constrictors, on his shining double-glanded chest, this dark giant props himself against the frame of the Bailiff's box. The Bailiff pats his cropped poll, then once more sinks into his torpor, his hanging under-lip nursing the whistle upon its scarlet brawn. From the direction of the nearest camp-dwellings a dozen figures are approaching. The flash of a hand-mirror held in one of their hands glances through the sunny mist. The stumbling form is straightening out, centrifugally, tangled eyebrows.

Along all the tracks converging upon the circus from the different parts of the camp groups are arriving, chattering and muttering, attending for examination, or to inform themselves of the procedure. Soon a hundred or more are collected, some giving the top of the morning to the functionaries, one prodding the grinning Jackie with a cane.

In the opposite direction to that from which the Bailiff and his retinue have arrived, that is to say, southwards, is at a distance of two or three hundred yards the butt of a decapitated tower and beyond it the rough shoulder of a submerged wall, running parallel to the river. The part next to the tower is cleared. It is made of large blocks, laid without mortar and marginally-draughted, of the size and appearance, in this cleared portion, of the Heit el

Maghreby or Wailing-place of the Jews. Cemented against it are a dozen hovels of sun-dried bricks. From one of these a handful of squat figures scrambles: Alf, Barney, Stan, Sid, Harold, and Ted.

Three premonitory trumpet-notes sound from the enclosure. Tying their chokers, trotting clowns hurrying at the crack of the magisterial circus-whip, the six scuttle and trip, but never fall, the ground rising in pustules at their feet to mock them, the wind clipping them on the ear, or pushing them upon the obstructions arranged for them to amuse the idiot-universe. They skip and dance on the bulky treacherous surface of the earth, stoic beneath nature's elemental hot-fisted cuffs, tumblers or Shakespearean clowns, punchballs got up as Pierrot. Alf is up and clearing a rock concealed beneath the sand-drift: Sid dances dexterously through a midden, kicking up a gaping wrecked boot buried in offal: Ted straddling leaps a little pit, doing the half-splits, reaching the farther side with a twang of corduroys as the fork of his extended legs snaps to. Harold says to Ted:

'Ere Tedboy! did yew 'ear woteesed yestday, yewknow timeyoungPerce pinched the lookinglass orfov the old toff?'

Bobbing along with a jaunty vibration their capped polls move forward in an irregular line. Their pride is that of their pack and its regular functioning. As he hurtles forward Harold reports with angry force across the foot of rushing air between Ted's ear and his own scolding tongue:

'E sez "Camel's yewrine turns the 'air white." Ah! *yewrine* eesez the genterlman I don't think! "Hirekker-mends" sezee "the water of the river inprefrence to the yewrine sold in the camp." The genterlman every inch of 'im!'

Insult for insult! Ted's face darkens: his sullen sagging jowl quivers with the momentum of his angry accelerated

163

trot. He gives Harold the tail of his bilious left eye for a breathless moment, his shaking pasty muzzle parting with the two words:

'Ignrant barstard!'

'Ahboy, yerright!'

A tongue of hair the colour of bleached grass sticks out from beneath Harold's cap, lolling over his right eye, striking his temple at each step.

Barney draws the knot of his orange and emerald handkerchief tightly on his shrivelled chicken's neck until the veins start out. His limpid glittering eye searches the Bailiff's personnel appearing at the side of the nearest booth.

Simultaneously quitting his throat, his red hands converge swiftly, with an obscene adroitness, thumb and index extended like meaty pincers, to a spot beneath his right ribs, where they go flea-catching up his jacket-flaps, intelligent crabs. The movement of their hunting backs can be observed under the cloth, as they track their quarry upwards. His armoured stomach comes into view, constricted in a wide studded and bossed leather cestus with a metallic blazonry of army crests letterings and numerals.

Barney's pair of hunting crabs make their spring beneath the cloth; his action, and the unctuous comfort of his lips, feed the fancy with the crack of the flea, as the claws nip-to through the shirt-stuff.

'Eezbin stuffin isself orfovme this arfar.'

One hand rushes out backwards, seizes a handful of soiled shirt, drags it up from under the stomacher and plunges in beneath it against the skin: it returns with the corpse of the parasite, embedded in the blunt fat of the thumb and index. He holds it up to Stan.

'Ere! wot price imboy! Eewuz properrot stuff eewuzan no mistake!'

Stan's jelly-eye signals approval, with mirthful eye-play in the direction of old hop-skip-and-jump, who is a fattun.

With natural small-scale ballistics Barney shoots the dead bloodsucker off his thumb forwards.

'Ere Stan! izzuntthat right wot theoldBailey wozzuntarf wild yestday time eearst forwhy I wozzunt alongov yew not the arftnoon timeoldAlf copptitt?'

'Ah! E went orf the deepend proper eedid.'

For a dozen paces Barney straddles rapidly forward, his knees thrust outward, while he ships and stows away his plucked-out shirt.

'Nomoreeazzunt I don't rekkon!' Sid is shouting. 'Eez a bloomin unicorn, same as old Bert Woods——'

'Wot old Bertwoods wotwurkt uppatt Knights alongov old Charlie Pierce?' Harold shoots in.

'Ah!' Alf agrees.

'Eewozzunt nar bloomin unicorn wozzuntold Bert.'

'Ere! diduntyew nevereer not ow oldBert gotisself pinched alongov young Ernie Baker?'

'A properlad eewoz youngErnie!'

'Ah! EeanoldErnie didduntarf cummitt alongov the females up BraunanRottens ormistiss!'

Barney shoots ahead, looking back, one hand in his trouser-pocket to show himself to the others, to be in it, bursting with a question.

'Ere, Alf, wot girls woz them? Orfficegirls alongov where oldBert worked?'

Alf sullenly refuses him the office-girls, scuttling forward shoulders squared, neck pumping in and out.

They have covered half the distance and draw together on an even stretch. Sid drags a fat bunch of drooping fingers across his brow, carrying away from it and discharging on the ground his heavy moisture.

'Ittaintarf warm, sweltmebob iffitaint!' he says.

Harold pulls his cap off: a mass of faded hair blows on his head. His feet rush beside the taller Alf's, hitting each

165

other when he gives himself a new direction. He bumps his neighbour as he closes up to speak.

'Ere, as it gorn whiteAlf, sameas the old barstard said it would? Ere Alf, as it gorn grayboy?'

'Ere Sid, whysole Bailley always pickin on me? Ere Sidboy——!'

Barney spanks out saliva as he speaks. Sid does not hear him; he is imparting innocence to the helpless swollen hole of his mouth, held open by face sores.

Barney is a well-favoured raw-faced coster-lad, on the sex border-line of boy and girl; his voice is loud juicy and coarse. Blatantly beauty-conscious, he propels himself with a long, swimming, pugnacious swagger. The idiom of The Elephant at a moke-gallop splashes in the gland-water of the 'loud-mouthed' Barney, his speech a luscious explosive pap, fiercened with cockney wit.

'Ere! Sidboy! wotzee always apickinnov onmeefor nar ennyar? Ime not afraidov im the great ugly sunovva-bitch!'

Barney chest-out delivers himself in hot pants of sloshy ferocity.

'Eesez to Alf wotyewwozzer Cissy. Thats woteesez alongov old Alf.'

'Eesez wot Iwozzer buttin Cissy? Ere, Alf, is that right, did theold sunovvabitch say wot Iwozzer Cisser! ere is that rightboy?'

'Naaar-boy! eenevversez nuffin Sids crackers! I never diddunteer nuffin.'

Barney's eyes flash raw fire.

'Eebetternot cumennyuv that oldbuck alongov me straight eeaddunt the loud-mouthed old barstard——!'

'Gaaarn enuffsed yewll coppitt youngBarn Ime tellin-yew, enuffsed boy wots theodds ifee did cumter that.'

Barney's face with hard righteous fierceness stares at an effeminate mincing image; he snorts, in injured scorn:

'Cisser! Cisser! iffee cum ennyer that——!'

'Ere! cummorfit!'

'Cuttittart boy!'

Barney's indignation darkens; put in the wrong, he hurries sulkily forward, his legs working at tense speed carrying him ahead, while he replies:

'Gaarn that's right, show yer ignrance!'

They arrive with a guilty rustle and patter, six compact slinking truants, at the left-hand extremity of the enclosure. There they manœuvre for some moments out of sight, wiping their dripping faces with their cuffs, ducking and dodging to avoid their master's eye. That large unwinking roaming orb plays hide-and-seek with the six nimble heads of the artful dodgers, a relish for the crude pastime uppermost with it for a moment. The ball of the detached eye, like a ball on a cord, is rushed up a hundred times within an ace of the disappearing heads: each time the skulking object is just allowed to escape, with its artful dodging, behind an attendant, or beneath the wall. The bland eye is sent out by the Bailiff innocently to watch a hole between two backs, while out of its corner it observes its prey exultantly disporting itself elsewhere. It flashes across them when they are not looking. (Did he see me? it's impossible to be quite positive.) Ted and Harold expose rows of decayed teeth beneath knowing winks, for the advantage of an attendant to whom they are known. The Bailiff's head is turned in the other direction then. The team of clowns, with perfect unanimity, tumble into the enclosure, with the same gesture, drawing the body up along the face of the wall by the arms, till they are poised, its sharp wale of brick their axis, then the oblique gymnastic tumble, the leg-fork vaulting over the top, the body rolling adroitly down the other side. All of them having swarmed over, they sit huddled together, quiet as mice. An usher vociferates:

'The Carnegie batch, those with Alfred Carnegie,

167

stand by!' The little pack sidle along towards the entrance-wicket.

Placing a trumpet to his lips, a man standing out before the booth of the protonotary blows a single deafening blast. A reeling shellback emerges with a small square flag which he runs up to the head of a flagstaff on the camp side.

The Bailiff rises, crosses himself, and with a pleasant strong voice of great cultivation addresses the crowd of appellants.

'Gentlemen! I am glad to see you all looking so well and so much yourselves. That is capital: to be oneself is after all the main concern of life, irrespective of what your particular version of self may be. It is remarkable how distinct you all are this morning. My warmest congratulations. The day's proceedings will open with the usual brief statement, for the benefit of newcomers. First, then, you are entitled to as many decisions as can be reasonably arrived at in a day, according to mean solar time or as you call it civil time. We abandoned the sidereal day in your favour thereby relinquishing three minutes and fifty-six seconds as a concession to your natural impatience. But before that we had already abandoned the system by which epacts, according to the Gregorian calendar, were considered as holidays. Then there is the anomalistic year, the correct period occupied by our earth in making its trip from perihelion to perihelion, which, to my mind, is a barbarous manner of reckoning I confess: but since it annually procures our honoured appellants an extra three minutes, that too we have adopted. In spite of these concessions, since the characteristic incandescence of our infernal neighbour has of recent years been so noticeably on the increase, we are as you are well aware very much in arrear as a consequence of the unfortunate climate. Although it is our constant endeavour to devote the fullest attention to each individual case, you are urged to

168

facilitate in every way in your power our efforts and to raise as few difficulties as possible. Those who can combine should do so—that is the rule: it saves time. Also such combinations ensure the maximum effect of reality —I have known cases of a man being completely restored to his true and essential identity after meeting an old friend it's most valuable it's the tip we always give the newcomer, dig out the old pal there's nothing like it. But in no case should the group be too large. These conditions observed, we shall then carefully note your points of difference and your claim to personal survival.'

An eager murmur of applause interrupts him.

Slowly driving out the decorous pomp of his magisterial manner, a half-baffled grin develops upon his face. A flush like the traditional red of anger makes its varnish glisten and redden. A retrograde movement of the hair gives suddenly a feline cast to the grinning, watching, incredulous mask. Leaning to one side upon the crutch or bludgeon which he has taken from its corner when rising to speak, slowly rolling his heavily-squinting eye up and down the side of his nose, he suffers the interruption attending on his marked popularity. When the response has subsided he bows and smiles in acknowledgment. A thick light of servile buffoonery illuminates his face. Then the mask of Punch-like decorum and solemnity is reinstated.

'Next I will summarily outline the system thanks to which you find yourselves in your present situation suitors for the coveted citizenship for which you have so far qualified that at least here you all are, only requiring to satisfy us that there has been no mechanical error by the way but that you are in truth the fittest who have survived.'

Thunders of spontaneous applause. The Bailiff affectedly gasps.

'To reassure you, gentlemen, I may add that few who

169

get so far are turned back by this tribunal. The system, then, is as follows. The souls forced peristaltically into this metropolis from the earth, as though almost by muscular propulsion, forget by a divine ordering of the mirrors of their consciousness the phases of their journey. They forget the progressive chemical action to which they have been subjected. In fact they appear to forget that they have ever encountered any chemical action at all. They feel as natural, I think you will bear me out, thanks to the efficient nature of what might be termed the process of psychic mummification they have undergone, as though it were their *natural life* that they were still enjoying. They arrive completely transformed, cooked in this posthumous odyssey. As we have compared this process with that of the human digestion, it will cause no surprise that they reach the anus symbolized by the circular gate over there more cloacal even than at the moment of their engulfing on their earthly deathbeds. They will be found to have assumed a more ultimate form as well (though equally cloacal) than was possible in terrestrial life.'

Suppressed giggles disturb the silence of the crowd. Handkerchiefs are freely stuffed into mouths choking with sly mirth. Lips made into puckered O's, these bullseyes of the masks-of-scandal lisp fiercely, with bashful eyes eclipsed. One figure, its small sparkling eyes discharging a flux of tears above a crushed handkerchief used as a stopper, explodes, the stopper striking a neighbour upon the nape of the neck.

The Bailiff remains impassible, pausing only long enough to allow the most sportive to vent their spirits; then he continues.

'But although that small postern you see yonder serves to symbolize the passage out of an organic system into an inorganic life, it is nevertheless an entrance, as well as, or even rather than, an exit. Men have their exits and entrances: but the son of man hath not and so forth my poor children, there it is and so forth and so forth. Salvation signifies the termination for those saved of that state of affairs.'

(General applause and laughter. A group of a dozen diminutive figures in the front of the audience and at the extremity of the tiers of seats nearest to the Bailiff, up at whom they gaze with round eyes of exaggerated reverence during his harangue, bursts into rapturous clapping. He proceeds.)

'Heaven is not, I need hardly say, a drainage system into which you drop but a system of orthodox posthumous—if you will excuse the pun, post-human life.'

(At the word 'pun' there is an immediate facetious response.)

'The adoption of this simple device as regards your introduction to Paradise may be understood to symbolize as no other method could the friendly intimacy of the terms upon which the soul fit to survive is received into the ultimate corpus of the mother Church. To arrive by way of animal ingestion, moreover, would have its disadvantages. This sort of rectal feeding of the paradisal body—if you will excuse this shoppy and officinal language—my master Shejx Kuschteri had been trained to medicine, it was from him I got the rather detestable trick—this device has been resorted to for one reason because few human personalities could hope to escape the vigilance of what stands for the medulla in the celestial internal economy where the "vomiting centre" would marshal the muscles, in other words its myrmidons such as you see here, for the violent emesis. This administration over which I preside is from that point of view a sort of nutrient enema—we are you might say the funnel. Without these precautions, tiresome as they may be, there would be no alternative for the despised and rejected but that uncomfortable spot over there to our left.'

(Laughter and applause, all eyes turned in the direction of the neighbouring Inferno.)

Some of the functionaries, listlessly following suit, fix their eyes upon a spot rather more northward on the same horizon. The crowd, now of several hundred souls, transfers its gaze to this spot. The Bailiff interrupts his harangue, turning his eyes in the same direction. Seeing everybody occupied elsewhere he sits down, removes his bonnet, his hair retreating spitefully from his forehead while his ears lie down flat against his head. He watches the groups of sightseers beneath him, tapping irritably the ledge of his box.

Two birds, one immediately above the other, appear to be approaching the heavenly city. As however their bodies get sufficiently near, they are seen to be not two birds but one. What seemed like two is a large bird of unusual size holding something in its beak. Crossing the highroad at the further extremity of the camp, it describes a wide arc that takes it southward and to the rear of the Bailiff's court. Thence, flying with unhesitating precision, it sweeps towards the watching crowd. Skimming the summit of the official box, neck outstretched, its face seems, as it rushes overhead, like that of an ecstatic runner. It flies directly to a basalt slab situated between the Bailiff's enclosure and the ferry station. As it touches the heavenly soil a roar of faint trumpets comes from the city. At the same time a mirage rises from the further edge of the water, having the consistency and tint of the wall of a cheese, but cut into terraces full of drowsy movement which are reflected in the stream.

Two ponderous sounds enter the atmosphere along with the image. They are Bab and Lun, of the continuous Babber'ln. The tumultuous name of the first giant metropolis echoes in the brains of the lookers-on. Heavily and remotely its syllables thud in the crowd-mind, out of its

172

arcanum—the *Lon* as the lumbering segment of the name of another nebulous city, and the mysterious pap of *Bab* that is the infant-food of Babel. A stolid breath of magic, they are manufactured, as they are uttered, as a spell: nothing but an almost assonantal tumbling upon the tongue and lips, preserving the dead thunder and spectacle of a fabric of gigantic walls. What would *Bab* be without its *Lon* or both robbed of their copula; evocative of twin strongholds—in the separation of their powerful vocables—eyewitnessed by the sightseeing Greek; these are two roaring towers of sound, connected by a chasm that causes them to reverberate.

There is a babble of awestruck voices.

'Oh look! That must be Babylon! I've seen it on the pictures. That is a ziggurat it's called.'

'Is that Bab' and there is a hiccup of surprise 'Lon?'

'No!' A cry gasps self-conscious infant-wonder. 'Bab?'

'Which is it? I see two, or is it one?'

'There is the sun Chris!' It has suddenly become dark, and there is a new pale sun shining in the shadow.

'Where is Nineveh?'

And then Zion!

The Jews of the lamentation should be somewhere within upon the plain of the eclipse, gazing with passionate envy from their latifundia upon this splendour, willing a Jewish Babel, stirred up by their prophets, like an infant ravening for the moon.

Sound and image sullenly mate, but the denser name doubly impending bears down the simulacrum. *Babber* is dominant, the crowd drums it with its tongues, an incantation to give substance to the phantom picture. All at last is sound.

'Shades of Strabo and Heliodorus!' sneers Pullman through his moustaches, with screwed-up eyes marvelling politely, little shoulders squared high to the spectacle. Satters with a florid posture of the hips droops and marvels

173

mournfully, with lazy fanning of eyelashes against the insidious yellow glare.

The crowd hushes its voice like a theatre audience upon the turning down of the lights.

'They've put the lights out!' a nymph-throat bleats in the dazzling yellow obscurity.

There is a suggestive scuffling in the darker corners of the circus. Satters, his mouth achieving without sound the organic shape of the paphian *Mimp*, sweeps round an arch gaze of honeyed understanding and his hand crawls in for protection beneath the masculine arm while without comment he timidly closes up.

Accents of velvet melt in melodiush lishp:

'Oh do stop. I feel so terribly nervousth do stop *pushing*!'

There is a muted fracas mixed with old-fashioned high-school-girlish anti-tickling sounds, with the passionate steam of exploding hisses, expostulant and rampant in muffled free-fight. 'No don't *pleaase-th*!' comes in mater-dolorosa-ish panting pig's-whisper, then the thud of a kidney punch. They have got down the most popular victim now shrieking for quarter and are gathered in concentrated knot to finish him off out of hand. Disappointed beauties turning away set up a disgusted *missum*! One heavily-painted lowering Charlotte-the-harlot pushes his haughty way past Pullman and Satters in a towering passion, his breast heaving, and striding mannishly, cross and lantern-jawed, takes up his station, eye fastened upon the babylonish past as far away as possible from the disturbance.

'Have with you to Saffron Walden!' Pullman exclaims gallantly and they follow in his boiling wake. But soon this great proud powdered and pampered lank-haired circus-Star has a surging following.

'I do wish you wouldn't push,' the furious Star pants passionately. 'I came here to get out of the crowd!'

Pullman shrugs his shoulders and they return rebuffed to the centre of the watching throngs.

A head in silhouette turning against the light drifts without compass.

'Which way is it coming?' it wheezes vacillating.

The image becomes more distinct.

'It's getting larger, isn't it?' a voice answers with sulky carelessness.

The head comes to rest.

'Is that it?'

'If people can't see I wonder why they go on looking! I do wish, if we must look at all this, people would keep their heads still!' Pullman's opinion is distinctly heard.

The head in black silhouette is galvanized into erratic movement and detonates with pugnacious lisp:

'Listeners-in at large as usual! If people would mind their own business it would be so much nicer, don't you agree, for everybody?'

'What's the matter now?' its voice's discouraging shadow answers. The annoying silhouette at that collapses and ceases from troubling.

'Oh do look, can't you see the hanging gardens I can!' In the darkness all the figures, diminished as an effect of the light, excitedly point.

'I do think that's too lovely, it's like a colossal cheese!'

'They were at the northern extremity.'

At last one sightseer tumbles from the wall as he obliviously advances into the air to get a closer view.

'I can see an evident an elephant and a howdah I am sure, like a biscuit.'

The most prominent grummet on board tiptoes; he has a bustling following treading on his tail in sedulous charleston corkscrew-dazzle, their eyes fixed slyly away on the defunct city. His hands are clapping in kiddish delight and a kiddish clapping is indeed then taken up on all hands even Pullman claps a clap if never another.

'Where, don't, *do* let me spot it! Yes *I* see it. Oh, do look, there's another, no, there under the other, both are red.'

'It *is* an elephant!'

As the end of a lengthy whisper, at its climax.

'And then they threw them to the alligators!'

Pullman and Satters standing silent, Satters greedily listens to a nursery-tale unfolded *sotto voce* by such a nice middle-aged auctioneer to an eager bright-eyed boy of not thirty-five yet, who droops in deferential awe nervously laughing, painfully anxious to catch the lovely story told by the middle-aged auctioneer, his solitary pick-up this side death.

'And the alligators, the hottest of the bunch, opened their great big hairy jaws, but just at that moment a great shout went up from the palace yard, *and——*'

Zooomp! There is the thudding pash of a flashlight. It is for the gazette (Camp Special).

Two voices come up behind them:

'It's a cinematograph!'

'No, it's not a cinematograph.'

'Very well have it your own way!' The speakers fall out.

Desultory voices seem to be exclaiming:

'Ah shud naver raspuct a mon hew kuddna kap his end up wi' a wewmun.'

'That must be a temple.'

Muttering temples, the ash of Ashtaroth.

'I should have expected.'

Engine-room bells clangour in the tent of the Protonotary, there is a flashing of signals, points of light perforate the mat mirage.

'They're not so high!'

Snorting *Battery*. Unseen scale-snob swells snorting in the darkness and is silenced in arithmetic.

'Who was the God of Babberl'n?'

'Babberl'n?'

'Bell.'

Bell was the god, Bell was the god.

A mock-scotch voice pawkies in Satters' ear and he feels a hand upon his ham. There is a compact pushing and shuffling suggesting an influx of new blood—a scottish fifteen fresh from the scrum with a rustle of stiff macintoshes.

'Och, stop ye guddling Jock, thuz ay na fushies een tha bruk!'

Satters breathes discreetly certain information in Pullman's ear and they move away to their right, Pullman leaving a flat glance of contemptuous rebuke with a pseudo-Scot.

Some newcomers spring up the steps and stand clustered watching; some avert their faces after gazing at the mirage for a few moments.

'You can't look at it for long can you?' says the foremost, waving his head as though it were a watch that had just stopped.

'It's the yellow light.'

'I know, it's like smoked glass. I can't see anything now.' Two groping men pass, brushing and prodding Pullman and Satters.

Pullman removes his glasses and wipes his eyes with his handkerchief.

'It's getting worse,' he says. 'I shouldn't stare too much if I were you. It's a great strain on the eyes.'

He replaces his glasses, putting his eyebrows and lids through strenuous ape-gymnastics for a half-dozen seconds.

'It's five thousand years away.'

'Is it—five thousand?'

'About that. They oughtn't to attempt it really.'

'Oh I think it's rather sweet, I much prefer it to Islington.'

'I recommend you to stop looking. It might perman: ently affect your eyes.'

177

A small man at Pullman's elbow whispers hypnotically:
'They think it is Babylon. It is not Babylon!'
'Is it not?' Pullman is distant.
'No. We have traversed the arc of the Heavens. That
town is Himenburg!'
Pullman looks steadily ahead in discouraging silence.
'That's not the only mistake they make!' the voice goes
on to insist, darkly. 'That would not matter. What is far
worse they believe this place to be Heaven!' There is a
pause without response. 'That is a strange mistake to
make! No one in his senses could mistake this for Paradise! What an idea! Paradise! A pretty Paradise! The man
that believes that must be mad!'
Pullman looks round quickly at this and surveys the
person who has volunteered the information. On noticing
the white folds of a classical drapery he pointedly moves
away drawing Satters along with him.
'One of those bolshies!' he remarks.
A voice hisses in Pullman's ear, this time on his other
flank.
'It is Niflheim! It is the home of the mist. Don't you
believe them if they tell you it is Babylon.—*Babylon!*'
Pullman spins about, indignantly quizzing this second
mesmerist. Again he remarks the livery of the pseudo-
Stagirite, he notes the peering fanatical countenance.
Looking behind him he discovers more sweeping dirty
robes, and intent faces.
'Look, let's get out of this!' he snorts, urging Satters
obliquely forward. 'We've got into the middle of the
Ku Klux Klan!'
The crowd is thick, its heads ascending the planes of
the amphitheatre on the city-side. Many Hyperideans
have come up behind.
Pullman and Satters force their way to a spot near the
head of the gangway where there are fewer people.
'What did he say to you?' Satters asks.

'Who? Oh he said it was Niflheim. He doesn't know what he's talking about. But they're all as mad as hatters.'

'Who?'

'That set—the high-brow circus you know, the followers of the so-called philosopher, Hyperides, not that that's his name either.'

'Isn't it?' Satters is gazing listlessly at the false sun. 'What is it?'

'Jones, I should think.'

They stand facing the highroad. The dark bird is squatting alone a short distance beneath them and to their right.

'Watch that bird! I wonder what that is, what's that he's got in his beak?'

The crowd begins flocking towards the entrance, pointing at the bird.

In the half-light it seems to be resting. It is russet in plumage and almost bald-headed, of stocky shape and about twice the size of a full-grown buzzard. In its mouth is what looks like a round dishevelled basket as large as itself. This rests upon the ground, still hooked within its beak now, circumspectly raising it the bird moves forward towards the basalt slab with a human deliberation. Its face is that of a solemn sly-eyed yiddischer-child: ungainly feathered buttocks have given it a waddle, resulting, with its energy, in a strut. A perfume of frankincense myrrh spikenard and balsam drifts back from it and from its burden.

It deposits the basket jerkily upon the slab butting it forward then, a little, with its head, till it exactly lies in the stone's centre. It stands back observing it for some minutes. As though talking to itself, or reciting some formula of worship, its beak works with a chattering movement. In its eyes is an aloof recognition of the presence of the watching crowd and its entire person is full of the important concentration of a ritualistic act. Then

179

it turns, but still avoiding the faces of the onlookers, in a sufficient silent loneliness, with the aplomb of the patriarch but its feathers in places scarcely covering its immature baldness.

It takes a few steps, portentously stiff, stalking with a parade of its uncouthness, as though to emphasize its bird-nature and the handicap of the air-born, or suggest unfamiliarity with the earth. It offers the obverse of its front-on waddle, that is its thickset silhouette. What can be seen of its eyes, annealed in the furnace of its repeated resurrections, is a half-iris, that weights, drugged and leaden, the lower hemisphere, swelling out from the nether line of the socket. It advances obliquely, knowing itself watched, perhaps striking fear, legendary and immortal, aware of its mystery. It is the child-bird as the secretary-bird is the secretary-bird; it stands a moment sublime in its confidence of a surprising destiny. Nothing can shake the archaic fixity of the ego with which it is replete. It tiptoes swelling with the music of self for a few instants. Then it spreads its wings, stretching out its neck, the filmy shutter of its eye opening and closing like a pulse for a moment, and launches itself off the ground. As it does so the dismal roar of the trumpets reaches the crowd again, a fanfare of farewell.

'That is the angelic host,' a ring-attendant remarks, 'saluting the nest of the Phoenix. That bird was the Phoenix.'

'This then is the City of the Sun?' inquires the elegant person to whom he has addressed this confidence. 'I should have expected it to proceed to its incineration within the walls.'

'No it is El Kuds. Heaven. It is the New Jerusalem. But the Phoenix always brings its nest here now. It prefers it.'

'Oh!'

The Phoenix rises quickly over the platoons of faces, almost touching those in its line of flight, its heat dust

180

and scent bursting into their upraised nostrils, staggering their senses. The puissant whirr and insuck of its wings become fainter as the trumpets break and stop suddenly upon a triumphant note. The mirage disappears, the dusty red daylight is reinstated and the walls of the customary city are there as before.

The Bailiff makes a sign to two guards with leather aprons tiaras and swords. These advance in perfect step across the central court, pass down the passage bisecting the auditorium, then, approaching the basalt slab, take up the basket, one on either side, and carry it away towards the landing-stage.

The Bailiff sits stock-still in his elevated box, biting his lip, with frowning abstracted eye. The comment aroused by this spectacle slowly subsides. The crowd one by one turn again towards the waiting magistrate. He does not move: his abstraction deepens. The auditorium becomes hushed. Then he rises and stands for a moment silently confronting the tiers of seats.

In surly lazy drawl, looking down his nose with a resentful glitter, he resumes his address.

'They always do that film business when the Phoenix comes. It's quite pretty, but as archæology it's all nonsense I'm afraid. I hope you enjoyed it.'

'Oh yes sir! It was *lovely!'*—'*Rather!'*—'I should think we jolly well did!' and similar exclamations rise with a fawning precipitation on all hands; eyes everywhere are dutifully lighted up, hands clapped, everything is one writhing spasm of appreciation. The Bailiff watches the obsequious ferment of the crescent-shaped wave of beings beneath him, smiles till his nose-tip touches his humped chin quickly, then proceeds, snapping his smile to in the manner of a telescope.

'That's capital!—Where had we got to when that tiresome bird arrived?—it makes all that fuss about its stupid nest every time it lays itself again or whatever it is that it

181

does, as though that could be of any interest to any one but itself or perhaps the dynasty of Noah! Why it should suppose that the feathering of its stuffy ill-smelling nest is so attractive and worthy of celebration or why it should regard its eternal reproduction of its ill-favoured self as a sign of God's favour baffles me: but there, you know the saying about people being taken at their own valuation! —it's only a bird, after all, a mere bird, we must excuse it—if it were a man that would be different—but then it would know better, would it not?'

'Please, sir, is it a real bird?' comes piping to appease him from his favourite where the pensive lad is attentively riveted, drinking in his every syllable.

'No, not real but quite real enough.' The saccharine amenity is reinstated with a wheezy rush. A sharp flurry of coughing springs up and dies down with the same suddenness.

'Oh, thank you sir I was sure it wasn't!'

The Bailiff beams. He clears his throat and takes up his story quickly.

'Ah yes, I remember I had just got off my jest about the anus, that went down well. I always rely on that to get us all into a good humour at the start.—We have now to be very serious for a short while: for the main problem of salvation—namely, what or who is to be saved—has to be canvassed at this point. Without splitting hairs—we shall have to split handfuls later on, I can assure you from experience—I am a plain man like yourselves, gentlemen, and would sooner be chopping firewood or I may frankly say it why not chopping up my fellow-sinners for that matter—the old Adam you know, in spite of the fact that my pacifism is a byword I'm even a little ridiculous about it—than perspiring here and cutting up things I can hardly see—let us get down to the business in hand. The sort of existence we are contemplating in the Paradise over there can only mean *personal* existence, that

I'm sure you will agree, since mere *individual* existence would not be worth troubling about, would it?'

An enthusiastic roar of 'No!' is released as he ceases.

'Please, sir!'

Another of the group of diminutive figures providing the tapette-chorus, eager minors as distinguished from the majors, which supports in the character of a confederated claque the utterance of the principal actor, holds up a hand. It is forced stiffly up and up into the air, the little fist clenched, while the buttocks of its owner wriggle excitedly upon the stone where he delicately perches or else jumps up and down in an ecstasy of suppressed inquiry.

'Sir! Please, sir!' he continues to vociferate, nudged and hissed at by his neighbours (who sibilate at him hoarsely behind their hands, breaking down in convulsive fun):

'You're not at school! Don't hold up your hand!'

He pouts and throws them off with a pettish toss of his shoulders.

At length the Bailiff smiles over at him, avuncular solicitude puckering the jolly features of Uncle Punch.

'Do you want to leave the room my little lad?' the matter-of-fact magistrate inquires, sleek sleepy and domesticated. The diminutive appellant thrusts down his hand: then tremulous, in a fit of stammering bashfulness, his head strained painfully on one side examining the border of his crested cricketing cap, which he pulls tightly over his knocking knee clinging to its brother-joint:

'Please, what is the difference between a person and an individual?'

'All the difference in the world, and out of it, all the difference between me and you my sympathetic little fellow!'

Absolutely everybody laughs who is attending, applauding the Bailiff's sally to the echo. Even Chris the most eminent among the favourites, a sort of leader of the dithyrambic choreutæ of the major order, in a perse-plum skirt-trousered suit, lavender-spatted, smiles slightly at the facetiousness, remarking in a dismal throaty cultured underbreath to his stern eyeglassed follower of forty-odd that he has never seen My Lud so young to which the follower replies No, he is very lively this morning, but that he believes he has something up his sleeve, that his laugh is a little raw and edgy. 'I do wish those young idiots would stop asking questions!' Chris testily replies intending the minors. When the laughter has expended itself the resourceful magistrate addresses himself once more to the audience at large, looking out over it comprehensively as a conductor with a numerous and complicated orchestra.

'Since the point has arisen, I will deal with it at once. Individuality then is identity without the idea of substance. And substance we insist on here, nothing else can hold any real interest for us, that is a cardinal fact about which you should all be perfectly clear. It is not the persistent life of a bare universal that any man, ever, is likely to covet. It is that crusted fruity complex-and-finite reality—the term by which we are accustomed to express the sensations of our own empirical life—emerging in the matrix of Space and Time or Space-Time—that all the fuss is about. It is the cuticle that the little colony of valves glands and tubes gets to cover it that is precious, just as it is the form of the Redeemer surrounding the *vesica piscis* that gives that emblem its importance. For us, whatever it may be for God, it is not the *laver* but the *fish* that matters—you understand me? The numerical identity of a particular existent, then, as it is catalogued in philosophy—am I right?—is not our affair at all.'

He pauses: dangling his pivetta as though it were a monocle he watches with ferocious pleased recognition a small bearded figure climbing with difficulty, for it is

184

lame, into the theatre. Leeringly he attends its ascent, notes ironically the histrionic swing of the cloak, with mock-courtesy attends until it is seated. At length he withdraws his eyes, publicly tempering the relish of his smile, and pursues:

'Substance, then, it is our aim to secure. But perhaps it may occur to you that my description of the especially concrete nature of what we seek to perpetuate precludes the idea of substance. I think that would be foolish, an effect of the snobbery of the old deep-seated dualism which attached disgrace to physical nature. When we set out to look for substance where else shall we find it but in the flesh? In the last analysis is not *substance* itself flesh? —as for that matter those excellent contemporary philosophers have shown who confound flesh and spirit to the advantage of the former and of physical law, just as *singularity* was for William of Occam the only true substance. Not that I recommend you Occam, his razor is a two-edged implement and makes him a dangerous doctor for beginners.—To return: there is no mind but the body; and there is no singularity but in that. Every step by which you remove yourself from it is a step towards the One. As we interpret it, that is towards nothingness.—So to be unique—no one quite like us, that is the idea, is it not?—and for that substantial uniqueness, as well, to be solid, so that we can pinch it, pat it, and poke it—that is, there you have—am I not right?—the bottom of our desire.'

The enthusiasm of the audience knows no bounds. The entire juvenile chorus, joined by other choruses throughout the assembly comparable in vivacity though not so well placed nor at all times on winking terms with God, shouts 'Hoorah!' Caps, mufflers, and even gym-shoes are thrown up into the air and deftly caught. One gib-cat, with one Jewish lip and one Polish one, slobbering with mischief, hurls an orange in the direction of the

185

Bailiff's box. It strikes Jackie upon the chest, a fat thud issuing from his black column. Jackie grins from ear to ear.

'Three cheers for good old Jackie!' is then given. 'Hip-hip-Hoorah!'

The Bailiff flings his own cap up into the air and bellows:

'Hurah! Hurah! Down with Hierosolyma! Ha Rou! Ha Rou! Up with the Gentile and down with the Jew!'

An attendant, dusting it, returns the Phrygian punch-bonnet, which has fallen outside upon the flags of the inner court.

The demonstration continues and is watched by the Bailiff with evident pleasure. Uncle Punch amongst his jolly children!—the solemn mask is off, the satiric on. He is all grinning vulpine teeth, puckered eyes, formidable declination of the ant-eating nose, rubicund cheeks, eyes of phosphor. The goatee waggles on the glazed bulbous chin; it is the diabolics of the most ancient mask in the world exulting in its appropriate setting. With an effort he repudiates the satiric grimace. As his face changes the audience becomes hushed. The tragic mask casts its spell, as well, upon him: as he feels it coming down over his skull and its awful shadow gathering upon his face he becomes another, the tragical, person.

In his deep faucal growl from a throat formed for a more guttural speech he commences:

'It is my duty—far more often than it should be!—to remind you that this tribunal is not a puppet-show. I am not a clown. You often presume on my good nature. I have to consider my trusted servants here this ill-paid and hard-working staff as much even as yourselves. Bearing this in mind please refrain from such exhibitions as the one that has just occurred.'

A deep mechanical silence ensues. Every one looks down on the ground or away into space-time. It is broken by a cringing pipe from the centre of the gangway, which asks in the midst of the mortuary hush:

'What is the difference, please sir, between Space-Time and Space and Time?'

Chris and the more elegant and grown-up of the juvenile chorus look round sharply in expressive indignation.

'Can't anyone make that young fool be quiet?' Chris asks, and his neighbours echo him.

The Bailiff pulls at his nose with his thumb and forefinger, squinting sideways at the Carnegie batch, then he replies a little absent-mindedly:

'Space-Time is merely the other two mixed together. What, dear? No, they are not the same: but henceforth they refuse to be parted just as body and soul refuse any longer to be considered separately. "If you have Time, then you must also have me for we are one!" says Space, and vice-versa. Oh, I beg your pardon! It was exceedingly fresh of me to call you "dear", it's my theatrical upbringing. I'm always saying dear when I shouldn't. Hadie is often very cross with me and says I will certainly offend people if I don't remember.'

He moistens his lips, which have become unmanageably dry and large, with feline thoroughness, waiting for questions. The same tiny oldtime tot, with an authentic cheap-High-school satchel at his side, squirms and blushes full of eager exhibitionism, and, the Time-problem the pretext, breathlessly whines:

'Some fellows say that Time does not exist, sir—Are they right, sir—?'

The Bailiff toasts him all over with a paternal eye till his blush has turned tomato-red; then he grumbles genially:

'No, my dear, I've told you—there is neither Space nor Time, now. There is only the one reality: and there is no reality without contact. Until things touch and act on each other they cannot be said to exist for each other, time commences for anything when it is in touch with something else. And further, one thing commences to have time for another when it is spatially present to it. Things are bearing down on us from all directions which we know nothing about at this moment, when they shall have struck us we shall term that an *event* and it will possess a certain temporal extension. All the times of all these potential spatial happenings are longer or shorter paths that are timeless until they touch us, when they set our personal clock or proper measure of time ticking, measuring the event in question for us. You see the idea?'

A voice so deep that it seems to fill the air with some thickening oil as it rolls out, begins tolling: a shudder of scandal at its alien contact shakes the assembly.

'Would it not be true, sir, to say that in your magical philosophy there is only Time, that it is essentially with *Time* that you operate?'

The Bailiff is electrified at the impact of the new voice, and he lights up all over. The sounds stagger his senses like a salvo from a gong announcing battle from the positions of a legendary enemy. It is a hail from the contrary pole, it opens for him by magic the universe that lies between which before the voice came was shut and dead. With eyes of the most velvet challenge he turns gladly to the interrupter. It is the bearded figure but recently arrived.

'How is my philosophy magical, Hyperides? Besides, I'm not a philosopher, as I have already said, so I don't see how I can have a philosophy.'

They are the oldest opposites in the universe, they eye each other: all this has been enacted before countless times, on unnumbered occasions all these things they are now about to say have been uttered, under every conceivable circumstance. He blinks his eyes in veiled welcome.

188

The voice roars out with the consummate accent of a rôle constantly rehearsed.

'I use magician in the ordinary sense of illusionist hypnotist or technical trick-performer: and whether your ostensible approach be that of mathematics, biology, medicine, epistemology, or moralistics, is all one. Men find what they desire. You do not expect me, at least, to be superstitious about your profession? With your convex and concave mirrors and with your witches' cauldron, Time, into which you cast all the objects of sense, softening and confusing them in your "futurist" or time-obsessed alchemy, are you not faithful to the traditions of the magician? Is your art, for all its mechanical subtlety, profounder than that of Protagoras that it took the greatest intellect of the Greek World all his time to confute?'

The kinked raven hair of the Bailiff starts back furibundly from his forehead. His ears cling sheepish and flattened against his skull. His underlip is extruded, and his eyes sparkling with the malice of battle dart hither and thither upon the faces of the audience, his cloud of witnesses. No verbal response comes from him at once: he plunges his little world into silence, in ambush, full of mute gusto, at its centre. But he peaks his mouth, strokes his jutting chin as though it were a beard enclosed in the varnished husk of a cartonnage: then in his most piping and nasal voice of extreme complaint starts off shrilly:

'This my children is the way the day always begins! What am I to do? I implore you to tell me! I have protested against the method imposed on us here of free debate. It isn't that I mind discussing these matters, they are most interesting—I know not to you but to me they are: and as you are aware, I think, I am all for freedom of speech, no one more so. Everything fair square and aboveboard is my motto and always has been let God be my witness! I don't regard you as my clients but as my *friends*. Let all opinion be ventilated, I'd rather see it that way!

189

But it is your *time* I am thinking about!' he wails, rolling his eyes about among them in startled gambols. 'It is your *time*, my poor children!'

He gazes at them in silent, passionate, protesting inquiry. Commiserative heads are shaken and wagged in chorus in time with his, and scornful glances cast towards Hyperides.

'Many of you have waited months, some even years, some so long you have ceased to know since when and have lost count, for your turn to come. It is the cruel *suspense*! There is a type of discussion—I won't say what it is for on no account would I do anything that could be interpreted as a discouragement of free-speech—which is in fact entirely otiose, it serves no possible purpose! What's more, it wastes a great deal of time, that is what I mean, *the time*, that's it, see? It is the *time* that is the trouble, that is troubling all of us the time in the waiting and the rest of it. But the *time*!—I enjoy it! The turning over the old things and finding new absurdities in them every day, all this time I'm turning over and over, for my part I love it simply—this is a confession mind! But no one else gets anything out of it. I reproach myself, oh! more often than not; I know I'm inclined to be a bit selfish in that respect. But I do realise that first and foremost I have to think of you that I do absolutely understand! Be just—now *that* I do! Business first is our motto, gentlemen! Our customers are our *friends*, that's another. It's a new ideal of friendship nothing less, the ideal of the modern age I might almost say. So there you are torn two ways see? duty and pleasure. Again I ask you is this the place for all that hot air? Phew!' (He mops his brow.) 'Not exactly!'

A slight cockney nasalness has shown itself in his voice. It appears from time to time throughout his discourse, bringing with it a slight vacillation in his vocabulary. Shooting his linen, throwing his fists out to get a draught

190

in his cuffs, flashing his fawneys, licking his lips to picture forth the dog-days, he shouts, laughing for his audience, speaking for them:

'*No it is not!*—Emphatically it is *not!*—God's will be done however every time, that's what we are out to stick out to stick up for and damn the whole of the bally rest! Excuse me! You know I'm a good old sport? *Weeel?*' (He starts back, lips thrust out, eyebrows raised, hands argumentatively extended as though posed for the climax of a hard bargain in the picture of a rustic bagman, gazing magnetically round in jocund intensive inquiry.) 'Weeel?' he drawls again, with more finality, answering for the audience up to the hilt, with humorous flourish thrown in. Catching the eye of Hyperides he pulls himself hastily together. In his stateliest manner he resumes, the bagman dropped out of sight in a trice:

'It is God's will that the utmost fairness should mark the proceedings of this ante-chamber of salvation. Every courtesy must be shown, those are my instructions. So it falls out that anybody who is so disposed can hold us up. This man *always* does!'

Hyperides remains with an indolent dreaminess above this *mêlée* of his own making. From habit he allows for the clattering descent of the thunder of buffoonery his earliest remarks must call down. He occasionally looks over to note what phase it has reached. Grandly outlandish, he is in the company of a tatterdemalion bodyguard. His smashed michelangelesque nose, with its vertical ridges of cartilage, deepset eyes, the centripetal ribs of wrinkles terracing his brows beneath black Vitruvian curls, remains stamped a mask of force, a dark cameo, in the centre of the crowds of faces.

Pullman is saying to Satters:

'A man called Dixon calls him the loud-speaker don't you agree it's rather a good description?' The wit of Dixon speaks neither one way nor the other to Satters, who is mesmerized. The prestigious play of the more fashionable part of the audience, the child-groups of the stallites, who continue to amuse themselves irrespective of what happens to be going forward otherwise, is his whole concern.

The voice of Hyperides rolls out again immediately:

'Is not your Space-Time for all practical purposes only the formula recently popularized to accommodate the empirical sensational chaos? Did not the human genius redeem us for a moment from that, building a world of human-divinity above that flux? Are not your kind betraying us again in the name of exact research to the savage and mechanical nature we had overcome; at the bidding, perhaps, of your maniacal and jealous God?'

'No.' The Bailiff shakes his head. 'We are on the contrary providing you with more rigorous methods in your battle with nature.' (Sotto-voce, then) 'Also, don't be offensive about God, I don't mind but the others do specially the servants.'

'So you say that your physics of "events", and the cult of the "dynamical" that substitutes for the antique repose an ideal of restless movement, is an "advance" for "us". But an advance in what? An advance for whom?'

'An advance for science: also, Hyperides, for the mass of men! You always leave them out of your calculations.'

'What are your intentions as regards the mass of men, wicked or charitable, old mole? You know, you sugary ruffian, of what quality is your *charita*! Heaven preserve us from—your Heaven!' (He waves his hand mournfully towards the neighbouring city.) 'Also some God release us soon from your demented itch for what you call *action*, from the insane fuss and rattle of your common, feverish, unhappy mind! That Time-factor that our kinsman the Greek removed and that you have put back to obsess, with its movement, everything—to put a jerk and a wriggle, a tic and a grimace, everywhere—what is that accomplishing except the breaking-down of all our concrete world into a dynamical flux, whose inhuman behests we must follow, instead of it waiting on us? *An eternity of intoxication!*—the platonic description of it—that is your great promise.'

'We promise nothing that we are not fully skilled to accomplish. *We hand over the goods,* as Joan of Arc remarked when she kissed the cow!' (heavy and spontaneous applause).

'And you still find that among the most profitable to deal in are drugs and philtres, pornography and lightning cures! You still live by prophecy, tumult, magic and terror: and "loving-kindness" is still your mask!'

The Bailiff's grin is sensitive, it is like a palate that sours on the instant at the contact of any unsuitable influence. The noble tolling of the voice of his antagonist has left it at full gala stretch from ear to ear and now the tongue comes out and sweeps the lips with the slow relish of canine tail-wagging when the beast is large and grave: his surroundings are not noticed any longer, lulled in that familiar organ-music. But this is not the Age of Messiah; he recalls himself with a burly shrug of the hump, with an effort clearly, to the twin-senses of duty and decorum. A red-armletted commissary has placed some papers upon the ledge for his attention and frowning he turns them over. Then he looks up to say:

'Have it which way you like, Hyperides, for the moment. I have you down here with your school for this morning. If we can despatch the earlier cases quickly we should be ready for you quite soon; then you can continue. We shall all I am sure be very interested to hear what you have to say.'

Throwing up his sandalled feet beside him and sinking upon one elbow, Hyperides turns the shallow ledge of his wide-shouldered back towards the Bailiff. As he does so he throws over his legs the curling ends of a garment like

193

a paludamentum but of dark substance. Beneath this is a plain sailor's jersey with a deep tightly-drawn canvas belt and tight black drawers. Turning his head back for a moment towards the Bailiff he releases a last lazy contemptuous thunder.

'Prove to this cattle that they are whatever you require them to be! It can matter very little. Only why give yourself so much trouble? You come down here every day to this paidagoguery: since you are its only begetter it must be to your taste, yet surely it cannot be for ever and for ever amen enough to entertain you to play the god to these drivelling fragments, up to your mouth in the very insanity of an artificially isolated animal function?'

The Bailiff nods his head eagerly and brightly many times, stuttering.

'Yes-it-is, yes-it-is, *yes-it-is*! For ever and ever amen!'

'What is your object, from the standpoint of your Paradise over there, in reducing all these creatures to the dead level of some kind of mad robot of sex?'

'What else is there but sex in life that is worth while, to be candid?'

'You mean that you refuse to admit, old despot, that your human slaves shall have any more ambitious interest—oh, unbecoming in a humble subject!—than the smelling and sucking propensities whose embodiments we see here, all garnished and dressed for the monotonous feast in the sickly finicks of the female pantry? No, there must be no competition with you! The clients must not aspire to the intellect of the patron, for then the patron's occupation would be gone, he would lose all interest in life—is that it? Hence those attacks of yours upon "the intellect": intellect would be a great mistake in the underworld of Plainmen and Plainwomen, and so the less attention men in general pay to intellect the better—it is not their business. The *senses* is their business, eh? To win your favour the subject, in consequence, should present himself solely as a sense-machine. And he cannot make exhibition of enough futility, never enough for you! There is no extreme of abasement or imbecility that would quite come up to your standards for *him?* Have I your secret—the more foolish you can make Mr. Everyman look, the better, else you would not be able to cut such a fine figure yourself?—But as opposed to this helpless mass of bottle-sucking cannon-fodder you regard the human male as your ambitious promethean enemy. The male principle is scarcely your favourite principle where the human herd is concerned! —that is so is it not? So you would drive back mankind into the protozoic slime for the purposes of your despotism where you can rule them like an undifferentiated marine underworld or like an insect-swarm: that is the big idea?—do we understand one another? Have I in my hand the secret of your complacent insistence upon the advertisement of super-sex old quacking Punch and Judy showman-puppet?—have I put my finger on the reason why you chuckle and cackle so light-heartedly when you observe yourself surrounded by this trooping of obsequious gazebos?—No, Mister Procurator, it is you who waste *time!*'

Many angry voices have expressed hatred of the interrupter amid a universal bawling and piping and minor cat-calling with many small hysteric explosions of shame-faced glee at the expression gazebo or upon the new word human-male.

'B.M.! B.M.! Bloody Male!' is bawled and sung.

Hyperides turns his bearded head away, and is offered a battered piggin from which after wiping its rim with his sleeve he drinks. He is at once engaged in conversation by an eager ring of disciples. But the Bailiff calls out loudly:

'Hyperides ler-ler-listen to me! Before bringing these foul charges in this indiscriminate way why don't you

195

look to your own followers? It is notorious you are not "Greeks" for nothing!'

'Yes those charges come strangely do they not from a "Greek"!' Pullman sneers up at them.

'But we will meet those charges later!' exclaims the Bailiff.

'Dirty puritan!' an aged pathic whistles through a severely disciplined plaster-mask of a suet-grey.

The disciples of Hyperides shake their fists speaking all together in a clamour of defiance and protest.

'I have made no "charges", as you know quite well,' (holding the piggin on his knee, Hyperides roars hoarsely, smacking his lips). 'Those are not *charges*. It is not a charge to describe a person as an addict of inverted sex-love if he dresses the part and insists on being recognized as such any more than to call us Hellenes, for as such we would be identified. It is the pattern on which you manufacture your pseudo-infant-minions about which I was talking and it is because they are organized self-consciously against all our more abstract and less feverish human values, under your direction: that is why we protest. What they do among themselves neither concerns nor interests us, we are as you say not Greeks for nothing though not in the sense you intended. As it is, you are drilling an army of tremulous earthworms to overthrow our human principle of life, not in open battle but by sentimental or cultural infection so that at last indeed there will be nothing but these sponges of your making left.—You do not believe in the sex-goods you deal in, we know that——'

'Ah thank you for that, thank you!'

'You need not—*power* is your vice we are well aware, it is your *complex*; with you sex like money is merely a congenial instrument in its service, and quite secondary; we know that too; if that had not been so you would not be where you are, bossing our universe—you like the rest

196

of us would long ago have fallen to pieces politically and all of you have faded into fellaheen, your Heaven a subject-province instead of an abominable capital with a world-monopoly to turn spirit into matter and farm Death. Congenial however I admit it is to you it must be, it helps you to stomach what otherwise even you would retch at or which else would cause you to yawn your head off or both together!'

A hearty burst of old-fashioned German laughter breaks forth from the Bailiff's box full of insulting self-congratulation. Holding his paunch in two-handed mid-wifery the Bailiff continues to be delivered of a litter of artificial-antique outsize laughs.

'Well well well! Weehl weehl weehl!' he comments in rapid nigger singsong.

'Get on with your session, puppet! Hurry up—we're waiting for you!' an Hyperidean shouts.

The Bailiff obeys, in mockery of guilty-schoolboy flurry.

Cocking his eye up for a moment, from the papers he has now turned to examine, downwards upon his nearest listeners, who sit up eagerly, grin and draw nearer, the magistrate says in the low voice of a confederate under the eye of the dominie:

'If you'd heard as much Hyperidean invective as I have in my time you'd think me the most patient of men. What a chap what a man! I had his head cut off once. But he was back here in a couple of months—after a short stay as an apparition at his old home on earth. He was very indignant. He was superb. I wish you could have heard him. Twice he has escaped from over there.' He jerks his head towards the city. 'It's difficult to know what to do with him. Do you want my job? You can have it!'

His confidants look at each other with merry delighted grins or with smiling condescension. Good old Bailie! The most animated glance back with roguish inquiry in the direction of Hyperides, surely discomfited by their resourceful champion.

Pullman says to Satters, settling himself comfortably upon an elbow:

'Give me the old Bailiff any day of the week in a scrap of that sort; loud-speaker's no match for him! To start with, he doesn't know a tenth as much—a tenth's a conservative estimate—the Bailiff has more knowledge in his little finger than that charlatan has in the whole of his body!'

Satters looks depressed: he listens to the Almighty Grown-up blowing-off steam in his ear and sits with his hands palm to palm, thrust flat between his thighs, and works his heels and knees up and down.

'He's the most suspicious cuss that I suppose you could find anywhere!' Pullman is whiling away the time in his club—his victim is securely landed, he lies luxuriously back propped on both elbows now, the hollows of his abdomen reposefully wrinkled, the little chest declaring itself extinct, the anchored fingers fiddling on either side in idle strumming, the meditative head sunken in the socket of the puny trunk, eyes dreamily fixed.

'Who is?'

'Loud-speaker!'

'Hyp——?'

'Quite.'

'Yes he seems awfully distrustful. Why does he interrupt like that?'

'Only to advertise himself! You can see the sort of person he is. Look at the way he dresses! He's one of those people who must be in the limelight else they're utterly wretched.'

'I suppose he's a frightful poseur.'

'Don't use that word I meant to tell you before—only very stupid people use it. It's what my aunt calls me!'

'All right. But some people do say that there's something in what he says.'

'Next time they say that to you, you ask them *what it is*!'

'Right Ho.'

'Try not to say *Right Ho*—it is so stupid! Don't—don't forget will you, I shall be most curious to hear what there is in that charlatan's rigmarole that I have missed.'

'I won't forget.'

'There, somebody's asking questions—I thought we were going to start.'

They listen, Pullman launching himself up and sitting bent forward, elbows on knees.

INTERRUPTER. 'That is not what I wanted to know.'

BAILIFF. 'By the tenor of my function, gentlemen, I am bound to answer these questions, though they lie as it happens outside my province. It is my duty to listen and to answer—duty first. I'll answer you.'

INTERRUPTER. 'By what authority do you state——'

BAILIFF. 'Gentlemen, gentlemen, this truculent gossip must be borne with—bear in mind our rule, be patient with him! Listen sir: I have a very ancient liturgy in my office' (he indicates the water-front, and its backgrounds, in an inclusive sweep of the head) 'which disposes at least of any Theory of the Presence involving objectivity and the annihilation of the substance of the outward elements. It is, I assure you, quite conclusive. I have had it here for over a millennium.—When this busy spot—as to-day you see it—was as peaceful as a rustic agora though now little better than a cat-market, my earliest little comelings used to perform it over there—they were little downy bearded beings like rabbits and chanted in the most ravishing way! Ah! Give me the early days of Christianity! However!—I had it taken down. I will bring it over with

199

me to-morrow if I remember. Then again, the Council of Trent is all very well in its way: but *we* have our Councils too, it is well to remember!'

ANOTHER APPELLANT. 'But is it not in any case a degrading doctrine to require that gross physical explanation of a supra-sensible mystery?'

BAILIFF. 'Of the first order! I'm absolutely with you! Gross isn't the word!'

APPELLANT. 'Of the first order—er—of the first order—quite. Then local considerations, too, are introduced, whereas——'

BAILIFF. 'Whereas the thing is supra-local? Yes? How I agree with you!'

APPELLANT. 'Such a *difficult* theory of substance——'

BAILIFF. 'Difficult ill conveys——!'

APPELLANT. 'It suggests unworthy questions——!'

BAILIFF. 'Ah, my dear sir, how right you are!'

(There is a slight confusion and clamour as a fresh figure seeks to place himself advantageously to bell-wether.)

FRESH INTERRUPTER. 'If ye have well received, ye are what ye have received!'

BAILIFF. 'Don't yell at me! What are you?'

INTERRUPTER. 'Ah!'

(The bellwetherer retires, having shot his bolt.)

ANOTHER APPELLANT. 'My lord may I ask you——? Milord!'

BAILIFF. 'Yes my little chicken?'

(He lends a fleshy accommodating ear to the voice of the little chicken.)

APPELLANT. 'What becomes of the Eucharist if an animal runs off with it and eats it?'

BAILIFF. 'The same that would happen to you if an animal ran off with you!'

(Laughter. A Ladies'-Tiddler-One-Penny is stealthily connected with the neck of the last speaker: he spins round, his hand clapped up to the seat of the formication, when he catches sight of the disappearing plume of the Tiddler. A scuffle ensues for its possession. Satters goes off in a haw-hawing peal of army-laughter and is noticed by a member of the juvenile chorus, who puts out a tongue at him. Satters protests vehemently to Pullman and adopts a threatening attitude to several people in his neighbourhood.)

PULLMAN. 'You mustn't pay any attention to those cheap little stallites, the Bailiff spoils them.—Even great men have their weaknesses!' Pullman smiles gently. 'They are appreciative! They are his claque in fact—he requires one heaven knows.'

SATTERS. 'But I shan't stand it if he's rude to me—he looks a perfect outsider! I'm a jolly good mind to go down and punch his head!'

PULLMAN. 'You'll do nothing of the sort! You're a perfect little cave-man!'

SATTERS. (His eyes still fixed upon the back of his enemy.) 'I don't care about that. Why should he try and be funny with me? I have as much right——'

PULLMAN. 'It was only high-spirits I expect—he didn't mean anything.'

SATTERS. 'That's all very well. I've done nothing to him——! Why should he——!'

PULLMAN. 'What did he do?'

SATTERS. 'He put out his tongue at me didn't you see him?—that one—no, the one next to the boy in blue—yes that's the one! If he's not jolly careful——!'

PULLMAN. 'Oh shut up! Pay attention to this, the fun's beginning now in earnest. The Bailiff's in great form, look at him!'

The Bailiff is in the greatest form, he is on top of everything on all-fours in the tensest fettle—why give a thought to Number One when it's where it is? *in excelsis*—hall-marked American—firmer than excalibur, while life's one singing thickset rough-and-tumble scrum moving towards the one and only goal provided of heart's-desire through which it will crash like a side of beef into other dimensions, ball-less and footless, and the one multitudinous team will fatally be the cupholders in that to-morrow-come-never which is the better-half of to-day? Ha Rou! Ha Rou! Ha Rou! Ha Rou!

But his voice is as bland as the sucking-dove as he gently tattoos for silence with his night-stick and clears his filmy throat.

BAILIFF. 'There are just one or two minor points with which I must detain you, gentlemen. It is a matter of great regret to the management that you are so cramped for space—although as regards time it's another matter. I refer of course to the dispositions of the encampment and the facilities for exercise. Beyond the restricted limits of the camp things are as you know by no means as they should be indeed they are all upside-down to put it plainly there's no concealing the fact, anything but orderly even chaotic. The least observant of you will have noticed that as you approach a certain well-defined limit the stability that we have secured for this small and necessary area is by no means maintained. Almost immediately unorthodox spaces and even unorthodox times betray their presence by untoward occurrences it must be admitted often of a distressing nature. We are able to guarantee nothing beyond those prescribed limits. We feel we owe you an apology for the fact that our provision of space is so stinted but no remedy so far has been found for this state of affairs.'

A sympathetic murmur rises and falls, while there is a sudden shuffling of feet and perfunctory whispering.

BAILIFF. 'The speed at which everything is regulated here is little inferior in quality to the admirable fixity in the Time-system that you encountered on earth, I think you will agree.'

There is a rapturous murmur of unqualified assent.

BAILIFF. 'We attempt to slow down everything as much as possible or as is compatible I should say with being thoroughly go-ahead. But we are of course creatures of Time, and it would be a most unfortunate circumstance which no one would regret more than the present speaker if one of you, too much venturing, found yourself suddenly caught in some Time-system, erratically cropping up when least expected, perhaps of a much greater acceleration than that you enjoy even so much greater that you might remain transfixed for a very great period in its midst—like Lot's wife for instance. But that is only one of the objectionable things that might happen.'

There is a murmur of law-abiding awe.

BAILIFF. 'It has come to my notice recently that there are some amongst you who are inclined to disregard these formal injunctions and in a spirit—I am afraid in some cases—of presumption to fly in the face of Providence and to roam in those problematical spaces—*and* times—that lie beyond the small but secure ground of existence which we are glad to say we have been able to put at your disposal.—This practice must cease! Those regions are in the most *absolute* sense, you understand, out-of-bounds. You will do well to remember that we are not so ignorant of what you do as you sometimes seem to suppose: although we are unable to control those regions as we should like we yet have access to them at all times and are able to detect the most insignificant happenings! With this warning I will pass on to another matter requiring our attention.'

With chided discomfort Satters' head bows before the silken storm for he understands which way the wind is blowing; his fingers stiffen and tighten upon his fellow-culprit's arm but Pullman is boldly unconscious, he stares round to endorse the Bailiff's censure his severe eyes sift the audience for delinquents. When he sees that the magistrate's attention is taken up with a servant bearing a message, with frightened eyes Satters whispers:

'Oh Pulley I'm certain he was looking at us!'

Pullman moves energetically in his place.

'Looking at us—what, the Bailiff?'

'Yes.'

'And if he was?—he was looking at everybody.'

'No, he meant us.'

Pullman drops away from Satters down upon an elbow, staring back steadfastly at his friend as if to decipher upon his face the secret of that capacity for misunderstanding everything that is his.

'No his warning was intended for people who are apt to stray outside in spite of orders to the contrary. It is a very timely one—he knows the dangers! I once found a man out there, at his last gasp, and had to bring him in pickaback.'

'But he had his eye on us all the time he was speaking, Pulley!'

After a further moment of contemplation of Satters Pullman sits up once more and transfers his attention elsewhere.

'It's the last time anyway I go for walks I may as well tell you!' Satters snaps with a hollow glower, violently removing his hand—which has left him to go down with

Pullman when he became partly recumbent and has returned with him when he sits up: flouncing right-about, Satters' shocked eyes call whoever it may concern to witness that he has washed his hands of all questionable adventures and is a distinct person.

'Wait till some one asks you!' Pullman retorts over his shoulder.

They sit with their backs to each other.

The Bailiff dismisses the messenger to return bon-homme and bustling to the enlargement of the safety-first regulations for appellants.

BAILIFF. 'As to the point I made just now, I daresay you think I was merely talking from the teeth outwards; it's a most awful bore I agree but during your stay without the gate you have to keep before your mind constantly the limitations—if I may say so, of the same nature as those imposed upon an aged person—which your present circumstances impose. To put it in another way, you may be said to resemble a company of veterans whom we have monkey-glanded and though we enable you to romp you must remember that it is only skin-deep, underneath there is nothing but *a corpse*—just as beneath the quick and animal flesh of living people there is always the skeleton.'

A restless movement of resentment and horror throughout the Bailiff's immediate following greets the unseemly image. The magistrate pulls up to gaze about him with mystified inquiry, then very severely remarks:

BAILIFF. 'Phocion—the real one, the Athenian, not the Hyperidean counterfeit here in camp—noticing himself applauded at a certain passage in his speech by the populace, turned to a friend and inquired, "What have I said amiss?" '

205

Pausing, he runs a supercilious eye over the assembly and exclaims:

BAILIFF. 'I am spoilt by popularity, gentlemen!—Am I wrong in believing I observed just now a gesture of disapprobation?'

There is a rebellious hissing of disgusted lisps and here and there the more venturesome favourites exchange unflattering views, of magistrates too big for their boots and Jacks-in-office, which is Chris's expression; while in the unfashionable backgrounds all sorts of personalities clubbed and clustered for argument, turning away from this new storm in a teacup noisily converse.

Pullman from their comfortable midway position frowns upon the fresh interruption.

'I do wish they'd stop carping and let him get down to it!'

Satters on his high ropes still affects not to hear.

BAILIFF. 'Hyperides is after all not quite mistaken; how I envy Hyperides sometimes his *beau rôle!*—he has all the noble things to say, if not all the intelligent. The whole nanny-hen shoot of us here my beloved tits could give a long start to the most punkish little whore of a spoilt-child ever thrown off by a peach-fed political duchess—I bear the blame boys I set the example! (it's my duty to, that's what I'm here for) that is all; do not let us enter upon recriminations, let let let let us stand or fall together as a company of jolly touchy darlings of the gods and s-s-say no more about it! Look the other way, ourselves is no fit sight! I have alluded to a matter of the most delicate nature—luckily I'm not called upon every day of the week to ventilate it—I apologize if I'se bin tackless—you exonerate me? Thank you!'

He gazes about vaguely with fierce amusement, many stars and lilies in his eyes, with a sweet-swooning ductile faraway finick.

BAILIFF. 'This place is an absolute paradise to what it used to be.'

The inconsequent statement is in the nature of a concession, his manner announces, it is to show that the subject is dropped. The tension is relaxed in his immediate following.

A FRONT-ROW APPELLANT. 'Which, sir? isn't it the same?—Oh *shoot* tup!'
(Scuffles and scraping of feet at underhand horseplay.)

This appellant at a first inspection would pass as a big public-schoolboy of about fifteen: his head is over-large, it has been coarsely upholstered from the pelt of a Highland shelty, untidy fingers of hair shoot out naïvely above eyes-to-match which in their expression offer themselves boldly as specimens of the most opaque and pathologic obtuseness that both love and money could fairly expect together to compass: a sensual value is involved, an animal claim staked out. The mouth, which is a coarse hole, promises as well complete absence of mind, nothing but matter and its gaping traps. The clothes are a size that has been overtaken by the furious animal budding of the boy-body; they make a theatrical eternal youngster and in places are burst at the seam and show the fresh leg-flesh. Of the elect of the circus this is a typical marionette of the schoolboy-pattern—he sits bolt upright, buxom and hieratic, with the air of a lumpish martyr to iron discipline. Should this figure become armorial, its escutcheon would contain only rods-in-pickle.

A VOICE. 'Baby Baby Bunting! Spoiltchild!'
A VOICE (spitting). 'Spoitchite! Spoitchite!'
   (A salvo of splutters succeeds *spoiltchild*.)
BAILIFF. 'Anything but. When first I officiated here
   there was a dense mist that was all, the original en-
   campment was invisible.'
APPELLANT. 'Where was that, sir?' A squeak. 'You cad!'

The appellant disappears heels-in-air. There is cuffing
and kicking at the interior where he has fallen.

BAILIFF. 'Here.' (He points down into the ground at
   his feet). 'I never landed. I used to interview people in
   the cabin of my state-barge, moored at that wharf.'
   (He points to the landing-stage at the state-barge.)

The correct façade of the Bailiff's front-row supporters
flashes with flattering exchanges of looks of wonder and
sympathetic interest in '*Fancy-that!*' poses of strained
politeness. Their thin pink line vibrates or is scandalously
broken, the sportive ferment that they affect uncon-
cernedly to mask getting the upper hand.

BAILIFF. 'It was much smaller that it is to-day—at that
   time the earth was not so thickly populated. A larger
   proportion moreover than at present was draughted to
   death into the ranks of the peons.'

The buoyancy of the more privileged audience returns
and they assist with growing enthusiasm.

APPELLANT. 'Why was that, sir? Weren't people in those
   days, weren't the people, weren't the——'
BAILIFF. 'Yes perfect brutes that's right; it was awful—
   for me. But the mist hung on all sides like clouds of
   powder, of dust and cinders, produced by a big erup-

tion; it was as black as night! It had a most depressing effect upon everybody.'

FRONT-ROW APPELLANTS IN CHORUS. {
'It must have been vile!'
'It must have been awful!'
'It must have been too foul for words, sir!'
}

BAILIFF. 'We've changed all that—very much for the better; if you could have seen the earlier dispensation I am sure you would agree there's no comparison at all.'

The Bailiff, the looker-on-that-sees-most-of-the-play would say, is proceeding with reluctance beyond a doubt, step by step it seems it is and with many wary stops as though afraid of putting his foot in it once having done so this morning already.

BAILIFF. 'Yes. It is true the mist still hangs about a little, ugh! ugh! ugh!' (Beating his chest he expels what has the appearance of mist, but in the demonstration falls into a tantrum of coughing, stamping in a croupy dance-of-death.) 'Hay fever! oh dear! well, eventually we hope to be able to eradicate it altogether I shall be glad when we do. Meantime the place does really look like *something*—we've got a mountain range in the distance and things generally have quite a normal appearance; they *look* all right, anyhow, even if on closer inspection they still leave much to be desired and that's half the battle, my tempting little titters!'

With little expansive laughs at this and the kindergarten tickled at being referred to as titters, everybody settles comfortably into the care-free hypothetic surroundings suggested, mountains mist hay-fever etc. The Bailiff relaxes more and more: he smiles mildly at himself as he detects a little human vanity peeping forth, but proceeds with a graceful haltingness.

BAILIFF. 'The mountains were an idea of mine!' (He suggests by his expression that his high colour is a bashful blush.) 'Yes, I thought of them one day as I was sitting here!' (He casts his eyes down with the shamefaced finicks of the female impersonator of broad comedy, raw-boned, with Wellington nose and wattled eyebrows.) 'They are as a matter of fact from Iceland, volcanic as you see I daresay—that is the Skapta Jokul —you can't see them but there are white columns of vapour rising up to a considerable height all over them; yes, most interesting, but they're too far off——'

He leans out of his box, talking in a wandering indolent voice, peering at the mountains as though not sure of his ground altogether and digging his finger out into the air while everybody turns in the same direction.

BAILIFF. 'They're there, I liked the idea when I was told about it.' (Rounding roguishly upon his noisy favour- ites.) 'Do keep quiet you naughty boys, I s'all have to spank oo if oo won't mind me else so-there!—pam- pam on Tomtit's big bad bold and bonny bot-bot of a B.T.M.! For two pins I'd short-coat you scut of smutty crazy shavers and send you in with bottle and crib in layettes and binders to worship for the rest of your un- natural days the Belly in the place of God—who "hath given us hands and swallowing and the belly" the sage has said, and so He deserves no more of us it's a mortal fact than to have you all wheeled into His presence in basinettes, it would serve Him right and you too and same here—for two pins I shall con- sider it!'

He rocks himself crooning upon the ledge Punch- hugging the truncheon, affecting to play for time. In the middle of his crooning he swiftly gabbles:

BAILIFF. 'Dat's my oozy swatch-cove patter!'

TWO BAILIFFITES. {'Is dat your swatch-cove patter?' 'Say, is dat your swatch-cove patter?'

He lifts his arm in comic fury, threatening a back-hander at least in gymnastic dumb-show.

BAILIFF. 'You dirty down-trodden darlings you for two tidy pins picked up on a frosty night for luck I'd come right down there and cuffoo cuffoo, yes I would you mind I don't.'

The nearest favourites make as though to parry a blow, affecting anxiety.

BAILIFF (coughs). 'Scoose my little language.'

He leans out towards the most egregious fledglings or impossible prank-heavy kittens as they pop and dodge in arch response and opening his mouth makes at them the sound solicited by the physician examining an inflamed tonsil.

BAILIFF. 'Aaaaah!'
APPELLANTS IN CHORUS. 'Aaaaah!'
BAILIFF. 'Aaaaah!'
APPELLANTS IN CHORUS. 'Haaahaahaaaah!'
BAILIFF. ''Ole black clam—see de roof? it's all baby-nigger.'

APPELLANTS IN CHORUS. {'All his roof is negro baby!' 'Oh how exciting! he's after all Afro, who'd have thought it!' 'Our black baby!'

BAILIFF. 'Yes Black Baby yes Black Baby!'

<table>
<tr><td>APPELLANTS
IN CHORUS.</td><td>'It's too marvellous he's Black! We thought he was White.'
'It's too marvellous he's not after all Blank!'<br>'He's not a dirty White as we have been led to suppose not a Blank which is too marvellous!'<br>'Oh our Bailiff's black inside him only his outside's dirty Paleface.'
'Hail Black Bailiff! We are lucky we are lucky!'</td></tr>
</table>

BAILIFF. 'With rabbit-palate see to rattle—rattle-snake for pretty baby!'

He seizes his unruly member.

BAILIFF. 'Tongue he too fat and forty for de White palaver!'

He shakes his head violently, the Punch puppet-egotist of the swatch-canon, full of the dumb negation proper to the wire-wagged noddle.

BAILIFF. 'Japhetic jargon he no belly fond of, truth-to-tell!'

With solemn whim he shakes his head to deny that any love is lost between him and the White Japhet's pompous patter. Slowly he despatches the gathering spittle called down by the exhibition.

BAILIFF. '*All* love-language oh boys all love-language love-cant and childer-chatter, dis poor swatch-cove'd never talk anything else if *he* had his way you just bet your death: he'd never never be the big cross Bailiff not he that'd be silly!'

Renewing his demonstration for the benefit of Chris's party, towards whom he turns, he stretches open his gills, seizes his fungus-tongue to liven it up and make it hop, and directs the light of an electric torch inside.

BAILIFF. 'Seen my prattling-chete—it's pretty! Seen my talking-tools, honey?'

He prods the torch-button, the light snaps out and snaps back several times.

BAILIFF. 'Seen this Kit, tongue lips glottis and velum all one penny-rattle! an that ole parrot-tongue he clappers on as he's taught—habit—habit he's a good clapper.'

He strokes its dark fur with a finger-tip.

BAILIFF. 'How worms talk in sounding-boxes—it's too marvellous Kit! Come now and I'll show you how it is that the words get melted, in glandmud-washing of de Swanee-bottom. I'll explain the last, that's the mud-flats where the dark words are dancing—I can't show them you—they get swamped.'

He rises from the ledge.

BAILIFF. '*Nigger-heaven* hell wat's zat but ze ganz same ding als baby-wallow! Am I right *aaam* I right? am I up to slum? Nexpleece!'

He jerks his head back in invitation.
'Aiisay! Hear! cumear Chriskit!'
Chris-Kit sways erecter.
'Cumeer Krisskt!'
To show it's for good that he's on all forepaws spread out to gossip and yarn as long as he likes, he drops down and rides at anchor upon his forearm rides back and forth

213

rockily and affects to wince at the buzzes caused in his funny-bone as he rolled to port too far a little and shipped a shock on his condyle.

'Mee 'umerus! Yaaaow!'

Facetious spot in excelsis of menkinds bodies (isn't it why where all the mad jokes sleep and hop hiccuping out when the spot's struck) it is frictioned while he pulls a humorous face of pain and complains:

'Me yewmrusbone's attit agen! me rheumrus me weak-watery spot's attit agen, it's tickled it's no use! I'm orf-agen! Hit's hit the Halpha-bit ho say boys! hit's hit that halphabit! hit's hit hit in me brain-pan and bin an mixt all the lettas! Ho Christ Chris hiffit hazzent mixt hall hiff hit hassunt hall the wordies up in me old tin brainpot wot I dropt in two at a time dayin dayout, at word-wide pains scrapped and scraped smelt-out sniffed-in collectioneered coined let slip and held tight got right side up an arse-overtip and toppled into me lucky-dip, I shall go to Folly Cliff I will I know you see and be fed at the bully-beef mammals of a bored jewish ogrish like a stuttering ten-monther, trussed and spanked *goodnight* by the bossy stenographer of the institute, if I can't get me tongue out of this tangle! Helf Chrisst helf!'

He cries 'Helf' in vain with seasick movements. Chris cries:

'Oh sir you'll tumble out!'

The Bailiff all of a piece and in a moment is as grave as a judge.

'Not so most eminent minx! Anny liffle mud which cometh out of Mam will doob, I guess, any lithle muth outh of Mump ull doofa tha mud-gland-washing of tha Swanee Bottom.'

He lurches forth his forepart and chucks back his head in *comeer* invitation again.

'Kumeer ant listnet fwot I sess lisden fwot I sess Kris-kerl-honey.'

Appealing to sundry super-ratings—
'Net Fret Tet! Tick tear, ant Mick! Howillowee Willee
and Fretty Frocklip *ant* Oliv Erminster *ant* Chrisst Walt-
shut! lisserndt termee!'

They lissent an he loosuns his tongue ant says:

'I'm as yewmrus as umerous an wot's the odds I'm a
walrus-Christ ant Carpenteer full of seabird-girl sob-
slobber and lunchcounter lacrymosishes and highschool-
girlish highfellafaloot, a bit of Bacon annegst, neggst
course ant nutter, an a bit of Shaks peer—a few slices orf
off that swan of Avon that swan that was some swan—
cut off the gristed wing next the flight-bone fer the high-
flights like eeguls—the pluckt het first, pleece, twitterlit
peepers, knucklescales claws serpent-lumber, crumbs
comb and parsonsnose (who wasn't him? it muzzd be neck
oder nudding and Shakss the bird that's cock of the dung-
pitch—*muzzzzzzd* haf *him*!—to make our shop clarssy
ant Maaa chestick!) ant add narfter thort wilt? ant say too
sumthin like dublinpubmumper on the rivolooshums-
highbrow-lowneck-racket mit a bag full of tricks mun
(for Arm scottish tew) full of wormeaten wordies infant-
bitten and granfer-mumbled, scotched gutted scuttled
and jettisoned in killeidoscoptic otts ents ant mitships
upon the coasts of Barbaree, where I stay—I'm the
wrecker get me? this is my stormdrum that's my wicked
light.'

BAILIFFITES IN
TREMULOUS
CHORUS.
{ 'Heavens man is that your wicked
light!'
'Say is that your wicket wanderlight
to catch the wanderlusting loafer on
your wicket rocks?'
'Is that your stormkettle, Steve?'

BAILIFF. 'Ant add narfter thort wilt? nope one mild one
just this dear Shaun as ever was comminxed wid Shem
Hanp ant Japhet for luck (for he's a great mixer is

Master Joys of Potluck, Joys of Jingles, whom men call Crossword-Joys for his apt circumsolutions but whom the gods call just Joys or Shimmy, shut and short.— "Sure and oi will bighorror!" sez the dedalan Sham-up-to-date with a most genteelest soft-budding gem of a hipcough. "Oh solvite me"—bolshing in ers fist most mannerly—"Parn pardoner tis the cratur that causes me to bolshie and all and sure I partook a drop over the nine impransus for ther lardner's empty save for the glassy skin of the cratur—short commons is short shrift and short weight ensues shortly upon the heels of Famine and the wind rises in voluntary in vacuo for we come like Irish and like wind we—arrah we're born in a thdrop of bogjuice and we pops off in a splutter of shamfiz or sham pain." I accepts the undertaking with good grace on the understanding. I then turns to the strange mixed marriage of false minds of a man and again:—"Ant add narfter thort wilt re *Sweet Will* honey?" sez I softly to the doomed Deedaldum cum Deedaldee. Ant Shorn o' Joys no John o' dreams but rarely pragmatical, to solemnly declare that he *will* nadd narfter thort he wilt, for it's all one to him seeing *orl* his thorts is *narfter thorts* for the mattero that come-to-think, ant one more nor less is all one and he'll accommodate as many narfter thorts as never narfter may come knocking for no spitality and hot-foot ad-mittance.—"Yes fire away!" sez he "ant may the divil take the hindmost!" and I ups and fires: tis an Irish bull's eye thwarts ther which me narfter thort wings its wilful wicket way. "Sure I was not dipped in Shan-non for nothing" sez he and he composes himself in his best foxy book-for-martyrs posture for the pot-shot, winking the while his with Nelson's optic, a cute little Cyclops with his one sad watery glim as he regards me as though I were some shrewd spudassin and he my martyred prey. But I exorcizing the man's privelege to change me mind (and wishing it's a fact no mortal harm to the stumer stammerer bless his brainweed and word-fungle) aims low for I only wished to wing him so I advizes his understandings and I dispatched me narfter thort thus.'

The magistrate describes the gestures of shooting play-fully low and winging, he pulls the imaginary trigger and then runs on.

BAILIFF. '*Sweet Will* as shop-sign is the best high-brow stop-sign—to say *We have* that Swan of Avon *right here inside* with us for-keeps, beard brogue pomes and all (in a hundred inedited poses from youth up to be seen on all hands tastefully snapshotted) ponderating "Neggs-in-progress" and "wirk-on-the-way" in our back office (with Vico the mechanical for guide in the musty lab-rinths of the latter-days to train him to circle true and make true orbit upon himself) so *STOP!*—but there is more, in confidence, for twixt me you the shop-sign and crooked counter Sweet Will is all very well but for tourists only, and there are others, non-tripping, that are surely stopping and wanting and quite otherwise wanting. So our sign's reversible—get me? there is a fourth dimension of introverted Swans of Avon unseen by the profane, we have *that* in the shop *too* ant many narfter thorts as well as swan-songs, so walk right in we'd be glad to be met by you.'

The Bailiff thrusts out the familiar mask of the War-wickshire Yeoman depicted as a serene dummy to the waist, painted upon a board, at the end of a stick, in the manner of a hanging-sign, he dandles it. The back is blank but the front has been supposed to be too, it's an empty business when all said and done.

BAILIFF. 'That was the first. I ups then and sayce: "Was it the tobacco tell me that scotched the fairies, plotcock's famous twilit spooks or wot was it, or perhaps wassernt tit not that synthetical spirit of the bloody bog orange man alive—and if so it was, why then my superstitious number-timid student of alphonsine-tables, tcharts of Zodiacs, my little decipherer of auspics, how comes it now that you make the *mano fico* in your little pantie-pockpocks what time you cross the cross-eyed pedestrians in the streets of the furious new kupfernickel cities and still will have it that God the Father is responsible for the safety of the premier-joint of the right-hand thumb and that crossed sticks be full of malific innuendos?"—But "*Shoot!*" he ups and sayce in the tone of *hoots-mon!* or as you'd see a film-star inviting a close-up shot at close-quarters but he meant *get it over*—"for be Jayzers I'm jumpy at the thort of your narfter thort, wot it may be Clodoveo, on me giltedged giltie conshie of a playboy of westend letters, it makes me heart hop for fear ant inscase its should be too foul a blow below the high waterlimit of a decent difficulty of piebald utterance and a real honesttogoodness obscurity." Upon which I ups and answers the resourceful impostor civilly but with a great show of flattering firmness as though he were a rare handful: "Put your mind at rest," says I, "me merciful slugs will merely unbed themselves within the postiche persiac wing of your time-honoured get-up and the negligible incognito of the draperies. No mortal organ is at the stake: except for immaterial injuries in borrowed plumes that do not matter it is O.K. and you're as safe with me as the licensed houses of Limerick at this moment. You may be hit in your Shaks-paw your postiche-fist quilled for a sonnet or a Hamlick or wotnot but that's nix: that's less than a glove. Only things that don't matter and regions to-match." At that he

218

H.A.—P

ripostes in extremely fluent ice-cream tinker-dough-boy *"Bast!"* But that was not the end of the interview. My prisoner Joys the swaddler is half Orange and quarter Bog-apple it is probable and in any case naturally half-hearted about Isis and Kadescha Papa and all that, not to say generally laodicean and a bit elegantly lily-languid as I knew, but his god is Chance and that as it chances is mine so as another narfter thort (talking all the time beeang ontong to you in the patois picked up in Targums, Titbits, Blickling Himolies, Centuruolas, Encyclepeeds, Boyle's Dictionary, the Liber Albus, Tamil and Lap Vademecums, set to the tune of the best Nash-patter) wetting me lips, with the attitudes of a deiblerish deathsman down on his luck and pining for a job, axe in hand (and—seeing that his lay's morbific—stepping it out) I bricks up a dragon of a word that was a perfect Walligraph Arm of a word-that-was-a-sentence only ferry ferry concrete, thus: *Faifeofeehehumphismeltztherbludofferbritterbumph!* Bomp! I lets fly me second and third narfter thorts ant he ducks, his lips labelling me in mossarabic "sunovverbitch".'

The Bailiff points his thumb at Hyperides.

BAILIFF. ' "Hycofrick," sez I, "come here an be spoilt": but no, as true mordant as Coventry blue with his cute dainty eye, in pathetic watch he keeps me under strict observation. "Well," it's for me to say to this disbelieving Shimmy, "Wot's the odds," say I, "if for once we jabbers heart to heart?" But no be jaybers he's not in the mood for confidences: so I breaks the ice for him and speaks out of his heart as follows. "To be patted *good-boy*," he sez by my leave, "by all the Troodies is me lay I'll bodily confess—what pays *is* and I'm for all the *is*es and let the pounds take care of themselves. I know me way about this vale of tears nicely without signposts and baedekers look you, I'm part of its cosmic divilment: so the Lord of French Letters and Bozartz be praised and more power to Old Erin's roguish monopoly of fun and fancy bedad and bighorrorea (all me jokes is for men only—claro! I've got what might be mentioned as the Limerick-mind but being Irish 'tis only natural, and Joys being jokey for sportive in roman why that's an added inducement) and the top of the evening to all the bhroths of bhoys and to spare that ever wove Old Ireland's winding sheets and partly them by proxy of the great-brits Scots and kims all in one with their perfectly irrepressible bulls puns quips and paddy-the-next-best-things and their entoirely irrepressible strong-spirits. Then as for that cross-word polyglottony in the which I indulges misself for recreation bighorror, why bighorror isn't it aysy the aysiest way right out of what you might call the postoddy-deucian dam dirty cul of a sack into which shure and bighorrer I've bin and gone and thropped misself and all, since s' help me Jayzers oiv sed all I haz to say and there's an end of the matter?'

CHRIS. 'Oh capital sir! I recognize him!'

TET AND TICK (jumping in an incontinent ecstasy of knowledgeable impatience). 'Oh sir wasn't it Belcanto that you were doing sir? It was Belcanto sir I know!'

BAILIFF (with a mournful monotony solemnly nodding to drive sadly home the name, he confesses). 'Yes Bel canto *yes* Bel canto!'

ANOTHER APPELLANT. 'Sparring wasn't it with Clodoveo milud?'

BAILIFF (pulling his nose and boring his index into the bird's-nest of his left ear). 'I was Clodoveo that rival clown cutting counter capers but did you notice when I winged him how he looked at me with his genteel canine pathos—he's as bourgeois as a goldmedalled spaniel and he gets as offended when you kick a few tears out of him as though the jest were not on the other leg as often as not. The vanity of authors, of women, and of dogs is a portion of eternity too great for the eye of man to measure, as Sterne his fellow-whimperer remarked—you'd say Bello had bought this heaven all because God thought fit to furnish him with an out-size gab but not enough wisdom to discount it for what it's worth which is little enough when these trumps are sounding.'

APPELLANT. 'Which trumps milud?'

BAILIFF. 'Never mind which you'll find out soon enough. Basta!—having explained to you the principle of my prattle, I hope you understood it. Nexpleece! Chris! Nexpleece!'

The Bailiff holds in his right hand the barrel of the electric torch he has used to illuminate his mouth when he was saying 'Ah!' and was showing the afro-roofing and gold gums; he points its shadowy flame at the super half-smile of the great Chris. One of the most savage and sad-faced of the heiduks stands near to Chris and the rest of the most elegant if less high-spirited favoured appellants, his bees-waxed hunting-crop barred across his thighs and a surly eye fixed homesickly upon his home-town across Styx. Pat, who is ringleader of the rag, fastens the muscles of his lissom stomach upon the fence and bangs this dreaming man's hat down over his eyes. Like greased lightning Pat has slipped back into the crowd, who clamour approval of his bonneting of the watch, and the victim in blind-man's-buff rush lashes the fence with his thong.

BAILIFF. 'Ah, Pat Pat! you'll come to a bad end and all!'

The Bailiff waggles his fat forefinger at the bubbling spot at which Pat has vanished.

BAILIFF. 'I'm sure I don't know what to do with you children; it's lucky I can remember the time when I was a mettlesome madcap myself—I've always been up to mischief.'

APPELLANT. 'Were you, sir; oh do tell us!'

BAILIFF. 'I am. What would you? one's only a mischief once, or twice, though mischief is always brewing; I should be sorry to look back on nothing, you compel me to say I was born mischief.'

APPELLANT. 'Are you never, never——?'

BAILIFF. 'Time-pleece, ladies and gents! The older staider and more serious part of the audience are growing restless—they are all thinking about their future lives; that is natural and they are beginning to betray some impatience at our frivolous way of going on down here—we must mind our P's and Q's. So let us return to the mountain-range, do you mind? Mountains are so respectable! Well then, there are the old mountains over there; there they are, one, two, three and a glimpse of a fourth, I had it fixed up as I told you. It was no easy matter to get 'em to make their appearance as you now can see them and settle down in the reliable way they have as pukka mountains, as they are. I went into the whole matter with our principal engineer as it happens a Scot—a Scot—a very able person: he was despatched to Iceland and he brought back the mountains with him or I should say their appearance. Once in a way they vanish even now, but they're a fairly dependable landmark on the whole as certain as most things. Don't look too hard at them, I didn't say they were to be taken too seriously.'

Every one turns back laughing and all agree that the mountains have a most natural air though of course they must not be taken too seriously. The Bailiff laughs as well, but as though to himself. He begins again slowly feeling his way painfully with his touchy pack, as jumpy as jumpy this morning.

BAILIFF. 'Now to the more thoughtful of you it will no doubt have occurred that perhaps you no more belong here than the rest of the stuff and I hope I have not undermined your confidence by what I have said. Demonstrably, my honoured split-men or half-men, you have not the fixity you had on earth, that would be way beyond our competence; we are sculptors of half-men or of split-men at most, we don't pretend to turn out the real thing—no. So the illusion is not of that perfection to which you were then accustomed— that has to be faced; we are not magicians, no my little hominies far from it—in spite of loud-speaker!'

He bats a friendly glance over to the slips for Hyperides to catch if he is looking and a nimble fielder for sudden looks, and putting his hand beneath the professional one-plank-stage upon which the true Swatch would strut and tread his triumphant measures, draws out and shows to his enemy the dejected corpse of Vampo, with a cluck-cluck-cluck and a half-crow, then returning the figure to its slum-fake beneath.

'Loud-speaker!' repeats Pullman to Satters and smiles with drowsy indulgence, flattered that that term should be known to that all-seeing Arbiter.

Now without ceremony the Bailiff switches to the calm lower key of conscientious expositor, frowning upon the setbacks of his morning's programme and its disadvantages.

BAILIFF. 'Normal you are not—though that is not an unmixed curse—still so far as this tribunal is concerned we are able to guarantee a large measure of normality; our proceedings here in this Court are not I am happy to say confused by any violent transformations on the part of our honoured appellants; a man presents himself with a head requiring a size-seven cap let us suppose, which we supply—and his head does not let him down by changing to size five overnight or as we watch him for instance; all in short is fair square and aboveboard so far as it concerns our proceedings in this charmed circle of regeneration. And in large measure the same holds good for the camp. Yes in a large measure that may be said—of the camp. But no farther. That's the end of it.'

He pauses with an apologetic glance around the audience and clears his throat.

BAILIFF. 'With me it's somewhat different. I am compelled occasionally to modify my appearance, of course.'

As he is speaking he grows appreciably smaller until he has lost about a foot in height. Then he climbs up again and broadens out in a gradual dizzy flowering until he is an inch or two above his former stature. He glances at the jamb of his festooned proscenium, and lays his head lovingly against it. Archly he rolls his eye sideways to take his measure from a test-gauge in bronze above which is inscribed *Bailiffs*. It gives the correct height for the functionary. He has overshot the mark. Back in the middle of his box, slowly he dilates his chest, then, with a constipated grunt, forcibly collapses, crushing himself down with a steady stertorous straining. This seems to have carried him too low. With another glance of reference at the test-gauge he inhales tip-toes and flaps his arms in a caricature of flight. Imperceptibly the approved altitude is reached. Thereupon he stands-easy, breaks into smiles and rolls out his genial relief at the successful issue of the test over the audience. General laughter accom-

panies the demonstration though in the background there
is some disapproval.

BAILIFF. 'With me it is different. I have to be up and
down and in and out, more or less, less and more of me
you will readily understand as circumstances dictate—
one day a salmon and the next a toad-poll, perhaps, a
snake or anything it's all one—that is the penalty of
not being a Hero! But as far as you are concerned it is
really O.K.: we do manage to keep things for you fairly
stiff and still so that we can transact the peculiar business we have to go through here without confusion.'

There is a salvo of instantaneous applause and some
hissing.

BAILIFF. 'I don't like that hissing at the back there!'

With heavy German mischief he stands for a moment
grinning down at the rows of good-boys and their excited
patrons; picking out smilingly this and that ménage or
couple personally known to him, he nods a *Go-to-it! Go-
to-it!* to all and sundry. Then he exclaims in one rattling
berserker-breath, sounding like a swan-song and death-
rattle in one—his graphic right eye yellow and dilated,
discharging a muddy fountain of images to jostle the
words:

BAILIFF. 'But I cannot but remind you that we are not
magicians as I have already done—you remember from
your first lessons in geography (why of course you do
that was but yesterday, don't call me *flatterer* yet be
patient!) what a thin time Thor had in Utgard—*ut*
ugh! the horrid humped word that it is! where he was
the unbidden guest—yes?—why of lovely Loki to be
sure! (*Who's-the-man-with-the-big-red-nose? Ra ra ra!*
227

rou rou rou!)—and how he wrestled with the nurse?—
Thor thought he had been thrown or sent to his knees
anyhow by the old cough-bag of jangled bones as brittle
as a brick—he a bull-breasted verrater, yes *sir* fire-
eating fair-*ratter!*—he was consequently crestfallen-is-
not-the-word and to the n'th degree on looking back
upon his performance—you remember how cheap and
cut-up when he came out of the city with his band of
brother he-gods all their nordic-blonde he-tails between their juffs?—I do!—and then how Loki—as real
honesttogoddamgoodnessaguy as ever crept or I've rats
in my cock-loft came to the poor distressed gentleman's
assistance and complimented him roundly at a safe distance quite-so—though it can be but a fool can it not
that makes a silly wedge with his fist and is apt to
swing hab-nab at the first-met? informing him that in
fact he had comported himself like the athletic divinity
that he was pardie, for that apparent nurse was none
other than Elli actually old-age in person, yes the thrilling Eld even so! that hag what dogs the poor lipsticked
and blossom-scented hominy, up and down and in and
out, like the shadow of a mad bum-bailiff treading upon
his prinking prim-set heel, at last dragging him down
beside her into her fetid bed the toothless vamp—
hominy does not make old-bones! is that a proverb of
the depressing days when we were suffocated in nordic
bogs for suspicious sterility or have I dreamed it? but
don't answer now—and though Ella was skinny and
yeller, quite feeble and gaga to look at naturally—
strengthless as a fairy's tear or as the genteelly suppressed perfumed hiccup of a homo—that yet she had
never lost or ever drawn a fight up-to-date except only .
against Sir Asa-Thor of Bilskinor the poorman's paladin
and last resort, in his inferior Valhalla, which was
very much to his credit though at the time he had certainly been under the impression that the beldame

was getting the better of it and indeed had him by the small-hairs at a given moment owing of course we now know it's easy to be wise after the event to Loki's magical arts—an error of judgment on the part of Thor but the muscles were Asa-sinews and the crackest of their kind, made of all the-things-that-are-not like the ponderous footfall of the pussycat the whiskers of women and the breath of fish.'

Pausing out of breath from his sudden saga, the most important portion of the audience lies sullenly low, scenting fresh mischief from the same quarter. Listlessness is the safe arm, its usual elegant weapon it chooses it, but come what will it will not play, that is flat, any longer with its boisterous Bailiff as it is accustomed to of a morning and help him along and butter-him-up. No.

He sinks back panting into the painted arms of the adolescent god of Thrace adorning as a hackcloth the interior of his lodge, and as a few here and there watch his honeyed collapse his person is observed to merge in the form of the divinity. As a result it is not Swatchel but a dark young man with a cheese-red clammy skin ornate baroque locks of moist blue-black (but suspiciously round-shouldered if not hump-backed), tossing a tumbled fawn-skin and chaplet of vine-leaves superciliously (but yet remarkable for a decidedly heavy wedge of nose far too swart arched and conspicuous), who next collides, unused to so cramped a scene, with the narrow counter from which a cataract of official forms falls into the court beneath as he leaps into the breach brandishing a goblet held aloft by a hand gleaming with magisterial jewellery.

BAILIFF-BACCHUS. 'Scowl!'

'Scowl!' shortly replies the quick-witted but abashed audience gazing tongue-tied at the reverse of the Bailiff.

229

The Thracian divinity skoal-drinks with dashing nordic abandon then crashes the goblet down bottom-up, true Thracian-Norse, upon the shelf before him. It cracks and rather slowly falls to pieces, some parts dropping within the box and some without.

'Scowl!' Viking-Bacchus huskily repeats but in the accents of the vanished Bailiff.

He wipes in a long wet caress his thick distinct lips, curved as a nigger out-cropping of lighter intestinal tissue, with a self-appreciative eye upon the mortal assembly.

'Scowl!' he repeats still more thick-tongued and husky, almost inaudible, castanetting the bacchanal moisture from his slack fingers forward into the court. He hangs indolently exhibitional for some moments in the royal box-front, basking in the publicity, giving all and sundry the full benefit of his beauty, a brooding smile distilling a slow obtuse molassine good-will-to-all-men of coarse-lipped luxury. The intensity of the will-to-please brings on a sultry squint; such crude good-nature suggesting a change of posture he cocks up a hip with a shuffling of ponderous legs, one knee going back while its mate comes forward the flesh of one limb piping-hot with its nap of harsh down brushing with auto-flattery its neighbour at its passage. An impatient panting 'Hch!' announces a hitch. With petty-pussy finger cocked up, the single crook of an index coquettishly claws back the Petticoat-lane fawnskin which has slipped its adipose-mooring and in sluggish descent is coming off the sleek expanse of nude shoulder, carved in sweaty Cheddar. From star to stage-struck there are tokens, signals; quickly he turns back and in response to the telepathic salvoes of sympathy and admiration registered, he shakes his head 'and screws his eyes still tighter: that dear stupid staring awe-struck thing—the eternal Public—that *will* have its favourite show himself again, heaven bless its big foolish heart! In this attitude a greatly enlarged mask of Chaplin,

230

but deeply-pigmented, in sickly-sweet serio-comic mockery, it shakes above the audience.

'Now that is the *real* Bailiff!' Pullman says to Satters with warmth. 'I think he's extraordinarily handsome don't you?'

Satters gazes with astonishment, on the whole displeased with the for him very much too exotic mannequin silently displaying his points where the Bailiff was some moments before.

'I prefer the Bailiff to that poseur!' he replies with a toss of the head.

'I do wish you wouldn't use that particularly stupid word, where on earth did you get it from?'

At last the Thracian-Bacchus drags himself away from his admirers. Rather suddenly he sinks into two-dimensional life once more. Simultaneously the familiar form of the Bailiff emerges from the god's face and chest a three-dimensional blossom of heavily-robed blubber and steps quietly up to the box-front. There is some shyness in his eye of the sort exhibited by schoolboys among their playmates after the departure of Governor Mater or sister, visiting the establishment for the first time. For a spell the embarrassed magistrate would fain be free to ask: 'Well what do you think of *him*?' But he has no need to ask. A thousand flattering eyes tell him that they think that *he* is too divine for words.

A whistling wind has sprung up and it is whipping the plumed vertex of the magisterial shelter, it slaps the canvas of the hustings, buffets the pontifical robes and rattles the phylactery dangling upon the convex face of the box like the clapper of a norse mill, while with the graphic hydra-headed roar of Pullman-Expresses in smelly Cimmerian tunnels a storm rolls up post-haste over the watercourse, preceded by darkness, at the same moment that an unmistakably Nordic chill and a suspicious damp together change the atmosphere in vain about the insensitive bodies of the appellants; but the personnel of janissaries scribes boot-catchers masseurs nominate-reporters doorkeepers runners deacons presbyters jazzing joggers blacks and the rest of the cast exhibit an animal restlessness at the portents of dirty weather.—The audience awaits events but disregards the weather, the nearer groups watching their Pappenheimer uneasily. The Bailiff looks dissatisfied. After putting two and two together the reception accorded the painting behind him in retrospect leaves something to be desired. Once or twice he glances over his shoulder with a critical eye of puzzled displeasure as though to ask *What is wrong?* The face of the god now reposes free of intermixture, with the purest Greco-renaissance perfection, smiling mockingly at the canonical hump and livid neck.

BAILIFF (wheezing disconsolately in sympathy with the oncoming gusts). 'But that was a god—I refer to Thor not the person you may have noticed embellishing the interior of my little room here—that was a god my poor defenceless hominies (except for me, I am your shepherd, use me as you will!) that was an immortal god as concrete in Valhalla as you in the Ballet Pit—we have no magic to make you into Thors—do not ask that of us just yet or perhaps ever and put us to shame my appealing shabbily-spatted bashful mincing moon-calves each complete with monocled attendant—obviously a gentleman!—who are really the pippins of your All-papa's All-seeing eye, as one day you will infallibly discover!'

There is a murmur of renewed disapprobation mingled with some applause.

Holding an umbrella over his head the followers of Hyperides accompany him out of the circus, hastening as the rain-fall commences.

'The Bailiff is out of sorts to-day,' remarks Pullman. 'He has been upset by that fellow,' indicating the departing philosopher.

'Is he?' yah-yahs the sleepy Satters.

'He's got his knife into some of them for some reason.'

'Which?'

Pullman waves towards the fashionable quarters.

BAILIFF. 'I only say all this because I should not like you to carry away the impression that my native cheerfulness gave you a sanction for feats for which there are other times and places but not these or here—I wish I could say they were!'

He interrupts himself to give a glance skyward.

Several weather-stained blow-hards in sou'-westers emerge with a foc-sle roll from the right-hand booth and flash hurricane-lamps to east and west, shading their eyes with tattooed fists while the storm begins to rattle upon the huts and tents.

BAILIFF. 'Stop here stop here! It is nothing it's a summer shower! Are you afraid of getting wet!' in response to a movement of dispersal amongst the audience he calls out irritably. 'We must not lose a minute, if we allowed these squalls to interrupt us we should never get any forrader.'

Some of the audience seek shelter to leeward of the enclosure, the majority nestle together in irrepressible joking knots or in whispering political clusters.

BAILIFF (wailing loudly above the wind). 'We are factors of Time factors of Time! and you must remember besides what we are—that we are only pretences, you and I; our blood is the death-dew of the Mystical Moon that the sun sucks up and leaves dry, our bodies are

233

just common-or-garden passages or reflections, at the most we are made out of the excrements of the substantial stuff of Time, we are phantoms oh! my little nanspits we are ghostie-ghostie-ghosties!'

The entire personnel of guards or of clerks take their cue from their master and throw themselves into a keening and sighing on all sides, stamping about in groups in the manner of a revivalist gathering in Afro-America, Southern-North or Old Dominion, made self-conscious of their earthly frailty.

'We are Phantoms!' the Bailiff screams at the stolid crowded ring of depressed spectators, making his nose resound with his wailing voice. 'Ah yes my poor latterday flock we are practically nothing—we can only *half* make you believe, only *half* if that, as we can only produce you as split-men or slices not persons a sort of puppets do not depend too much upon us, we too are only half-makers of split objects—realize our impotence we are nothing when it comes to the pinch—upside-down we are like anything else upside-down—nothing but one-way machines I assure you so do be careful!'

With solemn crashes and the butterfly-fluttering of a piercing violet light the dark cloud passes overhead. At the first roar of the thunder the Bailiff vanishes into the air. Red tendrils of lightning come and go about his box. The panic-stricken staff crowd back into their booths and shelters: the audience cowers together half-expecting some imminent judgment. In under a minute the storm-cloud has moved away, angrily discharging above the camp, and almost immediately the sun is shining and heat replaces the temporary chill. Wringing the rain from their clothes, wiping their hands and faces with their handkerchiefs and stamping about with roguish cries, powdering their faces from small surreptitious vanity-outfits, blackening lashes and reddening lips, the audience express their satisfaction, the staff recovering more gradually. But with a convulsion the Bailiff comes back, filling with a click of his insignia the gap left by his disappearance in the nick of Time. He peers out of his window, examining the lintel and running his eye over its surface, up and down, in business-like inspection after the bombardment. He fingers the woodwork where there is a discoloration and elsewhere where a splinter sticks out, which he pushes back into its place.

BAILIFF. 'One would have said Thor in person! No damage luckily this time!'

He sees he is not yet in the good books of the fashionable sections of his audience—he may be sent to Coventry for an hour or more for what he has said. He makes a sign to a commissary.

At a further signal from the Bailiff an usher exclaims 'The Carnegie batch! Forward!'

Vaulting over the fence, ducking under and between the bars of the wicket, tumbling and tripping, Alf, Ted, Barney, Sid, Stan and Harold respond to the summons. They form up in the centre of the court, cap in hand, in an irregular line. Changing from one foot to the other, looking everywhere but at their judge, studying the flags of the court, the patterns of their caps, they detach themselves and await orders.

Stan grins toothlessly at an attendant. Alfred Carnegie looks sullenly ahead, his trousers, twisted awkwardly, protrude behind, faithful to the pressures of his athletic legs and of his life of movement.

Upon the rapid departure of the storm Hyperides and his faction have returned to their old place, the bustle inseparable from the Hyperidean displacement attracts the Bailiff who glances up from his papers at the figures in the court beneath.

'Ah good morning Alfred! And what do you men want? Only to see you there all so brisk and trim one quite feels oneself back in Old England again!'

Alfred blushes at the mention of Old England: he wrings his cap and takes pose after pose each apologetic and grim.

'Give me Old England every time, the Englishman's the salt of the earth!'

The Bailiff bandies out his fleshy stumps, bangs stoutly down his cudgel to make a beefy tripod of his person, sinks the great red bud of his head to adumbrate the bludgeon-skull of the Britannic bulldog, all of a portly piece, as a compliment to his customers imitating the cartoon that incarnates Alf-land as the Music hall bog-trotter belies Fianna and Harry Lauder is the shadow of Fingal too.

'So you men want to be saved, eh?' bourgeois of bourgeoises he banters and chortles, looking them up and down, raking them with Mr. Bull's bluff eye from crown to toe, heavily quizzing. 'You don't want your immortal souls to go to you-know-where (I know you Englishmen don't like the name of the place in question being mentioned, small blame to you—I respect your sensitiveness) —no, not that! heaven forbid! I'm with you there for one! It's too jolly hot that's the truth of the matter what? You want to persist—just as you are without one flea and have the run of that little world of ours over there on which the sun never sets—all correct, I've got you Steve? Well, well, well, we'll see what we can do for you!'

The Bailiff begins scratching himself on the buttock, he turns his joke to account, he makes a gesture of retirement to the Carnegie batch. Three heiduks step quickly forward thong in hand and drive Alf's thin red-faced line back a half-dozen paces. The one flea to all appearance continues to operate.

In the rear and at the extreme end of the line stands young Barney, his chin stuck out at the battle-angle to his left flank. The profile of the male-animal coquette is tense as a cat's as he witheringly sweeps the front row of seats with his challenging eye, charged to the muzzle with the fierce false-pride of the gutter. This is the crisis of his feud, nothing else within the hustings is remembered, for the slosh sleeping in his right hand is about to bash out and connect with the jaw of its dreams, that is the situation; Barney and the group of grinning favourites-of-fortune have clashed, but here and now above-all is he hungry for the fresh flame of insult that will touch-off the charge. He stands as near as possible to the arch-offenders who are not backward and on their side nudge each other while sounds of imperfectly-checked pointed ravishment reach the scarlet-red ear of the slender young blue-eyed lion of the slums, while his enemies' eyes rest in fascinated amusement upon the details of his jaunty smartness and with languid eyes they marvel mischievously at the haughty carriage of the youthful coster-male.

The Bailiff affects to catch sight of Barney. Seizing his truncheon he strikes it upon the ledge, and cries:

'Why is that man skulking behind the others? Make him stand out where we can see him!'

But at this moment the cracker goes off, for a hissing whisper reaches Barney from the tittering stallites which his flaming ear interprets as *Cissy*. At this with the utmost intensity of proud coster passion he ejaculates between whistling teeth the one word 'Cisser!' *'Cisser!'* hisses madly as the storm breaks and with electric adroitness his little flashing fist has sped over the fence to its billet, the face of the principal mocker, into which with a neat sting it has darted with an imperceptible double-piston stroke upon the snub button-snout of the offensive cat in question, who with a huge scream tumbles back among his clamorous friends, his claret neatly tapped with the waspish little coster-pud.

As if stung, up in his beetling on-ended crate, by this

237

blow himself, the Bailiff who is the hen of the chick struck rampages frantically, he screams and clucks, impatiently flapping his sleeves.

'*What* is that man doing what on earth is all that about now, why I believe it's that same disgusting fellow I had to speak to the other day! Bring him out! Separate him from the others! We can't have violence of that sort in this place, what he won't come? drag the little blackguard here by his hair; kick the dog out here—give his dirty flea-bitten hide a taste of the bite of your whips!'

Barney ducks and sidesteps.

'Leave go yew dirty barstards!—I'll slosh yerrif—one on the ear'ole, ah never mind oossed I might! Take yer-rands orfov meeyer!—garnyer—yuss yew!'

The big heiduks seize Barney by the scruff of the neck, fling him down, then hoist him kicking forward like a live present for their master. He resists at every stage, skilfully in-fighting and letting-fly the nether-punch of his little dandy skipping hoof, which gets home on every shin in turn.

' 'Ere!—ooyerthink yersodyer pullin of! notsermuchov-vit narthen!'

He is halted a few paces before his companions: stationary he still aims kicks at the shins of the sheriffs: their whips descend on his legs and back.

Barney and the Bailiff look into each other's eyes, the big nigger-brown globe swimming round the bright aquamarine, a dark brown overblown satellite.

'What was the significance of that disturbance may I ask, what caused you to behave as you did just now, yes you! Well? Have you lost your tongue? Can't you answer have you been struck dumb or what? Speak up!'

Barney makes no reply. Leaping about in his open cock-loft, which rocks and trembles, the Bailiff rains blows upon the ledge with his truncheon and screams at the sullen coster lad held towards him stiffly:

'Answer at once you absurd gutter-snipe what made you think it an appropriate opening to your examination to display your savage temper by striking one of your betters under my nose—*under my nose?*'

'I sloshtimwunfer callin me a certain name wot I don't fancy the likesovvim callinmeov see no norno other dirty barstard neiver!'

'And what name was that? May we know?—so that we shall be able to avoid incurring your wrath ourselves for instance.'

Barney sullenly hesitates.

'Well? What was the great name what was it? I appreciate your squeamishness you know in not wishing a coarse word to pass your particularly dainty lips but that is an insufficient reason to keep us here all day coaxing you about it.'

A blubber-howl booms from the stricken party at this moment.

'Sir! I called the nasty little beast a *Cissy* and so he is! —That's why he hit me sir in the face sir with his fist— yes him sir!'

'Cissy?'

'Yes sir a Cissy sir.'

The lowering Bailiff receives the information with a majestic blankness and then addresses Barney in a mincing drawl:

'*Cissy*—so that is what his lordship mustn't be called is it? Cissy it is is it now, it is actually the *male* that we have offended? We are not quite good enough for him here we are too feminine that is the idea?'

He indulges in a long sneering laugh, enjoyed in instalments, with contemplation of Barney in between. His eyes run over the person of his glaring prisoner next with a long series of specific expressions of distaste, as though he had been asked to pick over a bundle of fetid rags.

'Soho soho if we are such a little male lord as all that

Mister Bill-Sikes Junior what do we get ourself up like that for—or isn't that a fair question? Why so much cost having so short a lease, why so much show if so little desiring to please? But that's for the ladies of course is it, all that's for the ladies God bless 'em—and unfortunately there are none here! Monsieur s'est trompé de guichet! And it would be a strange man who did not find you anything but ridiculous whatever the ladies might say about you! And I'll tell you something 'Arry—so nicely dolled-up for all the absent 'Arriets—I'll tell you something it is this: he was right about you the poor little lad you hit— you *are* a Cissy-man as you call it after all that's the joke —you follow? Joke. You. Why you a *man*! have you never looked at yourself in the glass? Spare us your blushes and your filthy temper and go over at once to that young gentleman you have injured and apologize—but properly! Get down on your mangy little knees gutter-snipe, tell him that you confess that he was absolutely right about you and that you are a dirty little Cissy-man you follow. I insist, then we'll get on with the business of the day, you hear me do you?'

Barney held in place by the magisterial police hears himself adjudged a *Cisser* from on high.

'I eersyew yew great loud-mouthed snitch!' he snarls while he prises this way and that the encircling band of bravos. 'I eerwot yew sez yerself wotzmor ah time yew was tellinorfov my mates fer leavin me bee yinde yestey!'

He attempts to free himself but is held.

'I arsts yew fernuffin get me—I don't want nuffin.'

He gives several heaves of regulation bulldog independence.

'Yew jest cum darnalongoveer an I'll lern yew witch is the man alongov us get me, same as wot yew sed, me or yew, ignrant great snitch!'

Barney stares up with a glittering fixity as if to mesmerize the magistrate into descending within reach of his little tingling bantam-fist. With an enraged impotent suspense the Bailiff returns his gaze unable to act, checkmated by the staring eyes of the youthful slum-lion, until Barney's attention is distracted, then his more ductile mercurial organs are set free and his tongue wags with sudden fury.

'What-what-what-what?' he breaks out in clucking guttural stutter. 'Whatareyoulookingatmelikethatfor?' He belabours the ledge with his baton.

'I sh'd beardup fer sumfin to do lookin at yew yew great ugly snitch!' Barney retorts reeling in the clutch of the cops.

'You shall no more!' in the puppet's fierce falsetto the Bailiff shrieks, tiptoeing and quivering motionless.

'Release him!' Barney's captors release him and step back.

The Bailiff makes a sign to Mannaei who comes nimbly forward drawing his hanger his eyes fixed upon his prey. Barney turns swiftly then stops in a twisted crouch, his legs braced for a backward leap, his face towards the samaritan headsman. The heiduks close up behind raising their whips. Mannaei approaches him with a wading-swimming movement, his cutlass held horizontally level with the eyes. Then with one rapid sweep the cutlass flashes forward and severs the head at a stroke. Barney's body falls stomach upwards, the head bounding against the fence, the trunk gushing upon the pavement.

A shriek has arisen from the assembly. The immediate chorus of prominent favourites retreats screaming up the steps in flight from the proximity of the tragic rink. All round the semicircle with decomposed and terrified faces the appellants rise, many crowding towards the opening. Syncope in the form of every graceful variety of suspended animation visits many of those present and the scene is strewn with pallid bodies: Satters collapses against Pullman in whose arms he sinks to the ground, Pullman pinching his cheeks and nose and resorting to all the usual remedies in turn. Meanwhile thirty guards heiduks and blacks advance sword in hand into the open, vigilant and menacing, watching the moving chattering crowd retiring with their wounded. Some attendants burn a bolster stuffed with feathers near the palisade: the stench of the burning of the cornified mass revives some of those prostrated, but it causes others to swoon, owing partly to fear at sight of the unexpected fire.

A hieratic huge-headed bat, with raised arms the Bailiff protests in a thick patter of expostulation, then in a tempestuous tattoo upon the ledge calls to order, his eyes hitting out madly to left and right: his pivetta is between his lips, he utters piercing cries with it to secure attention.

Mannaei, proceeding to the completion of his work is bending over Barney, dagger in hand, preparing for the ementulation. The violent discharge of the carotids has stopped, the coster finery is being torn open by the functionary.

'Mannaei! Mannaei! Come back! Come away! Order! Order!—Gentlemen! Take your seats again! I implore you! It was a mistake a dreadful mistake! One of those *terrible*——!'

He wrings his hands: then seizing his staff again delivers a tremendous rataplan upon the quivering flange of his one-man theatre.

'Mannaei! Mannaei!' he shakes his fist at the headsman. 'Come back here this instant you vile person, you snake in my bosom, you assassin you sadist—you *Samaritan*!'

Screaming at the heiduks, he nearly launches himself at the tail of his invective out of the shaking box.

'Back to your places reckless scum! Back! you bold reckless dogs! Obey your master! Obey me! Obey me! Obey me!'

The heiduks and blacks retire into the booths in serio-

242

comic slouch, twisted half-covert grins upon their faces, humorously hangdog. Mannaei returns with sullen strut to his position to the left of the magistrate, wiping the blade of his cutlass upon the skirt of his canvas vest. His eyes are rolled up in a dizzy ecstasy, giving a sluggish sickly cast to his face. Several of those who have fainted recover but succumb once more in the still disturbed atmosphere of the assembly.

'It's my evil star!' wails the Bailiff. 'To have the ill-starred services of this historic ruffian as though life were not already complicated enough. I am so upset!—Jenkins, a glass of water!'

The Bailiff attempts to pace up and down in his narrow box, his hands behind in Napoleonic clutch, but strikes his nose at once and desists.

Hyperides is now stretched out in the relaxed repose of the sistine Adam. One finger points inertly forward as though awaiting the touch of the hurrying Jehovah. Twisted backwards, his hollow melancholy face surveys the scene on which his back is turned, without interest.

'Gentlemen, gentlemen!' The Bailiff stamps and wrings his hands. 'How can I ever apologize enough to you for this abomination! It was a terrible error! My over-zealous servant——! (You inhuman beast!) Gentlemen! My halting tongue!'

He has the gesture of plucking out the infirm too-beefy member, so slow in the uptake with the japhetic machinery.

The Carnegie batch are as though they had never been, they have entirely vanished, only two caps remain to attest their recent presence.

'Where is Alfred Carnegie?'

No one has seen him, no one whatever has observed the exit of the Carnegie batch. Their five bodies fled into earth—the three heiduks point towards the earth. Others point to the passage-way. Some indicate the summit of

243

the wall and describe with their fingers the escalade, the scuttling exodus, of the missing Alf and his merry men. The Bailiff beckons to a commissary towards whom he bends to impress in solemn tones the features of an extraordinary mission.

'Find—you understand—find Alfred Carnegie and his friends at once but this instant, do you hear! Bring him to me. Express my deep regret for what has occurred. Explain to him the nature of the mistake—of the dreadful mistake! Tell him that there is no danger at all! Assure him of that! It is my one desire to make a public apology for what has happened. Tell him! Take no arms with you. Return with him here. Go!'

Janissaries are detailed for the Alf-hunt: the commissary charged with the affair hurries out with his posse.

The Bailiff slowly rolls his eyes down sideways in horror upon the self-possessed person of Mannaei as though becoming aware of an unwelcome apparition, and scarcely able to believe his eyes.

'Mannaei! *Please* withdraw. Mannaei! did you catch what I said you abhorrent person? You see what you have brought down on all of us! Do you really suppose that your further presence can be anything but painful to everybody present? You are the object of loathing to all of us! Withdraw on the spot—never let me see you again! *At* once! Hhrrrup!'

A number of appellants have hurriedly quitted the scene of the execution and are regaining the camp in cowed and dispirited parties. Many have not moved from their seats. The favoured section of the audience with blanched faces and hands that tremble as they cough and whisper, gradually resume their seats. For some time the front row is not occupied. Some bad cases remain prostrated outside the enclosure.

The Bailiff's distress is defined by his drooping lids his lax underlip—which he has folded outwards on to his chin—and the painful lines drawn down from nostril to mouth. No move is made to dispose of the body of Barney. An unusual silence is maintained throughout the audience but still the Bailiff does not speak, staring sadly away instead into the distance. Then in a funereally deep and muffled voice, as though swathed in the blackest crêpe, broken with emotion, he begins:

'Gentlemen! this is one of the darkest days of my life! I ask myself: How can I make up to those poor fellows for the brutal murder of their comrade? No answer, alas, is forthcoming! I wish I knew! I hardly know how I shall ever face them when they have been found and brought back here—if they are ever found! All I ask you, my children, is to believe me when I tell you that I would give anything I possess—which is not much, I am bound to say not much—I am only a poor man like yourselves—for this not to have happened!'

He allows his head to sink slowly upon his arm, which is in horizontal collapse along the ledge: completely sunk, the head hangs forward outside the box, he rolls it from side to side several times as a sign that he is inconsolable. Then his shoulders bearing the hump between them (which in his present position makes its appearance like an enormous bonnet from behind him) are shaken with sobs.

Several of the assistants are so moved by this that they take out their handkerchiefs and quietly cry into them. The hush is animated by a snuffling choking and sobbing. Satters buries his head upon Pullman's breast and shakes in sympathy with the general emotional atmosphere, though at the same time he is trembling from head to foot.

The arrival of the survivors of the Carnegie batch cuts short the epicedium brewing in the first mournful phases of the official grief, with the growing up around the central figure of a body of red-eyed deaf-mutes.

245

As handcuffed they come up the passage from the wicket they avert their eyes from the headless body of their comrade. Standing in a lifeless cluster they await cap in hand the recovery of the Bailiff.

Slowly the head of the chief-mourner is lifted, and a face hideously distorted with anguish is revealed, from which every one instinctively removes his eyes, out of modesty terror and sympathy. Except for Hyperides for a short interval he might have been alone for all that he is observed of anybody whatever. The remains of the Carnegie batch guiltily shuffle their feet; they too do not look in that direction.

So the Bailiff, the only person now who looks at anybody else, fixes Alf mournfully and long with a toffee-red eye and at length in a husky voice he whispers:

'Alfred!—May I call you Alfred?—my dear fellow may I ask you one thing?'

Alf keeps his conglomerate eye of bluish beer-and-water inclined to the pavement, which sends a pulsation of heat and light up into his white face.

'Alfred! will you, my dear feller' (at the stylish 'feller' the whining croak stylishly breaks, and he swallows noisily and greedily) 'will you give me your *hand*?'

The hand of Alfred dominates the assembly in the silence that ensues. Will he or won't he give it?

'Just once!'

Leaning far over the ledge of his box, the Bailiff extends a fat and flashing emblem of friendship and good-faith, rings embedded in its tawny meat.

Suddenly starting back the Bailiff screams and every one within earshot jumps to anxious attention.

'But my poor friend! what what what is this I see? Why heavens, you are manacled! No wonder you hung back when I asked you for your hand—for you are not able to offer it!' Then in a headlong drop to the bass to throw into relief this bitter paradox of the manacled

Alf and the handshake vainly solicited: 'How disgraceful to put those irons upon the wrists of a freeborn——! Here! Somebody! Anybody! Instanter! I never heard! Pull off those disgusting things, quicker quicker! and never let me see an Englishman in this condition again— or I shall want to know the reason why! do you hear? To everything there is the limit! Quicker! Quicker! I cannot bear this sight, these implements of slavery, this Briton's hands are the last straw! Who was responsible for this?— it is a scandal! How could you, who are slaves, presume to! Never! I am vexed—quickly!—*Poor* Alfred.'

The handcuffs are removed. Once more the Bailiff leans over the box towards the leader of the bereaved party.

'Again Alfred I am your petitioner! Will you give me your hand, will you take my hand stained with the blood of your comrade in yours?'

Taking his colossal poorman's discomfort by the horns, pushing every instinct down that paralyses his body the shamefaced street-hawker advances with a writhing of outraged reserve: he seizes the hand of the Bailiff, who breathing with adenoid-thickened heartiness, with both hands eagerly clasps his and drags him convulsively up towards him. The nightmare of a 'French-kiss' and a surging distrust and alarm grip Alf, he snatches his imprisoned hand back from out the man-trap of the false hot fist, his eyes raised involuntarily for the first time.

The Bailiff, squinting and blinking his eyes harmlessly in booby kittenish play and peaking his mouth, nods coaxingly, and sweetly mouths:

'Shake hands yes? shall we? *Yes!*—We have shaken hands, thank God, we are friends! *Once More!* You don't know what you are doing for me, Alfred!'

The voice rattles and breaks upon the disintegrating syllables of *Alfred*. Again Alf surrenders the limp hand. The hand of Alf is hotly squeezed, a great warm tear splashes upon it. In a quick upward-flashing glance of new dislike Alf takes in the Bailiff's bulb of an eye which has just discharged the tear and is in the act of manufacturing a second. A man is in the shining bulb that looks at him, peering at him entrenched behind the swollen lid, it is he that is preparing to launch another salt drop. The delicate soul of Alf rebels; the hand is again withdrawn with rough force. Changing from one foot to the other, fidgeting his big soiled cap he looks at the ground at his feet. Civilized Alf stands his ground aloof, repulsing the brazen savage Bailiff, repelled by his tear-baited traps, passive resister.

The audience holds its breath; there is an interval in which it is uncertain what turn this will take. The face of Mannaei is seen to reappear in the shadow of the magisterial box, his least movement is canvassed with anxiety and several of the more timid who so far have sat it out now discreetly slip away. But with the mask of the misunderstood-man complacently featuring, the Bailiff signals to the commissary who has brought in the fugitives, and exclaims:

'Take Alfred right in, and place him on the right hand of the Master of Heaven. Amen!'

A hoarse murmur of solemn 'Ahs!' rises from the neighbouring booths from the lips of the staff, overtaken by a whispered, piano, 'Menn'. The trumpeter steps out in front of the table of the Protonotary and sounds a jolly single flourish. Then he steps back, his instrument standing on its mouth upon his hip.

Turning to Alf the Bailiff remarks in a low and confidential voice:

'That's only a formula of course, it sounds rather alarming doesn't it? but it will secure you a shake-down for the night, that's what it's for, you won't have to tramp the streets which is the main thing.'

Jaw-set he thrusts out his hand fiercely-frank, a chum-in-a-thousand.

'Good-bye Alfred: or rather so-long, I hope. And good luck!'

The coveted hand goes up and gives its coveted British shake; Alf wheels about, the Carnegie batch in an elastic quick-time shuffle file out down the fenced gangway, tripping to phantom fife-and-drum, preceded by the commissary.

There is considerable applause. The auditorium assumes its normal aspect. All the elements in the gathering are chastened, but confidence falteringly returns.

'He's a real White Man isn't he the old Bailie? Those brutes get out of hand you know!' a large-size-boy's face remarks with eager conviction to a small-size-youth's. The youth's-face with a peace-at-any-price snub nose responds fiercely:

'I know, isn't he a topper, what! he'd clear all those brutes out if he had his way!'

'I shouldn't like to be in old Money-eyes' shoes, would you?' asks the other, a gleeful feverish quaver in his pipe, and is answered by an inarticulate gulp of emotional assent and a knowing-eye of vivid intelligence.

Pullman is administering smelling-salts to Satters, who has had a relapse on catching sight of Mannaei. He opens his eyes compelled by the salts but without conviction, he remains stretched out beside his friend.

'I feel as sick as a cat, Pulley,' he murmurs weakly. 'Don't you think we'd better go away?'

'No, let's wait a little. You'll soon get better.'

He chafes the slack hands with a tactful pressure and thoughtful reassuring eye.

'It was beastly: but it wasn't the Bailiff's fault, any one could see that.'

Satters sees nothing, a corpse-doll glassy-eyed he remains as near extinction as possible, ready to pop right in at the least alarm. Pullman keeps up an absent-minded friction.

249

'He was genuinely upset.'

His deliberate eye keeps in touch with his misunderstood hero-in-office, who with arms outspread at right angles, grasping the extremities of the ledge, his drooping head lolling mournfully, crucifies himself upon his puppet-stage, listening to a complaint of the clerus against the military police who have been surprised in the act of using the lavatory reserved for the clerical staff.

Pullman patters while he rubs:

'I believe the Bailiff hates this mediæval machinery as much as anybody. I've been told he's always trying to abolish it but he's overruled. It's always the way, where religion is concerned people are diabolically conservative. Oh there's that artist fellow going in! This should be amusing.'

'Joseph Potter! Joseph Potter!' the voices of the attendants are vociferating, while a tall figure enters the court by the wicket and advances slowly into the centre, gazing about him. He comes to a halt before the Bailiff, who is engaged bluepencilling the rough draught of the Carnegie dossier, which has just been passed up from the table of the Protonotary.

Barney's body and head have been thrust against the fence. The attention of the new appellant is immediately directed to this. Half-closing his eyes and inclining his head to one side, balancing his body backwards, he focuses his professional peepers and examines it. The Bailiff looks up and in friendly conversational tone addresses Joseph Potter without reference to the still-life that has taken his fancy.

BAILIFF. 'Well Joseph the Potter, I have read your statement: here it is. No this one: yes: Joseph James Potter, 33—thirty-three is I think a little under the mark, I should place it at forty-two, with a margin for growth. You have no objection? No. I will alter it, forty-two, so.'

250

He alters the description in the paper.

BAILIFF. 'I'm glad you take that so well—it's what we have most trouble over of course. *Painter*. Were you born a painter, Potter, or were you made one by adverse circumstances? Painters are born not made you know: if you were not born a painter then it would be better to say something else—bank-clerk, for instance. We much prefer bank-clerks to painters: shall I say *bank-clerk*? What do you think?'

The pencil poised above the paper he waits, but Potter is busy with the head of Barney the wonderful cézanne cocoanut or super still-life and the crumpled rampick at its side responsible for this solitary livid fruit.

BAILIFF. 'There is really a difficulty, Potter, where artists are concerned, I will explain it to you. In fact it is essential to be clear on that point at once. We are traditionally not very partial to pictures. In that we are almost Mahommedan. There are souls in those things you know—perhaps you don't—but you can take it from me there are. They always have been associated with worship. Although under the great Roman establishment and the Greek "orthodoxy" so-called we seem to welcome the image, here you are nearer our primitive sources. And we set our faces against such things. It was with great reluctance at first that in order to absorb the pagan cults, and as a means of early propaganda, we went in for images. Mani, the greatest heretic perhaps of any, whom we luckily succeeded in the end in getting crucified and stuffed with straw as you may have heard—as he most richly deserved —was a painter, advancing his wicked doctrines by means of little water-colours. We have not forgotten that significant fact! To go no further, Potter, we regard from of old your profession with great distrust; we do indeed make exceptions: but we have to be sure of our ground.'

He surveys Potter with a puzzled critical attention, with lifted brows at the quizzing question-mark of the ironist.

BAILIFF. '*Bank-clerk* I take it you do not favour. Well, I understand, it is an effect of the well-known aristocratical prejudice of the so-called "artist". You don't see your way I suppose to modify your outlook to the extent of refraining from sketching and scribbling?'

Joseph Potter shakes his head. His eyes are fixed keenly upon the Bailiff now, it is evident from his expression that some internal operation of the senses is in progress. The Bailiff after a moment's reflection, instinctively placing his hand before his face, arrives at a conclusion.

BAILIFF. 'I think I notice, Joseph Potter, that even at this solemn moment you are engaged in drawing a sort of mental picture of what is before you. Am I right?'

Potter smiles.

BAILIFF. 'Yes? I thought as much. So you are always busy prosecuting your art? When unable to do so on a piece of paper you continue inside your head?'

Potter looks pleasant and climbs with a nimble eye the structure above the head of the magistrate.

BAILIFF. 'Like most of your kind Potter you are not very articulate in the usual way. Now that is all in your favour. If there's one thing we dislike more than an *image*, it is a *word*. The logos we do not regard as an artistic trifle by any means. We're very serious about the word. With us the verb is The Verb and no nonsense, *Heaven admits no jest*. As a concession the creature is allowed to speak. But there is speaking and speaking. You follow me? We regard *words* from long experience of them and some small competence in their uses ourselves as extremely powerful engines and in consequence highly dangerous. We are tremendous realists! It is only the sentimentalist who ever makes the mistake of rating the sword above the pen.—(The rather slighting way in which we refer to "mere words" and so on from time to time does not, I am sure, take in a man of your acuteness.) We are not—I can confess to you, for you seem to be removed as far as is humanly possible from being an example of their unbridled use—we are not very fond of hearing a great many *words* from any creature. No, articulateness is not a recommendation to us (I do hope Hyperides is not listening!). Certain forms of prayer—exclamations of astonishment or of rapture at the mechanical marvels of creation—words of anger when confronted with God's enemies—hatred on the appearance of a heretic —the sounds indispensable for conducting the operations of hunting eating evacuating and lovemaking: that is one thing. We scarcely regard those as words. But the sort of engine that words may easily develop into when extended beyond those simple operations of stimulus-and-response, attending the fixed phases of the animal-life, is quite another matter. I can give you no better example than the fatuous and irresponsible discursive technique, serving the most irreconcilable of tempers, of such a person as Hyperides over there— that is a very different kettle of fish!—that we are anxious in every way to discourage.—Now you, my dear Potter, from that point of view are a model of

253

what we want! If anything you are too inarticulate. But it is a good fault, my man.'

Potter scratches his head. Scratch-scratch go the black nails upon the parchment of his scalp.

THE SCRATCH. 'I am confused at your words. What do those words mean?'

He catches sight of the large-size-boy's countenance stylized in a Flemish peasant-grin flowering for him as it happens, its present butt. Potter's eye hardens and fixes: still holding his hand up above his head but scratching ever slower and slower, he settles upon the contours of this new object and is soon absorbed in disembowelling it, by planes and tones, and rearranging everything in a logical order. The Bailiff gazes round in amused perplexity at the audience. He carries his hand to his head and sticking up two stout fingers beneath his cap scratches too, in comic time with Potter. The front-row is now in occupation once more by the elect and with Potter to reassure them the assembly is soon its lighthearted self again. A murmur of laughter and comment rises and grows. The Bailiff laughs outright at last.

BAILIFF. 'Well Potter you certainly answer to the stock requirements of "the painter" as that figure is understood at the present time and if you are as good a painter as you are a poor word-man you must be something quite out of the way I should say, in a class by yourself. But I will make a bargain with you Potter! If we let you in, if we let you in, will you promise to carry your profession altogether inside your head? Will you promise never to put pen to paper, will you agree to eschew all *outward* manifestations of your talent? Will you agree Potter?'

A superb negro underskinking for a wax-moustached furnace-flushed and grease-anointed French chef in blanched steeple-cap having stepped round from behind the booth on the extreme left to take the air, along with his master—a system of black glands and circles in the company of a sheaf of white cylinders—Potter, his hands now in his pockets, gets down to him on the spot, cutting him up into packets of zones of light and shade, bathing his eyes in the greasy tobacco-black, mustard, Stephens'-ink and sulphur (the wasp-colours and the oily silken night-Atlantic) picking out the bluish puckers of the lips, delighting in the white flashes of the eyeballs.

Peering round the edge of his box's frame inquisitively the Bailiff joins in the pictorial dissection of the shining copper nudity. Then with a sigh he remarks:

'Well I suppose it's all right! Luckily very little paper is manufactured by us, we have no books, pencils are unknown, he can't do much harm what do you think? Anyhow we'll risk it. Pass Joseph Potter in!'

A commissary hurries forward and indicates to Potter that he is to follow him.

The trumpet sounds as for Alfred, the painter is led off amid derisive applause. Cries of 'frightful sketcher!' 'Buster Bronx!' 'Long-hair!' 'High-brow!' and 'Alti-frons!' 'Come orf it!' 'Pavement-Artist!' 'Cubist!' 'Studio to let! No bottles!' 'Look pleasant!' 'Varnishing-day!' and 'Michelangelo!'

APPELLANTS AS POTTER PASSES.

{ 'I say look here how would you paint a face like mine, no mine, am I an awfully good subject? Joking apart! I say Potter—as a professional man—am I beautiful? Is my face worth sketching? What would you give me for a sketch? What should I get if I posed? What? A tenner a day do you think?'

255

APPELLANTS
AS
POTTER
PASSES.

'Take me Potter I say will you take me?
I've sat for masses of artists, are you
clever?'

'What will you take me for? Nothing?
For nothing?'

'Potter, come here! Would you like to
see my figure? It's a lovely one Potter
I'll sit for you later on! Would you like
me to no really? Shall I show you my
nude figure?'

'What photos do you do Potter—are you
a pot-boiler? Hop it! You're a dirty
pot-boiler! Oh!'

'Do you do groups are you dear? Take me
and this gentleman friend! We're a
quiet couple, we've just taken a studio.'

'Where's your camera?'

'I'll be your artist's model! With whiskers on!'

'I'm a sham-man mother says—do you
see any green in my eye? That's because I'm half-Irish. Do you do lan-
skips or oils?'

Chris strips to the waist amid jubilation and standing
on the front bench poses as the Venus of Milo.

Potter passes.

Crouching over the pile of papers that have now collected upon the ledge in front of him, the Bailiff is observed to be engaged in a novel occupation. Breathing
heavily, his lower lip thrust out, with symptoms of acute
mental discomfort, he labours secretly with a pencil-
stump, screening his activity schoolboy-fashion under
the pentroof of a fat hand. Like the butt of a stogy-cigar
his tongue sticks out from the corner of his mouth, he
grinds and rolls it. Every moment his breathing becomes

more oppressive. Straightening himself for a moment he squints evilly down his nose at something near the poised pencil. Then once more writhing and blowing he flings himself down, horizontal-chested and hump-on-high while his hand works upon the surface of the paper up and down and in and out. A furious impotent savage scratching is set up.

After five minutes passed in this way he suddenly scribbles about without design upon the sheet beneath his hand, and sits back. As though some tiny and baffling enemy were situated upon the sheet of paper before him, he seems unable for a moment to leave it with his eyes: he takes up the pencil again and begins madly graving and digging with its point; then once more he sits back, this time focusing his attention outside his box the spell of his nightmare occupation lifting.

'He's been drawing, I think,' Pullman says, observing almost tenderly the cross expression and the exhausted attitude of the magistrate.

'Is he artistic?' asks Satters.

'Yes, I believe he is, he knows a lot about art at all events. I should think he's very artistic—he has an artistic nature. I don't regard him as a scientific mind.'

'I think he's terribly clever, don't you Pulley?' Satters lisps, sticking his heavy prominent jaw out as a sign of meditation, and gazing into the distance where the dreams are.

The Bailiff recovers his good humour shouting to a clerk:

'Here, give me another one I've spoilt this.'

He throws him the paper with which he has been busy. Addressing the near-by spectators he says:

'I never could draw a line in my life, I don't know why, as a kid I was always scribbling but I can't draw a line now, not a line! That's as it should be however: it's a stupid imitative trick that fortunately does not survive into puberty. Can you draw?'

257

The appellant addressed giggles convulsively, violently shaking his head and biting his lips and looking up in frightened uncertainty.

'What did you think of Potter? Not much I'll be bound and small blame to you: I'm sure Potter's not an artist—what?—I know an artist when I see one! That was not an artist! We referred to him in that way, oh yes—we do from habit. Artist! That was an imbecile evidently with a mania for measuring and matching, *artist* doesn't mean that—rather the opposite I should say. Potter's talent consists in accepting all things at their face-value, he's a pure creature of the surface, if you understand me, like the ordinary practitioner of science—they're very alike those two. The *meaning* of anything it is almost his creed not to trouble about—he's a little technical fool in short, that describes that sort of artist. Did you observe him?—he was measuring me—did you remark? all the time the fellow was standing there he was matching my face the curtain and all the rest of it—he never saw *me* at all! It's typical—all your so-called artists are the same. I was completely concealed beneath my colour, this fine Hittite nose of mine, my hump, and this handsome furniture—completely. He *saw* nothing—in my sense. There are many things besides their *dumbness* which recommend artists to us. I didn't tell him. Never to see anything except the *outside*—what an admirable trait—for the other fellow! Did you notice how pleased he was with himself? —as pleased as Punch! They all are! It's an exceedingly healthy occupation— barring accidents the "artist" lives to a ripe old age, pottering about, never seeing anything, vastly impressed with his own importance!'

(The Bailiff strokes his nose.)

'I wish I hadn't sent him in now all the same, we've got masses of them: they're all alike. Shelah! *Shell—ah!*'

A swift-moving sleek-footed clerk shoots like a Jack-in-the-box out from the booth of the Protonotary.

'I will see no more artists! You hear me Shelah? That's the last. Send them back or better still despatch them as soon as they present themselves till further notice!'

He laughs heartily with lazy heaving of the belly.

'Shelah! You understand me eternal one, tell them they have either to be despatched or embrace the counting-house one or the other—the artist clings to life, he'll choose the counting-house!'

Shelah drops slickly back into the dark booth, a sallow wine-flush of sickly hatred on his neck and forehead, a painful fang-lifting bitter grin, darkest joke-hater of all. His eyes seek his fellow-scribes before speaking, when he breathes:

'No more artists to come up he says he doesn't want them.'

BAILIFF. 'Gentlemen!'

The Bailiff includes in his throaty summons all present. A sign that every one is for-it come this caudle-lecture is that he swells with dark and suggestive importance, looking down at his tumescent person, maturing his afflatus, and he breaks up at long-range with his soaring eye several minor meetings at the back of the conversazione.

BAILIFF (starting on a high-pitched snarl which deepens into a whine). 'Let me define my position a little further for you gentlemen: I am *uneasy*—I feel you have in the past perhaps expected *too much* of me, that I have *disappointed* you, I may be mistaken but that is certainly the impression I have received.'

He gives a few intense premonitory coughs of after-dinner-speech mettle: nagging voices at the rear still seek to have at all cost the last word in close theological disputes but the frivolous foreground has put away childish

259

things and disposes itself in a hundred attitudes of more than respectful attention (for the Seeing Eye counting its chickens before they are hatched, a catalogue of all sizes and shapes of kindergarten-lips in which butter-will-not-melt and of eyes that are the peep-of-day—some that do so languish and drip with milky-mouthed naïveness that there is sure no mother's super-Vesuvian bowels burning to litter millions of midgets or billions of bitch-lettes on one Ford-pattern, to be driven bleating to the bloody battle-market of Apocalypse, that would not welter and yearn and then burst with 1000° centigrade love all over the shop—it is now a massed babydom, scheduled fused and set to touch off at feather-trigger-contact all the maternal machinery concentrated in the most millennial of communist metropolises, to work double-tides and un-ending overtime).

The Bailiff examines his nails, one contemplative eye foremost, gnaws and prises at their quicks with his flanking teeth to allow sufficient time for those at the back to compose their differences and give him their undivided attention. He then begins with strong crashing accents a brand-new address.

BAILIFF. 'I am your appointed bugbear and my bug-word goes, my writ runs, at all events in these outlandish spaces and in this artificial temporary Time! It is not a nice position to be in believe me: I hope you credit that, yes, it is transparently true. My *bugaboo-and-baby work*, snatching a quote from Pippa-Passes in passing, is not a White Man's job I protest.'

There is a bated murmur of sympathetic doubt: several appellants kneel down and pray: a very small one bursts into bladders-full of tears because of the strain imposed upon his tiny organism by the necessity of keeping quiet, and is carried out at last by a burly spectacled cavaliere servente of-a-certain-age who shyly apologetic at the in-human howling of his little charge attempts to silence him by vigorous shakings and muffled scoldings.

BAILIFF. 'The hazards to which my office is exposed are not of the most trifling: at one time and another I have suffered every variety of violence. It is my duty to punish, to see that due process of law be awarded against any such offender against my person which is sacrosanct and if I do not do so my clemency may get me into difficulties over there, where I am described as over-kind.'

He looks down significantly at the body of Barney.

BAILIFF. 'In certain special cases (into that there is no need for me to enter now) I am supposed for form's sake to appoint a Jury of Inquest: in practice I never do so, I refuse to pander to this legal fiction I consider it un-English I even prefer to revert to the Ordeal—on my principle of *All fair square and above-board*. Often as a matter of fact I have resorted to the Ordeal in ticklish cases and have found it to answer very well it is most dependable if properly administered. Now let us come to you gentlemen and the nature of your rights. Of what nature are those rights—it is natural enough that you should be impatient to learn what they are as quickly as possible. Now they are as it happens embodied in no Bill, but I can describe them to you. I will.'

He pauses looking down to collect the clauses of an important sentence and looks up smiling.

BAILIFF. 'Your rights, gentlemen, can be summarized in one word, *Petition*. You are *petitioners*, for better or for worse. I am ashamed to have to tell you that no appellant is entitled to his Habeas Corpus or to anything resembling it, there is no Rule of Law for us, you are absolutely without rights independently of my will: that is the situation: a sorry one, an un-English one, one I am heartily ashamed to have to stand here and expose to you. I keep this fact out of the camp broadsides and notices because I prefer that you should come to it only in my presence, so that I can give it out to you man-to-man and I can explain to you what are—what are—the compensations. But there, the fact remains, you are entirely without rights. *For your share you shall have the rights of petitioning!* that my poor friends is your Bill of Rights—so has it been, so shall it always be—in that I can alter nothing. Call it a Bill of Wrongs, I cannot help you! I am not the Legislator. You are here exercising your right of petitioning: that no one not even I can take from you. You can petition and petition and petition! you can do so till you are black in the face and the worms eat you up. There is practically no limit to the amount you can *petition!*'

'Well come that's something!' Pullman shouts, in spite of himself, he has been following every syllable with breathless attention: everybody laughs led by the Bailiff and the atmosphere of doom is relaxed.

BAILIFF. 'Well yes something—and nothing!—but it is mainly its un-English character that distresses me and that I find it difficult to explain away, otherwise it is really not so bad. This is not a despotic legislature but it is also not a *curia*. However my personality is really the main factor in the whole thing, you need go no farther than me, I am your shepherd.'

A raging voice interrupts:
'You are our butcher!'

BAILIFF. 'No, shepherd.'

VOICE. 'Butcher!'

BAILIFF. 'Shepherd!'

A VOICE. 'What's the difference?'

BAILIFF. 'I started by saying I was your bugaboo but I exaggerate: I lighten your lot. I touch you with an opium-wand and you sleep obedience: if you describe this instrument of justice in terms of that sort, all I can retort is that you are very lucky to be supplied with such a costly and desirable drug and I only wish that some one would administer that heavenly sleep to me!'

There is a quick rattle of nervous applause.

BAILIFF. 'But in a sense there is worse to come even: for I must tell you that these persons, *peons* we rather contemptuously call them, these clerks for example that assist me in my arduous duties are privileged in a way that you are not. Their persons are sacrosanct even as my own: that, sirs, is a settled doctrine of this Court! Every one of these despised and rejected "peons" is able to plead his clergy, such is their peculiar and important privilege: for all my officers in its most absolute interpretation *Benefit of Clergy*, that archaic legal instrument—*archaic* I say but like most archaic things it is returning to favour— that is recognized and everywhere enforced! So if it were their wish—heaven avert the omen!—they could slay you with impunity, but no right possessed by you allows you to lift a finger against your problematical destroyer. You quite understand the position? I hope that in telling you all this you will learn to admire the commendable patience of these persons, who in all things model themselves upon me their chief!'

Hasty applause: the attendants strut about a little, showing their teeth nastily and conceitedly.

BAILIFF. 'These things have not gone unchallenged, I may add, for it is not English to sit down under a law of this description and as I have already said it is in the highest degree un-English to ask any one to do so. "What is a gentleman?" asked Samuel Taylor Coolidge — Coleridge, I mean, and he answered himself upon the spot in the following true and touching words. "A gentleman is one who in all the detail of ordinary life, and with all the consciousness of habit, shows respect to others in a way that implies anticipation of reciprocal respect to himself." I call that a beautiful definition of a beautiful thing! *Shows respect to others in a way that implies anticipation* of getting the same himself! Sam Taylor as you see was prepared to "respect" *anybody* who would "respect" him! Or was it only "show" respect? However that complicates the definition the spirit of it is obvious, no one can question its deeply democratic nature—it includes *every one*— provided he show Sam T. "respect". What I have to tell you is not only un-English but ungentlemanly I readily admit. I do everything in my power to make up to you for these lapses from what is English and what is gentlemanly in the ordering of the administration. But there have not been wanting rebellious brawlers to challenge us upon all these heads and stab them as I have said with shafts of disrespect and quarrelsome questions. Yes, I daresay you will scarcely credit it but to my face I have been called a *Trading Justice*—yes, sirs, a *Trading Justice*! and these self-sacrificing servants of mine have been described as "a pack of *runners*!", of runners, yes of *runners*! Gentlemen! On my word. Of runners.'

There is a murmur of resentment against a person or persons unknown.

A VOICE. 'And so you are!'

264

The bellwetherer tiptoes upon the wall near the entrance-wicket brandishing a fist, then yells again:

'And so you are—a pack of runners!'

He springs from the wall to the ground without and makes off forty to the dozen, occasionally looking behind him and shaking a fist.

BAILIFF. 'It is he! the very man who before made use of those expressions—a most violent man. I am very glad he has gone! very!'

A HYPERIDEAN. 'Is this a Court of Star Chamber?'

BAILIFF. 'No, sir, this is not a Court of Star Chamber!'

HYPERIDEAN. 'In what does it differ from a Court of Star Chamber—are we not summoned—?'

BAILIFF. 'Not by writ.'

HYPERIDEAN. 'That may be: but where are your jurors?'

BAILIFF. 'There are no jurors, as I have explained, except in special cases involving the appointment of a Jury of Inquest.'

HYPERIDEAN. 'And what may those occasions be?—you have been careful not to specify what they are.'

BAILIFF (stuttering). 'Yes, I have *not*—I am not answerable to *you*!—Stand down you coxcomb—I forbid you categorically! You are a coxcomb!'

HYPERIDEAN. 'Who are you, puppet, to issue orders, tell me that?'

BAILIFF (dancing with sudden spleen). 'I will show you who I am! Tomorrow at latest I will issue a commission of rebellion against all your faction!'

HYPERIDEAN. 'A la bonne heure, Periwinkle!'

ANOTHER HYPERIDEAN. 'Ah, death-flower!—fiore di morte! mad puppet!'

Hyperides rolled up in his cloak is fallen asleep with his back to the Court. A follower holds the umbrella over him to protect him from the sun, while others take it in turn to fan his head.

265

The two Hyperidean interrupters turn their backs upon the Bailiff.

BAILIFF (shrugging his hump and addressing himself to the audience at large). 'This is not as those ruffians suggest a Court of Star Chamber but I will not assert that it has no resemblance to the discretionary procedure of the Court of Equity as opposed to common law. It is by the principle of "grace" that I proceed; but what, sirs, is that precious principle at which we have arrived in this court by way of so-called Equity? What, sirs, after all is Equity but Equality? And is it not through the medium of "grace" (with I agree its mediæval implications) that I have been able to reach in this tribunal the ideal of *Equality*?—No oppressive feudal incidents of tenure will be found here; you are as free from obligations or restraint as a bird-on-the-bough. All we ask is a little love! It is not much!'

Rapturous applause from the Young Turks of Bailiff-ites.

HYPERIDEAN VOICES.
{ 'A bird on the bough *in your game preserve!*'
{ 'Beneath the knout of your heiduks!'

A VOICE. 'Your methods are inquisitional?'

BAILIFF (turning upon the last tentative bellwetherer—who shrinks—with gusto). 'You are a slanderer! And if we were an Inquisition? What then? Who are the beneficiaries of our system? Tom Dick and Harry, good luck to them! Not *you!*'

ANOTHER VOICE. 'Where are Tom Dick and Harry? Disclose their whereabouts?'

BAILIFF. 'This is assuming the proportions of a mutiny! I shall argue with you no more—I shall have the back of this Court cleared if I hear any more from such malicious objectors!'

During the altercation an usher shouts 'Tormodma-crob!' 'Tormodmacrob!' with a Welsh accent so that the two words become one. A large man leaves the body of the audience and comes down into the arena. The bench is prompt to note his approach and he receives a most affable greeting from it.

BAILIFF. 'Oh Macrob there you are! That is good. So at last your turn has come!'

The Bailiff searches among the files that have now col-lected in front of him, their numbers bearing no relation to the people who are heard, for the Macrob dossier; find-ing it he proceeds to its perusal.

Macrob wears the kilt: he advances with a mournful swagger, the oscillation of the short skirt so much a part of him that a massive time is introduced into the forward churning of his legs. It is a proud and dancing time, the Macrob is in ballast and it is the slow-time of a heavy body in almost reluctant displacement, light but not gay, that places its feet upon the ground even and deft and more deliberate than a cat. He has swung to his feet at the crying of his name as though struck in the centre of a dream with a potent impersonal watchword to awaken him; his body has swaggered and swung into the lime-light as if it had stepped out of the sombre ranks of its clan, alone of the innumerable silent clansmen, respond-ing to some summons of fate, to a wailing music privy to its ears as the tom-tom of the surf pulses in the revolu-tions of the shell. But that is all in the way of activity, for everything about him advertises a cadaveric decadence which takes the form of a dogmatic decay. Upon his clothes is the mud in which he has lain since his arrival in deliberate neglect; a senile rust is upon the stripes of his pale sandy hair, his rugged and splendid head is sug-gestive of the summit of a drab monument of a hero which has been cast too impractically colossal and so escaped the attention of the parish cleaners and scrubbers, so that the birds have nested in its chapleted locks and stained its face with their droppings. The eyes are the purest Highland amber, but they gleam ambushed in the cavities beneath the square earthen brow which is lifeless and unlighted. So this figure as it stands out and faces its new world appears determined upon being a braw corpse among corpses as is right and proper in the dwelling of the dead and as it surely is meant that bodies should be there, in spite of all fashions to the contrary, and looking to play-at-life as little as possible, being the body of a scrupulous person, that has died and left its world, to whom the frisking of a carrion must be abhorrent—that is the bearing of Tormod, but the Bailiff shows not the least sign of at all intending to countenance this morbid view of death and he smiles and smiles into the dour face in front of him to stare the stern ghost of the Scot out of countenance, but without success.

The foreground of the circus is in an uproar which shows no sign of abating and soon grows to a husky splutter of mirthful frenzy. Every one has at first view of the new male-animal exchanged deep and silent glances of fantastic inquiry, that are archly-guilty, lashing his lashes, with his especial fancy-man body-mate or personal baby-snatcher—or with another baby's—who by way of response lashes his indigo lashes too in a bashful fury, fiery-eyed with shocked understanding; then with febrile dainty fingers he catches from inside his scented breast a pocket-handkerchief to be a receptacle for the ecstatic tears of the explosion that must sooner or later occur if this strange brawny bristling hybrid persists in remaining there, planted under all their noses.

'What's he got on his legs?' one whispers to a shyer one.

'I don't know!' is booed and breathed shyly back in a still more awestruck frightened way.

Mutt-Geoffrey murmurs to Jeff-Maurice—both were borstalled early and escaped together and both since have been quodded, though separately, in tuscan fascist prisons:

'It's quickset or something I think, that's all—it's not anything horrid!'

'Oh are you *sure*! I do hope you're right I thought it was' (in a dying dreamy accent) '—*bristles*!'

Bursting into tempestuous fits of giggles quite the nearest speedily reduce themselves to helpless speechless wriggling masses that pop and jump like chinese crackers.

'He does make me feel so self-conscious!' Chris confesses to his bitter admirer with clever bald-head and a jealous nature, who is looking daggers at the Highlander. 'I'm not at all sure if I shall be able to go on sitting here! Then you'll get so dreadfully jealous in a moment!'

The voices of the Harpies redouble in mock energy around the lofty Phineas, who stands in sightless abstraction fingering the landscape-pebble of his shoulder-brooch.

HARPIES ADDRESSING THE BLIND PHINEAS.

'You horrid vamp! Go away! Go away! I protest you're a disgrace, a perfect disgrace!'

'Och! but what limbs the man has on him what!'

'What a carriage—what a bust! Doesn't he make you feel small? I wish he wouldn't stand so near, he makes me feel nervous—I'm positive he'll fall over what do you think? He looks as though he might faint soon.'

'It's not decent! Sir! Make him pull his thingimies up you can't see from where you are sir! I wish you could —we're respectable here—we don't like him at all!'

Pat bends over the parapet and attempts to attract the attention of Macrob.

'I say—sir!—excuse me! you're making me blush most terribly do you hear? *do move away*—go over to the other side do you mind most awfully? I wish you could see your way to! I mean no offence, you would be obliging me most terribly! as it is I can't help looking as though I were staring at you in a way that might be misinterpreted. Don't you hear me, are you deaf? You'll give me a bad name if you don't move away! *Please* go over to the other side—I do so wish you could see your way to!'

Another set of voices clamour from nearer the centre.

OTHER
VOICES.

'Kiltie! Look Kiltie, they're coming doon mon—aye it's not decent!'
'Kiltie! They're varra shurret behind mon! Had ye no stuff enough to mak a fool one? Is it ex-pain-seef?'

Pullman is standing up but sits down again with the remark:

'They'll have to have him taken away, I expect.'

The Macrob as he waits for the magistrate to terminate his brooding examination of the dossier begins at this point to shuffle his feet as if he is restless, a little in the manner of acrobats with the resin that prevents them from slipping. The air is rent with a piercing cry of alarm and horror and a voice screams:

'He's going *to dance*!'

The warning cry is taken up on all sides, with one movement of simultaneous panic the entire herd of nanmen, breathless hopping demireps and wicked debauchees, decamps in violent ebb, crushing back the appellant-mass in their immediate rear, screaming in a deadly gleeful scramble to safety. It resembles the exodus that took place following the accident to Barney: many apparently faint in the arms of protectors, and Chris remains prone in the danger-zone, lying stretched out in graceful abandoned corkscrew-languish across a fallen bench. Mr. Marshall goes down and drags him into safety.

CHORUS OF
BAILIFFITES
IN RETREAT.
{
'He's about to dance!'
'Stop him! it's not decent! he intends to dance.'
'It would be the most indecent thing that's ever happened, sir, use your influence to prevent it!'
'Sir! if you don't stop him he'll dance! He's dressed like a woman can't you see sir? Please look at him!'
'He's' (a shrill shriek) *beginning!*'
}

Pullman and Satters are flung back as the foremost of the crowd stampedes from the barrier.

'Damn!' shouts Pullman chasing his stick, which has been shot out of its slot and attempts to wriggle away among the press of feet. 'What's the matter now?'

'It's that disgusting crowd—they're ragging the poor Highlander. They say he's likely to dance,' Satters says in pursuit of Pullman.

'Likely to dance?' Pullman's voice is muffled and cross as he draws the stick out between a forest of legs.

He stands up, looking over at the Macrob.

'He doesn't look the kind of man who would want to dance.'

'I know!—He doesn't seem to mind does he?'

The Bailiff is immobile in the attitude of a carved rooster of bulbous red, conceived as congested in the act to crow, thrust forward over the cutwater of a galley. His eye alone moves travelling from face to face of his seething claque in retreat.

271

BAILIFF. 'Whatisthis! whatisthis!'

AN APPELLANT. 'He wants to dance, sir!'

2ND APPELLANT. 'He began to get ready to dance, sir, it would be too awful if he were to!'

3RD APPELLANT. 'Please sir, tell him he musn't dance—he's dressed like a woman. He's filthy too, I shouldn't think he ever washes! We couldn't possibly stop here if he danced!'

4TH APPELLANT. 'He's laughing to himself sir! he intends to it's obvious!'

2ND APPELLANT (moving away towards exit). 'I shall go outside till this dreadful man has gone! I think it's too much to ask us to remain in the same Court with such a creature!'

5TH APPELLANT. 'It's that exhibitionist sir down there! it's terribly upsetting to have him standing there like that, we don't know which way to look!'

6TH APPELLANT (shrieking). 'He's stamped his foot!—did you see him? I'm positive he's getting ready!'

There is a further universal movement of recoil.

A storm brews upon the Bailiff's face, his eye slowly moving over the gesticulating figures of the mob of nanmen backing with bleating lips in mock-panic. With a fine screeching voice in a key of ironic coaxing mastery he calls to them, pretty and quavering, a leaden loaded index dropping plumb down upon the vacated seats to fix the spot that it is his wish that they should at once reoccupy.

BAILIFF. 'Come back here! *Coome* back now and behave yourselves, yes come back! come *back*!' His voice goes up into pitches that are too brittle and fine to exist as evident sound.

There is suspense: no move is made but one of those in flight from the Highlander exclaims:

272

'I thinks it's most unkind of any one to ask us to come back while *he* is there—it's not respectable—he shouldn't be allowed to go about like that!'

The Bailiff turns quickly to his heiduks.

BAILIFF. 'Flagellants! Fetch back my gibbering fry of baby-buntings with your whips, back here! Let them taste your loaded tips!—This is rebellion! Bugaboos can't be choosers what next I never did and do!'

Thirty or more chuckers-out, whip in hand, vault the barrier.

'Will you come back?' screams the Bailiff at his quivering litter. 'Don't strike them if they will come they'd make such a noise if you did. Don't hit them if you can help it.'

The heiduks crack their whips: the Bailiffites swarm down chattering into their places and the guard is called off, reheaving themselves athwart the barrier and resuming their former positions, an aloof line of statues melting in the heat, their empty peon's eyes that are weary of space fixed nowhere.

BAILIFF. 'At last, gentlemen, we shall be allowed to proceed it seems with the business of the day!'

The Macrob stares dully on at the dancing shadow of the phylactery amid the dust kicked up by the disturbance: he has scarcely moved and no sign has escaped him that he is aware of what is going forward behind his back on account of his costume.

BAILIFF (examining the unkempt beggar-clansman, the glengarry khakied with caked mud, all the details of his dress that are unsightly). 'Well Macrob I'm sorry to see you in this condition!'

273

Chris whispers to his fuming champion: 'I do so agree with him, don't you?'

MACROB. 'What condition? Is this a condition?'
BAILIFF. 'I should certainly say that that was a condition!'
MACROB. 'Provided it is only a condition I am satisfied.'

Macrob folds his arms on his braw caber-tossing berserker bosom. With great kindness the Bailiff puts the regulation question as to nature of death and date, Christian burial, and so forth, but refers to the papers for the answers. He checks them, then puts himself at the disposal of the applicant.

MACROB. 'I have listened, sir, to what you have been saying to the people who have preceded me: that has enabled me to come to certain conclusions. I hope you will tell me if they are wrong.'

The Bailiff nods his head.

MACROB. 'I gather that you reject in your religion all idea of progression. Human life you regard as a term, the crystallization of a personality, which, once it has *become*, cannot ever not exist. Posthumously, you bake that into the displeasing forms we see around us.'

'Speak for yourself!' shouts a hunchback in the crowd, amid a delighted effervescence. The Bailiff laughs gaily at the kindred deformity.

CHRIS. 'If they're going to let him be as rude as he likes I shall simply leave!'
SHADOW OF CHRIS. 'If the fellow is insolent I shall have him removed—or go myself!'

BAILIFF (in his politest strain bending towards Macrob). 'You can put it that way if you like: I would prefer it if you said that we spare you further effort.'

MACROB. 'May I add to the burdens of your office by asking you some further questions?'

The magistrate nods, watching lazily.

BAILIFF. 'Certainly.'

MACROB. 'What sort of object are you?'

The Bailiff laughs faintly, his eyes closing, an amused contemptuous light squeezed out of the luminous slit.

BAILIFF. 'I can see with whom you've been associating, my poor Macrob! Had I known that I should have insisted upon your appearing with the Hyperideans.'

MACROB. 'You informed a questioner that you were not real?'

BAILIFF. 'Surely you are mistaken.'

Attending upon signs of unreality though still with the air of asking the apparition to confess, the Macrob fastens his naïve penetrating scrutiny upon the person of the Bailiff. A sudden disagreeable laugh cracks out of the Bailiff's face as his mouth opens to say:

BAILIFF. 'Macrob! You're absurd! Really totally absurd, yes.'

MACROB. 'If you are a dream these things must matter less,' argues Macrob sensibly with himself.

BAILIFF (heaving a pathologic opium-eating sigh). 'When I first knew you, Macrob—it's only a few weeks ago though it seems years doesn't it—you were a simple honest fellow, I took a fancy to you as you know. But this terrible poison of *mistrust* that that man there' (he points at Hyperides without looking) 'sows on all sides has entered into you—it's all up with you I'm afraid! Today you are full of questions that yesterday it would never have entered your head to ask.'

The Bailiff grins over at the dejected vault of the back of his arch-enemy still wrapped in sleep beneath the tent of the large umbrella.

BAILIFF. 'There are some people who spend their time spoiling everything for their more ignorant fellows!'

A darker expression of confused despair comes into the face of the Macrob. Painfully and steadily he drags the words one by one out of his mind, building up a sort of morose soliloquy.

MACROB. 'Orif' (becoming more Scotch) 'with drrrawing suffeeciently from this hallucination to observe it in its facteetious nature, you and the other objects so painfully present to me now are appearances only' (disturbances seriatim in the audience) 'one should regard all this as committing one to nothing—since it has no ground or meaning and can be wiped out like an arrangement of figures on a slate.'

The Bailiff leans civilly over towards him, finger-tips hieratically joined in the first position of the diver.

BAILIFF. 'I am not a hippogriff or a *golden mountain* if that is what you mean; my hump is quite normal, at least several gentlemen present, I am glad to notice, possess humps!' (fraternal laughter from the humps). 'I am as real as you—there that is what you want to be assured of is it not?'

MACROB. 'No that is not it. Here everything depends

upon the degree of your reality, not upon ours: it is the first and last thing in this situation.'

BAILIFF. 'Is it? Well, you can take it from me I'm real, devilish real, see?'

MACROB. 'If you are not real, if you are not so real as I am, then you cannot injure me.'

BAILIFF. 'How interesting! But I'm afraid even that does not follow.'

The Macrob peers at him from under sandy suspicious Scottish eyebrows.

MACROB. 'You are as customary as the average advertisement for causal reality, I suppose I must take you at your word.'

BAILIFF. 'I should! I should!' (he mocks negligently, performing the devil's tattoo beneath the ledge in front of him). 'Listen Macrob you have heard the story of your fellow-countryman, the one who it is reported went to a festive party one evening and subsequently took a very long time to reach his home, though it was only at the end of the street, because the shadows cast by the houses and trees appeared to him to be real so he had to walk round them, jump over them, or otherwise circumvent them. Are the shadows real however, and is the intoxicated Scot—or is the child before he has been taught our code of "reality"—right, after all, that is the question? If you will allow me to say so Macrob your whole outlook on what you term *reality* is very naïve indeed: you confuse yourself unnecessarily.'

MACROB. 'I consider myself real: so I don't see how I can withhold from you——'

BAILIFF. 'It would seem so: but the trouble is that you are *not!*' (He grins, scratching his upper lip while he draws down the centre of his mouth cat-wise.) 'I try to spare you all these painful revelations. It's no use. You

277

will have it your own way. I see what it is you really want to know. Your questions dissimulate a healthy curiosity about yourself, that is it am I not right?—what you have wanted to know all along is what kind of an object *you* are?'

MACROB. 'If you could speak the truth——' ponderously and wearily he reopens his interrogatory: he is asking for assistance from his judge.

BAILIFF. 'If you must listen to other people Macrob and learn distrust of your best friends it's difficult to know what to do to help you. If I could tell the truth! You accuse me of being untruthful? Very well. I will answer your questions truthfully, since you make such a point of it. It is the question of your *reality* that exercises you? Well, I'll give you the true answer you exact. You have a sort of reality—not very much. What every creature ought to understand is that he is never worth a fraction of the trouble we take with him here.'

MACROB. 'Are we on the same basis existentially here as we were on earth?'

BAILIFF. 'Oh yes about the same; there's not much in it, you were of no *more* consequence on earth if that is what you mean.'

Macrob stares at the oracle in silence. The Bailiff continues easily:

BAILIFF. 'At this celestial gateway into another and I hope a better life it is our duty to scrutinize and pass what is offered us as the most ideal specific fragment or cross-section of a certain human personality, itself a fragment—your terrestrial career having been satisfactorily terminated and duly recorded in our archives.'

On one breath of sustained inquiry Macrob then presses:

278

MACROB. 'But am I not, as it seems, in a world of imagination? are these objects contemplated now by me as real as earthly ones or are they built in a bare thinking cube innocent of the compass, a microcosm indifferent to physical position, nowhere in nothing?'

Slowly he beats out the terms of his question, docile and obstinate; the Bailiff keeps his eyes fixed upon the ground beneath him, then looks up and answers:

BAILIFF. 'Macrob, I have never cared much for the Scotch, until I met you: but I find that even you are too Scotch for me. I have told you that you are as real as ever you were. These terms you use, however, you make no attempt to define, it's like talking to a child. What for instance do you mean by *nothing*? However, let us use them as we suppose you intend them. First, then, were you not in Space-Time you could not exist at all, you can regard yourself as existing in a sort of mental excrescence, or annexe, of Space-Time: so all that you applied to the enigma of your earthly lot you can apply to this, with little modification. As near as damn it it's the same.'

MACROB. 'Am I an entity? Can I be put into Space and Time or taken out again, as you would put a pea into a glass of water and take it out again? Do I belong to empirical existence: or am I something apart from that, joined to it for a moment?'

The Bailiff ploughs irritably into the Scottish mist that is driving against him: in grating sing-song he begins intoning:

BAILIFF. '——*against your self you swore;*
Your former self, for every Hour your form
is chop'd and chang'd, like Winds before a Storm.

279

Now there is no more "chopping and changing", yet you are still there. But you still—oh human perversity! —seem dissatisfied. Once more however—there is no *you* apart from what you perceive: your senses and you with them *are* all that you habitually see and touch: I am a part of you at this moment: those battlements are becoming you; the *you* bodily and otherwise, which has been perpetuated, much to your disgust it seems, is all that at present you are witnessing and sensing. What is your difficulty in all this? Perhaps it is *me* to which you object, since you can claim me as an organic part of your consciousness—perhaps you would like to evacuate me? Please don't spare me if that is so, I am quite ready to go, I ask nothing better.'

MACROB. 'Are you a part of me now? What part?'

BAILIFF. 'Really! Well, of course a humble, an inconspicuous part. But *everything* can claim some part of you; if everything simultaneously put in its claim for its pound of flesh and pound of spirit where would poor little *you* be then? Of course you can put it the other way round if you like, namely that *we* are you: that interpretation is preferred by some people. The more highly developed the individual—and your development is evidently very high—clearly the more the exterior world is a part of him: the more sensitive he is to stimulus, the more of the world he registers and includes, and so forth and so forth. But—surely I need not remind you of that—the less to such a member of the sensitive *élite* the self matters as well or that should be so. Really a fool *is* the only thing to be if you are human: you are a spoilt-fool Macrob (that is worse than a spoilt-child in my opinion), quite a respectable fool gone wrong. Can't you see that? It's such a pity! Macrob! Did you hear me?"

He calls out sharply in response to the thickening look

upon the face in front of him. Then he leans forward towards the appellant and beckons him to approach a little, grating in an impressive sotto-voce, as Macrob moves reluctantly nearer:

BAILIFF. 'Nearer! that's better—I don't want the children to hear. All the same, Mr. Macrob after all, you are quite intelligent enough to know that the importance of your personality is very slight indeed, not more quite literally than that of a fly. There can be little doubt that you appreciate how this protracted conversation is therefore in fact an impertinence if looked at properly—though I should be the last person naturally to wish to insist upon that view of the matter, I have my job to think about! It is only imbeciles that suppose themselves of any importance: still self-importance is a weakmindedness that has to be humoured we always respect illusion—*of such stuff is the Kingdom of Heaven made!* It's our livelihood! Our show over there is in the truest sense an asylum; and our patients are our children. Look round you and you will observe a most characteristic lot. But let me warn you Macrob: with you and such as you there is no excuse! I should not feel myself justified in excusing you.' The Bailiff leans back. 'Do you wish to go on?'

During this address Macrob has stared forward with a gathering dullness like a shield to protect his consciousness against this adversary.

MACROB. 'I do.'
BAILIFF. 'Very well Macrob do as you like you're your own master. For my part I am prepared this moment to pass you in, as you stand, without further palaver. You are quite distinct. It is not I who am making the difficulties.'

MACROB. 'As I stand, yes that's it! Because I am what I am you owe me an explanation.'

BAILIFF. 'In that you are mistaken, no one owes you an explanation.'

MACROB. 'You represent the Deity. I insist upon an explanation, I refuse to pass you until you have satisfied me!'

BAILIFF. 'Hoity-toity Macrob hark at you! If you could only see yourself! Still, go on.'

As the Bailiff names him, he bestows on the uttering of the name at each fresh occasion some cumulative significance.

MACROB. 'How do I come to be? then, why am I like this?'

BAILIFF. 'To take your questions in the order you discharge them at me. The first is a stock Scottish question —Robert-Louis put it into doggerel—you would if you could. You are a habit, Macrob, a habit, merely, of Space-Time.'

MACROB. 'Is not Space-Time itself a habit?'

BAILIFF. 'Exactly, you are a habit of a habit—of a Habit. Whether you are a good habit or a bad one must always remain a matter of opinion, we isolate for you what we consider, as it works out according to our system, the most typical fragment of you and preserve to it its principle of identity and endow it with life. That's all we undertake to do.'

The Bailiff looks at him steadily, blank quiet and politely expectant. Macrob considers.

MACROB. 'I'm not obliged to you for that—whoever you are.'

The Bailiff laughs, a discreet volume of sound indolently occurring upon the surface, disturbing nothing underneath; while the vertex of the triangle beneath his nose is produced over his teeth with feline neatness.

BAILIFF. 'I myself have not been provided if it comes to that with a very captivating appearance: yet my exterior conveys even better than yours the human thing.'

Macrob looks at him with a pointed distaste.

MACROB. 'Your appearance appeals to me very little. It is not a human canon I recognize.'
BAILIFF. 'No I know it doesn't. You are still full of earth's old timid grace of course aren't you, at least in fancy! Beggars can't be choosers Tormie, you're a beggar it seems, your appearance suggests that that is your case—pocket your pride and go in. I can't send you back you're much too lifelike.'
MACROB. 'Why have you made me into a beggar? I never looked like this. What object had you in humiliating me?'
BAILIFF. 'Another delusion! No one cared in the least what became of you. You happen to have turned out as you have. The process is quite mechanical and absolutely impartial, Space-Time got the habit of you Macrob, and threw you up here. What after all is your history? You persisted for a certain number of years like a stammer. You were a *stammer*, if you like, of Space-Time. He—or it would be more proper to say *she* of the great Mother of all things' (he inclines his head, smiling, pausing for a moment)—'began saying "Macrob" and she went on stammering "Macrob" in a continuous present for the period of your natural life. The present "you" is the echo of that strange event. You are a keepsake. Having been uttered by Space-Time

you cannot die. We Space-Timers are a sentimental lot we make collections of *everything* that Space-Time has ever uttered, that is all, that is sufficiently articulate to hold together. So instead of happening once and for all sharp and sweet you meandered and rattled on through what must have seemed to you a never-ending lifetime, through countless numbers of stupid events "you" were dragged by slow heavily-moving Space-Time, you don't remember, we help you to forget all that: but it was not a very lively chapter in world-history I can promise you, the life of "Tormod Macrob Esquire". Well! There was all the filling up and evacuating of your stupid body was there not?—all the places that had to be built to house it, chairs for it to sit on, other animals to be killed, vegetables to be grown, collected, bought and sold, multitudes of things to be cooked, plates to be kept clean, clothes you had soiled to be washed, all on account of "you". And so with millions like you, here are a few of you at present. —Well, why this should be or have been I have often asked myself, I give it up! I must confess I do not know Macrob so for mercy's sake don't begin cross-questioning me! The upshot of it is however that Space-Time having borne you in this fashion has apparently some sentiment about it: and so here you are. How it can possibly matter to you whether you are "real" or not under the circumstances passes my understanding.'

MACROB. 'It passes mine too, that is why I asked you. You know don't you? If you don't wish to answer my questions why not say so at once?

BAILIFF. 'I have been answering you Macrob, to the best of my ability.'

While this has been in progress the followers of Hyperides have arrived in considerable numbers. Upwards of fifty are now collected at the highest point of the auditorium. They stand, their mock-antique draperies floating and flapping in the hot wind. With a picturesque gallery of sculptured frowns they look down upon the scene beneath them, their master, Hyperides, recumbent at their feet, his back still turned towards the centre of the circus.

The Macrob doggedly proceeds, his mind visibly grinds down upon its bone, his head canted and thrust out in tense mastication.

MACROB. 'Are you not in your present system merely extracting the creative principle from us and collecting our dead shells? This static degradation is the opposite, even, of the *becoming* to which you are so partial. Or is it the dregs of your *becoming* that we are asked now for ever to lap up?'

The Bailiff looks over at Hyperides with a smile. ('I draw your attention to this! Witness your handiwork!')

MACROB. 'In life is it not the thing that never *is* or *becomes* at all that is the most live part? That you cut out. It is as though you said "You wish to *be* rather than always to *become*, you chafe at the futility as you consider it of your magnificent *action*: very well, you shall have your wish!"—and then had composed a parody of eternity with the cheap and perishable material left over from all our *becomings*.'

BAILIFF. '*Eternity is in love with the productions of Time!* The Eternal loves Time if you do not! The only motive for His weakness for you is in your capacity of *factor of Time*, that is your principal not to say unique claim upon His interest. Some of you disregard your debt to Time in a really unaccountable way. Time is the mind of Space—Space is the mere body of Time. Time is life, Time is money, Time is all good things!— Time is God!'

285

His head up under the eave of his narrow chamber, in shadow, the Bailiff's eyes shine in his blood-red face with the beginnings of a mystical afflatus, furibundly darting them at this person and that, ceasing to look necessarily at his questioner. With rising irritability he begins listening to himself or calling any stranger to witness.

MACROB (cries impatiently). 'That is not my God!'

BAILIFF. 'What do you know about your God?'

MACROB (with a weary gesture of renunciation). 'There you hold the trumps always, you are the man-of-God, but you are welcome to your top Trump—keep Him up your sleeve, continue to trump everybody with Him till the trump of doom. Is it impossible to *die*? That's what I should like to know?'

The Bailiff with a shocked expression fixes a severe eye upon Macrob.

BAILIFF. 'I had feared that eventually we should come to that! That is quite out of the question!'

MACROB. 'The body you have supplied me with is the disgusting foetus only of my earthly self. Why do I have to remain always with this foetus? I thought death would translate me to another form or that I should die altogether. Yet here I am, still in a world of foetuses!'

(Exclamations of disapproval on all hands.)

BAILIFF. 'But you are shortly to enter a world of angels! It is you alone, in fact, who are postponing that happy moment. Death also, I may add, is not a miscarriage, as you represent it. It is an authentic birth: but not followed by the usual growing pains, since there is no growth.'

MACROB. 'When I contemplate myself from outside I see one thing: when I pass inward to my centre I experience another. Which is the true, the impersonal or the personal?'

BAILIFF. 'I should say that the former is the more true, but the latter the more satisfactory. It is your own affair if you insist on being impersonal as you call it with yourself. Your fellows here are much more sensible. *They* are not impersonal about themselves! Why don't you take a leaf out of their book?'

MACROB. 'What vision am I usurping in that interior contemplation?'

BAILIFF. 'The divine spark is of course the little lantern, which is locked up in you, of which you are making use in such moments. You are the vessel of an idea of Deity. That is why we cannot accommodate you if you ask to die.'

MACROB. 'But if I ask you to take away my spark for ever and to let this creation that is me die, are you not able to do that?'

BAILIFF. 'That, I've already told you Macrob, is out of the question—ask me anything but that! Brahman, my poor Tormod, is still your citizen! In one sense it must be admitted that human life is unfortunate: you are in the position of a suttee a Brahmanical bride, a woman sexually dedicated. When the man dies the woman is sacrificed, she is consumed at his side: you, on the same principle, but conversely, because of your divine spark must *live* for ever. Do you understand?'

MACROB. 'It is almost as though by living I had committed sacrilege?'

BAILIFF. 'Your death, if you like, would compromise the Deity.'

MACROB. 'But did not my life equally compromise Him?'

BAILIFF. 'Nothing but death is compromising to the Deity!'

MACROB. 'I am then a souvenir of life, as you have explained it: it is my lot to be preserved like a dance-card, a lock of hair, a rose-leaf, or a love-letter? How many of such trifles does He propose to collect and to what distances are the regions where He keeps such garbage liable to stretch?'

BAILIFF. 'Your existence is in that sense certainly illusory; in the human mind, how much more in the mind of God, there is room for everything that could exist, there is really no trouble at all about your *numbers*, that is a vulgar error to suppose the contrary.'

MACROB. 'Why should this luxurious and complacent divinity describe my "spark" as "divine"?'

BAILIFF. 'I never said He described it in that way. That's my description or yours, perhaps.'

MACROB. 'Was I created for His *pleasure*—in the sense that the Brahman's wife is dedicated to his?'

BAILIFF. 'The notion of pleasure plays no part in either —you are perhaps deliberately introducing that factor, though I am bound to confess that where the *pleasure* could come in in owning you as a creature I find it difficult to see.—You are coexistent with the Deity. You are in a sense His judge—much more than I am yours.'

MACROB. 'How can I judge God—any more than I can judge myself?'

BAILIFF. 'The creature is ipso facto a criticism of the creator is he not? You shouldn't foul your own nest. Your complaints disgrace your great Creator. Put yourself in His position! You complain because you are not *perfect*. It would make the most thorough nonsense of the world if you were, to that I suppose you will agree? God you should remember is naturally sensitive about His creations. He also is by no means as I have hinted— how shall I put it?—sure of His ground with them. Do you remember a remark of Socrates made in the course of conversation with Aristodemus—to this effect: "Surely the gods would not have put it into men's minds that they were able to benefit or injure them if it were not true"?'

MACROB. 'Do you imply that were men agreed on a condemnation of a god, they could will his destruction?'

BAILIFF. 'One man is able to will the death of a god. That is the only way I fear in which a man can die himself.'

MACROB. 'But if I am to be kept as a static souvenir of myself, in this celestial waxworks, how can I in future will anything?'

BAILIFF. 'Ah! the willing must occur during your terrestrial life. There is no more willing here! You have accepted God. It is now too late!'

MACROB. 'Who then is this God you are supposed to represent? I at least am not proud of this relationship, whatever He may be. I care less even than for one of the pant-buttons that in His infinite wisdom he has created for your divine master! Do you understand me? I say to you *damn* your God if you have such a thing which I don't believe: but if you should, by some evil chance, not be in this instance lying, then I say to you: I wish to make an immediate exit from His universe and yours!'

BAILIFF. 'Less heat my poor friend I beseech you, in such a climate as ours!'

MACROB. 'Look at this carcass you have served me out with, you say to symbolize my life on earth: what description of mockery is that?'

BAILIFF. 'I wish I could say that this is the first time I have heard complaints as to the personal appearance of our honoured clients. It is not. There's no pleasing some people and that's a fact, especially where their personal appearance is concerned. You no doubt found that during your life. I am glad that we don't deal with women at this gate as they do at the Yin; but it's often not much better than if we did, honestly. I can see nothing wrong with you Macrob: a little untidy perhaps—but what at this time of day can that possibly matter to you?'

MACROB. 'All your arguments are founded on our necessary despair. Also you gibe at us all the time. Evidently you are placed here on the threshold of your terrible heaven expressly to mock the wretched creatures who are passing into it!'

BAILIFF. 'No, I am placed here to expound the laws of this new existence when called upon to do so and to pass you in if I find you have reached the proper point of crystallization. I consider you personally have turned out extremely well Macrob and that you are ripe for an eternity of yourself.'

The face of Macrob is slowly changing its colour from the pale anger of the mind to the royal scarlet of physical battle. He opens his eyes upon the Bailiff for the first time since the match began: fierce indignant astonishment gives to his face a less simple look than when it had its heavy thinking cap. Slowly where before this alien menacing spectre was admitted into the darkened within, where he struggled mind-to-mind with it for an impossible decision, now it is driven out. Outside it is no longer a spectre. It stands above him, the Bloody Bailie in the flesh, helmeted in the semi-Phrygian red of Punch of Red Revolution and Red Passion, the red beast set there to mock and madden, at the gate of What? that Macrob as he steals out of his shell to see what is going on without ceases to question.

The Bailiff is saying:

BAILIFF. 'I cannot without reference to the sense and

interest of your worships, the souls of the innumerable dead, decide any matter above your heads. Are you Macrob satisfied in your mind or not that your case has been fairly and squarely dealt with?'

He holds his pencil poised above the spot on the dossier where he drops a flourish when the bargain is clinched.

MACROB. 'No!'

The Macrob is looking at him, but to look at the espada is not to play the game in this arena although the bull-killer of this bull is safe in the towering *burladero* of his puppet's-box.

BAILIFF. 'No? What further can I do for you? Tell me.'

MACROB. 'You can give me my quittance—I wish to end this transaction here and now! I wish for my discharge nothing short of that, choose you its manner—do you hear? I will not go on with it!'

BAILIFF. 'I am not only the supreme officer of this ad-ministration but (what is not so generally known) that appointment in no way derogates from the long-estab-lished sinecure of Gate-Beak to which appertains a quite distinct congeries of powers.'

MACROB. 'I don't care what Gate you are the Beak of, butcher!'

BAILIFF. 'All right. I thought you might care to know a little more about my powers.'

MACROB. 'Let me get out of your sponging-house, Mister Bailiff, or I'll break its locks!'

The Bailiff watches him for a moment, then taking a tabatière from his pocket he prises with a voluptuous snuffling. He nozzles and prises above his wagging beard, maniac and ape-masked with the expansion of the budding sneeze, taking no further notice of his man, grinding the twin shells of his nostrils down upon his snuff-laden yellow-shining finger-tips.

Emboldened by the pass to which the Highlander has been brought in gruelling keeling and basting up against the steam-roller of their prophet's mind, by his sunken popularity, or by his short-shrift soon to come—feebly scented of the blood-weasels—by the many portents, especially the snuff, the chorus shudders from tongue to instep. Souter says, crackling chorus-leader of the party of the left-centre, in muffled sing-song:

'Barts! seize Phineas and remove him to our operating theatre where we will chop his legs off for luck! He is the most improper mascot ever owned by a respectable hospital! Seize him and eject him from this theatre, militant medicos! He hasn't a leg to stand on, he'd argue a wolf-hound's hind-leg off if we let him, what he says is gutrot and ashes, he's a blot on the life of London! Up Barts and at him!'

'Phineas! Phineas!' his followers cry, pointing over at the stiff silhouette of the Macrob with the braw knee advanced bended and heraldic, as with head thrown back he parleys with the Bailiff in their final exchanges.

Chris restrains with scented tendril-fingers his partner (as bald as a coot but jealous to a fault and mettlesome to the marrow) who attempts a hostile demonstration against the tartanned legs, from the rolled stockings of which he seeks to pluck the dagger.

'I do wish you'd be quiet and not interfere with him! If you tickle him there's no knowing what will happen!' Chris complains, cross and caressing.

Mutt-Geoffrey says:

'He's riding for a fall—I can see the beastly brazen brute being suppressed quite soon now thank goodness, I shall be terribly pleased to see his back I mean not to see it.'

Jeff-Maurice echoes Mutt-Jeff:

'I can't tell you how thankful *I* shall be when he's gone, it makes me feel quite sick to look at him!' (He shudders against Mutt.)

The slow mind of Macrob leaves its shell inch by inch, horned blind and dazzled: then it is out, the shell stands apart statuesquely from its soul at last, staring and stark for a queasy second, and the unmitigated Macrob-clansman clicks into action. The muscular shell springs back, rebounds from the barrier (as it would look to the child-eye checking the event) and, intelligent gutta-percha missile, darts headlong in reverse and catapults up, a bolt from the abyss, in an animal parabola-on-its-back straight at its appointed target, it's bull's-eye the Bailiff. With a rattle and shock the charging body crashes into the bema which it tosses back half-a-foot upon its socket in the volcanic rock, the fletched topknot oscillating like an instrument set to register such upheavals: up sweeps the gaunt Scottish arm with beaked talon and then thumb and index snap-to upon the snish-tickled twitching snout, wallowing in its black bath of snuff. The powder from the snuff-box, batted upwards, explodes into the Bailiff's face, blackened like that of a man doctored by an apache on the sneeze-racket, and the body of the squealing nose is stuck fast like a fat rat in a trap.

As a dog with a rat seeking to stun it the Macrob tugs the nose violently this way and that.

'Aiiiiiiii mmmurder! Mummummu*mur*-ddd-er!'

Deafening squeaks continue to issue from the Bailiff's mouth. The entire pack of guards cooks clerks and runners as one man rush upon the aggressor issuing from every hole and cranny of the ramshackle steadings in full semi-articulate cry their eyes maliciously gleaming, some even convulsed with amusement. Three heiduks hang upon either arm, Jackie jumps in at the waist and attempts to rush away with the Scot's kicking trunk: but it

293

is observed that, as the negro makes headway and draws off with his burden, the Bailiff too is being dragged out of the magisterial chamber nose-first after the receding Macrob.

'Stop stop stop! Jackstop Jackstop!' the assistance clamours at the grinning black, who is crying cock with a happy jabber and would soon have both judge and appellant on the run in a squealing string. A halt is called in the tug-of-war.

'Aiiiiiiii! Iooouuu Jooouu!'

A despatch-box is hastily brought out of the office-tent and placed at the foot of the mêlée. An attendant mounts it and fixes a set of sharp strong teeth on the hand attached to the nose. Gradually the hand relaxes. At length the flesh is bitten down to the right spot but it succumbs with a disturbing suddenness. The fingers fly open, the nose escapes. On one side the human tree of compact limbs crashes down upon the pavement: on the other the Bailiff flies back into the bottom of his chamber with a piercing squeal of distress. There is a roar of alarm and laughter and salvoes of hand-clapping and stamping.

Jackie and Macrob hurled backwards fall with a dozen other zealous figures all biting kicking and kidney-punching fiercely inwards. Jackie forces his way out of the mass; gradually as figure by figure his assailants fall away Macrob is revealed upon his back, covered with blood, rolling in the quiet convulsions of the knock-out. He revolves upon his face and slowly rises. With a crash of his black fist Jackie floors him, and Pat leans over the barrier and with his hat begins counting him out.

'One!'

As Macrob reaches the ground Jackie takes a flying leap, landing with both feet upon the dazed upturned face, his lip wolfishly rolled back exposes a row of gold-stopped teeth. He kicks and tramples upon the face with fury. The others close round and Macrob disappears from view.

294

Sneeze upon sneeze in heavy heart-searching *atishoos* announces the recovery of the invisible magistrate. Then up he starts with a crowing scream, dragging himself off the floor. Holding his nose with one hand, with the other he points at the throng attacking the prostrate Scot out-of-sight.

'Stop that stop that! my merry wolves! I call you off— you hear me, harpies? Stop it—you'll kill him—I don't want it. Stop! Cart him off don't kill him, pass pass pass the brute beast in on the spot—treat him as he deserves not as you would he would do unto you!'

One of the doctors who was in constant attendance upon Darius, entrusted with the morning bulletin of his urine, with a magian beard reaching to the knees, a steeple-hat and bent with extreme age, arrives to examine the Bailiff's nose. He is waved away by the irritable magistrate, who instead dips his handkerchief in the tumbler of water at his side, so providing himself with an improvised poultice.

A large executioner's basket is brought out, and the fragments of Macrob are stuffed and stamped into it.

BAILIFF. 'That's right take him in—is he all there? No buttons missing? He'll come together within the magnetic walls, how angry he will be!'

While he poultices himself the Bailiff relieves his feelings in a muffled whine.

BAILIFF. 'Why do they always pick on me? Oh I don't know I'm about through, I've had my fill of kicks it's not as though I'd wished any harm what have I *ever* done not to a newt let alone anonrubble appellers, lick the foot that kicks, kicks, morons and yahoos, that's their style look up to you if you, yes but never a thank-you for your pains, you can sweat your guts out death's not

295

good enough, kindness yes back-foremost like the eye of the camel, giving-too-little and asking-too-much like the Dutch in the limerick, what are we different clay? no fellow-feeling no love nothing you'd say so to listen, where's the sense in where's the use? what's the— what's the end where does it all finish? one's no forrader at the end, one's always hated by this lot human cat-cattle though I say it who shouldn't one's not pop— not as once one was—*loved* I was!'

He heaves up his shoulders, speculative, despondent, while he secures the poultice with string at the back of the neck. His eyes look over the top of the bandage, his mouth asserts itself beneath it.

His immediate following wear a deeply guilty look, all their eyes upon the ground, a scolded class deliciously conscious of papa's wrath, all the world watched slyly through lowered eyelashes. Abruptly he turns on them his task completed, wagging his finger at the end of an outstretched arm.

BAILIFF. 'I wish all of you well from the bottom of my heart! You have if you only knew it the best friend you'll ever have in me! the best friend the most kind and helpful yet what do I get—nothing but insults, I'm held responsible for everything in heaven and earth, why I should like to know—I do my duty that is all any one would think the way some people behaved that I was at the bottom of the whole business! I'm not. Nothing to do. On the contrary I use myself up day in day out in trying to lighten the lot of you chickens. I know things are not ideal God knows—life is life I can't help it—I'm in it too aren't I? I get my nose pulled for my pains and what do you care?'

A murmur of sympathy rises on all hands.

BAILIFF. 'There will be an interval of fifteen minutes,' he announces with indignation: immediately he turns and disappears down the steps at his back.

In his precipitate flat-footed charge he rushes out and enters a tent immediately in the rear of the box, bolting without raising his eyes into the curtained door.

Every one has risen, the greater part clapping their hands as they stand, facing the empty seat of justice as though it were the rule for the principal actor to return and bow. An attendant mounts into the Punch-and-Judy theatre and draws the curtains.

Satters is threatening to swoon again, while Pullman watches the execution-basket being carried away towards the landing-stage.

PULLMAN. 'He's always massaged during the interval, the Bailiff's gone you see, let's stretch our legs shall we?'

The orchestra, assembled upon a trestle platform at the left-hand corner of the enclosure, with a mixed Jewish and negro personnel, begins tuning up on its 'cellos, xylophones, saxophones, kettle-drums, electric pianos, hooters and violins. The negro conductor rises with an imperious immobility, displaying his baton and flashing his eye upon his instrumentalists. The overture to *Don Giovanni* is begun. The minor chord of the opening is interpreted with traditional correctness. After that, first with the connivance, then at the suggestion, and finally in the midst of the furious insistence of the black *chef d'orchestre*, the Mozartian allegro becomes effaced beneath the melting ice-cream glaciers of the 'Blue Rockies', lapped up by the chocolate-cream breakers of the 'Blue Danube', rounded up by a Charleston, rescued momentarily by a jigging violin, lost again in a percussion attack.

The sun-heated tiers of the auditorium are alive with dancing couples. Pullman executes an old-fashioned shimmy, his stick wagging beneath his arm, in front of the drooping and protesting Satters. Nestling couples line the base of the wall outside. Several are picnicking in little pits like ancient shell-holes beyond the semi-circular promenade.

Pullman leads Satters in bourgeois dawdling down the stream of the theatre-queue in retreat, down the scent of the passage-way out of the congested spot where with bursting laughter and the hissing lips of the more elect the throng is evacuated. A fan-shaped maze of moving groups and pairs strolling hither and thither to the sound of the music is before them, without the enceinte. A regular track curves at a distance of a dozen feet corresponding to the circumference of the wall.

Dense centripetal knots or vortices of people collect marginally, beneath the wall or beyond the path, but a march is kept up where the ground is even by an active inquisitive crowd of promenaders passing each other back and forth like the chain of a funicular. The vortices forming beneath the wall are watched from above in the manner of the Eton wall-game by disputatious idlers who interrupt from their vantages with peremptory vetoes, or launch red-herrings into the centre of the scent. Sometimes they successfully disrupt small overheated groups by their unexpected interference at the critical moment. At the heart of the knots a handful of invisible protagonists wrangle intently at close-quarters. The argumentative heat of the interior of the ganglia is shown by sudden spasms at the surface or by a tendency to expand and contract. Occasionally such a compact circular mass or vortex will move bodily in this direction or that, without impairing its close formation; these will drift like icebergs into the fashionable fairway, as a discomfited protagonist seeks to escape or as he who has bested him in the symposium presses upon his heel his clacker at full-cock or as two absent-minded political-thinkers who have become surrounded by devotees or by objectors seek to continue their promenade as they discuss the day's events. There are many smaller circular bodies of a half-dozen figures, prospective nuclei of large groups.

Pullman, Satters upon his arm, stands observing these gatherings with a Sunday sight-seeing nonchalance.

'The Park one would say,' he says. 'Sunday afternoon. Loud-speaker should set up a rival tribune to the one inside to complete the illusion with a red flag at the mast-head, it would be perfect.'

'Shall we go?' says Satters.

They advance, Pullman approaches casually the nearest vortex without looking at the disputants, gazing away at the next-group-but-one as he aloofly listens. This is a chatty charwomanly description of lodge of persons not at their first application.

'Oddmanart!'

'Wasn't you?'

'Not likely!'

'This is my third bloomin turn.'

'Notyor third Bert?'

'Ah!'

'Go on!'

'I got a wrong feelin somar get me?'

'Avyer?'

'Ah! I ain't the goods notyet.'

'Ere Bert was yew ere Bert was yew——'

'I aint Bert Moody not yet not by a long shot get me?'

'Isn't you straight?'

'Nar-boy not proply.'

'Nar isthatright Bert?'

'Asn't yew got that Krooshun feelin?'

'Ah *that wrong feelin* that's right Old Bailey e orlers sez *Hazyew that wrong feelin* e sez.'

'That's right!'

'*Hay wrong feelin* he sez.'

'*That* boy. Not *hay* boy not when e arstyer.'

'Imemer sight berternwot I was timeIfustcumeer orgust that was.'

'Was yew plarrd Bert coz yew adder corfa summud?'

'Ah!'

'Ere yew was sent torspital that's right ain't it boy?'

'Ere e sez yew got summother blokescorf—isthatright what didn't belongovyer?'

'Nomoritdidn't e sez *corfssiz not reckonized* e sez. *Shofer weecorf* e sez *that wouldn't look notarf funnyanall* e sez.'

'Go on!'

'E's a fair nockart e is!'

'Ah e's a proper lad!'

'E dontarf make me larf straighteedont—itzorl Ikun do terkeep a straight face time e's onnat some bloke—yewknow arstin im particklers. E's a fair scream and no mistake!'

'*Dash mi buttons* e sez time ole Ben cummup *wasn't yew batman alongov Sir Spercyscott?—Nar* sez ole Ben *not Sir Spercyscott* e sez—*Yes yew was!* e sez. *E's not requirin a batman* sez e *yerplarr'd!* Ole Ben thorteed gottiz ticket. *But get along in* sez e *I'll see yew gets the job ov batman* e sez *to the Boss wots waitin himpaishunt ter welcumyer* e sez *eeaintarfgotter rotten one!*'

A new knowing voice interjects holding up Bert.

'Is you Mister Moody?'

'The same.'

'I thought you was summar. Glad termeet yew Mister Moody.'

'Owwer yew? Please termeet yew.'

'Pooterthairboy! I'm Ernie Watkins.'

'O ah! therwuz two Watkinses alongov old Arthur. Is yew young Ernie?'

300

A deep egg-like jowl leaden with stupidity, a mouth that is unable to open without appearing to smile, teeth frosty, always an indecent peep; veins and hair pigment making half the face blue while the other half is bilious tan, Mr. Moody it is.

'Time I was alive I wasn'tarf a rummen.'

'I bet yew wazzuntboy nottarf!'

'I didn't summarr seem to fit an that's a fact boy.'

The misfit pauses to allow singularity to sink in.

'We're all a bloomin pitchergallery of misfits wotIkanseeovvit!'

All the misfits laugh, their heads together.

'Ah yerrightboy we izzunt no bloomin hoilpaintins.'

Mr. Moody returns to himself.

'Time I was alive foreIcummeer I felt sameasIdonar I wasn't never proply not wotyewmightcorl yewman.'

'I never thorttitwazzunt nothin trite ome abart to be yewman.'

'Narmor didn't I!'

'Ah I never knew what other fellers meant timetheysez *yewman* as though that was summud to make a song abart.'

'Sweltmebob iffever I could Ernie not same alongasthemthort yewman meant.'

'Yewman! they was too bloomin yewman wotIcudseeorvit.'

'Ah!'

'Yewmantewyewman same as Obailysez yerright boy!'

'Thaywuz tew bloomin yewman ferthiss child ennyar an chance it!'

'Time I was alive I didn't think nothin of being yewman.'

'Yewman devils I corldum though I binner yewmanbeein mesself.'

Mr. Moody intervenes and draws attention to Number One.

'At the works I wazzentnotproply well yew know——'

'Wotworkswuz yewwat Bert?'

'Yewman, they treated yew worsennifyewwazzunt a dog! I opptit.'

'Wazyew a shofer Bert?'

'NottimeIopptit that was aforeIwazzuntter shofer I was only a young feller then.'

'When was that Bert?'

'Time I went tEastmutz.'

'Eastmutz, darn Norththendroad?'

'Ah cornerer Seddonrow I couldn't stick it.'

'Wazzittwurssenwot it is ere?'

'This is Evven terwotittwazzunt alongov Eastmutz.'

'Arkatold Bert! ere! ain't this Evven Bert where we is?'

'It ain't Evven nottyet, there a fat lot too many eryewblokes eerabarts for thiseer not to be Evven!'

'Wot price yesself Bert: ere! wot price yewboy?'

'I'll grow wings soonerenwotyew will boy.'

'Chance'd be a fine thing!'

'Ah! yerright!'

'Ere! Stan! there ain't nothin like avin a good opinion ovyesself. Berterloppitt alongov is bloomin wings wunnuvtheezeer bloomin days.'

'Ah old Bert ain't arfbackwardincominforward wiv is fevver racket.'

'I carntarffancy old Bert wiv wings!'

'Ere! do we avv wings, no isthatright do we avv wings saymazwotsumblokesez we as?'

'*Wings* yuss—yoolavver fat lot ov wings!'

Mr. Moody expresses boredom with the idea of wings with a gesture of dismissal and returns to himself.

'I sez tertherboss *Mister Eastmutz* I sez *fore yew fires me* sez I *Imegoin-toppitt* I sez. *Fire yew* e sez *yew must be mad!—Well I'm sorry Moody* Mr. Eastmutz sez. *Az yew summud aginsuss* e arst me. An I tells im straight. *I'm a square peg in a rarndole* I sez. *Since I bin ere start to finish I bin the oddmannart.*'

The vortex of workers murmurs approval.

'I bin the *oddmannart!*'

At odd-man-out he proudly challenges the rest with his aristocratic definition *per se* but of the Moody mint.

'Is you like that saymazyewsez Bert narboy?'

'Which is that Chorlie?'

'Saymazwot yew sez is yew yewknow wrong somar?'

'Imebetterenwot I used to be,' Mr. Moody replies with caution: 'Betterenwot I was time I come ere. Fore I come ere timeIwasalive me and my missis wazzavin argument —my missis she arstme where I bin. I start kiddiner yewknow I sez *Tomorrer* I sez *I was upalongov old Chorlie Coats* kiddinoverron. I let on I clean forgot where I bin time-she-arst, the forenoon thermonday that was, wotwuz yestezlike timeweeadd argument. I let on termorrer wuzyestezlike. The missis wasn't rattynotarff, she sez *Yor barmy*. After we'd argued where I bintomorrer oradduntbin or the day after next—we didn't arf goattitt-ammerantongs berleeve me!—I wasn't goin to letton I was kiddin not-then catchme! she sez waysheadd timewe-wasfirst manandwife—she was proper ot stuff wasmy-Addie—*I dunno* she sez *I someow feels timeannanother same assif I'd got somethin left over timeImarried yew.* Somethin left over yes Ishouldsaysso I sez. I diderntarf givver one onner bleedin jaw anchornsitt, yewknow a proper beauty!'

He shows his frost-giant's dental glaciers in white frozen mirth, the blow with its red blood was a flower—his missis.

'I lay theolewoman didderntarf cop it Bert timeshesez wotyewwaz leff-tover!

'Nottarf! ForeIcumeer timeIwasalive there wasn't nothin used to rile me sameazthat. All you bloominwelladd-tersay was *oddmanart* an I wentorfther deepend proper.'

303

'Go on!'

'I wanted to be same as the rest—yewknow.'

'Acorseyewbloominwelldid same as orlovuss time we was——'

'Ah!'

'Ittaintarf comic come terthinkovvit, eeritzther bloomin opper-zite, yew dontbloominwell want to be sameazeverybody.'

'Ah! Itztheruvverway rarnd alongovvus ain't it.'

'Yew dont summarmind wot yew are do yer? serlongazyer yer bloomin self it don't matteroo yer bloominwell are!'

'Ah yerrightboy there!'

They all chortle maliciously into their little vortex of confidences.

'Time I firstcummeer I come blame near settinerbart Obailey straight I did—arrwuz I terknow? e sez slappart yewknow sameaseeorllers do, e dont care what e sezter hennyone! same as people addbin intinov orl me bloomin life!'

'Wotwas that boy?'

'*Oddmanart!*'

'Ah!'

'Ah! It donttarf come funnylike first go-off.'

'When a bloke stand, the reantellsyeryer only her bloomin freak ah thatswotitcometo donttit well! I arst yer!'

'Yew gets yerbloominbackupproper yew do!'

'Nottarf!'

Bert is held up a second time by the same person as before.

'Wasn't yew sentorft orspital fer back-chat sameasthem gents corls it? Eer didn't the ole man say yor tongue-erd-be therbetterfer meddicurl er tenshun?'

Mr. Moody claps a quick eye upon this speaker.

'Nar-boy, not timeIfirstcummeer I didn't go there not

304

straightorfboy—that was orgust. I nevversed nuffin, I gone there abartter narsty ackin corf, see.'

'I thortIseeyew——'

'Nar-boy, yew got it mixed!'

'Nar isthatright, wasn't yew sent away for-why you sez *Slordstrewth if I azzuntgottinterrer bloomin Casey Court* timeyewfirst see Ole Bailey?'

'Nar-boy!' Mr. Moody reiterates still more firmly and fleshes his hawk's eye of the *odd-man-out* in the other's softer jelly. 'Yew're up the pole, that was ole Jackpilsher wotcopptit timeyewthinkinnon my son, that was ole Jack.'

The new man with the long memory has a barneyesque beau-catcher lolling from under a dazzling cap never worn out of sound of Bow Bells. He stands his ground.

'You sez—*If this ain't a bloomin Casey Court.*'

'I nevveraddnoargument no that'sright,' Mr. Moody then says. 'When e sez *Moody yewre a hodd feller!*—odd e sez *a odd-feller*, I'm not goin to say starttorf I adderntarffer mind nottertell the old barstard orf but there's somfin yewknow wotmakesyew feel yew wouldn't bloomin well mind what e sez time e arstyew anyfin—I flushessup like a two-year-old time I earrim say *hodd.* But yew cant bloominwellelp yesself, e explain it orl termee same as yewmight to a bloomin kid—yewknow. E sez *Bert, Hodds best* e sez *Haint hi hodd?* Hand hi hansers *yus* I sez *Hodds wot yewwiz Milord* sez I *as one man to another.*'

'E's a proper gent e is annomistake.'

'Ah! wunnerthebest.'

'What did he explain, I don't exactly follow you, was he explaining to you about the odd man out, or the persons who were not quite right yet—not quite *it* as you put it?'

Mr. Moody gazes at Pullman with the full force of his frost-giant's teeth. Then he says:

'Maybe yew're one of them—eer same as the others old lad! Is yew all right yet, I should find out if I was yew jestter make sure. Good harftermornin don't let me detain yew.'

The vortex laughs in hoarse chorus after their frost-giant leader: Pullman removes his nose from it delicately, with a flicker of fierce additional disdain as he moves on, drawing Satters with him. As they are repassing the wicket leading to the court he stops.

Two greybeards wag round dry parrot-tongues striking up upon gaping gums in dulled toothless palaver. Foggy eyes that are sick opals move behind spectacles, smouldering at the sound of the mighty words uttered in the feeble mouths.

'I heard a man say he had seen the Demiurge.'

'Indeed?'

'The fellow said he was extremely fat, stretched out naked upon a cube of ice his limbs following the figure of a cross composed of ashes—like Louis le Gros dying.'

'I heard he always stood I forget who told me. If he sat down he would die it appeared—or at least that is what he believes.'

'I have been told that his dreams are terrible. One man credibly informed me that a herd of celestial horses trampling on his chest produced earthquakes felt in the most susceptible spots of the earth's crust. I was in one once, the mountains moved about like frightened men, the sky became like chocolate spilt all over with vermilion veins.'

'Really! It must have been not unlike an inferno!'

'It was in Hell, as a matter of fact—of course it was, how stupid of me! what a fool you must think me! The infernal region is very sensitive to the sleep of the Demiurge they say,' the first elder croaks, his eyes watering and hands trembling with vexation at his forgetfulness.

A small and shabby inquisitive freelance, polt-footed,

a newspaper the Camp Special stuck in a jacket-pocket furnishing his hip, leans against the greybeards occupying a narrow space left by Pullman. He drinks in their discourse with his hungry marvel-loving ear. Mopping his face he turns to an attendant standing beside the gate, hands upon buttocks and legs planted firmly apart.

'This climate's a fair knock-out, ain't it guvnor? Ere! is that right—the Demiurge passes 'is time on a block of ice?'

'The Deity is not usually referred to as the demiurge here, we have nothing to do with gnostic systems nor platonizing heresies,' the man replies loftily, looking over the questioner's head.

'Sorry my mistake an all that boss: the old gent ere sez a party what e knows——' the small man turns apologetically in the direction of the wagging beards from which the word DEMIURGE is still heard issuing.

'You'd want something to do if you listened to half the things you heard hereabout my son. The Deity isn't a fish, you'd think he was to hear some of them talk,' the official pursues looking at Pullman, who listens closely, his eye fixed upon the Vortex of Elders. 'The pose known in Buddhist temple technique as *adamantine* is the most common to the Deity. He possesses a constitution of iron.'

With an expression of keen awe the small and shabby wandering listener-in turns to Pullman and whispers:

'E's a defrocked priest! No, that's right!' He nods his head energetically indicating the attendant. Pullman takes Satters by the arm and gently tugs him out of the Vortex of Elders into which he shows a tendency to sink.

Four dark figures in the tattered Græco-Roman livery of Hyperides, bearing a rough litter, with flying garments come hurrying through the crowds. They are challenged by the attendant at the wicket.

'What've you got there?' he asks.

'The litter of Hyperides. Make way!'

'Who is Hyperides?'

'Let us pass!'

Pullman, stopping a moment to observe this event, goes forward among the outer promenading crowds with Satters. He has removed his hand from his companion's arm and in reverse arrangement the big trembling forepaw of his nervous pal has slipped into its place working with sensitive spasms like a dank sucker upon his sleeve, wet at the spot where it is accustomed to lie immediately beneath the stick.

Many of those they pass are also arm-in-arm, immersed it appears, in a similar relationship, detachable masterspirit with rooster strut and bashful satellite, one who speaks bold and high, the other retiring and low with a sideway gazelle-like glitter of the eye. Both usually possess painted lips, but around the paint of the one is often a delicate whisker. Up till now Pullman has wandered alone amongst them as he went through the Rye. Several recognize him: these as he passes whisper and smile. Pullman steps briskly coolly and confidently, gazing about him, Satters drooping with the signs of distress of a wife at the termination of a cross-Channel passage.

The more brilliant bands of Bailiffites are gathered *en fête* near the orchestra in a close dancing mass. The two turn as they approach that violent vortex. A number of solitary mincing figures in addition to the couples pass them in a willowy one-step, and as each lonely devotee of purple passion (reverse-order, but fanatical pedant of the passionate canon) glides past with a rigid swimming gait or a rakish high-frequency trip, he cocks a brazen glittering abandoned eye upon the respectable spouses. Pullman's pal wilts beneath these disastrous solitary eyes and the shy hand has a spasm on his arm of perspiring bashfulness or secret temper.

Those they meet in the same situation as themselves are from every class and of all ages but tend to a uniformity that is strictly *passionel* and that confers upon them the cachet of a social class. Their class-life dominates them so that their responses to alien stimulus would be impersonal class-responses, or such as are proper to their prescribed function. Thus some would respond as the aggressive squaw-men that are highly intelligent, armed to the teeth with the tongue mainly but very fierce, and some as the female of the species, either adventurous or domesticated, whose fierceness is variable, as shy as doves or as bold as musk-rats, but in every instance responding truly as disciplined units of the great and prosperous hominy class. Or the use of the Proustian analogy would substitute race for class, and then it would be the hominy race which would seem to have the aloof and clannish habits of the romany race (the Proustian has it as the Jewish) with the relationship of *pen* and *pal* of *rai* and *rom*, with a system of hostile or self-protective practices at the expense of the alien world and a proselytizing ardour whetted with the glamours of martyrdom.

But having passed through the crucibles of salvation what is salved is different in this novel perpetuity. Over all, from the oldest powdered rake to the most elementary postulant, is an eager super-feminine youthfulness, and its salvage-value merges with its earthly one. For a canon there is the characteristic group of attributes of some imaginary adolescent at the acme of the hominy love-life. The *immature* is of the essence of this canon, and in the secret and painful urge to conform to the ideal of this passion-life, exaggeration must occur it seems still more under these abnormal salvational conditions. So here it is often simply in a diminutiveness that the desired end is achieved, and many almost dwarfish shapes swagger in their inverted scale-snobbery, proudly microscopic, accompanied by adoring monsters of Falstaffian proportions, whose immense and waggling hips accompany these tiny squires-of-dames or old-washerwoman's darlings, or pass

309

as the pocket males (on the principle of the epeira) of these mountainous spinsters.

The immaturity of the masks that throng the promenade is in full conformity with the canon of the passion-life as opposed to the human or classical canon, but their youthfulness is generally that of a moron in later life or of the faces of elderly dwarfs. Upon an adolescent ossature they are lined and puckered. But these wizened skins of an ageing gossip-column Lido-tart with lifted face and gorgon-eye (stiffened with an illusive masculinity of mind and body) are doctored with paste and pigment, which is obtained by them at the central canteen, where appellants are encouraged to improve upon nature or to put finishing touches to the chemical processes of mummification of the salvage-system here at work.

Some, since dogs are barred, drag at the end of a lead toy Sealyhams and Blenheim Spaniels, which can be obtained on application. Some carry Teddy-bears which they regard as mascots and play with when they think they are observed. Others support small Japanese parasols, canted against the sun.

A sprinkling of big rough-diamonds adds splendour to the scene, big middle-aged pairs in languishing embrace. These are the more loftily bohemian, their attitude is suggestive of cosy though not vulgarly large private incomes and the presence of the blood of great commercial undertakings in their veins—they are those who have dwelt in studios *d'outre tombe*, and in a bold studio-embrace in exciting pullovers or expressive plain jerseys, with pipe stuck mannishly in painted lips, they advance bareheaded, Byron-collared Adam's-appled and usually with a natural tonsure. Amongst these are to be remarked most of the richest of the great composers the great painters and the great dramatists who have in terrestrial life been the chief ornament of artistic circles, alternated with each other in the gossip-column, and occupied the largest ateliers in the principal European capitals. This is the true nobility, but there is also a sort of—Vielle Noblesse of Gomorrah, generally stationed in the midst of faithful retainers: these are people who have been famous propagandists and great fighters for votes for Homos, for the Homo's Rights (*My Passion right or wrong!* as a slogan for example) or just for Freedom.

Occupying more space than their importance warrants, on account of their matronly proportions, are the stock panting soss-paunched *Aunt-Marys* linked with dapper half-bred Middle-West midinettes, flappers from Innsbruck or Edinburgh or even Parisian counterfeiters—with one eye upon Loeb and Leopold and the other upon Nick Carter. Then there are the Proustite academic pairs who have veiled lids and are slyly superior, men and women of few words, exchanging brilliant confidences with their sly eloquent speaking eyes, in mercurial deaf-and-dumb show lifted above their vulgarer brothers.

The great majority of the aspirants for salvation not conforming to this canon are gathered in the vortices, but some promenade, and there are the classes and groups either occupational or social, but non-sex, that are met each with its archetype or leader, queen-bee or bellwether.

A thousand morse-messages are flashed into Pullman's arm at the contact of this world by Satters, but in him there is not a vibration. His response is an absolute denial of the existence of anything abnormal, within and without, and they advance in leisurely step a half-dozen times from one extremity to the other of the *paseo* without a word passing, until now they are returning to the riverine limit, the opposite to that occupied by the orchestra.

A crowd of men arriving from the waterside approaches in military formation, bearing arms. It is a family of gladiators, a hundred strong. Swaggering lazily in front

311

of them is a gigantic bareheaded lanista. The gladiators are mixed retiarii Thracians and Mirmillones. They advance with a clatter of shields greaves and other accoutrements, the retiarii in front, the *fascino* on their shoulder, with their nets gathered upon the opposite forearm.

'What on earth have *they* come for?' Pullman exclaims sighting this invasion. 'Evidently they expect a rough house.'

Satters' massive feminine hand has a convulsion and stickily clings while his lips go to pieces as he expresses his fear.

'Oh do let's go away, Pulley I do feel so frightened. What's the use of stopping here? Must we stop *is it* necessary? What for? you know it will all be the same we've seen all we want to, it's beastly, do let's go now!'

With masculine sang-froid Pullman examines the menacing fish-crests of the Mirmillones, casts a critical eye upon the galeri and man-nets of the retiarii.

'They're Baltic roughs, that one with the nose missing is a Gaul, what should you say? Yes, Gaul. His wife fought by his side like a windmill but he surrendered when she wasn't looking, he daren't go back! He prefers to face the wild beasts of Heaven and Hell what do you think?'

'I think the sooner we beat it the better I've had enough for one day, thank you!'

Pullman laughs appreciatively at the canine conceit of the lanista and turns on his heel, dragging Satters quickly about.

The music stops in a fierce brassy climax. The flag which has been hauled down during the interval is now run up by one of the plugchewing blow-hards in charge of the bunting. The belch of the stunning trumpet occurs. Every one makes for the entrance wicket with arch-scampering roguish crushing and pushing, or they swarm up the wall with delicate screams, in amorous ballistics.

'Hyperides Polemon Agatharcus Alectryon!' a half-dozen aggressive armletted commissaries fiercely exclaim, mouthing nasally the pompous Greek.

'Hyperides!' a solitary giant runner roars. 'Hyper-*ride*-es!'

Two men rush out of the booth of the Protonotary with the incontinent gallop of newsboys, flourishing broadsheets and vociferating:

'Gorgias Terpsion Parrhasius Hormogenes Photius Neobulus Planudes Hippias Meidon Hegemon Polynices Iophon!'

Wiping his mouth with a stealthy haste the Bailiff is observed plunging from the door of the bath-house towards the rear of his box, which shakes as he enters it. He appears radiant with expectation with winks and grimaces of understanding for his favourites.

More commissaries issue in swift succession from the booth.

COMMISSARIES. {'Evenor Evaemon Ecphantes Evenus Eteocles!'
'Mestor Mneseus Meton Mermerus Medon Mumactes Milichius!'

BAILIFF (frictioning his hands in excited delight). 'Talk about a heaven fit for heroes to live in! we shall have to provide palaces for a pantheon!'

A stately town-crier holding a galley-sheet begins reading from the top in a deliberate boom:

COMMISSARY. 'Epaphus. Battus. Biton. Otus. Alcman. Porus. Magus. Ops. Epops. Pops. Thon. Boethus. Medon. Bumps. Bopp. Pott. As. Tar. Kar. Da. Dada. Ma. Pa. Thor. Har. Acca. Hos. Finn. Nidhogg. Fogolt. Lodhus. Haco. Don. Got.'

The Bailiff places his fingers to his ears: the pivetta

313

buried in the pulp of his mouth he utters tremulous
thunders of consternation. None acknowledge the sum-
monses. His fashionable friends echo in every key the
vocables exploding from the blunderbusses of the mouths
of the ushers and runners. A long wail of *Pa-pa!* goes up
and a super *Da* is syncopated and trumpeted by a hundred
contralto throats.

BAILIFF. 'Come along my glottogonic geese tumble to it
shift your kitties! Where is Acca? What has happened
to Pops? Look lively Lod-huss! Bopp and Pott my
panting worthies you're backward in coming forward!
You're blackballed Bumps—I refuse to have any
Bumps.'

COMMISSARY. 'Bromios!'

No one appears at the name to say *Here sir!*

BAILIFF (mysteriously whispering). 'He is not there!'

Pullman stands in his place looking keenly on every
hand. The first shouting ushers have gone back empty-
handed into the booth and return with further files:
names and more names stream out of their distended
mouths as they turn their faces hither and thither, hurrying feverishly about expecting their owners to spring up
and respond.

COMMISSARIES.
'Aspalion Autochthon Atlas Ampheres
Androtion Adrastus Aristomenes
Agoracritus Apollodorus.'
'Scopas Simmias Simonides Stratonius
Strato Sumerledes Sigemund Skar-
phedin Sigurtrudinsteinar Sindri
Snotra Skilfinger Skunk.'
'Timocharis Telamon Thases Themis-
tocles Timotheus Tanngniost Tann-
grisnir.'

314

The Bailiff with ever-rising excitement thrusts out his head the lips moving restlessly around his purring comforter while his eyes dart among the undergrowth of his expectant passionate backing as if looking for something mislaid but never indulging his eyes with the spectacle of the hostile clan, whose names are constantly repeated, now at full strength. Clucking in his noisy mouthpiece he beckons a runner who springs towards him and stands trembling like a tense bow.

BAILIFF. 'The procurator! Where is he? Send me the procurator.'

RUNNER. 'The lanista, excellency?'

BAILIFF. 'The procurator, schweinhund!'

RUNNER. 'Pardon, excellency! He is here! The procurator! The procurator!'

The master of the gladiatorial 'family' appears in the passage-way: he hastens with a head-cocker's beefy strut towards the Bailiff with whom he holds a whispered conversation, which the nearest assistants attempt to overhear, then he withdraws, rejoining his gladiators, who remain outside. The bands of heiduks and of blacks heavily reinforced draw up in a line on either side of the magistrate.

Without individual recognition of the names that are bellowed at them the followers of Hyperides, to the number of several hundred, push their way roughly through the banks of spectators and gather in the court, while Hyperides himself, limping, is assisted down by a group of dark-robed stalwart postulants, who, shouting angrily, thrust violently aside the clusters of people obstructing their way. The litter appears in the parados: as it reaches the wicket, they lift Hyperides upon it, and he is borne into the centre of the enclosure. A tall young man in a tattered blue smock-frock trimmed with black wool, a Phrygian

mitre and hessian boots, steps out and sounds a prolonged full-blooded flourish that is at once the plaint of
the stag the gaiety of the huntsman and the mournful
distances of the aisles of the forest. As he performs his
companions shout repeatedly

'Long live Diana!'

Thereupon some of those nearest to Hyperides violently
seize the shafts of the litter and start in procession around
the enclosure, while others, hurrying beside and before
them, apostrophize the spectators as they pass.

All the Hyperideans affect some variety of the Greek
investment; they have pelisses of black wool, sweeping
black cloaks of canvas or linen; some wear a workman's
pilos or dogskin kune, there are many different shapes of
the more elegant and languishing petasus, the unequal
brim drawn down over the ear and tied beneath the chin:
motor-helmets with buttoned cheekpieces surmount a
leather thorax and a chiton. Several are naked except for
girdles: these are the more athletic. There is also an intermixture of Norse head-dress, where the Phrygian mitre
merges in the piratic cap of Edda-legend, the Greek
helmet with lophos of horsehair combining with the
Scandinavian horned helmet. When resting they lean
generally upon staves or shepherd's crooks: when they
hurry about they are seen with the trailing black wings
of their cloaks scudding in their wake. They cover the
ground with great rapidity, with the rush of the intent
supers of a highly-disciplined Miracle. At the slightest
hint they take fire, in everything over-zealous, they leap
into every suggestion of a breach, theirs is the Legion of
Lost-Causes, they have the tattered grandeur of an
Imperial Guard at its Waterloo, a cambronnesque *The
Guards die, they do not surrender* is painted all over them,
they advertise doom in all their attitudes with a heroic
rejoicing.

As the Hyperideans deploy and open their ceremonial

march the gladiatorial family push into the gangway which, standing three-deep, they block, withdrawing as the last of the demonstrators comes to a standstill.

Satters remains seated but Pullman, like many of the appellants placed at some distance from the arena, is standing.

'The Lord Mayor's Show has started,' Pullman sneers: he sits down, the pretentious sightseer, beside his contemptuous better-half, who squats in the crush hot bothered but fallen flouch, unbuttoned and unbuckramed, wrestling with the Victorian vapours borrowed from the obsolete *fair-sex*, fanning a large red face.

'Are you hot?' Pullman's hand passes a bare second upon the dewy top of Satters' in elusive alightal.

'Not more than usual,' replies Satters with the lofty resignation of the Anglo-Saxon matron, suffering the callous puerilities of her lord and master.

'That circus is an awful bore it's all dick and worry for everybody.'

'Why did we stop, we needn't have stopped here need we?'

'Look at them! What a pompous clown the fellow is! Really!'

'What are they doing?'

Satters is bewildered by the wild bustle: he takes a peep to reassure himself.

'Nothing. Absolutely nothing, except talk, I wish the Bailiff would clear them all out!'

'Perhaps he will.'

'He may mean to at last, it looks as though he meant to do something this time.'

The Hyperideans rush with heavy shouting round and round the enclosure, their manœuvre suggestive of the passage of a circular stage-army organized to represent a colossal rout. The litter of Hyperides passes and repasses beneath the Bailiff's box.

A giant with a metal swastika sewn upon his breast, who leads the unpolished horde, bellows:

'This is your last chance to join our great revolution! to join up—our great revolution!'

FOLLOWERS OF HYPERIDES.

'Down on your knees! Down, fools, lost souls, cardboard-men, sticks, fuel for the World-bonfire, fashionplates, pseudo-niggers, poor white trash, bought and fooled, Nanmen and Pipsqueaks.'

'This is the last Aryan hero that you are seeing! Salute him!'

'This is Hyperides! Do not you know Hyperides? Yes Hyperides!'

A furious hand shoots out over the fence and sweeps three hats off covered heads.

Squinting in an intensity of impotent anguish, the followers of Hyperides thrust their bearded muzzles out at the rows of faces beneath them as they pass, admonishing collectively their fellow-appellants.

A lean and rushing shape, the Cassandra of the Circus, clamours mechanically:

'Delenda est Europa!'

In a mooing throaty voice one denounces:

'Fools! Take off your sly smirk! It is *you* who still are to be butchered.—Sheep!'

These proceedings are surveyed from above by the smiling Bailiff with a stolid satisfaction, his staff hugged in the canonical Punch-like position proper to puppet-sleeves with no arms inside or hands to direct it.

'They think they're still alive!' he remarks to the black poll of his negro, which he pats, gurgling pigeon-fashion in his pivetta. 'His leg's bad to-day.' He refers to Hyperides, whom he notices wearily dragging himself from one position to another to retain his balance as he is swept around by eight impetuous brown-limbed gymnasts.

'And still as you go
Tread on your toe!'

is chanted by the Bailiff as he watches.

The chahut completes its fifteenth revolution, the litter is set down at right-angles to the justice-box, its forward shafts directly beneath the figure of the magistrate. The remainder of the Hyperideans throng into the arena contemptuously pushing aside people not of their sect who are in their path.

The Bailiff remains in the best of good humours. To a favourite appellant, who is leaning over the fence and exchanging amused glances of understanding with him, he remarks:

'I had a man here yesterday from the Appalachian Mountains, he tried to talk to me in yiddish of the time of Elizabeth! I sent him over to our Berlitz for a spell.'

Pullman on his legs again crossly quizzes the school of Hyperides.

'Their fancy-dresses don't look violently expensive do they? nor archæologically speaking above reproach!'

'Some of them seem to have dispensed——' Satters' eyes are fixed in bovine expressionless trance upon the naked ones. They stalk athletically, massaging their flanks, stroking their biceps and surveying aloofly the populo.

The sea of rough hair and red and white flesh and of every hue from cinnamon to vermilion now beneath the bema ranges itself slowly into two or three menacing stationary waves. The small group of the more immediate disciples of Hyperides converse at the side of the litter.

Hyperides from his lectal seat, lying in shabby state, gazes away without change of expression. His forearm is still balanced upon his right knee, which is raised, while the other leg flows out to his pointed sandalled foot.

With the gesture of the auctioneer the Bailiff raises his truncheon and then loudly raps, chuckling in appealing roulades of alarm and expostulation with his pivetta, the mouthpiece thrust out, his head down, forehead furrowed—in the butting position, but that of a peevish feminine bull, threatening a charge if not obeyed by its moon-calves in the absence of ma-ma. Roaring 'Silence!' the commissaries and runners start forward. The trumpeter blows his one blast. The Hyperidean clan is not yet quiet.

Leaning out of his box and speaking in his most civilized nasal and high-pitched voice, the Bailiff opens the sitting.

BAILIFF. 'Gentlemen! As you see we are about to make the attempt to dispose of this heretical faction, which has established itself in the heart of this little community of ours, composed of those among you who, on the threshold of a glorious existence, have been misled by the subversive utterances of that man styling himself Hyperides, that enormous offender.'

A mass of wild faces is now turned towards him and a constant rain of words rises from their grimacing lips. Moulded into every shape of insult, these grin-twisted mouths, ragged spits of teeth or white insulting rows flashing frosty mockery of menace, bristling fringes of hair, eyes that wink dark sub-rosa messages with juicy hints of shameful secrets that must-go-no-further, or that squint as if to squirt contempt, or glare their black light with the impact of a high-power salvage hose, express every variety of mocking hatred.

At the name *Hyperides* one starts forward furiously shaking an immense pistol-like hand at the Bailiff.

'Liar! What is your filthy name? Answer!'

'Answer! Answer!' a hundred voices bay at him.

HYPERIDEANS.	'Your name! Name yourself! Give us your *name*!'
	'Baphomet!'
	'Hell-bird!'
	'Swine-rose!'
	'What is it? Answer!'
	'Name yourself or be named by us!'
	'Urine and cinders! Are your bones wood?'

'Hang your three golden balls out pop-eye! You have forgotten that ornament!' with a rich schoolboy vehemence an Irish voice exclaims.

Polemon steps forward and pacifies them.

POLEMON. 'Let him speak. Let us hear and confute him. Do not let him say we gagged him.'

The faces relapse into a ferocious dumbness. Malevolent leeches, a crowd of eyes hang upon the Bailiff's. The upturned disks with an intensity of invitation offer themselves as mirrors to him, each one a grimacing reflection. As for the Bailiff, he is beside himself: his spirit dances upon this mesmeric sea, he bobs buoyantly in his appointed box. He is the arch trick-performer, the ideal Impostor of Impostors, surrounded by his most sensational properties: a star-turn is in preparation, he continually winks at his assistants, throwing his cap at the Protonotary to attract his attention, tickling Jackie in the neck to make him grin, then half hiding behind his curtain peeping with a ravished splutter when spotted. But according to Bailiff-canon, on the principle of rigid juxtapositions, he turns almost in full state upon the audience at large without transition, decorous in a twinkle, and abruptly thunders:

'This virulent faction has become an intolerable scandal!

I have winked at it! I—have—winked—at—it!' he howls
above the tumult. 'I can wink at it no longer!' He
thumps the ledge with his fist, squealing with his pivetta:
then an answering grin upon his face, leaning out towards the interrupting throngs, he shrieks spluttering
with crazy mirth.

BAILIFF. 'Silence! Silence! I say *silence*!'

SEVERAL
VOICES OF
HYPERIDEANS.

'It says silence! The master-puppet
commands!'
'Whom are you addressing? Snout!'
'Silence for the arch love-bird who
would coo!'
'Let us hearken to the dove of peace!'
'Silence for the little Baphomet who
wishes to perform to us. *Oh silence!*'

Upon the audience a hush of alarm and uncertainty
has fallen. It is separated from its Bailiff by a turbulent
sea of factious figures who seem able to master this dancing deformity in the seat of justice or who at least are not
mastered, and who blot out everything with their vitality.
The Bailiff watches his stocks fall with an evil contemptuous scowl: then addressing the main body of the
audience over the heads of the hellenizing crowd, he
trumpets with the full pomp of the Living Punch:

BAILIFF. 'Gentlemen! You see the kind of persons we
have to deal with. They are a violent and lawless sect
who would stick at nothing to secure the success of
their wild theories. Do not be intimidated, I will see
that no harm comes to you, I am your trusty shepherd
and I will defend your ideals to the last breath in my
body. We have an ample force here devoted to the
cause of law and order to cope with any threat to the
Freedom of the Individual. I shall not hesitate to use

it if necessary. Were we not provided with these guards
—whose presence I regret as much as any one can if
not more for on principle I loathe coercion—we should
as you see be torn limb from limb by these ruffians.
I am taking no chances—for you for you not for myself, for myself I care little enough I can promise you.'

He ends on a quavering flourish of throaty pathos. On
all sides the Hyperidean standing-crowd apostrophizes the
neutral seated-crowd behind it. The voice of the Bailiff
is completely drowned at the end in the turmoil.

FOLLOWERS
OF
HYPERIDES.

'Fool! Examine what he is saying to you.
Consider what he *does*! They are
words that he is using now, *words*,
they are not true words, are all words
true that are spoken? his are not: they
are never true with him. All his
words are false.'

'It is not music you are listening to.
Take his words and weigh them, you
will find they are all short weight!'

'He is the arch-impostor. He has usurped
that throne of justice. He does not
know what justice means!'

'Enrol yourself, come to Hyperides, he
alone can show you the secret of this
felon's trick!'

'Shut your eyes and open your mouth!
The jolly lollypop! *Freedom!* Min-
now! Did you hear him say *Individual*, did you hear him when he
said *Freedom*? Blockhead!'

BAILIFF (screaming down at Hyperides). 'To-morrow I
will issue a writ of capias against you, sir!'

Hyperides lies in his former attitude his profile towards

323

the Bailiff. Polemon his adjutant starts out in front of the insurgent crowd with both hands raised, palms to the front. When the voices are become less clamorous, he exclaims:

POLEMON. 'Listen to him. Let him speak.'
SEVERAL VOICES. 'Yes let the puppet speak!'

In a relative calm, the ring of grinning masks beneath him blasting away in the silence, responding sentence by sentence in scorifying dumb-show, the Bailiff resumes his address. Sometimes a hand shoots out and points at him dumbly retorting to something said. Like the effect of a nomad wind travelling a forest with each sentence some section of the crowd is stirred and murmurs.

BAILIFF. 'And these are the people, gentlemen, who would convict me of brutality! I am a devil for this sodality of angels! To believe them there is nothing of which I am not capable. Well, you must judge between us. These are no ordinary revolutionaries, mark you, gentlemen: this revolt is not aimed at an earthly and therefore fallible power but at the infallible throne of the one and only God. Summoned to His presence these amazing subjects refuse, and stop without the gate. And then they call in question His fallibility and very existence, describing the whole scene in which we find ourselves as an effect of magic—and I become a Circe for these *swine*!'

There is a rushing gasp, the trigger snaps, a roar of protest is released.

HYPERIDEANS.
$$\begin{cases} \text{'Swine!'} \\ \text{'Swine!'} \\ \text{'Swine!'} \\ \text{'Swine!'} \end{cases}$$

324

Tempered and timid applause among the second audience is completely eclipsed.

Polemon advances in front of the litter, and faces the Bailiff.

POLEMON. 'Will you withdraw that epithet?'
BAILIFF. 'Which?'
POLEMON. 'The one you have just used.'
BAILIFF. 'In connection with Circe?'
POLEMON. 'Yes.'
BAILIFF. 'But what else could I say consistently with my image? You will admit, Polemon, that that is a very irrational request! It is quite clear that "swine" was used to signify the transfigured followers of Ulysses, not those of Hyperides.'

Polemon gives a short nod and resumes his place at the side of the litter.

A fresh but milder roar occurs as he retires.

BAILIFF. 'These subversive doubters call in question *everything*! All that marvellous edifice of Progress, those prodigies of Science, which have provided us moderns with a new soul and a consciousness different from that of any other epoch, that have borne man to a pinnacle of knowledge and of power——'
   (He licks his lips as though there were a great 'sexual appeal' in the word 'power' and gazes fiercely round the audience, allowing his eyes to rest especially upon the goggling round-mouthed countenances of the youngest, smallest, seated listeners, to his immediate left: then he continues.)
   '—all that staggering scientific advance that has made modern man into a god, almost, dominating nature in a manner beyond the wildest dreams of Antiquity—all *that* these hot-heads you see here deny

325

and call in question excited to insurgent zeal by that
man who styles himself Hyperides——'

An indignant roar leaps up at once at the name. After a
few minutes the young priest-like figure of Polemon steps
forward. With a slow cool histrionic emphasis his Ulster
accent steadily advances:

POLEMON. 'I think, sir, if you could refrain from using
the name of our beloved master that that would be an
advantage. You would not then be exposed to inter-
ruptions which, you must agree, are provoked in any
case by your manner.'

BAILIFF. 'I cannot be dictated to by you Polemon. Other
people beside you and your friends have claims on me
in this assembly. I will not be gagged.'

The Bailiff turns to the audience a blood-reddened
'fighting-face'; the glands of combat advertised in the
Bulldog Drummond out-thrust of the head, locked-to in
nutcracker toothless death-grip—veteran of a thousand
sham-fights upon dire forensic or financial fields—but
above all in the wennish cyst of the nuque bloated in
verbal battle, while the eyes flash righteousness.

BAILIFF (throatily inflating various parts of his person).
'No man, no nor yet any devil, shall gag me!'

POLEMON. 'That is not true, we do not gag you.'

BAILIFF. 'They refer to this man as you notice as a "beloved master", these pagans under the very Eye of the
One and Only One set up their cults! Observe them
hark back to their saints and heroes under the very
shadow of that great Unity, the Omnipotent Abstraction in person, in person set up here by us as an immense awful magnet to engulf all souls to Itself. They
carry on just as though we had not set up and so on.
At last I have summoned all these disturbers of the
peace here today to account for their disobedience. It

will be a Day of Judgment for them! But I shall not be
their judge—you shall be. Or we will judge them together: this same wheel of mischief has been set turning and we'll keep it running! The nature of their
revolutionary heresy you are about to hear from their
own lips: we will judge those heretical opinions in the
light of our ideas. If these cynics in open debate receive
the stamp of popular allowance, I withdraw, but I
know they will not.'

(Applause from the seated audience, mock counter-
applause from Hyperideans.)

BAILIFF. 'We are challenged by these savages upon the
ground that they are the true children of the Hellenic
Culture (though far more contentious even than their
prototypes) and upon the ground that we are not. Let's
cocker-up our answer under their noses and forestall
them! *Our acts our angels are*—well we have an angelic
host of absolutely fresh ideas, we'll marshal it. Mon-
tanus peace be with him called me unpneumatic, watch
me and judge of his error. What ideas have we? Whatever they may be they are today everybody's so we
must be all right! That is not an idle boast. Except for
these few malcontents there is an absolute flat unanimity it's almost monotonous. We are the humble
children of Progress. By the light of the great orthodoxy of Science we will judge these Greeks—Greeks!
What an absurd costume! But what—I should be glad
to be told—can the Greeks mean to us at this time of
the day or night? We are not Greeks the Lord of Hosts
be praised, we are Modern Men and proud of it—we
of the jazz-age who have killed sexishness and en-
throned sensible sex, who have liberated the working-
mass and gutted every palace within sight making a
prince of the mechanic with their spoils, we deride the
childish statecraft, the insensitive morals, the fleshly-
material art, the naïve philosophy of the Hellene.'

327

A raucous murmur rises from the Hyperideans, silenced by Polemon.

BAILIFF. 'The Greek is our enemy, perhaps our arch-enemy, why should we disguise that fact? Do not let us be superstitious about the word "Greek". Classical Man must be the target for our hatred then, remember that. You wish to hear my reasons for that sweeping statement? Gentlemen I am quite ready to oblige you: the reasons are numerous and excellent. We are not neighbours of the Greeks in Time it is true; neverthe-less they are as truly our enemies as though they marched with us in Space. Greek idealism is the enemy of our reality. It is the enemy therefore of our God. For the famous Greek Idealism, of which Plato is the principal illustration, we have no use at all: we are Plain-men and ideals cost too much. No thanks! We can't afford them, so we spurn them! Why can't we afford them, gentlemen? Because today we have a true understanding of economics, we know that Plain-men cannot afford ideals. Besides ideals are aristocratic. This, gentlemen, is another dispensation. To the *idea* of the Greek "gentleman" we oppose the flesh of Demos. Are we afraid to be "barbarians"? That is only *a word* after all, a word of that word-man the Hellene. Did he not get his civilization even from the very "barbarians" he professed to despise? His pelasgic slaves even provided him with its foundation. Never be stopped by a word brothers! We are primitive and proud of it! God is primitive, as you will presently dis-cover. He is no quietist, the God we have over there waiting for you! Against the puny humanism of the Greek we set up God, that great theologic machine.— The Greek is the first Occidental—his athleticism (which even all his own sages condemned), his offen-sive animal health, his aristocratism, his logic, his secularity, his ridiculous optimism (in a word the "Greek miracle" if you please!), those are our antitheses, those are the features of the pagan, the now discredited, European world—of the heretical, promethean, insurgent mind of the West. That is dog to our cat for ever!'

The head of the Bailiff goes back like the beak of a tortoise into its shell-covered socket: beneath the shadow of the ornamented eaves the eyes blaze enthusiastically, the nostrils bulging with vaticinatory fervour. A thunder of abuse mixed with applause pursues the retreating head and reverberates in the roofs of the hotly flapping tents.

Hyperides motions to Polemon: after speaking with him for a moment the latter rushes forward and holding up his hand as before addresses the crowd:

'Our master wishes to hear why he has been summoned here. He wishes us to cut short this scene and compel this strange magistrate at once to expose the ground and circumstances of this summons.'

In a moment the entire Hyperidean crowd is silent. The voices of the audience beyond the pale fall silent too. Then the universal silence succeeds to the universal din.

For several minutes this hush endures, everybody within sight now waits upon the Bailiff. Clasping the ledge with his hands, his truncheon stuck beneath his arm, he, but as silent as the rest, gazes down sideways at the figure upon the litter.

At length, slightly turning his head towards the magistrate, a voice from a sepulchre or the mouth of Sheol, hidden from all but the Bailiff by the crowding bodies of his followers, with the same thrilling intonation as before the voice of Hyperides is heard by everybody.

HYPERIDES. 'You have summoned me here. What do you want with me, sir?'

329

BAILIFF. 'You know what I want with you without my telling you: are you prepared, accompanied by your faction, to return to Heaven: or do you persist in remaining here the focus for disaffection and every lawless impulse?'

HYPERIDES. 'Before I answer may I first put a few questions to you?'

BAILIFF. 'A few? Any number as far as I am concerned. But——! Well you know I've always listened patiently to all you have had to say: I may even add—to you— against my clear duty I have entertained at all times the most affectionate feelings for you. Perhaps I could be accused of having fallen under your charm to some extent!'

HYPERIDES. 'The magic, as you know, Impostor, is all on your side.'

BAILIFF. 'There I can't agree. I think you underestimate *your* magic, and overstate *mine*. Your vitality is magical. Whether you will or not you infect people with it. When you're here I feel twice as alive too much so sometimes: I'm sure—to me you can admit—you never pass a dull moment. Do you now? Be honest!'

(The Bailiff turns towards a commissary.)

BAILIFF. 'How's the enemy?'

COMMISSARY (jumping to attention: while a movement of instantaneous martial watchfulness transfixes the line of blacks and heiduks). 'What enemy excellency?'

BAILIFF. 'I mean the time.'

Voices from all sides. 'Eleven A.M. sir.'

BAILIFF. 'The best of friends must part, Hyperides, I fear I can only give you till noon.'

A spasm of furious resentment agitates the Hyperidean crowd.

VOICES OF HYPERIDEANS.	'*You* can give till noon! Who are you to give *time* to Hyperides?'
	'We have come, and we shall go, when we choose.'
	'Make time for others, not for us!'
	'Swine-face! Withdraw! Hide your face, or before noon we shall have marked it.'

BAILIFF. 'Your followers always return to my face. That is not only unkind but unintelligent. I am like Socrates, outside I am deformed and repulsive. But like those figures of Silenus called Hermae inside I am——'

VOICES OF HYPERIDEANS.	'Sacrilege!—Socrates!—Swine!'
	'Compare yourself to nothing human, puppet!'
	'Hide your face goat's-dung! We shall hear your rotten squeal just as well from behind a screen. Draw-to your curtains!'

BAILIFF. 'Many hold that my appearance, my beak, this hump—is not a compliment to mankind. In taking human form I might have adopted a more flattering view of the race, that's the idea. This exterior has its advantages but of course I should like very much to make a good impression especially upon you Hyperides, there I've confessed! But the image of my person on the retinas of other people is not indifferent to me: I should not be extant now truth to tell, you must see that, had I not become sensitive to looks of approval and disapproval on the faces among which my life has been cast.'

POLEMON. 'Rather say had you been as sensitive as you describe yourself you would not be extant at present! The history of your continued existence is a long and dirty tale of a very thick skin.'

BAILIFF (shakes his head sadly). 'If you only knew.'

POLEMON. 'Your history is one of *separation* and your appearance is what it is to cut you off from other men so that you may remain primitive and barbarous. It was no doubt Nature's idea but it is displeasing enough.'

BAILIFF (sighing). 'You have learnt your lesson of distrust too well, young man! Nature I can promise you had no part in my appearance. It was entirely my own idea. You are a conventional person, it repels you—I can't help that.' (Addressing the audience beyond.) 'Does it not strike you as strange that these men, most of them in the flower of life' (he dilates his nostrils at life's flower and passes his tongue across his lips) 'should pass their time in this way, unkempt and scorning pleasure, all for the sake of *truth*? How powerful the unknown is: like a god. They all believe this dreamer here, too, sooner than they do me although they get truth from me alone: that is the paradox.—What do you think Hyperides?'

Hyperides' inert profile concedes no response.

BAILIFF. 'You're not interested like me in the truth, Hyperides—that is always our difficulty of course.'

HYPERIDES. 'I'm not so interested in the *dead*——'

BAILIFF. 'But my dear Hyperides I *must* be interested in the *dead*—they are my clients! I sometimes think you oughtn't to be here at all you know—you're so much alive! I don't know how you ever came to die.'

HYPERIDES. 'Well, what is your "truth" today sir? For it changes every day that I come here. In that it resembles most things that men call truth.'

The Bailiff leans forward crouching upon the sill of his box and in a much lower key that sinks at times to a hurried whispering embarks upon a full-dress *tête-à-tête*. This dialogue of the two principals forthwith and up to its conclusion shuts out the choruses, the Hyperideans standing a little back at a signal from their master.

BAILIFF. 'I have a truth for your private ear Hyperides.'

HYPERIDES. 'My what?'

BAILIFF. 'Yes, it is one that it would be pure loss to evulgate before this mob you are out here with. Will you give it your attention?'

HYPERIDES. 'Yes, I will hear you. Having brought ourselves to submit to this public farce, I suppose we must lend ourselves to that too and give hospitality to your asides. But my friends will overhear you. Try not to refer to them as *mob* and as *herd*.'

BAILIFF. 'The mob are beasts, exclaims the King of Daggers!'

HYPERIDES. 'But since they do not recognize you as a person, as you know, *mob* on your lips is for them a simple offence without meaning.'

BAILIFF. 'I am the conjurer for their conceit: I will show them who is *mob* and who is not! *Le mob c'est moi!*'

HYPERIDES. 'I can see you are in a bad mood, puppet. Under such extraordinary dispatch as you observe in your judicial procedure, will not our time soon be exhausted?'

BAILIFF. 'You leave that to me: I am one of the ten Princes of Time.'

HYPERIDES. 'It's as you please. In this preposterous divan of yours you keep madman's time in any case. Well? I am at your disposal. Do not be coy with this exclusive truth that is too delicate for the ear of the Many. You should get behind your curtain like Pythagoras and take up your esoterics one by one into your mysterious parlour, you know, not lean down and mumble these oracles to me like a common impostor.'

BAILIFF. 'Listen Hyperides. I am not an impostor. That is what I have to tell you as a matter of fact. But I am

333

anxious that no one but you should know. It is essential that they should believe me to be an impostor—that is what was once called the plot.'

HYPERIDES. 'No one will ever suspect that you are not, not even I, you can put your mind at rest on that point. The plot is safe.'

BAILIFF. 'Bene bene! as our polyglot chum Belcanto would say—did you see him here this morning?'

HYPERIDES. 'I can't say I did.'

BAILIFF. 'No matter. Well then, Hyperides! In behalf of your clap-trap tribe you lie there in a sumptuous cynicism, but the head is at cross-purposes with the heart. You are the head and not the head. You have united together in one rebellious purpose all those spirits least like yourself, least swayed by reason—far less so than my doll-men here—by appeals to passion that no reason, except yours, is any longer able to subdue.'

HYPERIDES. 'That is your first lie for my ear alone. Go on.'

BAILIFF. 'So it is to your reason that I must appeal, in order that it may intercede—I don't want a scrap. Shelah! ask those bitches to be quiet I can't hear what Hyperides says!—See? You see sir? Now lend me your ear, will you be patient?'

HYPERIDES. 'It's useless to listen. Besides you're growing more excited, I know the symptoms.'

BAILIFF. 'Wrong again. I wish Hyperides I might vanquish your distrust—if you would only submit to own me more particularly, but to the modest extent of glancing from time to time in my direction, calling me by my name or even casting a smile up at me! It would look better too. Your people grow restless.'

HYPERIDES. 'Have you anything to say except that? If not bring your whispering to an end and unfold your plans for us all openly.'

BAILIFF. 'First let me have my say. I wonder if you heard Polemon girding at me just now? Never mind, he was abusive. He attacked my skin on the score that it was thick, yes, that is a subject to which *le sieur* Polemon is very partial. After a few minutes' conversation with him I feel myself encased in a bullet-proof epidermis. I believe that a thick skin covers a number of facts that have escaped your attention. Have I your permission to reveal to you a few of the secrets of the Thick-skins?—the history of the Redskins pales beside theirs in stirring romance.'

HYPERIDES. 'I have come in contact with enough Thick-skins to know that they do not wait for any one's permission to enlarge upon the many beauties and curiosities of their persons.'

BAILIFF. 'Of course, but listen. Here or elsewhere I have never been popular, invariably I have been surrounded with a bitter criticism my ways have not been the ways of other men—I have often told you though how much I have had to put up with.'

HYPERIDES. 'Often.'

BAILIFF. 'In conflict with the reality of Polemon and his kind, and that is most of the human kind, my reality has proved impervious. I have indeed not given a foot —my identity is *virgo intacta*. Locked—dead—thick get me? How much for this fine virgin ego—no offers? A ravishing hideous beauty all its own, ladies and gents, guaranteed with this fine prime virginity because it *is* so primitive!—I know you hate that but it is so real for that cause—you believe it's unreal but that's why I'm surprised at your not getting that. That's not what I have to say it is this— this is history! (I am a poor degenerate Thick-skin but I know the fakirlike feats of our historical skins—we are pioneers to a man —I won't tell them you now.) I wish to drag out and pin down the assumption sticking out of Polemon's

335

gibe—is that a bull? It is pointless, Polemon is a silly-billy, I needn't tell you know.—*Primitive and proud of it* that's my motto. Never mind. Now prick up your shaggy ears this is the moment for the extraction. Polly says I'm a Thick-skin (I *am* proud of it) because I don't give a hoot what Polly and his lot think of me and my lot. What, not what Polly!—how on earth was that? Why I must be as mad as a hatter to be so jolly insensitive—not to say dirty at once, that comes after a bit of argument when the *no-gentlemans* are on the carpet—as to decline to believe about myself all that some Polyphemon believes about me! But there is a solution, I hesitate but will expose it. Can it be that I have had my private thoughts on the subject of Pol on my side all along? Treason! Yet so indeed it has been. Bitter as their thoughts have been about me, gentle sir, mine have been still more bitter. I, in this box—at last Jack-in-the-box has popped up to say—I am the bitterest creature in the universe. For why? Because *I'm primitive and proud of it!*—the slogan of the Thick-skins of whom I'm an outstanding personal member.—Well!'

HYPERIDES. 'You are giving us at least an accurate account of the motives of your war upon humankind, it is the outcast's bitter creed that we are hearing. When the time comes for the inquisition for blood your sorrows will have to be allowed to you, to give some sort of human value to your murderous bias.'

BAILIFF. 'My murderous bias! Have you then been slow in shedding blood!'

POLEMON. 'If what you have to communicate to Hyperides is nothing but divers complaints about me I submit there is no necessity to affect this stage-whisper or to pretend that it is a message for his ear alone.'

BAILIFF. 'You are eavesdropping Polemon!—Hyperides, be just, if only in retrospect. Mine is not a war upon mankind at all. What is mankind? Since we have gone upright we have been parted, but on all-fours we were all of one persuasion, in the sodality of beasts. Now it is snobbish distinctions, then it was only the mechanical distinctions of competing machines, like walking tanks at war, there was no snobbery of work or manufacture, or at all events it would have been unavailing. Snobbery and advertisement—they are largely commutative being generated in the same instinct to bluff—there you have all that is specifically human. To be human is to bluff. In the bluff-market I have no standing, I am not a beneficiary, the canons of human bluff for some reason have passed me over. So it is said that I am not human at all. I, a man, have been hunted like a wild beast, and it may be I have acquired some of the savagery of the wilderness—you say I am retrograde, but I say you are a snob. To be a snob is to be the cruellest of the animal creation, it is my experience. I have attempted to covenant with men often but I have found them as treacherous as they are violent. Men are my enemies because they falsify, without changing, the mechanical energies of nature. They call their composition *justice*, *truth*, *God*—you know the names of the snob-lexicon.'

HYPERIDES. 'I know the names and the last one mentioned by you is also your particular property.'

BAILIFF. 'No more than other men's. The only difference is that I sink all others in it, for me there is only God.'

HYPERIDES. 'Which, for us, is the same as no God.'

BAILIFF. 'But I have my ferver, which is also my jechidah!'

(He lifts up from under the shelf, and exhibits, a blank rice-powdered puppet of thumbling length, a quarter-span.)

HYPERIDES. 'Yes, characteristically an inert abstraction with the minimum of the person about it—in fact just such a thing as one would anticipate—a kind of embryon of Pierrot. Put it back in its slot. If you possess a god it is no doubt Khordad, and your daimon would be as a wrist-watch is to a municipal timepiece—a little Khordad: or you should have a dial fixed in the face of your dolly, if it has a front—or instal one in its belly.'

BAILIFF. 'It is scarcely in a spirit of friendly accommodation, is it, that you approach me? Well I will not be easily discouraged—thank your stars I am a Thick-skin. I am also a Hump, next after my skin comes that and I suppose my face. This weighs more with your neo-hellenic sentimentalists than the skin—but I am jumped on if I mention that memorable Athenian who transgressed against the facial canon of the profile-proud freiherrenkeit of Athens so grossly that at last they poisoned him like a rat.' (He clears his throat.) 'May I speak of the human mouth, or should I be overheard? Do you think all these lips would hear me and begin sneering at me? The mouth's important. As a source of expression we find it ugliest says the good Ruskin where it has none, as mostly in fish. The beaks of birds he says obtain an increase of expression by various ways of setting the mandibles as seen in the bills of ducks and in the eagle. But the carnivora says he lose their beauty-of-lip in the actions of snarling and biting he tells us. So he traces *expression* which says he is *beauty* up through the horse camel and tiger to man. So far all is smooth sailing. But up to which man (or woman should it be) upon his principle? All that amuses me, I don't know if it does you there is no occasion to say. How are we to decide between the lips of St. Theresa and those of the Jersey Lily I'd like to know—where do the lips of Leibniz come in or the good Ruskin's eloquent pulp? If snarling and biting destroy the beauty of carnivorous lips are not those of all the most lovely women carnivorous (bloater-eating and chop-tasting) in a quieter way certainly, and should not all lips be distorted by snoring if not by snarling? (But why exclude snarling if it comes to that —your followers are human averages.) The neat drinking-cups that are birds' bills take higher marks in my eyes than any pair of pulps of dirty pink, however much their owner may have to express—I do hope I have offended nobody here who has a great deal to express?'

HYPERIDES. 'You would sell us to the birds, if you could, to the fishes or ants, your aversion for all that is human would make you reverse the whole of nature. You would start of course by degrading all that is highest in the human and making it fetch and carry for Caliban. Revenge and envy can go no farther—that is the history of the Humps is it not, ably abetted by the Thick-skins? But after all your chatter of bloater-eating lips what then, you disgusting person?'

BAILIFF. 'Well I will tell you what that leads to—but what with your averting your head from me as from a bad smell, for ever trussing up to be gone, or throwing your arm out to dangle upon your knee as though to get more air in your armpit, or to disturb the pertinacity of an incubus, it is not so easy as it might be. You cause me to raise my voice. Even now I do not know if I am heard or if I only molest you with something like the rattle of a clap-dish in your dreamy ear.'

HYPERIDES. 'You molest me, you molest everything by your mere existence, nothing is easy because of you, you are the chief intellectual mosquito, it is as though God were suddenly a parasite, what you think stinks before you speak, but, alas, I *hear* you, everybody *hears* you, no one is able to stop his ears against your tongue.'

BAILIFF. 'Then I will still not despair. Perhaps I shall

melt your heart before I am through. That I am a respectable jolly Punch-like person who is sadly misjudged, that is my case of course that is the plot. I am jolly I am misjudged I am a Punch-like person (jolly and misjudged) the idea in a nutshell, neat and sweetly pretty. But I'm not going to say that I am like this by accident, oh dear no! oh dear dear dear dear no! I can account for every ounce of my hump and I *grow* this nose on purpose, I feed it with fine nasal fodder imported from my sweated plantations (poor black-and-white-trash mixed) in the tropic of Cancer. Now will you lisserndt termee Hipe ant not pee so silly-pillie! Wilt? Hipe? No no no no no no no no no no no no no no no no no no no! Not go! I promise!—you irritated me—I'll not go-off-the-track again—never—honssthinj!—hearmeout!—hoppitnot!—Hipe!—this once! —having putter hand turrer plar—take no denial— Ime rights rain—one chance more—lovely ladies— beautiful bilgewater—bloomingasblooming—one of the best—never say die—top o' the morning—Kilkenny cats—very!'

Dickensjingling and swatchelstammering he stops with the soft clatter of his ornaments as he shudders shaking off his little fit.

BAILIFF. 'Hyperides this is serious. Lisserndt—listen to me. Listen. (I'm quite recovered.) Let us come to these objections and really grapple with them as man to man—I should say as one objection with another. I'm the objection. For why? I will explain. I once was but am no longer sure that I know where the misunderstanding crept in but I know when I first noticed it, 'twas on a summer's evening in its tent (Li was there) I spotted the misunderstanding and I recognized it for such without much difficulty but the gist of the matter was that to eradicate it would be a long business, so by way of short-circuiting it I invented a password, all and sundry could creep in and then obviously we should be near the solution, that's how it presented itself to me at the time and for the moment I heard no more about it. The misunderstanding centres round if it's not actually and in very fact this horrible gibbosity, so it's hump-begotten first and foremost—if it were a matter of the nose only that would pass—what should be cleared up, I owe it to you, is the why and the wherefore. There is really no difficulty it is simply a question of method. Objection number one: I am a judge. Objection—am I a fit and proper person? Objection number two: those I am called upon to justify or justivate can feel no confidence in my æsthetic judgments (I'm an aesthetic judge—beauty-parlour bench and so its import). For why? Objection number three: I am odd. Were I shaped like the winged wonders of *Peter Wilkins* ethereal and berkleian ah that would be another pair of sleeves but I should be æsthetic. Like would call to like. As it is. Objection number four: should not I have been chosen (or if it lay with me should not I have chosen myself) with a view to satisfying a somewhat higher human canon? Granted! As it is. Objection number five: I violently compromise this administration. Absolutely! Objection number six: my appearance cannot lend itself to the secret approbation of the vigilant newcomer (who is often little better than an offcomer) and so is suggestive (very subtly) of insult or something or other, well of insult let's go no farther—insult's no joke, assaults have been known for less. As it is. Objection number-seven-and-eight: you give me a bad name and I don't hang you, you call me a dog and treat me worse, if I am innocent and no dog why don't I lock stock and barrel? That's the worst. Let's take them one by one and wrestle

341

with them. First. If I were inviting misunderstanding
I should only be doing what others are doing—it is
the misunderstanding of the doing that is the un-
making of the American in man that is American in
both, when it is not, as most often happens, but un-
making, and great suspenders. Fi fo fee fum. *But*—
and that is very very. I'm not! Well then let's come
down to brass screwdrivers and see if we can't mop
up the understanding that others missed in the un-
making but that's not my funeral, though conscientious. Object number one (not mine): Is this right?'

POLEMON. 'What's the game, puppet?'

BAILIFF. 'Oh hark at Robert. Oh dear Mabel!'

POLEMON. 'Have you quite finished?'

BAILIFF. 'No.'

POLEMON. 'What are you clappering away about
there in your sleeve? Is it for this that you have summoned us? When are we to be heard?'

BAILIFF. 'When I am ready.'

POLEMON. 'And when will that be may I make so bold
as to inquire?'

BAILIFF. 'Oh almost any moment now, I still have a most
important matter to discuss with him.'

HYPERIDES. 'How long will it take you, have you any
idea?'

BAILIFF. 'That depends how closely you follow me.'

HYPERIDES. 'Give him another five minutes.'

TERPSION. 'He's playing for time I believe.'

HYPERIDES. 'It's his time not ours.'

BAILIFF. 'Thank you Hyperides. What I waste here is
bought and paid for, with blood. Will you dispose yourself to listen—I am your conscience. If I have sound
ears and my companion speaks to me I may persuade
him that I did not hear (this is a quotation) but myself
is not so easy to persuade (I change it). But when my
conscience speaks to me (as now yours does in me) I can,

by repeated efforts, render myself finally insensible. You see the idea? To which add this other difference in the case of conscience, namely, that to make myself deaf is one and the same thing as making my conscience dumb, till at length I become unconscious of my conscience. You will perhaps make me dumb if you go on pretending to be deaf; that would be disastrous—consider! all the chat and chutzpah and the clatter of the prattling chete gone west—you would be without a conscience.'

HYPERIDES. 'Enough. I hear you.'

BAILIFF. 'I am glad. Insanity or apostasy is the alternative for him that hath ears and shuts them up. You would all be somnambulists in this concentration camp of dead fish except for me and live in dreams like the animals. I stand to you in the capacity of *will* which is conscience too, that is why I get a little alarmed when I see you collapsing into a torpor.'

HYPERIDES. 'Go on old mesmerist. You have just described your opposite, you have not sent me to sleep. You will have to deal with me awake.'

BAILIFF. 'No. Well we'll get back to those objections, those objections from one to ten I should like to answer as they deserve. With you I can do so without fear of giving offence or inviting misunderstanding—I have a complex about being misunderstood but only by you. Now then, it is not only, illustrious sir, that your obedient humble servant is expected to be comely, that same worm is also expected to be *great*. Men are used to that: they have—accordin' to 'ow their superstitious society is arranged *pro tem.*—their supermen or "great men"—they have invented a value they call "greatness". It applies to the brain that's the difficulty. Seeing me stuck up here a Jackass in Office earning my keep, spotting the celestial fleur-de-lys upon my sleeves, however, they say to themselves: "Ha!

evidently a very clever man—he must be great": and, what is far worse, proceed to treat me accordin'. Democratic prescriptions for muzzling the mastodon come into play, they open up into polite and humble pies and puddings but in a way peculiar to men dealing with their great—it's exceedingly awkward. I naturally don't encourage that sort of thing. Men don't alarm me in a general way but when they think they're in the presence of a great man they do by gum, fi fo fee fum! I get the wind up proper. They're beyond compare dangerous when their littleness is aroused. I put them off in every way I can. But no. By reason of my awful function, my surprising parts, my immense responsibilities (they say) I should certainly occupy that rôle, and, in short, be great. They will not let me baulk it, nothing will shake them off, they have smelt blood, they think they have detected greatness, it's no use. I am expected to be dignified as it is called—like you for example—as serious as an alderman about this highly important matter of animal survival—all the things that I am not that is the long and short of it; they will have it that way, they refuse to hear of anything else. They have scented their victim and they believe that I *must* be great—they don't see how I can possibly escape them situated as I am. That is how the matter stands.'

HYPERIDES (nods his head). 'Go on, I'm listening.'

BAILIFF. 'I have other ideas for myself I need hardly tell you. I know all about the penalties of the state they propose these little average men. I know better than to be caught in that trap.'

HYPERIDES. 'Is there a trap? I thought all the traps were yours, but perhaps you are afraid of being caught in one of your own traps you mean?'

BAILIFF. 'Sure it's a trap! Didn't you know? You have a lot to learn. A great man is a standing joke with them

344

—that any one can be so silly you know. They hate them like poison—didn't you know?'

HYPERIDES. 'Who do?'

BAILIFF. 'Why, the great men—I mean they do, they simply detest them—the others. But they can't help themselves.'

HYPERIDES. 'Who can't?'

BAILIFF. 'Why the poor devils the great men you know, they're a bunch of bums I call them, they haven't the gumption of mice, try as they will they seem quite unable to reduce to the necessary scale that of all around them, it's pathetic—it's a matter of the glands of internal secretion—they have no control at all over their rate of development and there they are a sort of Gogmagog of a silly staring giant before they know it and all the fat's in the fire. A price is on their head at once there is an immediate hutesium. They're too big. Everybody's terrified of them and when they're not frightened they grin and split their sides with malignant merriment at the forlorn albatross—you know *ses ailes de géant l'empêchent de circuler—tres pénible*— terrible. That enrages the monster and then they are terrified again and they plot to suppress him. So it goes on.'

HYPERIDES. 'Is that so?'

BAILIFF. 'Of course! The really uproarious part of the whole matter is that these Gogs (who are made into a sort of Antichrist or anthropophagos at the least and hunted up hill and down dale and from pillar to post) are generally the gentlest of creatures. That is really a delightful touch don't you think of Mother Nature? I've had several of them here oh hundreds of them. They wouldn't say bo to a goose in nine cases out of ten.'

HYPERIDES. 'What of the tenth?'

BAILIFF. 'Oh well there are exceptions of course; but it's

345

usually safe to say the bigger the gentler, and it leads to the most ludicrous situations. What makes it particularly funny is that of course they are the same size—you understand me, physically—as the others, it's difficult to know which is which sometimes. I have made mistakes occasionally though as a rule I can spot them—and I've had some nasty jars. They are exceedingly intelligent sometimes. I try and separate them from their inferiors as far as possible but there again a laughable situation arises; for although upon the worst of bad terms with the average run of their fellow-men and much as they fear them, that's a fleabite to their treatment of each other with whom they are at daggers drawn. I wish you had the job just for once of getting these odd monstrosities to consort together, you would get many a good laugh out of *that*!'

HYPERIDES. 'Are they so stubborn?'

BAILIFF. 'It's not so much that they're stubborn it's something else. In spite of their really tragic situation, you know, which, you would think, would leave them little concern for anything except the safeguarding of themselves against the incessant attacks that must be expected from beneath, in spite of that they actually—one can scarcely credit it I know—they actually feel a mysterious pride in their predicament, as though there were some abstruse merit in it: and as to other "greats" they eye them with the most inveterate distaste hatred and scorn, and they positively are *jealous* of each other's misery!'

HYPERIDES. 'That I find it difficult to credit.'

BAILIFF. 'Yet it is so. I do all I can for them. They're nice lovable creatures by themselves, and of course to their undying misfortune twice as intelligent as the rest and I get on with them most awfully well. (One gets to appreciate a little sense almost inordinately at this job and as to gentleness—that is a characteristic worth its weight in gold—one is hardly able to believe in it any longer.)'

HYPERIDES. 'I can quite understand that. Would you consider it indiscreet if I asked you if you have any of these strange people you have been describing in camp at present?'

BAILIFF. 'Why yes, several as it happens. There's Belcanto he's one. You know him? He's rather jealous is Bello, you wouldn't get on well with him—you take up too much of the limelight he's averse to that in others is my Bello but he's a rare pleasant bhroth of a bhoy in his cups—when he is able to forget his situation which when sober he is not more's the pity. He lives by himself and never speaks, except for a few disjointed phrases in ice-cream English or counterfeit Latin with a sprinkling of tinker and Greek, in fact he's made up a cant of his own which is founded upon the stuttering of a particular moron that for some time we kept before destroying hoping she might get better— she never did: and with that he mixes his odds and ends and it seems that except for this cant in which he communes with himself by the hour together like an old maid at her Patience he is grown particularly silent, almost deaf and dumb, indeed, it is said. Bello is not one of the greatest of the great you know, he's only moderately monstrous, though extremely self-conscious. But he is a most gentle humorous and nimble person with a fine nose for the *mot juste* and a rare tongue for an old brandy and a lovely melodiush tenor. My Bello! Why there he is I do declare! No it is not he. I'm glad. He becomes rather abusive sometimes when he discovers me talking about him—but as it's in his bellocanto cant it's as though you were being called *no gentleman* or *you're another* in singsong pedlar's French. He once however got so angry with a fellow-great that as he knew he could not make himself understood in his thieves'-stammer he drew a picture of the offender with compasses upon that wall there, which I had to have rubbed off because it looked a little obscene in places and I have to be very careful with all these children about.'

HYPERIDES. 'You needn't tell me about Belcanto, puppet, it is not a subject that interests me.'

BAILIFF. 'Ah there now! What did I say, there you are you see!—when Greek meets Greek—if Ulysses could meet you on the leeside of the port of Heaven the feathers would fly as soon as you sighted each other's coxcombs a mile off—you would take to your wings you would make a cockpit of the firmament. But it's seldom I fall foul of the exceptional persons as I have said, we hit it off. But that is nothing to do with my own predicament whatever—I have excited you so much by the mention of Bello that that I can see is forgotten. Not so by me. I have half a mind to tell it you in Hottentot clicks stutters of atonic jazz and with an epithet-mongering that would stagger you, a Greek, in fact in my own swatch-cove patter which is more than a match for Bello's cant but I will not now.'

HYPERIDES. 'You are getting nervous again.'

BAILIFF. 'Not really very nervous, thank you, I will try and explain with exemplary distinctness where the shoe pinches and see if I am rewarded by your raising the ban and exalting me from the classes of the misunderstood—for come-we-must to a settlement of this hellish dispute. I am up every day at six and I have had enough of it. So when I take my stand in this place-of-sitting—I have a wool-pack but I use it to throw at people's heads—they arrive and look at me and say to themselves—*This is one of those great ones evidently* and as I have remarked grow immediately most ironically polite for they think they have got me on the analogy of *their* great—I can see their minds working. "That at least," they say to themselves, "we have at our fingers-tips, as for Milud and His-Highness why we know how to put *them* in their place, keep them in their place, nail them in it, crucify them on it —that much every mother's-son-of-a-punk of us, poor as our parts may otherwise be, was taught as an alphabet—anything we don't know as to how to clip muzzle and castrate the great why that decidedly is not worth knowing!"—And so they get to work as eager as a band of sickly house-breakers but as civil as possible, prostrated as their slave-Teacher prescribed in his slave-slogans of meekness, as *He who humbleth himself* and *The last shall be first*—so they flatten themselves like worms persuaded they will soon all be popped into the coffin to feast off the Mighty Fallen—I *don't* think! —the sacrificial corpses of the wonder-workers slain by their cunning priests. No but they reckon without their host that is me in this instance. I too have it all at my finger-tips!—"Little men, little men!" I say to myself "go easy! I have my eye on you now I have the charts of your narrow hearts and you will hardly wreck me on your pasteboard rocks—if Ulysses was expert I am a better sailor than he and I am in league with the hurricane as likely as not, so go easy little men, lay-off with your baits from your red leviathan a second while I whisper a breathless word or two I have been keeping hot for you this twelve-month."—Directly I see one of them after that I crook my finger and beckon him. "Little superstitious whiteaveragefellow come here now till I tell you!" I gently cry "you are a sharp Charlie, too sharp by Charlie half, you'll do but you'll sure get a shock in your hum-drum your centre I'm telling you and this will be the way it will all come to happen and all your world will go down snap, then you and I and all of us will go down snap while bloody treason will fix the costs it'll be a tidy bit. This will

come to pass one morning. Of course it is all written—
you're for it, it's nice to know all the same. Shake!
that's as it should be! No ill-feeling? None. Good!
Next time we meet it'll be on you! But I'm showing
you now, watch me. In your Krooshtian teaching
there's a flaw, get me, you've made a big mistake for
a wee man you're up the garden and not what's more
of Eden worse luck and God's the man what's led you
up the garden and that's the end of the matter, but
for pure sport I will show you little averagefellow
where the snag is—come here an' I'll point it out without more ado gratis, it's because I'm no sport I'm
gratis—others abide our question, I'm free! You little
machine-minding cheese-mite lisserndt termee! Who
oh yes! may that good fairy be what makes you all these
powerful presents? they *are* lovely! I *do* congratulate
you, you *are* lucky! but never mind to answer you've
got one there just now has been brought up-to-date
for you—I admire that. Look, I'll tell you. You work
it all-right but the first word of its workings is the last
thing that you'd guess. Follow me! It's the big-game-
plant for the nursery lion-hunt with live lions and
escapes to match—when there was a Time did you
never think the big things of life could be trapped except by expensive Lady Leohunters in private saloons?
Down with privilege! Down with Leohunters up
with lions-for-all with breads and circuses! It's all
fixed up now though. Bitted baited, shot-at-while-
hobbled, caged and bun-fed, all alive-oh and no members'-days nor close-seasons for the big-game when it's
human! No. All the greatness is cheap at last, that's
high time but it's a bit of a surprise—so their bright-
ness *can* be used to light your pigsty with electricity
and be made to supply your kennel with cheap heat. I
always thought it was poetry—it only shows how mistaken one can be. There's none of that any longer

that goes idle that's a dead cert, that power's tapped easy enough, given the instruments that's child's-play in fact it is now child's-play now it's child's-play all along. Still listen the fraction of a moment—you general-run-of-little-averages you have the trick now! but look you at this cunning matter from the side of the force tapped who is human full of *idées forces* thoughts and all that. Listen to the sad song of the waterfall as you sit blinkered with earphones little listenerin." '

HYPERIDES. 'Are you telling me what you do say or what you should?'

BAILIFF. 'What I should stupid!—if I weren't so awful despotic—you could say it but you wouldn't—you're too democratic so it never gets said. Don't think I think all this. I only say it since it has to be said and I have to say everything one side and another, no one else will so two sets of dirty work fall to me—but only in private. Still see how it goes on, the best is yet to be, I lead him up the garden after the big-game (which I tell him is hiding in the shrubbery) and there I leave him as I found him. What can you say to such people?'

HYPERIDES. 'You seem to have a good deal to say to them.'

BAILIFF. 'A bagatelle to what I think I promise you! As it is when he approaches me I approach him still more rapidly hat-in-hand on both sides but mine sweeps in the dust and I set up this whispering across the lines and routes of his strategies like a flurry of sand to perplex the campaigning of an ant—he goes back. His orders contain nothing as to the indiscretions of the wind which he regards as a fourth dimension of space —one two three as steady as steady then this chaotic blowing. "Littlewhiteaveragefellow stop trotting while I tell you," I cry after him softly, "you're but a lost one I'll show you where you took the wrong turning!" He does not stop so scampering top-speed we press on while I hastily mutter, "Look you now! Goodman God like a Mister Drage in His infinite power with wisdom, but especially wisdom, has given you an Earth to sack. Be plenty! go to it! 'tis the Promised Land of worm's-desire. Fancy putting all these preposterous forces at your disposal! you wouldn't think He'd have trusted you would one? It's evidently His great love that's what it must be. That's obvious. *Too good to be true!*—what blackguard did I hear snort that? As you pop in the bath-salts or ram down the clutch it would be sacrilege to question the gift-horse in the mouth or look for catches in the hire-purchase system. If the average lot is cast in a paradise of exploded giants—on all hands they succumb like ninepins and the effluviums of the decay of the splendid plunder fill you with an agreeable confusion, it is *embarrassderschwah* for all—that is kismet and top-notch kismet at that! To *pick brains* has been your expressive Saxanglish tropology and they grow bigger and bigger Pelion on Ossa one damned thing after another—I'm sure I don't know where we shall end! what with the mountains instead of molehills and still only moles to account for the mountain except for dead giants dropping like flies on Ossa, it's a pell-mell magnification. That is magic, no one sees, it is the shaft that flieth by night. His love would have to be seen to be believed else gasp is all one can do, gasp."—From time to time as I stand here off my guard I find I am caught even now napping and once I allowed myself to be great for a whole day. What a day! It's my usual routine however to place at the disposal of his lordship Thomas Thumb Earl of Earth all the advantages of the great establishment for preserving his highness's personality absolutely inviolate that we have over there and he comes up modestly, secure in the conviction of being passionately loved for his little blinking *beaux yeux* by an omniscient All-papa waiting to receive him inside. I am his flunkey standing statuesque to attention more or less at the gate to receive him, to take my little lordship's hat and coat and announce his arrival to the expectant Deity. Here he is met by me and it is my duty to give him a foretaste of the prodigious favours to be lavished upon him inside. What a pastime! On that occasion when I played *the great* I ticked him off at the end of the performance. I drew myself up to my full height—I believe that day I was an inch or two above par and in my grandest manner I began:— "Worshipful Sir, I would solicit of your lordship's grace, seeing you be a choice, honest, small stout, upstanding downtrodden loco-foco, that I might have the unique advantage of your opinion in a matter we have in stentorophonic controversy in the Seventh Heaven (where no one is smaller than Ma Erda your mater and mine and the rest's so when they fall there to argument it is impossible to withstand the vibrations, the least of which hits you like an Atlantic roller each time they employ the definite article or change from singular to plural) I would have something minted in your matchless understanding which would recommend itself to their lasting approbation so that finally we might have peace in the silver and aluminium sub-skies and those of blanched gold and more especially at this poor exposed spot which is neither fish nor fowl nor good Red Heaven yet not out of reach of those storms of discourse into which the Abrahamic clowns drop on the least provocation, frequented by daily doubt of their security as Heaven grows redder and redder with the revolutionary influx of ever redder and redder corpuscles." He was as you may suppose considerably flattered by my address and I then slipped in quickly my questions, veiled at first still by the Mohammedan mummery borrowed to sidetrack him.

"Do not run away with the idea or the picture of the great ones of the superior heavens as human kings pontiffs generals or proconsuls. They are quite different, there is no state. To convey to your mind a faint reflection of the conditions but don't press it too far, think of genius or if you like think of geniuses, that's much easier, suppose Napoleon lying in a strawberry-bed surrounded by attar of roses and next to him Stendhal (his grocer and Boswell) and Nietzsche and Corneille and the Cid in a heap, Sappho De Quincey and Wilde, all the size of the Moon (it's easier to think of than the Earth, we see it) and suppose them all devastated with suspicion, for the strawberry-bed shakes very slightly now every time they move, they have been infected with the belief that they may be growing too big for their strawberry-bed. Obliterate that picture!—I believe it will mislead you after all. Genius at all events comes nearest to these strange essences. For instance amongst these quiddities are numbered oh all the *mottoes* that are spirits with their bodily heraldry, there are the draumkonur or dream-wives of the Abrahamic clowns and the other clowns, some possess several of these creatures, embodiments of personal luck tower leagues above their human client, that is such as were met on their way to Glum, there are the functional *gipta* that follow the historical Asa like a dog umbra or suspended star after the manner of Napoleon's—I have met such an out-of-the-way person as the Decorated Lady, who is the tenant of the eighth room of Darkness and her combatant ghosts, called The Travellers Along the Wild Ginger Leaves— Ravana with the midday sun passing beneath the arches of his enormous Cingalese palace is a common sight and hundreds of feudal giants, then the abstractions of literary myth, Love hidden in one of the crevices of Crashaw's mistress, the shadows of Plato's cave and the spirit of Night who dosses with Bysshe somewhere east of Suez, lastly there is Time, I won't describe him, there are lots but they are quite unassuming. As a matter of fact that is no merit. They've never imagined much less seen anything so small as yourself—you don't mind my putting it in that crude way? Then this is the trouble, this is why we consult and want your tip. We're up against these monsters (this must go no further) and we should be glad of your advice in the matter. You must have some valuable hints you are a man of the world: how, sir, how would you stop the mouths of these enormous terribly indolent conversationalists? We know that you have a short way with *your* great—we are keen students and I may add admirers of your terrestrial methods—we feel convinced you might point out a short-cut with ours. Now it is significant that our great never gave a hoot about your affairs so long as it was merely your hereditary royal and other public houses that were being suppressed and wound up. It is quite different at present since you've begun on your local genii. Lately they have grown unaccountably restless. We can only suppose it must be that they have got wind of your determined scientific classwar of great-versus-little but from every possible aspect and point of the compass. They feel at last that *they* are involved in some novel and alarming manner, that's all we can think. (I wish we knew what's upset them.) However that may be they're a handful just at present. They scarcely ever stop talking about *the nothings* as they call them, the particles of which they are composed. As to your methods I may have been misinformed, and now I should esteem it a very great favour if you would allow me to run through with you my impressions of your celebrated memoranda and correct them where they are mistaken. In a general way you are described

355

as making war upon *the great* in every form but especially where mind not money is in question (indeed we understand that it could be simplified in such a way that it would appear that it was money that was pitted against mind and that your admirable campaign derives from policies of embattled capital) by means of progressive systems of isolation. *Class-consciousness* is the keystone or cornerstone of the destructive edifice? But *class-consciousness* is merely another word for segregation, I believe I am right in saying. The more you can invent *classes* or excite to *consciousness* those already in existence, the more you isolate men from each other? Hence—on the analogy of the cast-iron caste-system so successfully imposed upon the Hindu—the easier they are to govern. Side by side with the segregation of classes or syndics or that of sex from sex for instance (directed at that loathsome invention the family) you have evolved a similar policy with what you label *great* to cut it off totally from what you label little. (Of course by great here you mean only the individually great, those put in a false position by the undisciplined action of nature and not the great in the sense of the concentrated mass-power or money-power, which is the only truly great.) So, if we are not misinformed, of a person born into that odd and awkward minority you exact, am I right? perfections, peculiar hardships and inhuman control of his human principles of being, sacrifices of all his passionate wishes, in short of everything that has value to you—things naturally that in your own small sickly way you would not dream of attempting—I need hardly say—but you exact these things, we have been told, with a fervent punctilio and really admirably savage malice, which suggests that some instinct of revenge is at work. (We know that that cannot be the case of course, sir, but at first sight it would have that appearance.) All this

356

effects gradually, through your skilful arrangements for their segregation, a sort of living death for those objectionable persons. But since they are cold-shouldered and *cut* as it were by what was originally and is still ostensibly their kind, and are forced into a corral apart, they must cease to be effective or to exercise the influence that their powers, if they were not dealt with in this way, would secure to them. In fact of course where the treatment is entirely successful these objectionable freaks could as well be dead for all the living they are permitted to do. But when I said *cut* (I saw you wished at that to take me up) you do, it is true, cut them or send them to Coventry (do stop me if you find I have not got the hang of the thing) not ostensibly because you disapprove of them, never that, of course (on that point we follow perfectly the drift), on the contrary you say you avoid them out of respect and admiration. That is a capital point. If you will allow me to say so it is a device that I admired greatly when it was first explained to me. In fact I found it difficult to understand why no one had ever thought of it before, it so perfectly answers to the case. But there were obstacles, before the machine-age the personal factor or the human meant so much no one would have allowed it to be touched, governors no more than governed, and greatness of course was bound up with that factor, perhaps I should say that they are the same thing. In fact it would have been totally impracticable before. So there we have the rough draught of your stratagem: first you shut them off entirely from all participation in active public life, political and even as far as possible social, since social with you is a form only of politics or business—you neither have nor wish for art (all this does not hold, in parenthesis, for the old ones who are harmless and scarcely any longer much different from yourselves) only you do it

357

with all the gestures of a frightened veneration, with a salvo of ironical kowtows for their sublime capacities, their incomparable gifts, which, you say, would never consort with yours. This behaviour makes it seem that their enforced splendid isolation has come about through your heightened appreciation of all that is noble and bewitching. Or on the other hand you can affect to believe that it is they who have withdrawn from your society and left you severely alone much to your regret. But whichever way it is done, the important thing is to enlist all 'the little' into a self-consciously 'little' class, and leave all these great Untouchables by themselves, in an inhuman category of other-worldliness, where they can no longer interfere in the affairs of this world. If you can persuade them, once they have been locked-out and marked 'great', to invent a cant of their own, which is a further barrier to communication, why then the thing is as near perfect as mortal hands can make it. That last is a very special touch and I must frankly confess that as I survey one of you class-conscious herd-midgets instructed in intensive propaganda for mass-action, I cannot quite see how you can yourselves have ever brought to perfection such a far-reaching plan. It was not you, no? Indeed I suspected as much. It is not only beyond your compass, it belongs to another order of things. That is the work of your great crowd-masters, those great engineers in the human-plastic. On your side you are rightly adamant: as the greatness of the great is all shut up in their greatness ('greatness' or 'highbrow' in the cant of revolution branded upon them as an incomprehensible 'highbrow' thing reserved for beings of another clay) so littleness becomes fanatically little. Any suggestion that *you* might adopt with advantage some of these disciplines of the unhappy great ones, why that you receive with a stern indignation. In order to approach the great those fools of the Past used to have to affect a little greatness themselves, history is there to show us that comedy. No. Not *this* child, you say, it is your axiom that *you* should be *human*. It must be conceded you as a natural right that by your life and nature you should for ever blandly contradict all that the 'greatness' (on which admittedly we are all in one manner or another dependent—but what, as you say, of that!) illustrates. A strange situation! A splendid discovery! Everything now is simplified and as plain as a pikestaff. If my account is substantially accurate we will immediately adopt this device so that it shall be in heaven as it is on earth. So please tell me at once if I have understood." He was still rather flattered though disoriented, at that I left him but I don't see how I can leave you in the air in that way. You say you are astonished to discover me in this shape: you are so literal you will not admit the possibility of disguise. My form is unprepossessing, it is not worthy of the occasion—I should have put my best clothes on, have had myself massaged and anointed!—I am told that I behave "beneath my dignity!". That means that I behave in a *human manner*. But do not men always exclaim in that fashion when they detect one of those unfortunates whom we have just been discussing behaving like one of themselves? Well I *always* behave "beneath my dignity", it is my most settled policy, I would not be my own equal for worlds, I would not contaminate myself by being myself with these carrion. So I cheat the vulgar of *that* handicap, at all events, which they immediately with the most implacable malice impose upon you the moment you have betrayed the compromising fact that you are their *better*. What handicap is that?—why the handicap of being their eternal *souffre-douleur* which could only be supportable if you took them at

359

their own estimation of being held to the impeccable inhumanity of a *noblesse oblige* watched over by a thousand jealous eyes, and yet for some reason of wearing a human shape—a shape *too good* for the human nature that is beneath it—to be in short, a sort of humbug like *you*!'

The nearest Hyperideans rush forward with exclamations of violent disapproval but Hyperides makes a sign to them to go back.

HYPERIDES. 'I wish to hear a little more of his private persuasiveness before he takes up his public rôle.'
BAILIFF. 'Thank you Hyperides! I so much prefer being a private person I was not cut out for a public figure and that's a fact. I hope we may be able to settle it all in private, highcontracting parties and all that you know, that is what I particularly hope.'
HYPERIDES. 'What I understand you to say is that, given what men in the average are and their native hatred of excellence, then even a presentable human form symbolizes too much—that, called upon to be symbolic, the wise man would choose the most unpleasant body he could find?'

The Bailiff assents by a smile.

HYPERIDES. 'Your discourse is as full of hatred as your acts, on the score of frankness you leave nothing to be desired. I cannot see you ever becoming reconciled to our kind.'
BAILIFF. 'What is your kind? Not I hope the kind I symbolize with this body.'
HYPERIDES. 'Then why should our kind be perpetuated?'
BAILIFF. 'Ah, why? Can you guess? I cannot. But I

360

want an answer to this. Was my view of the human average, as just developed, so different from your own?'

HYPERIDES. 'I should not indulge in the descriptions of averages in which you delight.'

BAILIFF. 'You would not indulge yourself but can you deny that our opinions are much of a muchness? No. Here is your crowd, over there is mine. In quality they differ little. What is it that excites you to this indignant effort on behalf of this mass of uninteresting people?'

HYPERIDES. 'It is not people that interest me so much as the principles that determine their actions.'

BAILIFF. 'You are stimulated by an idea, which you perceive behind this crowd? Perhaps then it is crowds that interest you—for clearly none of these persons taken singly would correspond to any idea capable of exciting you. Further it is an idea that no person singly could sustain.'

HYPERIDES. 'Why not?'

BAILIFF. 'You mean yourself? But you are a crowd, not a person perhaps at all.'

HYPERIDES. 'You wish to turn the tables on me, puppet, by suggesting that I am no more a person than yourself I see.'

BAILIFF. 'Well I am sure you are not, I should not like you if you were. The fact remains that a crowd is composed of persons. It is material to know what is the quality of its units. You realize—or do you not?—what means you have employed to get this crowd together? —This is what I wish to point out: the idea by which you are excited cannot be incarnated in this crowd of men. They have nothing to do with it. They follow you know for the most elementary motives, except for your two or three spot talkers, Polemon I except for instance. It is because they are a snarling pack of herdmen, brought up to hunting and sport. You got them to follow you by vulgar appeals. Yes it was to their violent instincts you addressed yourself. It would be idle to appeal to anything else, that was patent to you.'

HYPERIDES. 'Your favourite appeal is through the excitements of sex, and I use war or sport in the same manner, is that it? But your behaviour conceals affinities with some higher principle, you imply, for which, with the human material, you are unable to find an expression—your disappointment provokes you to go to the other extreme with it. So you refuse any expression to those you control and disdainfully refuse to adopt any for yourself.'

BAILIFF. 'No that is immaterial I am thinking of you. Let me get in a little closer still. These people with whom you identify yourself have no incentive but that of violence They would turn upon you if your star set or it suited them or if there were nothing else there outside themselves except you, they don't care who it is they tear to pieces. What else does all this rush and roar signify? They are out for blood. They care as little for persons as do you, but for ideas not at all, in your sense. Impossible indeed it is, admittedly, to gather together a better crowd than that, you've done your best, but in what have they the advantage over mine? That being so—the nature of the force that propels them being as I describe it, namely a love of dressing-up, of excitement, and of breaking other people's heads—where then is the superiority of the Hyper-idean idea over mine—that is unless you repudiate this crowd?'

HYPERIDES. 'What is *your* idea—but to that you will come presently?'

BAILIFF. 'When you accuse my administration of barbarous practices cannot I convict you of hypocrisy, for the animating principle of yours is barbarous certainly, whatever mine may be and you must be aware of that.'

HYPERIDES (indicating Barney's body). 'What is that body doing there? Why has it not been removed?'

BAILIFF. 'Oh that? You would drag that in! I left it there as a King Charles head purposely. No, the truth is I like to see a few corpses about, it makes the others seem almost alive.'

HYPERIDES. 'It is you who invite us to violence.'

BAILIFF. 'Your followers do not require much prompting, what do you think? You cannot evade my criticism of the manners of your followers: these men are howling here for the same reason that makes Mannaei an efficient headsman. When they come to dispute, and sometimes they do that well, it is the same instinct of physical battle sublimated. They are wolves. I shall eventually, when this is all over, employ them as peons in my police.'

HYPERIDES. 'Is not the battle-instinct sublimated sex, in your doctrine?'

BAILIFF. 'Nothing would ever happen here if we had not those raw propensities of the offending Adam to fall back upon—you can pick which you choose to revolve the merry-go-round and grind out the tune. So, I submit, it has been by vulgar appeals that you have got all these people together: but why have you taken the trouble, condescending to demagogic methods? That is to me a puzzle. You exert yourself for them, you say, or for some idea underlying you or them or both together. But they are not only inferior to you, they are of a different clay. Actually they are more like me —I come much nearer to all that. Polemon and I understand each other better than Polemon and you. Why, you may be of the same stature and as like as you can stare to your blood-brothers but, though the issue of the same belly, in character your precious blood-brothers may resemble other mothers'-sons far more than they do you or each other. Now these men collected behind you are moved by motives the reverse of yours. They like dressing up and breaking heads. What has all that got to do with Hyperides? What is brewing here is a dust-storm you understand or an event of no more importance—this is a very arid place, I try to make it a little juicy as you have often observed with displeasure, it is the Plain of Death and is full of an empty whirling underneath—its movements signify nothing: these myrmidons will whirl about and my particles there will agitate and collide, vortex within vortex, mine and thine, with a buzzing of meum and tuum, a fine angry senseless music, it will be an unintelligible beating of the air if we go on just as it will be if we do not.'

HYPERIDES. 'In that case let us go on!'

BAILIFF. 'There spoke Hyperides! But before you decide that we shall you should recall perhaps that you don't really enjoy it, whereas, from habit, I do. Along with my thick-skin, agelong habit has given me an insane hectic appetite for this. If there is any *winning* to be done in this game I am certain to be the winner since I am in a sort of way—it is a fatality—interested in all the squalid details of the thing where you are not. We are unequally matched. You are far too finely made for this, I warn you off this dunghill, it is mine, it has been given me by God, it is mine by divine right and I have a certain fondness for it—not for itself you understand but simply because it is my property.'

HYPERIDES. 'Thank you, puppet, I am your debtor, you are a good kind puppet!—So you think from my standpoint that life should be given up as a bad job, is that your message for my private ear?'

BAILIFF. 'What else can I believe, knowing you as I do? Strictly I do not see how you can justify action, in any shape, with your sort of nature. Yet, as I have pointed out to you, with the average human herdman it is only through the promise of stupid action that we crowd-masters can get results. No. You should really have nothing at all to do with human life, I don't know at all since you ask me what you're doing here with this sect at your back. You must have been very surprised when you found it all about you for the first time? I daresay you suspected me of putting it there. Did you? Not now but then.'

HYPERIDES. 'That is all you have to say I gather, so let us cast up our private accounts. It is a short addition. You scorn the human idea but you claim it as your personal property on account of some mysterious un-assimilable right. Here you stand surrounded by armed bodyguards. Your storm-clouds sail up and down above us in our prison camp but rather ineffectively with their tired electricity flash round our heads and sometimes scorch our coat-tails. Individually, that is in the flesh and to talk to, you do not seem very powerful; yet a pull somewhere in a very high or it may be very low place you certainly seem to possess and you come in and out of that unpopulated-looking place that con-fronts us yonder and you appear to have bought or stolen the secret of our fate and you hold the necessary sanctions to farm us. What are we and what are you? What do you do with us when we pass across that water? What is that place over there? Those are the things we want to know. That's all the answer I need give you. As to my questions, please broadcast your answers now, we have nothing more to say to each other as man-to-man as you call it.'

Hyperides motions to his bearers that his litter should be moved back and shows that the interview is at an end: these fling themselves with alacrity upon the shafts and remove Hyperides out of range where no privacy can be expected, at a position considerably in the rear of his first

365

one. During the interview between their master and the magistrate many of the Hyperideans have leant over the barrier in eager propaganda addressing their arguments to the seated audience. Others have stood in a vigilant throng their eyes fastened upon their champion, moving angrily in response to any gesture of impatience on his part, jealously anxious should his attitude hint of conciliation.

As Hyperides is taken back the Bailiff springs up full of a claptrap mechanical fury, admonishes him with playful spanking movements of his hand, sawed up and down from the wrist, and shouts after him:

BAILIFF. 'Very well, as-you-were, then you go back and I go back, everymantohispost but don't say I didn't because I did! Let all our world be given over to madness I'm not to blame. Let vituperation thrive—it's your fault. Unchain these revolutionary harpies *you* have unchained them, up with Apocalypse *you* say it I never said it. Let everything turn back to the primitive—it's on your head. I'm a salon-cat really—I hates fights! Let there be nothing serene and noble left I am as calm as a yogi and as distinguished as a fashion-plate, it's your doing you savage quarrelsome monster!'

Turning to the crowd, he points to Hyperides.

BAILIFF. 'You pack of little revolutionary averages, you may have him, that keeper of misrule patron of ruffians, you may have him for keeps. He wishes to be great he told me so, it's no use. Hyperides can sacrifice himself if he likes but as for me I would see you *damned* first I would really—was that emphatic? Damned. Hell. You know!'

The Hyperideans respond with a defiant roaring.

BAILIFF (turning to Polemon, who is standing in front of the litter). 'Begin your questions.'

Standing beside Polemon is a young man a head taller than the Hyperidean chief whip who has listened throughout to the discourse of the Bailiff, delivered generally at such a pitch as to be easily heard by those near the litter. He is the handsomest of all the Hyperideans with a large and languishing russet *petasus* tied beneath the chin. A black cloak falls straight to his heels fastened with a Bangkok swastika temple design imposed upon a rough brooch and he carries a black leather portfolio of continental cut. His face has no feminine imperfections but is cast on the severest lines of an eager and wolfish symmetry, in lean silver-bronze, that olive that might be fancied as the moon's variety of sun-burn of a pallor incorruptible by anything vulgarly hot, as though he had been a nocturnal lunar votary divinely protected from the grilling heat of the day-star. He appears scarcely more than adolescent: his manners are of such a striking gentleness as to suggest some romantic postulant of a much-tried order in a militant epoch and his expression conveys no blemish of passion at all except settled pity too formal to be oppressive. When he is smiling it is an inaccessible radiation: it gives some idea of his remoteness but he shows no discomfort at this, though conscious what the smile does it seems. As he bends down gravely towards his master, Hyperides looks up at his astonishing disciple with a pleased surprise. They confer for a few moments. Hyperides signals, Polemon rushes zealously to the spot. After that Polemon and Alectryon leave the side of the litter together and the former places himself in front of the Bailiff.

POLEMON. 'As you are aware sir your remarks have been heard by most of those in your neighbourhood. There

367

are some aspects of your argument that we should like
to see taken up and put in a clearer light than you
have cared or for that matter were able to do. Alectryon
here who was within earshot and has marked what
you said has been deputed by us to correct you. Have
you any objection to debating publicly what you have
just now advanced in private?'

The Bailiff rolls about majestically, like Dr. Johnson
upon the seashore bidding adieu to his friend, before he
replies, looking askance at Alectryon.

BAILIFF. 'Yes there are several things I should not care
   to discuss publicly which I was willing to communicate
   to your leader in good faith sub rosa.'
POLEMON. 'We should not violate your secrets.'
BAILIFF (eyeing Alectryon). 'I am not at all sure that he
   would not.'

Alectryon stands with a submissive modesty his eyes
upon the ground.

POLEMON. 'He is the last person to do so.'
BAILIFF. 'All is not gold that glitters—I've had some!'
POLEMON. 'Have you any objection to the person we
   have chosen?'
BAILIFF. 'First let me have a word or two with him.'

A long wooden structure of rough struts and trestles is
at a sign from Polemon rapidly produced from the body
of the crowd. Set on end it assumes the appearance of a
rough tribune. This is installed in the centre of the court
in such a way that any one mounting it would face the
Bailiff, but its platform is enclosed on three sides, a compass of 135° of this circular rostrum available for the
orator. Alectryon gives no sign of participating in the

issue, either to notice that his suitability had been called in question or that a decision had been arrived at with regard to his recent request. His passivity expresses the aloofness of the instrument whose private interest is in no way involved in the event. When called upon by Polemon it is almost as an automaton that he approaches the tribune and swings himself up on to its platform. He deposits his portfolio upon the narrow lectern that is provided, opens it, and produces an assortment of closely written manuscript. Then he raises his eyes to the Bailiff who is studying him with a heavy disapproval.

ALECTRYON. 'I am at your disposal sir.'

BAILIFF. 'We have met before!'

ALECTRYON. 'I am aware of that, under other circumstances.'

BAILIFF. 'You were one of those students of *French-Action* type?'

ALECTRYON. '*French-Action* yes.'

BAILIFF. 'Who went to Austria where you met students of *Steel-helmet* type?'

ALECTRYON. 'I met students of *Steel-helmet* type.'

BAILIFF. 'Who believe in Odin?'

ALECTRYON. 'Not that I know of—what has that got to do with this?'

BAILIFF. 'Your mother was English and you are English too?'

ALECTRYON. 'As far as I know I, like my mother, am—but please what is that to you sir, you're not a censor of mothers that I am aware of.'

BAILIFF. 'You are in fact a cosmopolitan student associated with students of *Steel-helmet* type only you have an English domicile—hence your peculiar continental politics.—Give me the Anglo-Saxon! Faugh!'

ALECTRYON (smiling). 'I am Alectryon.'

BAILIFF. 'And come from London?'

ALECTRYON (*mildly*). 'No.'

BAILIFF. 'I remember you well, you are a Breton baron-
ette with an English barmaid for a mother.'

ALECTRYON. 'Your memory plays you tricks I humbly
submit; I was a Breton duke's son with an English
Big-Steel Jewess for mama—I had a magnate-mother
but my papa was poor.'

BAILIFF. 'That's a fib you have nothing Jewish, your
good mother was a mere Seven-Dials barmaid poor-
white-trash all bitter beer and skittles. You have
disguised her in expensive steel.'

ALECTRYON. 'Have it that way if you prefer it, sir, in a
steel-helmet if you wish. To me that is all one.'

BAILIFF. 'Your opinions were so very unorthodox, I re-
collect that had you not retired to the camp of Hyperides I should have had no option but to dismiss you to
the Dago-Heaven.'

ALECTRYON. 'Dago-Heaven!'

BAILIFF. 'Why not? You can't mix Anglo-Saxons with
Dagos of *French-Action* or *Steel-helmet* type who still
worship Thor and hear God in the wind it isn't done!
They won't mix. I'm not sure it's in order to allow you
to speak to me.'

ALECTRYON. 'Is yours a Dago-Heaven puppet?'

BAILIFFITES IN SUDDEN CHORUS. } 'Say is yours a Dago-Heaven?'
'You didn't tell us! *Dago-Heaven!*'

BAILIFF. 'Shut up!—There was an impasse?'

ALECTRYON (in flat recitative). 'An absolute incompati-
bility existed between my views and those you expressed.'

BAILIFF. 'Yours were hopelessly aristocratic.'

ALECTRYON. 'That was not the trouble.'

BAILIFF. 'The great pride of Anglosaxondom is its sporting radicalism is not that so?—the A.-S. is so daring,
it's so shocking! How could you a Breton baron-ette, a

continental student of *French-Action* type who had unluckily been sent to Vienna——'

ALECTRYON. 'Never!'

BAILIFF. 'You couldn't! You simply couldn't do it—the Steerage Heaven for Dagos I remember saying was about your mark, that was too good for you.'

ALECTRYON. 'You said that.'

BAILIFF. 'Exactly.'

ALECTRYON. 'But there *is* no Dago-Heaven any more than any other Heaven here. So!'

BAILIFF. 'And now you've found a congenial atmosphere under the wings of this rebel?'

ALECTRYON. 'Yes.'

BAILIFF. 'And now you are going to put me in my place?'

ALECTRYON. 'Now I am going to show you up.'

BAILIFF. 'I'm not sure I shall let a Dago like you show me up!'

ALECTRYON (with a dreamy breathlessness). 'You better quickly—I'm impatient.'

HYPERIDEAN CHORUS.
'He's impatient puppet he wants to show you up!'
'We are impatient, you'd better hurry—we're not waiting!'
'WE're set on his showing you up and quickly!'
'The time to be lost is not is not is not—here.'
'And now—enough!'

BAILIFF. 'I'm not at all certain I intend to be shown up by a Dago!'

ALECTRYON (in automatic chant). 'I simply can't wait, you must be.'

BAILIFF. 'I relish being shown up fearfully but not by Dagos.'

ALECTRYON. 'I think it's too bad that you should refuse! Consider my position.'

371

BAILIFF. 'Polemon have you no pure Anglo-Saxon?'

ALECTRYON. 'I am purely that except for Breton, no worse than Irish. You cannot object.'

BAILIFF. 'But the magnate-mother?'

ALECTRYON. 'That doesn't matter.'

BAILIFF. 'What was the barmaid?'

ALECTRYON. 'I refuse to be tempted.'

BAILIFF. 'You'll be the death of me! You're a Breton adventurer!'

POLEMON. 'How many more objections puppet are you going to raise? Aren't you going to get on with the war? All our men are picked carefully this is a first-rate debater and it's only because you're afraid of being shown up that you make all this fuss!'

BAILIFF. 'Really it is not, you know there's nothing I like better than being shown up by a nice boy but he must be Anglo-Saxon it's no use. This dark-featured young person is distasteful to me. Have you no blond? *Gentlemen prefer.*'

POLEMON. 'Alectryon has specialized in what has to be gone through now. When you said *Untouchables* that was his cue. You simply must accept him—he's the only man who can show you up as you richly deserve at this point—*show you up!* what ridiculous things you make us say! but a show-up it will be! Proceed!'

BAILIFF (wailing). 'I waaant to be nicely shown up but it must be Anglo-Saxon!'

HYPERIDES (in sepulchral sing-song). 'Literature is too good—for ever waiting!'

Hyperides closes his eyes. One of his attendants sponges his face.

BAILIFF. 'I like that! I want a blond and will have one why shouldn't I? all that I ask is a blond—I waive the Saxon, go ahead! But not *this*. He has that wretched

372

earnestness of the continental—it must be an island
blond, mild muggy and matey, they never hurt—I
refuse to be dressed down by a dirty Dago! They're so
savage and so rough! We're all *gentlemen* here, no hay
sinon caballeros aqui como non como non! is that good
dago? and true *gentlemen* do *prefer* you can't get away
from it siempre los rubios pero verdaderos sabe, no
me gustan estos diegos sabe, dagos get up me nose com-
prenny! Gentlemen prefer pure island blonds that is
burly British business gentlemen of my kidney and
ilk. I won't be handled by a Dago it's no use—I'm a
gentleman.'

POLEMON. 'This man is not a Dago.'

BAILIFF. 'Oh!'

POLEMON. 'He is not.'

BAILIFF. 'But look at him! And then consider what he
    thinks. No gentleman would think what he thinks or
    he'd be jolly careful not to say it if he did or no Anglo-
    Saxon and I flatly refuse to be questioned in a brutal
    way that will leave me no alternative but to turn my
    back and stop my ears—you don't know him as well
    as I do.'

POLEMON. 'He is a baron. You can't say he's not gentle.'

ALECTRYON (gently). 'A duke's son.'

BAILIFF. 'He's rough I tell you, he has absolutely no feel-
    ing for the fine shades that the Anglo-Saxon is never
    without even in America sometimes who *never* hurts
    anybody he'd sooner die first and is as kind as can be,
    liberally loving and even worshipping black red and
    yellow men as his brothers and teachers and he's my
    man. I like 'em kind and soft and shy and not hard and
    fierce, for it's all about nothing so why get excited?—
    look I still have the marks of this ruffian's teeth upon
    my mind where his hideous sharp thoughts bit—he is
    a bloodthirsty Dago savage who does not know that fair-
    play's-a-jewel because he's never been taught at school

373

—he's a cowardly ungentlemanly ruffian and I refuse
to have him show me up: he is the sort of man who
wouldn't lift a finger to help a poor anarchist to put a
bomb under his child's cradle and would be as likely
as not to electrocute him if he did afterwards in the
teeth of an indignant universe and might even show
up oh! absolutely anybody—he's no gentleman he's a
rank outsider. It wouldn't be a square deal he's a crook
it's no use.'

POLEMON. 'So you say. Well we will humour you. You
shall have Terpsion. He is irreproachably Welsh.—
Terpsion!'

BAILIFF (screaming and holding out his hands in immediate panic). 'No no no no no not that not him.
Terpsion!—never! I'll have the Dago every time give
me my Dago! Send him away! Give me Alectryon at
once where's my darling Dago got to? Ah! I want to be
shown up by Alectryon please without delay—he's
my man! I apologize! Polemon! tell Terps to go back I
won't stand it! You did that on purpose! Not him!'

Polemon waves Terpsion back.

POLEMON. 'That's all right!—Proceed Alectryon!'

ALECTRYON. 'May I show you up sir now?'

BAILIFF. 'Yes for heaven's sake go on but don't rub it in
too much that's all.'

ALECTRYON. 'I will do my best sir not to rub it in too
much.'

BAILIFF. 'I suppose I must.'

ALECTRYON. 'Thank you sir.'

BAILIFF. 'But just a little gentleness.'

ALECTRYON. 'It will be my best endeavour.'

BAILIFF. 'I know I shall be roughly handled. I can see
it in your eye.'

The Bailiff settles himself upon his stool to be shown up

374

and making up his mind quickly which way to look looks over at Pullman: his trusty and well-beloved Anglo-Saxon admirer gazes back at him through his glasses in steadfast silence while the sucker-like fore-paw of Satters wakes into activity and massages the muscles of his patron's arm in secret.

ALECTRYON. 'The tenor of my new questions, lofty sir, derives from the nature of the task laid upon me by our prolocutor, namely Polemon, who in his turn is answerable to the great Hyperides, and it is by virtue of the power derived to me from that great headpiece of our faction that, ultimately, I speak; and if I speak well it is through his influence, though this task of mine, I humbly conceive, be by no means above my parts, which in their turn derive to me from the hardy conjunction of an armorican duke with a Big-Steel Jewess (albeit such descent in certain quarters smack of attainder) the last devisee of the historic blood of him who brought back the blocks of the decalogue out of the cloud from which archetypal puppet I inherit the slight stammer you m-m-may have rem-m-marked.'

BAILIFF. 'No. Did Moses stammer?'

ALECTRYON. 'He, sir, was named the Stammerer in consequence of his stammer: Aaaron did all the s-s-s-s-s-s-speaking.'

BAILIFF. 'I thought sometimes you seemed to hesitate.'

ALECTRYON. 'It's very distant, but it is there. However such, sir, are my credentials: I am neither unquiet nor pragmatical I would have you believe, I speak under orders, civilly and according to a deeply-meditated plan. It is all right.'

BAILIFF. 'All right.'

ALECTRYON. 'It is with what in your brilliant diatribe, O terrific officer of Heaven, were styled the great Untouchables of our revolutionary Western World that my business opens. It is upon that vesture that I first would browse before passing on to my pastures-new. To make a mystery and a trade of the machinery of our defence is not our object so under correction I will speak without ceremony, but if I come too sharply to the point you must check me—you know, if I am brutal, and continental. That we choose to commence with these new pariahs is perhaps natural for you will not object to my saying, illustrious patron of our decay, that the whole picture was pinched; and as it was from *us* as it happens that you were so good as to steal it there is all the more reason why, feeling at home in the midst of that material, we should turn to it first and reclaim it a little from your swatch-cove exegetics.'

BAILIFF. 'The charge is preposterous! It is trumped up.'

ALECTRYON. 'Let that be as it may be, exalted nobody —though I apologize. It was certainly we who the first nicknamed those unhappy exiles from the communion of their kind.'

BAILIFF (dropping into scornful laughter). 'I who have sat upon the lap of the Queen of Sheba and have been the companion of the Seven Champions of Christendom—*I* come to the likes of you for my views!'

ALECTRYON (laughing). 'We know all about that—but you slipped off the lap of the Arabian queen you were a doll in those days before you grew so great in your peevish expansion.'

BAILIFF. 'I knew this would happen!—it is in vain that I have devoted irrecapturable minutes to the smelling out and expelling of metics. This is too much!'

POLEMON. 'You have accepted Alectryon and we will not have you when you are discomfited throwing up his Breton origin in his teeth!'

BAILIFF. 'Can't you come to the point?—He is playing with me like a cat with a mouse, he is not showing me up as I was promised, he's letting me down. I am impatient, mind you, I'm not waiting, not-very-likely!'

POLEMON (menacingly). 'Silence puppet! Little puppets should be seen and not heard!'

ALECTRYON (sedately). 'Silence!'

BAILIFF. 'I said you were a bully. You show it in your face.'

POLEMON. 'Proceed gentle Alectryon he is nothing.'

ALECTRYON. 'Then it was the Hyperidean speakers, there are clouds of witnesses, who first pointed out that parallel. The position of those "great" by nature (whose pathos has followed hot-foot upon that of the Western kings and nobles politically "great" alone) and that of the Indian *parayer*, the pariah—the analogy no one detected except we emancipated from convention. (I refer to the "revolutionary" convention of the sentimental poor lost West hypnotized into self-destruction—that is the convention of Christian duty and the other conventions.) Persons possessed of conspicuous undemocratic abilities—this we showed all men without boastfulness—must become *outcaste* in the midst of the modernist class-conscious orthodoxy. (I refer to the orthodoxy of "revolution"—red pink yellow or even white, the orthodoxy that establishes the conventions.) The fanatical "proletariat" of mediocrity must exclude them or attack them in its holy-war against privilege, the privileges of nature being even less palatable than privilege that is the benefice of men. We indicated how these exceptional persons would be considered as *too noble* to be allowed to mix with others perhaps (the isolation of the most gifted, the natural leaders, lest they upset the revolutionary apple-cart). It would be a good idea. It has in part happened, we were endowed with prophetic reason. Therefore we are pariahs—prophets are stoned are they not? We are the new Western prophets. We are a totally new type of prophet, to match the times—it would have to be something out of the way. The Brahmanical system would thus be inverted if we if they were thus isolated. So the Western World as today shattered and ungoverned is busy erecting a barbedwire-entanglement about a super-caste of Untouchables of its own to match the oriental, only with characteristic "originality" it is creating it out of the noblest material to its hand. The first shall be last it is the notorious slave-ethic: it suffocated the first Western Empire it is a trick that never loses its efficacy. The class-war of the low and high brow started in insidious comic dress but is ending in sullen appeals to the hatred of the average. The little man dragooned into a self-conscious "littleness" is mobilized and the gifts of a leader are misrepresented according to class-war canons as the enormity of "pride". We proclaimed all that: we had ourselves for the pariah-pattern, we had your operations here to guide us in deciphering the enigma.'

BAILIFF. 'I am but a poor copy-cat.'

ALECTRYON. 'But independent thought bursts out. The most cunningly woven ring of obstacles can be overridden or broken up. That is by reason of the demonic force of genius you understand nothing else would do it. However such an irruption is a scandal of the first magnitude. There the intellectual intruder stands featuring as an armed housebreaker among a herd of swallow-tailed boiled-shirted fashion-plates surprised in the midst of the ritual of a saccharine African dirge stopped upon a comic clang and wallop, as the masked high brow crashes in at the window pamphlet or cubist-picture in hand.'

BAILIFF. 'Why cubist?'

ALECTRYON. 'Why not? Would not the Willow Pattern be too wild where such gentlemanly barbarities of sugar-stick melt-and-wobble are afoot?'

BAILIFF. 'Your sect condemns jazz?'

ALECTRYON. 'To that ice-cream tomtom of the savage New-Rich, that is our post-war Magnate-Plebs, who have adopted jazz as their folk-music, we are indifferent.'

BAILIFF. 'You are indifferent to the ice-cream tomtom of the savage New-Rich you are off-hand with their folk-music?'

ALECTRYON. 'Not I—that sugared savagery for the salon makes me sea-sick my stomach is delicate. That's my private reaction.'

BAILIFF. 'Oh that is your private reaction?'

ALECTRYON. 'You invented the moral sense?'

BAILIFF. 'How absurd it's as old as the hills who invented it I expect—go and ask them there are the mountains they are moral.'

ALECTRYON. 'Then listen. If we were showing you up we should show up your morals.'

BAILIFF. 'Oh would you show me up as an immoral character? That would be very intriguing though it would give me a bad name, I do wish you could see your way to do that at once.'

ALECTRYON. 'No we should show you up as a mass of morals as the Old Man of the Sea of morals.'

BAILIFF. 'I am moral.'

ALECTRYON. 'Peep with us puppet into the theatres that are the hot-beds of suburban "vice"—those nurseries full of rocking-horses tired stallions triangles-for-Tooting-Beck Lesbos and lechery for the Millionaire Filmmind.'

BAILIFF. 'Oh I am pleased! Do take me to the play! Consider me at your side, a perfect peeping-Tom.'

ALECTRYON. 'There densely-stacked sit the Millionaire-class and the grinning Suburbia of its polite employees.'

BAILIFF. 'Oh how dull!'

ALECTRYON. 'There sit the reporters and the gossip-column slysleuths.

BAILIFF. 'Worse and worse.'

ALECTRYON. 'The puppets - by - appointment to the Millionaire-class exhibit upon the stage the devilish sex-wickedness of the Millionaire-class.'

BAILIFF. 'Oh what an awfully dull play!'

ALECTRYON. 'In the Pit the employee is struck down with appropriate horror.'

BAILIFF. 'I'm not at all surprised.'

ALECTRYON. 'He sees a *fils de famille* correctly emancipated a flower of the Millions (not the Masses, of the Millionaires—he only has pocket-money you know) who plays a ukelele in his bachelor-flat. On the floor is the corpse of the young cockney window-cleaner who has taken arsenic a sort of Barney.'

BAILIFF. 'What for?'

ALECTRYON. 'There is worse behind, but I will not tell you, you know the old old story.'

BAILIFF. 'Aren't you going to tell me? It is equivalent to turning the lights out. What is the use of your taking me to the play if you suppress the plot?'

ALECTRYON. 'It is finished. The hack-pressman shoots off to boil with indignation, as ordered, over his article, at the novel wickedness of the class of his employer, as testified by the behaviour of the puppets. *See what our children can do they are devils!* The play is a dream of old age, it is in fact the Millionaire's dream of perfect arrogant and wicked Youth. There is a father who has a fit upon the stage at the revelation of his child's addiction to vice and jazz but he is not a Millionaire-father he is marked Middleclass in the book-of-words.'

BAILIFF. 'That's better—he would have syncope if he were marked like that in the book-of-words, that is life-like.'

ALECTRYON. 'The employee at breakfast next morning

380

in the Suburbs devours the report of the hack-press-man. They are both disgusted his young wife is there, their marrows are frozen their sex is all topsyturvy and turned turtle. The critic with the beau rôle follows upon the heels of the hack. He pours scorn upon the Middleclass.'

BAILIFF. 'And rightly so.'

ALECTRYON. 'Yes. Middleclass is what the upper-servants of Big Business are called in a general way. Everybody is some sort of servant of Big Business one assumes. But that is not what the super-critic means by "Middleclasses".'

BAILIFF. 'No. He's got it mixed perhaps.'

ALECTRYON. 'The hack reporter has to stand up for the "Middleclass".'

BAILIFF. 'What a dirty shame!'

ALECTRYON. 'But some one has to, that is most important.'

BAILIFF. 'Why does the "Middleclass" have to be represented in this way—is it so important?'

ALECTRYON. 'Yes most. It doesn't exist. If it weren't officially represented people might guess that it didn't.'

BAILIFF. 'That accounts for it.'

ALECTRYON. 'The Millionaire-class has to have some one to score off you see and its employees in the Pit would take no interest if they did not think somebody was excited. That makes them disgusted and excited. It's funny that they have to get excited to-order against their patrons and be disgusted with their wickedness on purpose.'

BAILIFF. 'Well that is comprehensible.'

ALECTRYON. 'Yes morals is the main aphrodisiac of the Christian nations: morals at all costs have to be kept going for-and-against pro-and-con vice-and-virtue.'

BAILIFF. 'I don't understand you, I question if you're amusing.'

381

ALECTRYON. 'Morals have to be kept going for *scandal* is essential, morals are a great institution.'

BAILIFF. 'I follow you with some difficulty.'

ALECTRYON. 'Morals are the backbone of scandal, you must have morals they are the salt. No "virtue" no "vice".'

BAILIFF. 'You are trifling with me—why morals?'

ALECTRYON. 'Morals have to be kept boiling.'

BAILIFF. 'Whose morals?'

ALECTRYON. 'The underdogs at boiling pitch.'

BAILIFF. 'You won't get me to swallow the underdogs.'

ALECTRYON. 'Well where would be the beauty of immorals without morals, you are dense!'

BAILIFF (in heavy aside). 'I feel I may soon be for it!— I always instinctively disliked you. And what of the play we went to together have you forgotten that my mercurial young companion?'

ALECTRYON. 'Next all the ghosts rise up, it is the mythical background coming into action, that is in the newspapers. They write letters to their daily paper after the play's first-night.'

BAILIFF. 'Messages from the Spirit-world?'

ALECTRYON. 'Yes: indignant letters from the Astral-plane. But they do not say they are from the Astral-plane, they are printed as coming from living people— the "Middleclass".'

BAILIFF. 'But how did those spooks get into the theatre— is it haunted?'

ALECTRYON. 'They never got into the theatre. It was the hack-pressmen in the Millionaire newspaper-offices who wrote the letters from the Middleclasses.'

BAILIFF. 'Impossible!'

ALECTRYON. 'No. It was to create interest.'

BAILIFF. 'I see, to create interest.'

ALECTRYON. 'In the newspaper offices there are the stock-figures of the myths that write letters.'

BAILIFF. 'Of the Middleclasses?'

ALECTRYON. 'Every fresh outbreak of sex-daring on the part of the puppets that stand for the Millionaire-circles encounters this chorus in the columns of the Millionaire papers.'

BAILIFF. 'The chorus of the myths of the Middleclasses?'

ALECTRYON. 'Such myths. They fall into three heads. First there is the *Old Clergyman from Lincolnshire*. Sometimes he comes from Somerset. There is one in one office to judge from the addresses that comes from the Isle of Wight. Isle of Wight has it is felt an ideally middleclass sound, an island it has the advantage of an insular position. It is doubly insular.'

BAILIFF. 'What is his function?'

ALECTRYON. 'He is the best ad. of the lot he draws big houses. He is the standard myth. He is both "Clergy" and "Middleclasses". He is very powerful. When he writes his letter of protest the employees of the Millionaires are gleeful.'

BAILIFF. 'Have they in the newspaper-offices in a docket a formulary marked *Old Clergymen's letters?*'

ALECTRYON. 'In all the best—those that is with first-class popular circulations.'

BAILIFF. 'That is what I thought.'

ALECTRYON. 'There are the letters too from soured-up Victorian Spinsters: and there are the letters from the Old Colonels.'

BAILIFF. 'What do the Spinsters mutter?'

ALECTRYON. 'The Spinsters anathematize cocktails and foam at the mouth at jazz. They are invaluable—it is like the Music-Hall. But next to the Old Clergymen come the Old Colonels, they are the heaviest ammunition. We have an ex-hack here who specialized in his time in Colonels.'

BAILIFF. 'Do you believe what journalists tell you?'

ALECTRYON. 'Not as a rule. Gouty red-faced and mon-ocled retired Old Colonels of the time of Pendennis but who are as extinct as the Dodo, who sit all day long purple in the face in the bay windows of Clubs that were long since pulled down, shouting "demme sir the country's going to the dogs!" are the backbone and mainstay of the Millionaire Classes' social advertisement, equally for theatres nightclubs beaches and novels: without them the Plebs of Das Kapital would lose its lustre and perhaps crumble. That is why they have to be preserved in the imagination of the people, or sub-plebs, which is conservative and readily embalms them in a posthumous flower.'

BAILIFF. 'It's not so bad as all that I hope.'

ALECTRYON. 'It is possible. The Old Colonels and the Old Clergymen are of capital importance in its domestic economy, of Das Kapital. I should not like to say that without them the Millionaire World would survive a minute.'

BAILIFF. 'It is a dark picture.'

ALECTRYON. 'We are realists.'

BAILIFF (furiously and all of a sudden). 'You are a damned impertinent young puppy and if I have much more of your nonsense you young ruffian I will have you horse-whipped you hear me sir!'

ALECTRYON. 'Oh sir! you overdo it. You are never *the real thing*. All your imitations ring false in some particular.'

Bailiff, as red-faced *Old Colonel in the Club-window* remains speechless with indignation in his magisterial sentry-box glaring at the *Young Puppy*. Alectryon casts down his eyes with a mournful and drawn expression, to suffer his vis-à-vis to expend his frivolous unreal rage of an imaginary Old Colonel.

ALECTRYON. 'We are accused of laughing at homosexuals instead of being impressed.'

Polemon quickly signals: the Hyperidean guards are strengthened around the tribune from which Alectryon is speaking.

The Bailiff watches the composed and half-shamefaced mask of the Hyperidean orator with doubt, pulling violently at his nose.

BAILIFF. 'Yes?'

ALECTRYON. 'It is said that the homosexual fashion should either arouse our indignation or moral passion or else nothing, we should affect blindness or else be it. It is in claiming as our humble right a third position, neither that of moral passion nor one that is complacent nor helpful, that we meet with a difficulty at your hands.'

BAILIFF (shouting hotly). 'The vice to which you refer is a filthy one it is an outrage, its addicts should in my opinion be hounded out of decent society! Indignation indeed! I should jolly well think so!'

ALECTRYON. 'There speaks the eternal moralist; your heated epithets supply that cult with its main advertisement, each "filthy" and each "decent" is worth its weight in gold in Sodom.'

BAILIFF. 'Do you not find it an abomination?'

ALECTRYON. 'We take no interest in it. We are indifferent to homosexuality.'

BAILIFF. 'It is disgraceful to be indifferent!'

ALECTRYON. 'No. We claim that our attitude is highly disinfectant.'

BAILIFF. 'It is immoral. Indifferentism is hideous of all attitudes the most rotten, it is spineless! You are worse than out-and-outers of whatever colour, your group are rotters!'

ALECTRYON. 'We are sorry.'

BAILIFF (still Old Colonel). 'Sorry! It's no use being sorry!'

385

The Bailiff springs up with fussing affected impatience and stands his hands squarely upon the ledge, his arms in bandy bulldog arches, a hectoring lowering person.

ALECTRYON. 'We suggest that you know that your passionate attitude in all things breeds passion like rabbits in feverish swarms both of its like and opposite but always passionate and that often with you those change places: your "vice" and "virtue" are nearer together since they are created for each other than contradictory principles in the system of our values. For with us they are not equally personal and so not so passionate. Two passionate people that are opposites meet in their extremes of passion: witness the moralist who merges in the immoralist and the ecstasies of his goodness express themselves when at their intensest in the opposite diabolics of his erotics—witness the mystic.'

BAILIFF. 'I prefer hot-blood to your beastly intellects.' (Floridly fiercely and irresponsibly) 'God is hot-blooded!'

ALECTRYON. 'God and blood!'

BAILIFF (stamping flat-handed upon the ledge). 'Yes! God and *blood*!'

The guards are further reinforced in the neighbourhood of the Hyperidean tribune by Polemon. As he proceeds Alectryon's manner becomes more silken still with a more and more caressing precision. His chanting voice echoes with a monotonous gentleness over the attentive partisans, while he raises it slightly at any competition from beyond the Hyperideans where disputes are continually maturing and exploding.

ALECTRYON. 'May I dare to clothe my words in the chaste accompaniments of reason or will that act as a red rag to you and be unbearably irritating? Your intolerance of the hard-bitten moralist is as strange to our classical pre-Christian intelligence as if you were to fall into a rage at the sight of say the Bearded Griffin because it did not conform to your simian canon. You conceive of nothing purely as lying outside your ego and its irritable poles. You must either explode against a thing or you must melt into it, so excellently coarse and simple is your mind—*primitive and proud of it* as you call it, puppet.'

BAILIFF. 'Do not call me *puppet*! I've had enough of you!'

ALECTRYON. 'Still you are a puppet though God may be at the end of your wire when you are not at the end of His—showmen by turns—the doll-God and his officer.'

A rain of cinders that turn out to be the charred bodies of flies occurs. In most cases as they come in contact with the heavenly soil they vanish as raindrops would but with a crackling spark. The umbrella is opened and held over the litter of the Master. The Bailiff consults with a commissary and an activity reigns within the tents. The shower of flies is of short duration. The atmosphere is appreciably hotter and the magistrate wipes his face with his red bandana returning to the sitting position.

BAILIFF. 'Come back to your accusation.'

ALECTRYON. 'We do not "laugh" at the homosexual fashion we only can be accused of discreetly appreciating that sentimental oddity that it breeds, he was surely sent for our mirth as the *Précieuses Ridicules* were given into Molière's hands for his immortal amusement. Certainly, though, we experience contempt more than compassion. Detachment with us does not reduce all things to a dead level.'

BAILIFF. 'That's capital! Thank you so very much for assuring me of that and indeed for all the rest of your numerous condescensions.'

ALECTRYON. 'There is quite a different aspect of homosexuality as you are aware. That you refuse to see, you insist on seeing nothing in it but the raptures and roses of vice. We will now interpret homosexuality for you politically.'

BAILIFF. 'That will be very nice for me!'

ALECTRYON. 'There we should satisfy you better in so far as we provide powerful reasons against this fashion.'

BAILIFF. 'I know, but go on.'

ALECTRYON. 'Politically this is how it looks to us, the rest is negligible, it is a private matter for each to adjust himself to according to his inclination.'

BAILIFF (moving nervously upon his stool). 'I don't object to being bored stiff but it is your abominable manners that revolt me!'

ALECTRYON. 'You are such a great gentleman, sir, it would be impossible for the humble members of a cynic sect to come up to your palatial standards. I respectfully submit on the other hand that we have the strictest orders not to give you unnecessary pain.'

Many of the Bailiffites have gradually left the circus: vortices have again begun to form without, beneath the wall. Some of the magistrate's personal chorus are sleeping in their places others languish in a painful idleness staring dully from time to time at the Hyperidean crowd or the black figure of the young orator.

BAILIFF (yawning). 'Oh yes!'

ALECTRYON. 'To all we shall have to advance you will object with violence, we shall enrage you. To save you trouble I will answer for you. I will use this convention: *Non sequitur it's a lie.* These are alternatives. I use "lie" so that your feelings should not go unrelieved as I proceed. Suitably interjected every now and then that should cover the requirements of the case.'

(Alectryon pauses to mark the opening of his set statement.)

'We do not pretend to any sort of statistics but it is safe to say that at present there are a hundred homosexuals for every one a decade ago. That is the sort of statistic that every observant person can check quite roughly so we need not waste time in arguments as to the proportions in which they have multiplied.

'*Non sequitur it's a lie!*

'Homosexuality is a branch of the Feminist Revolution. The pathic is the political twin of the suffragette or he is her immediate political successor. Large-scale male perversion is the logical male answer to the New Woman, in short it is the New Man.—Homosexuality is a department of Social Revolution.

'*Non sequitur it's a lie!*

'It is described romantically in terms of a secret sect (with intense esprit-de-corps) in the great work of Proust. To be homosexual was to be persecuted to be misunderstood. In pre-war Europe it was as a minority of Untouchables that homosexuals lived: and it was as an Oppressed Class that they "revolted"—almost as an Oppressed Sex like their sisters the Suffragettes.— Proust might have been, had he cared, the Ibsen of the homo instead of the privileged historian and popularizer of homosexual "emancipation".

'*Non sequitur it's a lie!*

'The homosexual and the woman are by reason of their functional specialization necessary conscripts for Social Revolution. Both have been emotionally mobilized as the enemies of Man.

'The homosexual is apt to be as class-conscious as a revolutionary navvy.

'No militant feminist woman can be more militant than many homosexuals.

'We will now bring on the Man who is neither

389

womanly nor homosexual, not very intelligent only very manly. He is to be pitied. Both for the feminist woman and the militant class-conscious homosexual, "Man" features as the *brutal insensitive clumsy childish unintellectual domineering egotistic alien slave-driving* Enemy. The only point of difference is, an important one, that the homosexual is in equally violent "revolt" against Woman as well, who is for him a *shallow unintellectual over-sexed stupid animal treacherous childish* Enemy. It is "the Man" remaining in the nan-man that arrives at this estimate of Woman. It is "the woman" in him that decides his attitude to "the man". His constant imitation or caricature of the feminine does not in any way prevent the homosexual from objecting to women on the same grounds upon which he could be objected to himself. Hence a new and powerful factor of falsity and social confusion we are under correction suggesting.

'*Non sequitur it's a lie!*

'The romance homosexuality attributes to itself is deliberately out-of-date. Its principal advertisement for the young today is still that it is a cult of romantic Untouchability. The glamour of persecution is artificially preserved. This no longer corresponds to the reality, since these powerful "pariahs" with the full cosmic organization of Social Revolution at their back are in a position to persecute "man", who, in his turn, is today anything but the tyrant or oppressive figure of the Revolutionary fairy-tale or the socialist or feminist cartoon. The "male" has today been thrust into the defensive and watchful rôle. Life for the young male of the species requires as much cunning as formerly it did to be an outcast pervert, that is what we are saying.

'The young male of the species today we are saying frequently resorts to protective colouring to escape

390

attack. He affects to be homosexual that is not to attract attention. He also finds it useful for escaping women. '*Non sequitur it's a lie!*

'Homosexuality is referred to invariably as *one thing* which is confusing. It is not one thing. There are as many forms of this relationship as there are historical cycles and time-groupings and differing race-consciousnesses or personal consciousness. Puritan and Anglo-Saxon Machine-age Post-war homosexuality must be an exceedingly different thing from that practised in the cities of Greek antiquity that should be easy understanding: also its political effects must be widely differing, that is surely certain. It is essential to regard homosexuality more as a sentimental than a physical thing, that is what we are saying, since the physical is always the same but the consciousness is not and it is the latter that gives everything its political colouring. We are considering it chiefly as a snobbery or cult, and there are today a dozen sentimental fashionable addicts to one physiological pervert, that almost any one we think should be capable of seeing.

'*Non sequitur it's a lie!*

'We see the exploiting of the homosexuals and of their peculiar feminine freemasoning. The same revolutionary forces as have encouraged Feminism have been the mainstays of homosexualism, for, whether this or that, it is disintegrating. The idea has been to lay the foundations of a neuter-class of childless workers in both instances. The Machine-age has doomed the European *Family* and its integrating. The worker-paterfamilias with a wife who is little more than a private unsupervised body-servant is economically indefensible. Against this wasteful unit, the traditional Aryan family and its integrating, both Feminism and Homosexuality are directing their engines. The Male is the objective in both cases of the aggressive impulse.

391

Behind "the Male" is "the Father", behind him the White Man. It is desired eventually to reduce the expensive conceited White Male, whose "home is his castle", to the status of a sepoy black-boy or coolie in the ordinary average labouring and living. As a merely machine-minding automaton or inefficient adding-machine his position as a privileged "Male", as an amateur "Father", and as a not very intelligent "White Man", but with lordly pretensions, has become absurd and is incredibly out-of-date, so it is ending. As it is, because White he is still six times as expensive as if he were black or yellow, though perhaps half as quick strong or intelligent, which economically is super-stition, so that he is *white* is perhaps worse than that he is a *man*, that is what the Machine-age is saying. So now that is its burden.—That sir is all: have my responses been correct, sir? Has not my statement proved a series of *non-sequiturs* or alternatively of lies? Now I am going.'

BAILIFF (lowering and still, biting his nails, savagely directing the onslaught of his teeth into their quicks). 'When you have quite done I will give you my answer, sir.'

ALECTRYON. 'All who do not follow the beaten track of orthodox economic Revolution named Radicalism in America must be opposed to homosexuality—it leads to the goal of the Machine direct, that is what we have been saying. There is its comedy it should not be neglected. Revolutionary Emancipation of Women re-presented as freedom-to-love often which is resulting in the disappearance of the Man and so the Lover from the scene, that is an event that as we watch it is partly comic. But we are too compassionate to relish it alto-gether for we see too all the unhappiness of the future of the disintegrating and the mechanizing. The mobil-ization—conducted beneath the comic stutter of the

Afro-American tom-toms—of the neuter-classes (misinterpreted by the mobilized entirely and seen as a summons to purple passion) fills us first with a sad amusement but then comes the bitterness of conscience again, of the only persons who are not blindfolded in all this gigantic bluffing, and a little roughly perhaps we turn to attempt to wrench off the blinkers from this doomed herd.'

BAILIFF. 'A doomed herd?'

ALECTRYON. 'It is everywhere.'

BAILIFF. 'It is useless and they would not thank you.'

ALECTRYON. 'I said it was our conscience, you are forgetting that we are human that is fearful.'

BAILIFF. 'Oh ah of course you are not animals like the rest of us I forgot. But I can tell you this—to be serious for a moment—that if you are human *they* are not: and if you succeeded in removing the bandages they would trample you to death for robbing them of their illusions, that's what they are like. We understand these herds, you do not, we are expert drovers. I suggest you would do well to leave us to deal with them and I'm telling you, it is not such bad advice I am offering.'

ALECTRYON. 'Thank you sir.'

BAILIFF. 'All that you have said I agree with except that your attitude does not follow from what you have said, *non sequitur* but it is not a lie. The Family as found in the bourgeois countries is an abomination—below a certain level of intelligence life is not worth the trouble to yourself and others, the European democracies have fallen beneath that mark of what is possible. Thus the pretentious woman of chivalry and equally the manly man is a bigger figure for comedy than are the evolving neuters you describe, though I confess that they are mildly comic but of a vulgar order. Middleclass mating —the amenities of the chocolate-box beauty that is

393

throwing her nets to catch the bank-clerk the adding-machine and retire with him to his semi-detached "castle", his home, to be his body-servant and to reproduce themselves in squalid dignity—is *not* so uncommonly lovely as a picture. The neuter is possessed of many qualities of intelligent ones that are absent in these conventional opposites—your own arguments lead to that. These social revolutions are painful and exacting but they are necessary. They will establish rigid limits for self-indulgence and folly and all that, all the pigheaded futility. In the future fools will not be suffered gladly, the weak will not be encouraged to go on living and suppressing the strong.'

ALECTRYON. 'What a pity that you are in charge!'

BAILIFF. 'Who else could effect it tell me that?'

ALECTRYON. 'The trouble is that only your hatred is creative it is your only way of being creative. Can you really pretend that what you have to give or even *want* to give is worth the trouble of all the dramatic reversals you contemplate? Are *you* the super-man? No. You are not even a man. Sir, now I am going.'

BAILIFF. 'Oh oh oh oh!' (A pause.) 'I am an alkahest!'

ALECTRYON. 'That is all sir. Now I am going.'

BAILIFF. 'Will that be all for today? Thank you so much. *Good* day.'

Alectryon replaces his notes in his portfolio and vaults down from the edge of the tribune to the accompaniment of a continuous applause from his faction.

The thunder of the master is now heard in an obscure opening rumble and Polemon who has advanced in front of the Bailiff steps quickly aside to make way for his master's voice.

HYPERIDES. 'Before Alectryon showed up the dishonesty of your last obtestations for my private ear you asked us to begin our questions. Well, my questions as you know are always the same. Why am I and my friends here? What do you want with us? What is this farce we are required to play? And for whose benefit are we supposed to be playing it?'

BAILIFF. 'In that form, as you know, your questions cannot be answered.'

HYPERIDES. 'You described your God as a magnet some time since. Have you discovered some secret of nature that enables you to draw people into your magical net? Are we trapped: and why, for even if we are I cannot see the object. What is the use to you of all these numbers? Is your God a miser, who hoards men instead of money?'

BAILIFF. 'As you have often heard me say, the Kingdom of God is composed as far as possible of *children*. God is essentially a father. Heaven is a very large family in fact the city of God is a strictly communistic abode. If you don't like large families I can't help it. It is frankly *large*. It is a swarming litter! That is God's will, not mine. If you really wanted to be a popular figure in Heaven, now, you would be as childish as possible—you know *kiddish* in yankee—instead of giving yourself these great airs of a master—posing as a sort of *father* yourself. In life you may have got something out of it but here really there's nothing to be got out of being a father at all. There is only *one* father in Heaven, that is our Father Which Art. I'm very sorry Hyperides.'

HYPERIDES. 'It would be a poor God indeed who was jealous of me. However it is clear enough that that sort of question is never likely to get a reply. I am not quite myself today.'

BAILIFF (jumps as if shot. An expression of acute dismay distorts his face). 'What what what's that I hear? Not *yourself*? Not yourself! You've made my heart hop up into my mouth man alive or my god I hope you are! Without warning—just like that: *yourself*! Oh! I'll have my own physician examine you at once! I would not for worlds have—how is it that you feel are you certain that it is so or is it a passing—— I *am* so upset! What sort of *change* do you notice, is the——' (his voice hesitates and drops) 'is the *self*-feeling less—did you say your *self* is that where you feel it? You have absolutely stunned me!'

HYPERIDES. 'No: I didn't mean *not myself* in that way, compose yourself. I shall not *die*. But my friends here must speak for me today. It tires me to speak at any length.'

BAILIFF (sinking back in immediate relief). 'Tires you! Of course, that—— It must do with a voice like yours. It must actually weigh—why don't you learn to throw it into your head? As it is if you asked a man to pass the salt it would sound as though you were predicting the destruction of the world!'

HYPERIDES. 'And if you were destroying the world you would do it with a dove-like voice and the gestures of a saviour.'

BAILIFF. 'Ah my one and only Hyperides! How we adore you!' (He blows him several kisses.)

(The gathering storm breaks among the followers of the philosopher. The kisses like little frisky sparks detonate the rage that has been held in check so that the beloved master should be able to speak. Polemon at last quells this outbreak.)

HYPERIDES (to his followers). 'Let us try argument first with this sagacious puppet. Never forget that he is only half-human, if he is that—never treat him as though he were human you would be wasting your breath. Still let us give him a hearing. One of our trusted leaders will state our position for us: as arranged, he will outline our argument.'

BAILIFF. 'I'd rather have it from the horse's mouth, Hyperides.'

HYPERIDES. 'I will speak after my followers. I am here and you can refer to me if you wish to.'

BAILIFF. 'But it is not so much a doctrine as a person with which I have to deal: and a very peculiar one at that, you do realize that I hope. You do not look like a Florentine painter for nothing, my berserking sistine prophet. It is only when we *close our eyes*—and open our ears for instance—that we realize how strangely unlike the purely visual world our datum can be. You are so overwhelmed with the concrete reality of every-thing—your intellect has it all its own way.'

HYPERIDES. 'You of course are the *philosopher*. When you begin thinking you lie down and close your eyes that is true. In your discourse you philosophers always speak as though men were heavily-muffled thickly-myopic percipient automata: you show them peering into a metaphysical fog in which they intuit painfully and dimly in the black recesses of their neural regions the forms and utterances of other men. What could be further from the truth? The whole universe except at night is brilliantly electro-magnetically illuminated. Men can examine each other and note every muscular change, every flash of an eyelash, with the utmost distinctness. There is between the percipient and the object, when that object is a human organism, the closest contact of the spirit, because of this brilliant physical light. Seeing this, it seems as strange to me that two men should set about each other, for instance, as that the left hand should attack the right.'

BAILIFF. 'How true all that is, thank you for saying so much better what I am always trying to say myself to my inquiring audiences—and, with that baying voice

397

if I closed my eyes I could believe that God was speaking! No wonder these crowds follow you! It is your *voice*—for they are probably anything but creatures of the ocular sense.'

HYPERIDES. 'You gibe at my predilection for the solid. You are a religionist: the less plastic senses serve your turn better, that is understood. That is why music goes hand in hand with religion.'

BAILIFF. 'Yes. It is your voice that awakens the *religious* response. And once that has been aroused, your plastic pagan philosophy is *blindly* accepted!'

HYPERIDES. 'You are quite mistaken. We are not all born musicians. These men here are not even like you in that.'

BAILIFF. 'I suspect that they are more like me than you think! But men do become fishes again the moment they commence to think, that's what I say!'

POLEMON. 'Of course you say it, ape that you are! Do you know who was saying it a moment ago!'

BAILIFF. 'People who live in glass houses, Polemon! Are you not a disciple? What is that but an ape?'

POLEMON. 'Not of your species!'

BAILIFF. 'People do *not*—I don't care who says it after me—keep abreast of the other appointments with which evolution has supplied them. The mind *is* the body, as you should not need a Spinoza to tell you or me. If it's not, it illuminates the body like fifty arc-lamps, men and women are all as transparent as though they were in show cases. My God, I shall be down there soon beside you, with the rest of them, spitting up at this box! Quite without knowing it I've become your disciple, but you'll repudiate me!'

A flame appears to be hovering in the air on a level with the Bailiff's face. As he finishes his remarks it abruptly darts into his chamber and vanishes. He affects confusion when first noticing it. He goes through the form of cocking a wary and embarrassed eye in its direction. When it disappears, and so near, he shakes his cloak as though to dispose of some insect, with an expression of great distaste.

Seeing that Satters has his eye fixed upon the spot in deep alarm Pullman says offhandedly,

'Lambent flames and apparitions! It's all done with Nantz brandy.'

'Who does it?'

A neighbour who has been bridling, flinging himself hotly into a new posture, explodes pouting, over his shoulder:

'What do you know about it? Je sais tout *too too*!'

Pullman examines him coldly, depressing the point of his stick though a little under an inch.

Polemon steps forward and addresses the Bailiff.

POLEMON. 'Before we submit ourselves to examination we wish to be enlightened as to the nature of this court.'

BAILIFF. 'Look here, Polemon, as I remarked earlier in the day my position as gate-beak takes with it the privilege of hanging you on the gate-post without trial if I don't like your face. Up till now I have kept an open mind about your face. But——!'

POLEMON. 'I do not wish to hear a catalogue of your sinecures: no one supposes that with your appearance of a walking flesh-pot of Egypt—which has displeased *me* I may say from the first moment I set eyes on it— you have not fattened upon every official and un-official tid-bit under this particular sun.'

BAILIFF. 'Wrong again! I'm as poor as a church mouse. I can see you don't believe me, for once I wish you were right. I possess absolutely no realty, either legal or equitable, terrestrial or celestial, no feoffment, copyhold, seisin, liveryment, interests in expectancy, fiduciary benefits, special tail, regalia: I am not a tenant by courtesy, neither wills nor intestacies, secured either in common form or in solemn form, have I ever tasted, not an asset by descent, no chose in suspense is to my account—only a little trash on my wrists and fingers, and an empty portmanteau on my back—that is the extent of my wealth, Polemon!—What would you say is my *damaged value*—examine me more closely—what would you say, on second thoughts?'

He turns up his soiled sleeve and displays a ragged lining depending upon the mustard-fat of his bare arm.

POLEMON. 'That only demonstrates that you are as mean as you are rich, and that against your carrion body you wear a filthy worm-marked sheath of cloth. But it is useless, I can see, expecting anything but crooked answers from you puppet, so proceed.'

BAILIFF. 'Very well, I shall proceed. (You're most offensive Polemon! I suffer most awfully from worms, there you got between the ribs without knowing it! No dead man ever suffered from worms as I do!) You're all of you as mad as May butter but I'll go through the form of examining you or of being cross-examined by you, that's what it will amount to.'

POLEMON. 'Agreed, puppet, and we on our side will treat you as though you were real for the purposes of this examination. So the battle for the reality can be joined at once for the idea of reality. Who is to be *real*—this hyperbolical puppet or we? Answer, oh destiny!'

The Hyperideans, with outstretched arms, acclaim Polemon.

'For my part,' said the Bailiff, 'I will return at once to the citadel of Unreality.'

A trumpeter steps forward and blows a blast to summon to the Unreal all the Bailiff's cortège. At once there is a thudding of hundreds of feet.

SATTERS. 'Pulley!'
PULLMAN. 'Yes?'
SATTERS. 'I do so loathe that man's voice, Pulley.'
PULLMAN. 'Whose voice?'
SATTERS. 'Oh, the one with the dirty jumper.'
PULLMAN. 'Ah!'
SATTERS. 'Can't we go, Pulley?'
PULLMAN. 'Don't you want to find out which of the two is real?'
SATTERS. 'I couldn't care less, Pulley! Could you? What does it matter which isn't real! I was never real. Am I?'
PULLMAN. 'I suppose you *were*. In the way that a toadstool is.'
SATTERS. 'Cat! You do fancy your luck, *beaver*! I suppose you think a beard ... ...'
PULLMAN. 'Exit Sancho Panza. Get yourself wound up.'
SATTERS. 'I suppose you think that *you* are ... ...'
PULLMAN. 'Take my arm. Don't stumble. Don't walk with your head screwed round to look at those boys.'
SATTERS. 'Stop twisting my arm. I think you get more horrid every minute! Bully Pulley!'
PULLMAN. 'Step out. Pick your feet up. If you must go nowhere, step out.'